Lusting for Infinity

A Spiritual Odyssey

Tom W. Boyd

∼

LiP
Line-in
Publishing

Line-in Publishing
Norman, Oklahoma

Published by:

LiP
Line-in Publishing
Custom Print, eBooks & Audiobooks

Line-in ™ Publishing
Norman, OK
Copyright © 2015 Line-in ™ Publishing, Norman, Oklahoma

No part of this publication may be reproduced, stored in a retrieval system, or transmitted in any form or by any means, electronic, mechanical, photocopying, recording, scanning, or otherwise, except as permitted under Section 107 or 108 of the 1976 United States Copyright Act, without prior written permission of the Publisher.

Parts of this work are in the public domain. No copyright to that work is claimed.

Line-in ™ Publishing issues a number of textbooks and academic titles in print, ebook and audio format.

Visit us at our websites: lineinpub.com and audiobook101.com

Book Design and Graphic Design:
David Fetter

ISBN: 978-1-62667-024-2

Dedication

to **Barbara**
Alias, Skye Dancer—but not for
everyone. She met me on
Elk Mountain in the Wichitas
Or did I meet her?
Either way, we met—
and that has made all the difference.

Tom W. Boyd

Tom W. Boyd (Ph.D. in Religion, Vanderbilt University) is currently the David Ross Boyd Professor Emeritus of Philosophy and Professor of Religious Studies at the University of Oklahoma. He taught philosophy at the university for 28 years, concentrating in philosophy of religion, ethics, and value theory. During the last seven of those years he served as Kingfisher Chair in Philosophy of Religion and Ethics. In 1997 he retired to join his wife in Denver, where she took a position. In 2002 he and his wife returned to the university to assist in founding the newly established Religious Studies Program. He taught in that program for eleven years, specializing in upper division theoretical courses and introductory courses in religion. He has won nine teaching awards at the university as well as the Oklahoma Award for Teaching Excellence in 1995. He retired, along with his wife, in May of 2013. At the final commencement the university awarded him an honorary Doctor of Humane Letters degree.

Tom's current concentration is on the interplay of religions in a global context, the problem of religious pluralism, and the relation between culture and religion. He also studies the impact of religion on ethics. He seeks through his studies and teaching to understand and appreciate religion in its contemporary setting and in light of an emerging planetary culture. His writings, made up of articles and book chapters, have focused on the interface between religion and culture. They include such pieces as "Is Spirituality Possible without Religion?" "Is Humanism an Ideology?" "On Saving the Sacred Text…with a Nod to Derrida," "Positive Thinking: Magic, Science, or Religion," "Is Rabbit Running with Jesus?" and "Christ of the Rising Sun: Japanese Christianity in the Fiction of Shusaku Endo."

∼

Contents

First Movement: Orientation
- One — 7
- Two — 22
- Three — 38
- Four — 51

Second Movement: Exploration
- Five — 63
- Six — 72
- Seven — 80
- Eight — 91
- Nine — 99
- Ten — 109
- Eleven — 123
- Twelve — 137
- Thirteen — 149
- Fourteen — 158
- Fifteen — 168

Third Movement: Formation
- Sixteen — 181
- Seventeen — 195
- Eighteen — 210
- Nineteen — 223
- Twenty — 238
- Twenty-One — 253
- Twenty-Two — 267

Fourth Movement: Transformation
- Twenty-Three — 285
- Twenty-Four — 303
- Twenty-Five — 320
- Twenty-Six — 334
- Twenty-Seven — 351
- Twenty-Eight — 367
- Twenty-Nine — 382

First Movement: Orientation

One

Nature is a temple from whose living columns commingling voices emerge at times;
Here man wanders through forests of symbols which seem to observe him with familiar eyes.

Baudelaire

~

Down six flights of stairs, two at a time, sideways. Grades are in for the semester, and I'm dancing my way to earth, to meet Ethan.

He waits in the parking lot, leans against his aging green pickup, and watches for me to exit the building. Ethan's a plumber and a poet who occasionally howls at the moon. On the door of his truck an oval sign declares, "Suss and Son, Plumbers." Across the middle of the sign in bold script: "**Artists in the Dark.**" As I say, Ethan's a poet, but he looks like a plumber, large-boned, beefy, a dense shock of hair waving in rebellion, massive hands, and always a ready grin that cracks his jowls into creases ranging from mischief to delight.

I peer into the back of the truck. "It's all there," Ethan reassures. "I just picked yours up." I see two stuffed backpacks, mine red and his green. They represent our life-line for the next three weeks. Once in the cab our doors shut bluntly and simultaneously. Ethan lets out a whoop and we're in motion, headed west.

As we make our way through the familiar maze of roads and highways leading to I-40, Ethan presses a button and Bob Dylan, our favorite prophetic minstrel, rasps out his first tune from *Slow Train Comin'*, We grin at each other. By the time "Everybody's Got to Serve Somebody" wafts through the cab for the second time, we're beyond Oklahoma City and bound for Amarillo.

This trip's only partly for pleasure. Who wouldn't find pleasure spending three weeks in high country wilderness? But we've planned it as something more akin to a mission. Both of us, each in different ways, have studied one primary subject for most of our adult lives. I mean that literally. We were both born into zealous middle-American versions of Christian piety and so imprinted by our experiences that our adult lives have oriented themselves to making sense of religion as a primary feature of the human enterprise. We've long since left the religious forms of our childhoods, with only rare nostalgic glances back toward them, but the theme that marked those years continues to occupy us: religion and how to make sense of it.

This trip began in our imaginations one night, when a clutch of friends chased ideas in a café near the university. Someone, I don't remember whom, turned to Ethan and said, "Why do you always bring up religion? Man, get over it. There're other things—serious stuff—we can discuss besides that." This led to an hour's clamoring as to whether and how religion is important even in this "God-forsaken" age. That's the way someone put it. Ethan ended the free-for-all by remarking, "See, you all think it's important too. Otherwise, why all the fuss?"

Ethan gave me a ride back to my place, and on the way we decided that the subject deserves some truly careful and sustained attention, some foundational rethinking, as we put it. That's when this trip took shape. He said, "We need time to think this thing through—this religion thing. It's bugged both of us our whole lives…long enough, and we ought to find a good reason for it still hangin' around after all those Enlightenment pundits declared that it was in its death throes." I agreed.

I proposed the backpack idea, and as much as Ethan hates to sleep on the ground, he went for it. He often says, when anyone mentions packing, that in Vietnam he'd had enough sleeping on the ground for two lifetimes.

So, this trip's our attempt to think through religion. We're not complete fools. We know it's been worked and reworked since people started talking—and especially since they started writing. And today the endless discussions, speeches, and books on the subject are as prolific and often as zealous and loaded with conflict and nonsense as ever. Our run at it isn't going to settle the matter, not by a long shot. Still, it draws us. I've taught about religion from a philosophical angle for twenty years, but I've not been able to dig down to religious bedrock. That's what I want to do, scope out what in the human condition really requires—and I do believe it does—*the religious sensibility.*

I like that term, "religious sensibility." It suggests something near the core of human existence, well ahead of what we commonly call religion. Something primordial, necessary, that won't go away. A student asked me in the heat of a frustrated discussion, "Why the hell is anyone religious anyway? You know, what makes a person interested in religion in the first place?" That's the question, in a nutshell, that Ethan and I want to examine on this adventure.

What I have in mind is a special kind of *pilgrimage.* This is a very old word and a common one in the lexicon of religion, but it seems to be right for what we want to pursue. Traditional practices of pilgrimage involved journeys to sacred sites—shrines, mountains, temples, and the like. People made pilgrimages to worship, or to find either healing or renewal of some sort. In other words, pilgrims move toward a destination, and the going, the arrival, and the return are acts of religious devotion. This sort of journey cannot be reduced to its external form, traveling to a sacred destination and back. Earnest pilgrims enter the journey either from within themselves or in an effort to go there. The external journey is only the shell of pilgrimage. The kernel lies within the pilgrim. The great descriptions of pilgrimage stress this. The external journey is metaphor for the internal. I'm thinking of John Bunyan's *Pilgrim's Progress* or the Islamic *hajj.*

My introduction to pilgrimage came through the forced reading of *The Canterbury Tales* in college. The stories recounted by the pilgrims, some enticingly ribald and bawdy, enthralled me. I wanted to tag along with them just for the stories. This feature of the pilgrimage—stories along the way—is part of our own invitation for readers to join our trek. I propose something of a *sacred* journey, that is, a reverential venture into the very stuff of religion insofar as it bears the sacred, and along the way stories of the way may illumine the *way.*

"Yeah, I remember those tales," Ethan recalls. "Ole' Chaucer probably couldn't get away with yarns like those even today in some places. My own idea of a pilgrimage came when I read about Santiago de Compostela. Bein' a Baptist I'd never heard of such a thing. Too Catholic! The pilgrim's road to Santiago starts in southern France and ends in northeastern Spain. Thought about goin' there between hitches in Nam but couldn't scrape up the funds."

"Maybe we should've tried goin' there instead of the wilderness," I propose.

"Nah, too far for me, but I've had the perverse fantasy of sneaking into Mecca during *hajj*. All those Muslims convergin' from around the world, all dressed in white and doin' such serious prayers and marches around that Ka'aba. That'd be somethin' to behold. Remember Malcolm X? It changed his whole life and his point of view about people who weren't black."

"But he was a Muslim. He wasn't faking his way into the place."

Ethan shrugged, "I don't care about that. A pilgrimage is a pilgrimage. I'm not a Catholic either."

"But…"

"To suggest that a backpack into the Rocky Mountain wilderness might become a pilgrimage appears weird enough to me," Ethan counters. "Or downright wrong headed. What, for instance, is the sacred destination?"

"Good question," I admit. "I've thought about it. Human ingenuity and industry have produced for us, especially in the technologically advanced West, a *constructed* world. Because this 'artifice' is the work of our own hands and because it has been so successful…or so it seems for everyone who enjoys its benefits… we're easily duped into the illusion that everything is subject to our own control."

"Right," Ethan enthuses. "We say, 'Technology will take care of it,' no matter what 'it' is. Despite the occasional 'act of God,' we quickly repair the damage and go right on with the illusion that we're masters of the universe."

"And this is exactly what *secularization* means and why the last three hundred years in the West is often described as 'the secular age.' And furthermore this term is sometimes taken to include the idea that religion is obsolete, a kind of hangover from our primitive past, or at most, a secondary and strictly private feature of modern life."

Ethan pounds the steering wheel. "Oh yeah, these days religion's nothin' but the great epiphenomenon! Now you're preachin'!"

Suddenly this notion occurs to me: in nature there is no *secular* process. I dislike the phrase, *in nature*, because we're *in* and *of* nature totally. In a strict sense there's nothing else. All of our contrivances remain rooted there. We have no choice. Still, there is a difference between the way we live within the cocoon of civilization and the way we're confronted when its security recedes and the uncontrived world engulfs us. Everything that takes place without human bidding, including breathing and having skin, might best be called, not *the natural world*, but the *uncontrived natural world*.

To go into nature—the uncontrived world—is itself a fitting pilgrimage, because somehow nature bears the origins of the sacred. When I say *sacred*, I'm pointing to any direct confrontation with whatever is over against us and yet sustains our very selves. It's the awareness of ourselves being engulfed by what is not us but without which we would not be. I'm not quite sure how best to explain this notion that the sacred comes to humanity through nature, or at least that it is most directly realized through our experience of uncontrived nature. But I want to try. What I don't want to do is romanticize nature the way it was in the nineteenth century, but I can't abide deliberately treating nature as though it were a neutral reservoir of resources for our exploitation. As though we were not part of it or were immune from it or, worst of all, in command of it. Silly and disgusting!

I'd rather speak of the way the uncontrived world is experienced when we engage it without all of the protective gadgets of civilization. We find ourselves more directly *dependent* on the uncontrived. Of course, I make no claim to be a Tom Brown primitivist, surviving totally from what the wilderness, what's left of it, provides. As much as I admire that, my backpack and its contents are state-of-the-art, and although I've tried to minimize excess—all my gear must be hauled on my back—I have a number of labor-saving gizmos stashed inside. But the wilderness still speaks the message that originally prompted the human experience of the sacred. I'm speaking of the sheer mystery—and terror—of the encounter with that experience over which we have no control but into which we enter to experience it, to respond to it, and to learn from it.

When I encounter nature unfettered by human ingenuity and design, it both includes me and confronts me. I'm at the same time wrapped and sustained in it and also bounded by it. I'm subject to it. This must surely have been the earliest archaic awareness that originated the sense of the sacred as that which stands apart and is nevertheless utterly present to us and within us. This sense is what Owen Barfield has called the "original participation" of the earliest peoples, a primordial awareness that subsequent humanity—with fewer and fewer exceptions—has simply lost. This loss is especially evident in the Euro-American West. Modern humanity, no doubt, has also gained much, but the loss remains substantial—and could be fatal. We may be overwhelming ourselves by our own success and distancing ourselves from the wisdom of nature that could correct our folly.

The sacred arises in human consciousness with the knowledge and feeling that humanity is contained beyond itself and yet fully included in what contains it. Nature, in its uncontrived and uncontrolled presence and vitality, provides the most elemental milieu of sacrality. Without the experience of the sacred through the force of nature, I believe, religion would never have come into existence. Hence, this pilgrimage into a wilderness!

****

The child attends his first funeral. He is seven. His Sunday-school teacher contracted scarlet fever and died of complications. At the funeral he feels sad for his teacher, but he doesn't understand exactly what it means that she is dead. He has only seen his dead dog, but it was a dog, not a human.

The funeral is outside on a sunny day. When the time comes for the viewing, the child's father takes him by the hand, and they line up in a procession moving solemnly past the large off-white box at the front. They reach the box, and the father turns to the child and without a word lifts him up so he can see. The child looks into the box, but it is covered by glass (to protect the mourners from contagion). The sun shines on the glass, and all the child can see is his own reflection. This startles him, but he peers further through the glass and dimly makes out a pale face and a pale pink garment. The face does not look like his teacher's but like a mannequin lying prone behind a store window. Already she appears to be far off, in some other world.

Two weeks later the child is sick. The doctor comes to the home and says he has scarlet fever. When the child hears this, he begins to cry. The mother thinks he is crying because the father must live away from the home during the quarantine, but this is not why the child cries. He does not want to go to the white box and live under the glass. He cannot explain this fear. His crying increases, although he is assured repeatedly that he will be all right.

For six weeks the child remains in bed becoming weak, his skin peeling away. He lives in the parents' bedroom. Every day the father comes to the front window and stands outside, talking with the child. The child looks forward to this visit, assuming that the father is living under the house or in the barn. The child's brother comes to the door of the bedroom and they talk. The mother reads adventure stories to him, and his imagination bears him away to distant places.

When he is finally well enough to leave the room and at last to walk outside, he wobbles on his feet, and on a sparkling spring morning ventures into the yard. Something dramatic has happened. When the child entered his sick room, winter lingered, but now, he walks out into spring. He had not noticed this transformation while inside the room. The shock of spring engulfs him, and he is transfixed.

The child walks further into the yard, where the grass is damp from the morning dew. The grass caresses his bare feet, and he looks down to see blades protruding between his toes. At that instant a dramatic feeling of unity with everything overwhelms him. He is connected to the whole universe! His toes meet the grass, which binds him to the earth beneath and somehow to the sun above. The "vision" only lasts for seconds, but it is enough.

****

Road noise and the blaring of Dylan, now from *Blood on the Tracks*, insist that we sit quietly, hypnotized by the unfolding highway stretching across the prairies of western Oklahoma and into the Texas panhandle. When the tape ends, I say something about nature and locating the sacred in the wilderness. Ethan glances at me but doesn't say anything. I can tell he's thinking.

"Yeah," he eventually begins. "nature's very informative, but its truth is not necessarily sweetness and light. It can be such a monster. In the bush, humping through rice paddies, fightin' all kinds of living and deadly critters, the whole thing takes on a different face. And if you add other people shootin' back at you, it's a mess. In the heaviest slogging I used to repeat that old description, 'Nature, red in tooth and claw.'" He glances at me, waiting for my response, but I simply nod. He's right, but he never seems to let go of Nam as the source and inspiration for almost everything he says.

"Ole' mother nature may give rise to the sacred, like we've discussed before," Ethan adds, "but 'sacred' is not the same thing as 'good,' I mean not any kind of moral thing. Nature never gives a hoot about good or bad. She just is!"

It strikes me once again that the problem with any talk of the sacred so easily slides off into moralisms such as "sacred equals good." But when the notion of the sacred first struck human consciousness, I wager it had nothing to do with goodness or badness. It had to do with *power*, the overwhelming force vitally present as nature, and yet, flowing through human veins. Nature was that force early humans could not even pretend to escape and were obliged to embrace directly. To be able to do that, they had to face it as the sacred.

Already the language becomes sticky. "Sacred," for instance, is loaded. Everything from mama's apple pie to the American flag and on to God can be considered or can become an expression of the sacred. The problem is not with what we call sacred but what makes anything whatever sacred at all. Both "sacred" and "holy" mean roughly the same thing: "to be separate or set apart." But set apart from what? The common answer is that sacred or holy things are set apart from profane or ordinary things, *secular* things. In fact, one noted religious scholar, Mircea Eliade, and he's not the only one, describes religion around the human effort to distinguish sacred or holy things from profane or ordinary things. I suppose the sacred sets apart whatever represents the sense of the enduring or abiding as opposed to the passing flux of our ordinary experienced world.

The difficulty begins with the fact that it's ordinary things that become set apart and called sacred. Trees, water, stones, mountains, sticks, you name it, and it has probably at one time or another been "set apart," and this says nothing about humanly constructed things, from flags to monuments or temples, that we make in order to "set apart." But none of this seems to strike at the heart of the sacred itself. Things set apart are simply representations or pointing gestures toward something else. This is why we call such things, whatever the thing may be, "symbols." With the introduction of that word the discussion becomes even more complicated, but one word at a time. What stands behind, if I can put it that way, the "things" we call sacred? Or, what do sacred things reveal?

I can't shake what I said earlier. Sacred, when we move past all of the objects we call *sacred*, must be about power, enduring power. If we return to the imagined earliest humans and how they must have experienced the weight of nature, they surely met its force and experienced their intimate identification with, participation in, and their overwhelming dependence on it. Of course, power or force is not a thing. It is closer to what interpenetrates everything and allows it all to exist, behave, and relate. When I say power, I have in mind the capacity of everything and the whole of things to keep on being, doing, and influencing surrounding environments, mostly without the aid of human effort or creative genius.

When humans recognize this power and the place of humanity in it, the sacred is manifest. But it's so unfathomable, so compelling and threatening at the same time, that we somehow need to represent it so we can refer to it. This is how symbols come into play. They strive to indicate—and in a sense to *unveil*—this mysterious quality we call "sacred." Symbols give shape to the force of the sacred and allow humans to draw near and respond to it without being vanquished by it. The Greek word *symbolein* means "to throw together"—that is, a kind of harmonizing—what might otherwise be experienced as sheer overwhelming chaotic might.

"Know how I like to put it?" Ethan chimes in. "I came up with this while teaching a poetry class at the community college. Signs are referential, symbols are revelational." He lets the statement hang in the air before adding, "What I'm sayin' is that signs 'point out' things, and symbols 'point through' things to what lies ineffably beyond things as things."

"Right," I agree. "Symbols unveil meanings. They don't *signify*, they disclose *significance*." Ethan nods in agreement, and I continue. "Our problem is that we keep confusing these symbolic representations of the sacred with the sacred quality itself, and we stumble about, lost in the details of our sacred symbology. Symbols of the sacred are actually more like windows onto the mysterious manifold of the cosmos in its relentless, inundating, and urgent givenness."

If we're going to rescue ourselves from confusion over the sacred, we might best begin with the common distinction between the sacred and the profane. First of all, from what I've already said, it should be quite clear that the sacred is not simply good and the profane bad. In childhood we were warned against "profanity," but that meant the use of inappropriate—usually middle-class taboo—language. This definition didn't leave much room for a positive take on the profane. Same thing with "vulgar." I had the early impression that it only meant cheap or low. It actually refers pretty much to the same thing as profane: the common or ordinary conditions and functions of existence. Street-corner stuff.

Why, then, is there a split between sacred and profane? Why isn't everything sacred? Or everything profane? Or both? Well, in a sense everything and the whole of things are both. Sacred and profane, in the end, are not about some things over against other things. These two terms more nearly refer to two different ways of experiencing everything. Let me explain this because I've given it much thought, and if we're to make any headway on the subject of religion, we best begin here.

When we encounter our world in a sacred way, we confront the overwhelming power of what lies beyond ourselves and in which we nevertheless necessarily participate. At times this is only modestly and momentarily recognized; at others, it can engulf us and take us over. We become stretched between infatuation and virtual horror at how we're contained. This is the truly appropriate place for calling upon that much used and abused word, *awesome*! In fact, the only truly awesome thing is the sacred: the sacred is what calls forth awe in us.

Most of the time for most of us, especially in this present age, the profane or ordinary way of relating to ourselves and our world dominates. Our world is, first of all, the domain for sheer survival, and then it becomes habitat, where we can engage our interests to extend and enhance both our contrived world and ourselves. Then, when we dominate the world and claim to control it for ourselves, the profane itself becomes reduced to human resources or commodities. Everything is profane! That's the secularist message. The sacred is swallowed up in the profane.

If we describe the profane in this rather off-handed way, however, it may be confusing, because the profane is also about power no less than the sacred. The profane is about a particular relation humans have to power. It is the province of effort, where humans set their own purposes and strive to achieve them. This includes everything from staying alive to exploring Mars. We're bound to do these things because we're that sort of creature. The profane encounter with power has to do with our endless efforts at mastery over all of nature, the attitude of conquest and dominion. We *have* nature *for* ourselves.

From a so-called First World point of view, we are especially devoted to this profane way of treating everything. A more common word for this today is "secular." We are, as I've noted, the secular age. We might just as well call it the profane age. "Profane" originally referred to what goes on "outside the temple" or put another way, *the street-corner stuff*. Similarly, "secular," basically means something like "the present world," and both point to the ordinary conditions of human existence pursued by human effort toward achievement of our own proposed ends.

In the West, and increasingly around the planet, this profane, cum secular, way has been astonishingly successful. Under the guidance of science and its practical off-spring, technology, we've extended the profane powers to such an extent that sacred power appears to recede toward insignificance. We are *awesome* to ourselves! The only sacred thing left—what we truly worship—seems to be our own power to exploit the profane. Or, because we still very much need what the sense of the sacred offers us, we give to more mundane things the attributes of the sacred. I'm thinking of nations, heroes (military, athletic, or other), and memorials as common cases of this sacralization. There are also more personal examples because anything whatever may take on the guise of the sacred and be used to represent it. In other words, the sacred is reduced so that it fits more readily into our dominant profane-secular organization of the world. We have created a "disenchanted" world. Yet, the echo of the sacred still haunts it.

So, although the sacred visits our dreams and appears in tamed expressions, it is nevertheless in crisis. Or, perhaps we're in crisis because we've ignored the weight of sacrality. The bent of the age is to diminish the sacred or reduce it to one more object of our control. Part of the evidence for this tendency is that those who most ardently insist on returning to the sacred, or on perpetuating it above the profane, represent increasingly strident, and often fanatical, exploitation of the profane to achieve their ends.

Fanatics are fanatical, however, because they sense the weakness of their case, and their own confidence is threatened at every turn. Either that or they seek a supernatural power to challenge mundane or profane power or to offset the felt lack of sufficient mundane power. This madness can take on apocalyptic proportions, and it often has. The voices of fanaticism can be loud and at times notably dangerous. This extremism is unfortunate for the proper appreciation of the sacred, particularly in this profane-secular age, and it is for this reason, among others, that we want to probe the farthest reaches of the religious forms humans give to the domain of the sacred. What I most want to do is salvage religion from its worst distortions, or at least to find out whether that's possible.

"Know what?" Ethan asks. "Maybe our first chore is to see how this talk of the sacred connects to religion. Are they the same thing, or if they're different, how do they relate to each other? What we've said leaves this in a muddle, it seems to me."

I nod and add, "But we can't do everything at once. For starters, I believe the sacred and religion are intimately related, entangled with each other, if you will. It seems to me that the root of all religion, what we've called the religious sensibility, is the urge to articulate or give shape to the experience of the sacred. When we respond to the sacred with symbolic schemes of any sort, we have the makings of religion. It begins with an attitude, or better, a sensitivity to the sacred."

"That's gotta' be fleshed out for me. I'm still not sure." With these words still hanging in the air, Ethan moves rapidly to the inside lane surging ahead to pass a long cattle truck loaded with stock. "We need to get around that truck. I don't wanna' smell cow shit all the way to Amarillo."

Two

> And in the same way a child in the cradle, if you watch it at leisure, has the infinite in its eyes.
>
> Van Gogh

~

Ethan exits abruptly and slows. I wake up.

"We need gas already?" I ask.

"Nope. I just saw a sign you won't believe." We stop at the intersection and turn left. "See that huge cross over there?"

He points to the right, where a white cross looms above the horizon as if to dominate the sky. Then he reports that he'd seen a sign on the highway: "Tallest Cross in the Western Hemisphere."

"Can you imagine? Right here in Groom, Texas! I gotta see this."

We turn west toward the cross and arrive at a parking lot near its foot. A number of statuary figures circle the massive cross, and three smaller crosses, to more human scale, rise from a prominence to the west. It takes me a few moments to realize that the figures around the circle represent the Stations of the Cross. The first sign of Catholic influence, one of their own great symbolic pilgrimages.

A few cars and an eighteen-wheeler are parked and people move around quietly and solemnly, staring. I try to imagine what they must be thinking. A burly bewhiskered man dressed in black T-shirt with a slogan: "Truckin' for Jesus." *Maybe he's here to worship*, I mutter to myself.

Ethan turns to me, grins, and says, "Damn! This is phallic Christianity with a vengeance."

"What would make somebody—anybody—put up such a thing out here on this barren expanse?" I ask vaguely.

"Advertising," Ethan ventures.

"But for what? Everybody in this part of the country relates in one way or another to Christianity. Why do they need to scream it? Why so in your face?" We stare up the length of the monument until our necks throb. "I think these people somehow feel threatened. The larger cosmopolitan world presses on them from every direction, and they don't understand it—or like it. When you're feelin' powerless, you grab for the grandest power you can imagine—for them, religion—big Texas-style religion."

"Nah," Ethan insists with his mischievous tone. "It's advertising. Gets people to stop here and buy gas and snacks. You can't beat religion for sellin' things." He poses as if to ponder, "Unless it's sex, and they go together better'n most folk think. Especially religious folk! That's why this is a phallic monster, I tell ya'."

I read a small hot-pink leaflet thrust into my hand with a "God bless you" from the man delivering it. The message declares that the cross in the center of the spectacle is 190 feet high (nineteen stories), 110 feet wide at the cross beam (eleven stories), and weighs two and a half million pounds. I concur that it's big.

To the east and outside the circle of figures marking the journey of Jesus up the Via Della Rosa we see a bronze figure kneeling before what appears to be a tombstone. We investigate and find that the monument is inscribed, "Tomb for the Unborn." Uh oh, the agenda of the builders discloses itself! A dogma inserts itself among the classic Catholic imagery and intrudes on the mood. This intrusion becomes accentuated when Ethan points out a tiny fetus in the cupped hands of the kneeling figure of Jesus. "That's rude," Ethan grumbles. "Ideology in bronze! Jesus co-opted once again!" And he walks away.

"Well, it all seems like ideology to me," I respond, waving my arm to indicate the whole panorama.

"Know what I think?" Ethan asks, pondering. "When symbols become confused and take the place of what they symbolize, then you have ideology, and that's only a step away from sheer idolatry. Ideologies are rationalized and frozen systems of symbolic meaning." There is marked passion in his voice. I mull it over but do not respond.

Later we find a small building to the southwest dedicated to the Shroud of Turin with, as the sign reads, "an exact replica" inside. A reliquary of sorts. But with the Shroud there is this additional muddled notion that it is some sort of *evidence* for the story of crucifixion and resurrection, though evidence for what I've never been able to grasp or appreciate.

We wander back to the truck and climb inside, leaving the doors open to allow the prairie winds through. It's already hot. I open a bag of nuts mixed with raisins and we snack. I think about how Ethan always starts with the crassest explanation of things before he digs around for more serious ones. I chide myself for being too serious. Well, sometimes, but religion is a way of being serious, holy hilarity aside, and I'm troubled whenever I sense it's being used. And, of course, religion's always been used for all sorts of special pleading, abortion being only one example. One way I can tell is that people keep killing each other over it. I stare across at the scattered houses that make up the nearby town and wonder if some of those fine citizens, the ones who helped put up that cross, would kill for it. Probably. But I don't plan to stir them up.

For reasons I can't explain, I think about how riled up people in Illinois became over the Mormons in their midst. Did they hate the religion or simply the strangeness of Joseph Smith's version of religion? Probably a combination of both, but most of the locals likely had their own religion and didn't like aliens in their midst. In any case, that mob didn't flinch from assassinating Smith while he was in jail. Whether you're for or against it, religion can spawn violent passions. It always has.

"We don't really need gas," Ethan says, "but since we've stopped, I'll top her off."

First, we go inside the typical interstate station with rows of this and that, and in the rear, near the restrooms, we find a display of newspaper clippings about the cross glued to a display wall and covered with plastic. The community is proud of their achievement. We read through the clippings, and I realize that these Texans see themselves making a statement to the world about who they are, and their piety shows as boldly as their monument. They identify with Big. It serves as a confirmation.

As we prepare to drive away, I have a sense that we've just visited the first shrine on our pilgrimage. My feelings, as they often are in response to religion, are ambivalent at best.

Ethan leaves me standing in front of the store, drives around to the pump, and begins to work it. I decide to walk over for one last stretch before the next leg. As I Look at him across the bed of the truck, his movements remind me of a combination of a Neanderthal and a prince of the realm, mixed up and muddled in the same person. This observation takes me back to the first time I met him. An older student and virtually straight from the bush in Southeast Asia, he sat in the back of my ethics class. His eyes, shaded by a prominent forehead and bushy brows, gave him a brooding look, and I surmised at once that he had a cynical aspect and that I would contend with him.

After the class he walked by me as I placed materials in my satchel and said, "I have a strong crap detector. This was all right." And for the first time I saw his broad mischievous grin. My initial assessment of him was both confirmed and amended, and I knew we would have more encounters. They would not be boring.

True to form, I became Ethan's thesis director. He worked on Albert Camus, not a subject encouraged in the department, but he persisted, as if in defiance. His love-hate relation to the department and the university became evident in the process, and his singular character revealed itself along the way.

Here is how he put it one night when several of us were sharing our various ways of approaching and coping with philosophy. These are not his exact words, but they're close enough.

> I'm not a philosopher. I'm a poet and a plumber, and both are equally important to me. Through them I seek order without losing the rage and wildness that should never be lost. When I crawl under a house to plumb it or to correct some failure in the system, my whole aim is to restore the orderly flow of pure water, gray water, and shit. Order is necessary. But the aim is to keep the action, the movement, the flow happening. Everybody wants their plumbing to be 'nice' and to take care of them without exposing what's really going on in the bowels of their homes. It's always the same action, pure water for intake and sustenance, acrid watery sludge to chase away all that betrays our deeper fellowship with beasts. But it's still there, moving away into the nether world. That's the system.

Everyone at the table stopped drinking and stared at him with dumbfounded attention. Of course, he loved this reaction and continued with hardly a pause.

> It's the same with the work of a poet. As water is chaotic without the help of plumbing, so words are chaotic without the close attention of the poetic imagination. I'm a poet, and I order words with tight economy so that they allow a flow of appreciative insight. The wildness of words must not be lost or stifled in this process. Their ordering must conspire to release the passion, delight, and rage of language. To let if flow! The aim is vision…and at best, ecstatic vision. The heavenly must never blot out the earthy, or the poetry is phony.

Ethan's recitation was bluntly interrupted by an advanced doctoral student. "Then why in the devil are you doing philosophy?"

"Discipline," Ethan shot back. "The torrent of rage—no, outrage—in my mind needs to be sufficiently brought to heel so my poetry can include—well, intelligibility, I suppose."

A young professor asked, "Is it working?"

"Not really. The academy is a system of clogged pipes, like a poet who's too preoccupied with his own words to actually let them run free—and—actually *reveal* something." He stressed that one word, "reveal." He continued, "Schools of thought, ideologies galore, 'little systems' constipate academic thought, to use a most apt image."

"Then why don't you study poetry?" someone queried.

"That's worse! Nothing can evaporate the creative juices as quickly as 'studying' it."

Recalling these moments in my close and ongoing friendship with Ethan, I watch him finish fueling the truck. We both slide into the cab as if in synchronized movement, and I reflect on how he is such a peculiar synthesis of powerful intellect and visceral force: too expansive and unpredictable, too untamed for the demands of academic life or perhaps of any institution. True, he eventually taught poetry at a community college, but only on condition that they allowed him great latitude in pedagogy. His classes became—and are—events!

That's Ethan, I think to myself.

When Ethan turns toward the interstate, we both hear a clicking sound under the hood. "That can't be good," he notes, but we take to the highway, driving west.

If I tried to separate out the religious from the political, social, or economic motives guiding the people of Groom, Texas, I couldn't really do it. All of the forces that shape them are entangled with each other in the way they think and live. They don't seem to have difficulty mixing the layers of their lives and even confusing them. I grew up in places like this, and I can recall how the threads of personal and communal life seemed to form a fabric of seamless but rough design. Religion was crucial to the whole thing and related to it all, but it was not clearly distinct, except at times of formal practice or in a crisis. When people went to their respective places of worship, differences stood out, and occasionally considerable controversy could surface. Mostly, however, people tolerated each other on the generally unstated assumption that they had far more in common than not. Though some might have believed that other religious groups were ultimately doomed to perdition, they seldom went public with it. A strange version of "live and let live," at least for *now*, prevailed.

Of course, there were always the outsiders, people who never quite fit into the fabric. Even they served the purpose of being the exception. They helped define the edges. A town drunk or someone who "cussed" boldly, for instance, was an object lesson to every child. If these irregulars were especially religious and if their religion wasn't too strange, they might be allowed a certain grudging inclusion or be tolerated at a distance. They served as the accepted exception. In Amish country the same sort of tolerance is common.

If we're going to discuss religion, setting it apart for that purpose is not easy. It belongs to actual people in communities living particular lives all over the planet. Most of them do not talk about religion in an abstract way. They simply live religiously much the same way that they live politically and economically. Yet, for the most part people who are serious about their religion—like at least some in Groom, Texas—do not really see their religion as one thing among others. It more nearly binds it all together and makes the whole thing legitimate for them. It ties heaven and earth together.

The idea that religion is simply one thing among others has been popular for a long time among scholars who study religion. This point of view can be traced back at least to the eighteenth century and the beginning of what is often referred to as Modernity. Many of these thinkers are not themselves religious, and this raises questions about how far they are able to understand religion from such outsider positions. I wonder about that myself, and I have a hunch that there's a limit to how far anyone can grasp anything without participating in it in some way. Genuine knowing, I believe, is itself a kind of participation. Ethan and I agree to explore this idea later.

People who believe that religion is only one thing among others usually try to explain it by seeing it in relation to something else. A psychologist explains religion psychologically. A sociologist sees it as social in nature, an economist, economically. The list could be extended, but all of them have the same goal in mind: to *reduce* religion to something that it is not but that explains it. The effort to do this has continued for a couple of centuries and still dominates attempts to understand religion.

The hidden mission of this entire way of thinking is either to somehow do away with religion or to domesticate it. Most of all, such interpreters are trying either to reject or sidestep this basic question: *Is religion in any way true in its claims to make connection with a higher order of things on which all humans and the entire universe depend?* "And in the end, dammit," Ethan adds, "you can't bracket or ignore the issue of truth and authenticity in what religious people claim."

The question has two parts: whether there is any such thing as a higher order, and if so, whether religions can legitimately claim to make a connection with it. This is the Achilles heel of every effort to explain religion, if the effort begins with the conviction that the answer to this question is clearly negative or that it can be bracketed without ever removing the brackets. People who seriously practice any religion assume that the question is answered affirmatively for them. They do not hold to their religious orientation as a convenient comfort in the face of suffering and death, or as an illusion, much less as delusional. They embrace their religion as *true* connection between them and whatever ultimately claims and fulfills them. Perhaps they are duped but it might appear that way to me simply because we don't concur. There's no good reason to rush to the general conclusion that they are either duped or trying to achieve something else or playing tricks on the rest of us, or on themselves. This very notion of how to authenticate religious claims calls for further consideration of the sacred, as we discussed earlier, and its relation to religion.

I realize that we must agree with scholars who, like myself, study religion: religious people may be mistaken or deluded. Anyone can live an illusion without knowing it, and this includes the most devoutly religious, to say nothing of scholars. All of us, to one degree or another, do live in and with illusions. The belief that religious people are mistaken or deluded is widely embraced by those who wish to set aside or deny any truth in religious claims, but beginning there it is arbitrary and foolish.

If the sense of the sacred, as we discussed it this morning, is widespread among us humans, it will express itself in one way or another, and we will use symbols to do it. This whole process is what I call religion, what we're trying to examine. Simply put, it doesn't do to begin with denying or diminishing something as pervasive and persistent as the religious manifestation of our sense of the sacred.

One of the earliest and most influential ways of explaining the "mistake" of the religious was to call it a *projection*. A German named Ludwig Feuerbach made the most careful study of this idea early in the nineteenth century. It is deceptively simple. Human beings have needs and ideals for meeting those needs, but they do not have the power or capacity to fulfill all of their needs or to reach their ideals. To overcome the frustration this lack of power surely causes, humans have developed the brilliant strategy of projecting their wishes and longings out into the universe, as it were, and attaching them to a "god." Feuerbach's most famous statement summarizing this notion is that "all theological statements are anthropological statements." If I may put it another way, when we speak of "God," we are actually only speaking of our idealized selves as humans. Feuerbach believes that this process remains important and that religion is therefore potentially very useful to human fulfillment. At the same time, however, it is not true that there is a god or anything of substance "out there" to receive our projections. They are self-referential.

Let's admit that this interpretation of god is a brilliant way of explaining religion. Intriguing, to say the least! Many other thinkers who tried to understand religion for the next hundred years used this idea or some variation of it. The most notable example is Freud.

Still others have said that religion once had a purpose, but we have now developed as human beings to the point that we no longer need it. Religion is a mistake in human understanding that we have now uncovered and are in the process of overcoming. Or—and this is part of Sigmund Freud's explanation—religion is a human neurosis, a kind of low-grade illness of mind that humans need to overcome in order to be psychologically healthy. In all such cases, religion is taken to be either a mistaken or illusory *projection*, and as such, humanity should be rid of it.

Another variation on this same way of understanding religion is to declare that religion is both true and useful to human beings but not in the way it claims to be. It is not true in saying that through it we are connected to any higher order of things, but it may truly connect us to our social order. Or it may provide us a legitimate sense of hope and well-being. In other words, religion has a worthwhile role, at least potentially, to serve human fulfillment. These are ways of affirming a positive place for religion while denying or setting aside the most fundamental convictions of those who actually practice any given religion.

Here's a new angle for explaining religion away. There is simply no such thing as religion, only religions. Some go so far as to say that "religion" is a modern and western word invented to account for this or that. Or, religions are so many and so different from each other that comparing them or lumping them together under one overarching concept is impossible. This might be called the "divide and conquer" notion. About all we can do, they claim, is carefully study particular religions and find out how they work in their specific contexts within a given culture.

There's something to this because a hasty blending of distinct religious forms can produce an unsavory religious stew. Still, it seems to me that there are enough similarities, along with the differences, among what we call religions that they can be best understood by comparing them and especially by going beyond them to their primordial motivation. This kind of investigation isn't easy, but it can be done. I want to explore how to do it by seeking the ground of the whole enterprise, which has been tried before, and so to take it up again has pitfalls. We must walk gingerly on this terrain.

Even religious people have taken up this suspicion of religion. Imagine that! Popular religious movements sometimes maintain that theirs is not a religion but a *faith*, or in any case something else besides a religion. With so many religions, each so different from the others and each making competing claims, this response has been used to make a particular religion the *exception* by insisting that it actually does not belong to the category of religion.

This claim to exceptionality is most common among some Christian interpreters. They insist that Jesus was either against religion or certainly that he did not found a religion. Thus, to be a follower, all one need do is have faith in Christ. In this way, Christianity can avoid being compared to other religions. It is different qualitatively from religion. This move is clever, and it often rests on the truth that Jesus did not seek to found a new religion at all. But history will not allow this ploy to stand. The movement called Christianity shortly became, by virtually any standard, a religion with all of the forms and practices associated with a religion, and it continues as a religion as much among those who deny its religious character as among those who embrace it as their religion.

Others, for different reasons, prefer to call what they do *spirituality* in contrast to religion. They tend to be disillusioned with traditional religions and their trappings. Hence, the idea is to be spiritual without being religious—or better, without belonging to a religion. This notion is especially popular in the New Age movement, where it appears to have begun, but it also surfaces in the general population for people who want to replace formal religions with something vaguely related to it but somehow more liberating, free flowing—and superior.

When people say they are spiritual but not religious, I wonder what they can possibly mean. Is spirituality an attitude toward life and the universe? Does it involve a more specific way of living not followed by those who are not spiritual? And if this "spiritual" way of life is expressed in the world, doesn't it appear as religion? The concept of being spiritual but not religious is never clear to me. And how is spirituality actually distinct from or related to religion? I'm not saying the idea is misguided or simply false, but it is odd, and not immediately clear. Since spirituality is often set against or in contrast to religion, I keep thinking that surely there must be a relation between the two. Could it all be a judgment on religion for not being spiritual enough, whatever that might mean? In the end I'm left with two questions: Is it possible to be religious—or to practice a religion—and not be spiritual, and is it possible to be spiritual without a religion?

For starters *being religious* and *practicing a religion* are not the same thing, though they are related. I can see people practicing a religion in a nominal or conventional way without seriously and consistently shaping their lives by it. I'll go so far as to venture that the majority of people in all religious traditions appear to practice in this way. They exercise their religion as little more than an extension of their culture. In this sense they are not especially *religious*. Or should the word be "spiritual?" On the other hand, I can imagine a person being religious—I mean by this that they are devout in relation to the whole of things, possessing a sense of the sacred and a religious sensibility—without practicing any specific religion. But if they live their lives this way, what leads them to call themselves religious or for me to describe them as religious? I ask again, would the better word be "spiritual?" Or, again, might they be simply self-actualizing naturalists? If we're going to make sense of this muddle, we will want to begin by becoming clearer about these words: spiritual(ity), religious, religion.

The taller structures of Amarillo rise on the horizon, breaking the straight line of the earth's edge. I ask about food. We have groceries in the truck, but I want a break. Ethan talks about a steakhouse on the east side of town. It doesn't especially appeal to me. Too heavy. But I say nothing. I can do with a salad. In the edge of town we glide off the interstate and into the parking lot of a brash establishment that challenges anyone to eat their seventy-two ounce steak in one sitting. The reward: a free steak! I feel gorged thinking about it! The idea is very Texan—like that cross back at Groom!

The place is called Big Texan Steak Ranch. The crude image of a huge steak adorns a nearby billboard. "Sometimes I like 'big,' but these folk ratchet the whole idea out of proportion." As usual, Ethan is testy. "Big crosses—big steaks—big Texan! A fella could get the idea that big is the same thing as *good*. Whatever happened to *subtle* or *diminutive*?" We slide into a booth and stare blankly at gaudy menus.

With food to tame us, Ethan takes up the subject again. "What's the biggest thing?"

I stare at him, my mouth brimming with salad. "Well, the whole thing. That's the biggest thing."

"But the whole thing can't be a thing, because there's nothing else to measure it by."

"Not true. The whole thing is measured against no-thing," I contend. We fall into one of our free-flowing confabulations, throwing out whatever comes to mind and playing without any outcome expected. We simply follow the line of ideas for no other reason than to see where they lead. Some of my most useful insights have come through this process.

"All and nothing. The great either/or," he muses. "Then is God the All or the Nothing?"

"Yes!" I strike the table for emphasis and patrons turn to assess us both. Ethan pretends he's serious. "If we're gonna' have this idea of God at all," I continue, "It—and I prefer that impersonal pronoun—cannot be a thing or even the sum of things or over against things. It is at once in, through, and beyond—"

"Gobbledegook!" Ethan shouts. His plumber's practicality and poetic imagination combine to sidetrack my abstractions. "We'd better stick to something closer to us, like that distinction you brought up just before we escaped the interstate."

"You mean those words 'spiritual' and 'religious'?" I ask.

"Yeah, I have something to say about 'religion' and 'religious.' They go together somewhat, but they're not the same thing at all. When I talk about religion as a general idea, I'm thinking about a particular way people express their relation to whatever it is they find to be ultimate or final. Know what I mean? Any scheme of beliefs, actions, or attitudes that claims and forms this relation is a religion. It can be fairly informal, but most of the time it is formal and understandable to other people with similar beliefs, actions, and attitudes."

Ethan glances to check my face before continuing, "But people can do this without being especially religious." He puts up his two index fingers to indicate quotation marks. "If I think about a person being religious, I think of something like an unconditional and intense involvement. It has to do with the way they relate to the religion and through it to what they hold to be ultimate. I know that the word can be used in other ways, such as playing the stock market 'religiously,' but in its strict sense, being religious describes the sort of devotion people have to—or is it 'through'—their religion. The devotion to their religion aims to go beyond the religion to what the religion is about. And you can't be religious without having some fixed and concentrated way of doing it—and showing it. So, religion!"

I think he's through, but then he throws up a hand and adds, "And all religions are in the business of encouraging their folk to become more religious, I mean, devoted and intense about whatever the religion claims."

"So, being religious has to do with the *passion* people have for their religion?" I ask, stressing the word, passion.

"Something like that. Yep, I like that. It sounds close to 'lust.'" He beams. "You remember how Jonathan Edwards wrote about 'religious affections'? He was searching for this same idea, and passion may do as well as affection, but the point is that being religious is a personal matter of life-defining engagement. If that's passion, then I can buy it. How's that for fancy talk?" Ethan becomes what he considers too serious and backs away with his dismissive question.

****

The child lives near a railroad track. Trains traverse the countryside to punctuate the day. Their shrill blast announces their approach. When the child hears the chilling report, he is momentarily paralyzed. Then he races around to the other side of the house, where he can hide near the back steps.

The child is terrified of trains. They are black, gigantic, moving, and belching dark smoke that wafts across the yard as they pass, darkening the day. He does not know why the trains fill him with such anguish, but he does know one thing: he must never let the train see him. He must especially keep the headlight from seeing him. The only way to do this is not to see the train. This is why he rushes into hiding.

He hides near the kitchen, where he can usually hear the mother bustling through her routine. But he knows she is close, and this knowledge is his abiding consolation. As he crouches by the back steps, his body quivers, and he dare not come forth until he can no longer hear the train's rumble and roar. The feeling mixes horror with ecstasy and brews a darkly compelling moment.

The child never speaks of this. What would he say? How could he ex-

plain his terror? It is so much larger than his child's words can capture. It is only his experience of power and its threatening nearness. His father has worked for the railroad and often tells stories connected to the work. He sees his father as courage itself, the one who can tangle with trains and live to tell of it.

It will be half a lifetime before the child-cum-man realizes the force of the "locomotive-god." That is another story, another revelation.

****

I wipe my mouth before asking, "Then you'd say that people can have a religion and not be especially religious, but if you're religious, you need some form of religion."

"That sounds right, but I need to think more about it. The key word there is *form*. We thrive on form. We spend our days forming, unforming, reforming, and uh—transforming *everything*. That's the way we handle the otherwise chaotic world coming at us. We need to give it some order to make sense of it. So, if we're passionate, we'll have a passion for form, to use the going word here." He pauses, and gestures that he's now going in another direction.

"It's like we discussed earlier, we encounter the sacred but we can only do so by generating symbols and in that way we are already moving into the religious and toward religion." He grins broadly. "I hope I've sufficiently confused you for now," and he stands to leave.

I pay for lunch, and we walk toward the exit. Outside, the sun itself is big, blazing. We stand squinting beside each other, digesting. I ask, "But then where does that other word, 'spiritual', fit in relation to being religious and having a religion? Where's the confusion?"

Ethan walks toward the truck in silence. As we turn the truck around in the parking lot, there's that sound again, this time stronger. "Damn," Ethan says, "I hope that's not an omen. Next time we gas up, I'll check." I think, *Always the risk taker*.

We head for the entrance ramp to I-40 and he says. "I think that 'spiritual' and 'religious' are nearly the same thing. What folk are trying to say, when they insist that they're spiritual but not religious, is that they're not affiliated with any formal practice of a given system of religion."

"Well, not necessarily," I insist. "I find that all of this spiritual talk means too many different things to be only a synonym for 'religious'."

Ethan baits me, "All right, smart boy, lay it out." Then he reads the highway sign: "'Tucumcari,' dead ahead."

When we speak of spirituality, I believe we're referring to the vital uniting force of our very selves in its quest for meaning. It's what holds us together in our humanity and concentrates our energy so we can *live* in the qualitative sense. It is the intimate tie between our power to live and our drive to express that power in a significant way. Spirituality is that convergence! If this is true, then spirituality can be expressed in all of the basic ways we organize our existence: culture, morality, personality, and so forth. For instance, art is a singular expression of our spirituality.

The rub comes in relation to religion. Since so many people contrast spirituality with religion today—or bind them together in some fashion—that is what we need to untangle. Here's my attempt. Spiritual life, as I just described it, includes more than religion, but only in relation to religion does it reach its fullest expression. The religious aspect of spirituality is expressed in the effort to find the *connection* between the whole of our humanity and the ultimate order of things. I believe this effort is implicit even in such things as art, but religion makes it explicit and direct. Still, spirituality remains especially present in art as the most *creative* and *generative* way in which we express spirit. In art we strive to break out of our bondage to time, space, and to our embodied life by turning those boundaries into a vision, or spectacle, of whatever lies beyond while remaining close and, as it were, available to us. Art never fully or finally succeeds, but it is our most humanly fulfilling attempt. But when we more directly seek our relation to the larger order, the whole, spirituality reaches for and opens up to all that is beyond us. Religion is our inevitable attempt to order and express this quest.

Going back to the word "form" that Ethan brought up, religion is form. It gives form to the religious dimension of spiritual life, and the religious dimension of spiritual life is spawned by the encounter with the sacred that he and I discussed earlier. If this is true, then people may be religious without a religion—that is, without a specific form.

But the religious sensibility of spirituality will strive toward form and thus toward religion. It could be put this way: spirituality is the *dynamic* of religion, its "religiousness," and religion is the *form* spirituality takes in embodying our ultimate orientation. Symbols are the means of that embodiment. This way of understanding the matter has led me to the conclusion that a sharp separation between spirituality and religion is more confusing than helpful.

Form, of course, is itself a problem. Ethan is right: our whole lives are marked by an urge to give things form. I'm making this pilgrimage because I am committed to giving form to my *understanding* of religion. At the same time form is always limiting. Form confines, because it thrives on edges and boundaries. Not only is it limiting, it is limited. It establishes what belongs in bounds and what remains out of bounds. We are caught in this double bind: form is a necessary urge of spirit and at the same time a kind of binding and potentially bondage.

This double bind is the bottleneck for any and all religions: how can their forms express the dynamic of the religious sensibility without it turning into bondage? The same is true of all ways in which we form things, whether political, social, economic, aesthetic, or other. In relation to religion, however, the potential trap is especially threatening, because the form of religion claims to engage and articulate our connection to what is of ultimate significance for us, the *boundless*.

This dilemma lies at the heart of our pilgrimage.

Three

> In order for man to live he must either be unaware of the infinite, or he must have some explanation of the meaning of life by which the finite can be equated with the infinite.
>
> Leo Tolstoy

∼

On the east side of Santa Rosa Ethan pulls off the highway and stops. He points back. "Did you see that sign? It points toward Roswell and says it's the UFO capital of the world. I wonder how far it is down there."

I'm puzzled by his exuberance. "So?" I ask.

"There are some real freaky groups who believe we're being visited. It's a spooky kind of religion. Don't you remember when we all read *Chariots of the Gods*? I knew guys who swore that the reason people believe in gods and angels and all that is that we have a collective memory of visits from them. You know, from extraterrestrials."

Again, I respond, "So?"

"Oh, I don't know. Just thought it was interestin,' given what we're talkin' about." I pick up his drift at this point and offer an irrelevant comment that leaves him staring at me. He continues. "What I don't get is that they call these things they see in the sky, Unidentified Flying Objects!" He speaks with emphasis. "If they're 'unidentified,' how can we know what they are? Every tale that tries to explain them, especially the more mysterious ones about beings from other worlds, is pure fancy. I mean, made up from whole cloth—"

Ethan sits quietly, looking somber and becoming morose. "Sometimes I think all of the tales of religions and their endless web of symbols and rituals are just so much fancy. The harsh realities of life are just too much for us, so we conjure great epics of escape from it all." I've often discussed this sort of visceral skepticism with Ethan, and we've both wrestled it considerably. But he's more anguished about it, because of all he's seen and done. What he remembers.

Abruptly he concludes, "But what if they're right? One thing's for sure, whatever and whoever is right, we'll all be surprised by how things turn out." He starts the truck and struggles to steer it back onto the highway. Whatever the problem is with the truck, I notice it's getting worse.

At Santa Rosa we decide to stop for the night. It's not that late, but by the time we could reach Pecos, it would be. Besides, we're tired from the excitement of preparing and the adrenalin rush of the first day on the road. Our lodging requirements for the night are simple: cheap and clean.

As Ethan turns off the interstate and onto a road through town, the noise under the hood is stronger. "I think we've got a problem with the automatic steering. Damn!" I can tell he's turning the steering wheel with increased effort, and I'm glad we're at least in town.

We spot a motel off the interstate, but before paying we insist on checking the room. Marginally standard. The clerk wears a white turban. I ask him about it. He's a Sikh. He smiles when he announces it. America!

We discuss whether to haul our backpacks into the room, but Ethan has a locking system that should discourage scroungers. He grabs a small bag and enters the room before me, while I dig around for a toothbrush I forgot to pack in my overnight bag. Inside the dimly lit room, once my eyes adapt, I spy, first thing, an impressive 357 magnum on the stand beside Ethan's bed. "What the hell's that?" I ask, pointing.

"That's my baby," Ethan responds, patting the gun. "In places like this, I'm never without it." He notices that I'm restive. "Man, its security. Once you've been in the bush, you're always vigilant."

Then I realize. Vietnam is never entirely absent from Ethan's mind. By now, I think to myself for the umpteenth time, he should surely have some relief, but I dare not even suggest as much. As he reminds me over and over, "You weren't there."

Right! That dark war still shows its scars in people who endured it, while the rest of the world forgets its way into yet other wars.

Ethan can talk about his "drama in blood and bones"—his poetic way of describing it—endlessly, especially when drunk or stoned, but I'm in no mood at the moment to take up that wearisome topic. I go to the bathroom.

When I come out, Ethan has two books spread open on the table between the beds: a *Gideon Bible* and the *Book of Mormon*. I can tell that he wants to say something about them.

"Dueling Bibles," he says, pointing.

"Not quite. More like the original and the supplement or something like that," I retort.

"Yeah, I guess. They'd say the *Book of Mormon* completes what the other one started. Funny how so many religions try to be nice by saying what went before them is *good*, even important, but this latest thing—their thing—is better—and don't forget, *final*."

We head out the door to find food, still jabbering, until I point to the blazing horizon. We stand hushed in the parking lot, while the sun offers a lustrous adieu to the day. What draws me to this country is the surprise of nature, despite its ceaseless sameness.

Albert Camus concluded that the world is mute and, when all is said and done, "absurd." Not true. It speaks with a bold wordless voice, and when it does, we become speechless. Or, we break into poetry. I can tell Ethan is in the thrall of the moment. He stands transfixed for a couple of minutes before muttering, "What great round thing is that! It comes and goes but never leaves. . . I spy all life in it."

Trudging along the roadside toward a sign celebrating Gustavo's Kitchen, we settle for the consolation of silence. We say nothing until seated in a booth, staring once again at a one-page laminated menu.

"When a spectacle like that confronts me, the business of UFOs or dueling Bibles and everything they represent becomes a kind of joke. Who the devil are we to pose and posture ourselves, 'our little systems' as. . . what? As *if* we had . . .the final Word! We're such clowns, and the problem is we don't know we're clowning."

Ethan's neither angry nor cynical, but seeing that UFO sign and those sacred books has set him off. He speaks as though stumped by what he so often calls the "Circus of Folly," referring to the whole human undertaking. Vietnam still lies just below the surface in images of defoliation, desecration of the earth, and ripped bodies.

I'm surprised at how tired we seem to be. After dinner we stroll back to the motel, turn on the television for half an hour, surfing the sparse channel options, and then Ethan yawns and stretches. "Man, I'm about ready to sack out."

"Me too," I admit.

"We'll need to check that steering problem in the morning," Ethan says with an edge of anxiety in his voice. "Should'a done it yesterday." After he brushes his teeth, he adds, "I'm piss-poor at takin' care of business like that. Don't want to hear bad news, I guess."

After a breakfast of huevos rancheros the next morning at Gustavo's place, we ask about a mechanic. When we pull out to follow directions to the mechanic, it takes both of us to turn the steering wheel. We wonder whether we can make it, but there's little traffic. We sputter into the driveway of a little business, Pauli's Auto Shop, and chug to a halt.

Ethan goes into the shop, and he and Pauli come out. Pauli wipes his hands on an orange rag and opens the hood. I step out and join them in time to hear him say, "Dry as a bone. You needed fluid way back there." He steps in the truck, starts it, and turns the steering wheel. "She's frozen." After checking more, he concludes "Now I see. Fluid wouldn't do much good. Seal's busted. It'd leak right out."

We discuss options, and after a phone call we learn there isn't a replacement in town but there is one back in Tucumcari. We could try a junk yard on the other side of town, but that would be a "crap shoot," as he puts it. Pauli says his wife could go for the part and be back in a couple of hours, but with another two jobs already promised, it'd take most of the day for the repair. Pauli apologizes, "I'm a one-man show here, and. . . " He did not finish and did not need to.

Ethan and I confer and decide to go ahead. What else can we do, really? Pauli's wife comes out with some cans of Coke and a flask of water for us. We're surprised. She says, "You can go around behind the house where there's some lawn furniture you can use. I'll be back as soon as I can." We thank her profusely, and she drives away. Pauli is already back inside the garage, and we don't see him again until she returns at almost noon.

We both go to the truck to retrieve books, and I bring along my journal. We haul the beverages to the backyard and take chairs around a dusty glass-topped table. Green. Everything is some shade of green. I can tell Ethan's brooding over this hitch in our plan, but he says nothing. He's reading a novel by Hermann Hesse, currently his favorite author. I take up my journal and review conversations from yesterday.

Ethan sets his novel aside, and we launch a discussion on the great diversity of religions and how they're increasingly in our backyards in America. I mention the lively Sikh we met at Gustavo's, but this subject is old terrain and at first we're not enthusiastic about plowing it again. After a few random exchanges, we drift into silence. Ethan takes up the novel again, while my mind continues to ruminate on the subject of so many religions in the world.

People have encountered religious differences from antiquity. There's no doubt of that, but however this fact may have been treated in the past, it is now before us with unprecedented urgency. In the first place, religions from all over the planet are accessible to each other, and in the second place, new religions are arising to challenge or supplant more traditional ones. Beyond that, religions are being forced to accommodate to the fact that no one of them can claim superiority or finality without being opposed by another. Some religions have more adherents and are more widely distributed around the world, but this only has to do with a quantitative advantage, as in "my religion is bigger than yours."

On this pilgrimage, if we're going to gain a more adequate grasp of religion, we might as well begin with this obvious fact: there are so many religions so distinct from each other that the one word "religion" may not be adequate to account for them all. This is the view of one American philosopher, John Dewey. He wrote a little book on the subject in which he says that we cannot properly use the terms *religion* or *religions*, because what is included under them is far too diverse. I disagree with Dewey, but he does alert me to the need for some explanation. So, I want to answer this question: What is *religion*, given the fact that there are so many different versions of it? But I don't want to start with some general definition. Too abstract, and premature.

Among people who seriously study religion today, two ways of sorting out the answer, along with variations, are common. One answer, Dewey's, is that religions are simply too distinct and too many for anyone to adequately comprehend them all under one umbrella concept. The only solution is to study particular religions for what they are and leave it at that. Some allow for limited generalizations about the character of all or most religions, but others won't even go that far. I call this way of thinking *atomism*.

The opposite answer usually has to do with the idea that religion has a surface form and expression—what anyone can observe—and a deeper underlying pattern. If we study particular religions carefully enough, we can uncover or discern a larger pattern which it shares with other religions—and in principle in all religions. No religion includes all elements of the pattern, but when enough are present, we can reasonably conclude that a religion is being practiced.

Those who don't like this notion of a unifying underlying pattern often call it *essentialism*, and they believe that nothing, including religion, has an essence, or if it does, we cannot get at it. I'm not an essentialist, but I certainly lean more in that direction than toward *atomism*. My reason: things are connected, and it's more important to discover connections than simply to make distinctions and leave it at that. Making distinctions best serves our interest in connection and is only preliminary to making connections. This is a bias I heartily confess!

Atomism is right to insist that every religion is *particular*. For instance, any given religion belongs to a culture and expresses itself in specific ways by specific people in a specific time and place. If we do not recognize and honor this fact, we'll never begin to understand any religion. Even the same religion—say, Islam—is noticeably different in different settings and at different times. Anthropologist Clifford Geertz studied Islam in Morocco and in Indonesia and concluded that, while both countries practice the same religion, the way it is expressed is profoundly different due to differences in cultural background and social practice. This is to say nothing of differences among sects, denominations, or other internal varieties within a given religion. The most casual attention to various forms of Christianity in one typical American town—say, Groom, Texas—is enough to show this.

But notice! Despite the differences between Moroccan and Indonesian Muslims, the religion itself remains Islam. It is sufficiently *the same* to bear the same name. If this is true of one religion, might it not also be true of different religions insofar as they are expressions of the umbrella concept, *religion*? To what extent can we say of quite distinct religions that they remain somehow the same?

These days it is popular to solve the entire problem of religious diversity by using such clichés as "we're all in different boats headed for the same shore" or "there are many ways up the mountain." Such glib comments sound much too naive and dismissive of the question, utterly ignoring significant differences among religions. Simply to decree that all religions are the same will not do. I find this point of view too superficial and sometimes even deprecating of the uniqueness of given religions or all religions.

Yet, this popular way of thinking may possibly point in the right direction. By paying close attention to the variety of religions, their differences as well as their common patterns, we may come closer to a proper grasp and appreciation of religion as such. I like to think such progress is possible.

If I'm asked whether religions can and should be compared with each other, I come down in favor of doing so. If for no other reason, comparing religions may help each religion to better understand itself. In fact, any attempt to understand anything, beginning with myself, requires comparison. It's not easily done well, and it can be overdone or underdone. Even more, comparison is often done to make one thing superior to another, usually the one with which we identify ourselves when making the comparison. Still, all learning includes comparison, and no one should be surprised that this applies to religion.

More importantly, comparison has the potential to cause change within religions. While this potential can be threatening to religions that see themselves as the exception, or superior in one way or another, no religion is a fixed thing, frozen in time; and no religion has simply arrived.

Religions, living ones at least, have an ongoing history. No doubt this is bad news for some, but if it is the case, and I believe it is, then history reveals that change is not the enemy of religion. Simply put, religions constantly change, either toward greater adequacy or toward decline, and within the history of any religion, it tends to undergo both processes. Religions flourish and fade, rise and fall, wax and wane. The terrain of history is scattered with dead religions, and no religion is immune to the possibility that it will not survive.

More positively, any phenomenon expressing the human spirit, if it is *alive*—that is, viable—is engaged in a process of *challenge and response*, if I may put it that way, in relation to the context in which it finds itself. At the heart of our current global context, one dominant challenge is the immanent presence of religions other than our own, and the issue before us is our response. How do we change to meet this challenge?

All orderly systems and institutions established by human beings tend to be conservative. They strive to survive and to preserve and perpetuate themselves. Thus, they resist change or at least strive to maintain maximum continuity as they endure changes. This resistance to change is especially true of religion, because, in general, it claims to provide both cosmic and personal stability and assurance of continued, eternal, stability. Relatively modest changes can threaten this constancy, and an encounter with another religion, even a "friendly" one, can lead to trauma and reaction within a religion. Such an encounter is one way that any religion today may suffer an *identity crisis*. While some religions are more likely than others to see this as a threat, any religion can be threatened by other religions within its cultural habitat, and these days that habitat, more and more, includes the planet.

Up to this point I'm not advocating any particular change in any religion. I am only reviewing what appears to me to be the current situation for any religion. Perhaps it will help to indicate what I'm not advocating.

First, I am not asking that religions deliberately blend or join with other religions. I do not insist on any particular syncretism. I do believe that such blending inevitably happens in religions: they borrow from each other and mutually influence each other, often in unconscious ways. This even happens between religions that are quite hostile to each other. However, I do not and would not suggest a deliberate syncretism as the way to deal with the encounter of one religion with others. Every religion best continues by sustaining its identity and character as well as it can, but it need *not* be hostile or dominating. At the same time I also believe that, when religions encounter each other in any basic or sustained way, they will affect each other. Enough said.

Second, and even more emphatically, I do not advocate any sort of move toward one universal religion. While I do believe that religion is now evolving and will continue to evolve in ways I would not dare try to predict, it is not likely to evolve into a monolithic super-religion. I would not even favor such a prospect. The lively engagement of difference and the examination of common ground are far too promising for me to want that possibility to disappear. Nevertheless, in the process of such an engagement religions will alter in unpredictable and, potentially, both positive and negative ways, but the encounter of any religion with other religions can enhance all of them.

One of the rewards of comparing religions and of religions comparing themselves to others is the possibility I mentioned earlier: the disclosure of *underlying patterns* that expose the deeper common character of religion across its many expressions. I do not intend to seek those patterns here. That will come later, after we first examine the bedrock that makes religion possible, and feasible, in the first place.

Here I only want to make it clear that I do believe there are such patterns and that they are fairly evident through careful attention to the "family" of religions. This does not necessarily lead to the idea that there is a fixed nature or essence to religion, but there are sufficient common features among religions to suggest that its subterranean vitality within human experience moves toward universality. I may revisit this later, but for now I want to stake out some broad boundaries for this inquiry into religion.

"But that only leads to another connected question," Ethan, having set Hesse aside and considered the subject with me, insists. "How may one religion be superior to another? This is a bear of a question for more than one reason, but we can begin by admitting that every religion likely sees itself as, if not superior to all others, at least fully adequate among religions. I'm not inclined to question this way of seeing one's religion. It may even be inevitable. If nothing else, it belongs to the universal ego tendency to favor the familiar over the strange or alien."

I chime in, "But beyond this, the question remains whether there is a reliable basis for ever saying that one religion is objectively superior in any sense whatever to any other."

"One way to solve this," Ethan proposes, "is to say that, as long as a religion is alive for those who practice it and as long as it doesn't threaten the equally legitimate religions of others, then all religions are pretty much on the same footing. This sounds nobly inclusive, and many will readily agree. It's the 'tolerant' attitude to hold." He makes his quotation marks in the air.

Pauli comes out to check on us and promises that his wife should return in about half an hour. "She called to make sure she had the right part." He turns and walks back to the shop, wiping his hands on that same orange cloth, a mechanic's habit I've noticed.

"But this doesn't seem to get at the deeper problem," I resume abruptly. "Can a religion be more or less *adequate* than others? Or, more strongly, can one religion be universally the best to the exclusion of all others?"

Ethan says with a grin, "Maybe we've got a steering problem! What if we have turned the whole discussion in a wrong direction and can't seem to turn back. For instance, I'd rather raise a radically different sort of question. Maybe the first question of all! Is religion itself, when push comes to shove, fatally flawed? I mean, so damaged at its very roots that it needs to be rooted out. . . eliminated? I can say this much, that religions can do and have done horrendous things in their names, but does this mean that the religion itself, in its character as religion, is fatally flawed?"

"Well," I retort, "if we do agree that some religions, as religions, are inherently flawed in ways that others are not, then we're obligated to examine the basis for saying so. By what standard are they to be judged? Don't we have to find out what makes a 'good' religion? Or maybe we need to ask when a religion is being most genuinely. . .or authentically religious? Man, that's a jungle!"

"That's not quite what I asked," Ethan insists. "I didn't say 'some religions.' I'm talkin' about any or all of 'em. . .about religion, plain and simple. Start at the beginning." Ethan's always into beginnings, and I can tell he's still working on his reaction to that UFO sign.

"Is any religion 'good'?" I pose. "Maybe religion is somehow a bad thing, a human dis-ease of some sort. Or maybe, like ole' E. B.

Tylor says, it's obsolete...a kind of mistake of the primitive mind. Could this be a fatal flaw?

"That can't be ruled out. We've talked about this many times. Religion might be only a distraction to keep us pacified. Or, we may, like Tylor says, have outgrown the need for it. We both agree on that possibility. Could it be that it once worked for 'primitive' people, when they felt more limited and less adequate, but now we really don't need it?"

"Yeah," Ethan chimes in, "it's just a *superstition*... I hate that word. What the hell does it really mean anyway? Usually people apply it to what they don't believe, you know, as a way to put down what they don't believe."

"Don't get off the subject," I insist. "We're tryin' to give reasons for doing away with religion altogether. Here's one: religion is not 'true,' but it still meets a need for consolation and feelings of security."

"But that's no argument to get rid of religion. That only placates religious people for being religious. Very condescending! Sounds like a putdown to me."

"It is, no doubt. That's my point. It makes religion something else besides what religions are all claimed to be by the people who practice them. So, it's taking the religiousness out of religion and making it a sop... and an illusion. Nietzsche believed something like this about religion and especially about Christianity, but he had the guts to go ahead and insist that we do away with it altogether on that account. He thought it encouraged people to be 'weak and pitiful.'"

Ethan places a beefy hand on my shoulder and mockingly consoles. He adds in feigned sympathy, "What's the matter, partner, have you lost your *ubermensch* again?"

Pauli's wife drives into their front yard and takes the automatic steering mechanism directly to the shop. Pauli comes out, holds it up for us to see, and disappears back into his world of work. We walk a mile or so to a diner for a burger and stroll back in the mild spring warmth.

I return to our earlier discussion. "The strongest criticisms of religion I've run across are that it's either pathological or evil, or both."

"Like I said," Ethan reminds me, "religion can be horrendous.

Just look at the record. It has blood on its robes and plenty of it." He gestures broadly, "And that says nothing about how many people are screwed up by it. Sometimes I do think it might be better to get rid of it, but that'll be the day. Besides, it may not be the fault of religion. It's what people can do with it. If we can mess up every other bit and piece of our existence, why should religion be the exception?"

"But. . ." I begin.

He interrupts. "I know what you're gonna say. You're gonna ask that question you always bring up. If some religion is sick or downright evil, does it mean that evil is all religion amounts to?

"Something like that," I add, "because if that's the case, then we can turn around and go home. This dilemma is really what we said we're goin' to work on for the next three weeks."

Ethan's eyes light up, and he exclaims, "No brother, we don't have to turn around. I've heard there are people up in 'them thar hills' who like to party." He gives a knowing grin, then adds, "I still can't believe I agreed to do this whole thing. The hard ground for three weeks! Have I lost my mind or what?"

"Oh, that happened some time ago," I assure him. "You're only now noticin'." Ethan responds by making his lunatic face.

I insist, pounding on the glass table, "I do, I do, I do believe there's something down at bedrock that makes religion, not only inevitable, but crucial. . .even if it is dangerous and often becomes distorted in one way or another."

"We'll see," Ethan says wryly as he glances my way.

I realize we haven't really faced up to the other question, the one about how we distinguish among religions and which one or ones might be more adequate than others. Maybe that can't be answered, but I can at least say this much: I do not believe any one religion can be superior to all others and certainly not to the exclusion of all others! Not actually, not ideally. Since religion, like everything else that belongs to being human, is dynamic and changes in response to the conditions of time and space, no religion can be final or perfect. Beyond this I don't have a need to go further, at least for now.

Here's a more important idea. If religion did not serve some basic purpose for human beings, at least possessed some minimal survival value, it would disappear. Any biologist might say as much.

Since it hasn't done so, despite the tremendous pressure of our secular age to diminish its significance, I've proposed to Ethan that we seek that grounding purpose that explains the continued presence and force of religion. This entire pilgrimage could be our attempt, at least implicitly, to unearth the purpose of religion within the stuff of human existence and thereby discover a basis for assessing the adequacy of any religion. This is perhaps more than ambitious, and it could be foolhardy. Nothing's to be lost, however, by inquiring into the possibility.

We walk out to the truck, where Pauli's had his head under the hood on and off for almost an hour. "I've 'bout got her ready," he announces as we approach. "A couple of contrary bolts slowed me down." We stand watching as he tightens a bolt and says, "That should do it." I stare at the spanking new mechanism amid the worn partners around it as Ethan follows Pauli into the shop. He shortly returns with a receipt, and Pauli comes out behind him. We both thank him.

"I guess we'll just stay for another night," Ethan says as we drive away. I immediately agree. Like yesterday, it's too far to Collins' cabin, where we're headed, and there's no place to stay in between.

We're not thrilled about another meal at Gustavo's, but we endure it, mostly in silence, as we listen to Hispanic music. In the early evening we read, exchange a few random observations and reflections, and let sleep gradually take over.

Four

If the doors of perception were cleansed, everything would appear to man as it is: infinite. For man has closed himself up, till he sees all things through narrow chinks of his cavern.

William Blake

∼

Ethan's up and stirring around the room. Early for him. As I come to life, I can tell he's moody. He's usually quiet in the mornings, but this is different. We begin the day without a word. Only after we've dressed, made our way to one last feeding at Gustavo's, and ordered from the menu does Ethan speak.

"Had that damn dream again last night," he begins as his hands caress a warm mug of coffee.

"Which one?" I ask.

"Oh, I mentioned it the other day, when I said I thought my mind was tryin' to make me ready for this trip."

"How's that?" I want to penetrate his opaque references without setting him off. It's too early in the day for that.

As if in a trance, Ethan recites his dream:

> I'm back in the bush. We've had this blinding melee of a battle, and I'm the only one left. I've lost my rifle and gear and I'm running through the jungle. I run fast, faster than a human can run. It's like I'm not runnin' away but trying to find something or somebody. I cry out as I run, 'Oh God, Oh God! You've gotta help me.'
> And this voice says to me, while I'm runnin' like fury, 'Slow down. You're not going to die. You've just begun.' The voice is soothing, and I slow down. I'm walking in a normal way, despite an urge in my gut to begin running again. When I've slowed to a kind of stroll, the voice comes again: 'There now. That's better. See, you're not going to die. You're only going to wish you had!' And the voice begins this distant loud laugh, as though it's a joke.

"I tell ya' man, it's the scariest screwball dream I've ever had. It's worse than all those gory blood-bath ones I've told you about." He looks out the window for half a minute before saying, "Here's what it feels like. God's making a riddle I'm supposed to solve, but I'm the riddle!" He sits back as though exhausted.

Our hearty huevos rancheros come, and we eat. Ethan continues. "Tell you what. I think everything we've discussed in the last two days is beside the point. Academic falderal! Here we are, making the same distinctions we keep making and tryin' to clear the deck for. . .I don't really know what, I guess for clarification. But you cannot begin at any sort of beginning." He strikes the table with his hand, and his face takes on a momentary angry aspect. "We all wake up in the middle, with the whole mess all around us, and we have to make sense of it from there or from nowhere. That goes for religion and for everything else."

I can tell he's fed up with what he calls my academic egghead way of trying to make sense of things. That's nothing new, and I know he's at least partly, maybe totally, right. I ask, "Where do you think we should start?"

"Maybe with that crazy dream," he blurts. "I don't know, but this much I'll stand on: religion's somehow a special kind of subject. I can't really nail it down, but maybe it's like. . .well, you know. . . the basis of everything else in our lives, but, like in that dream, it comes at us in a gigantic riddle with a laugh added to it."

I stumble over words before admitting, "I think you're right, and I want to go there, but I'm lookin' for a way to begin."

"All right. Let's start right in the middle." He stands for effect. "Religion's all around us. Everywhere there are humans, religion shows up, and all of the attempts to get rid of it have failed. So, we gotta' take it as it is, right here in front of our faces. I recommend we go back to that one question, where we started out, and this time stay with it. Why in hell are people religious in the first place. . . I mean, religious at all? If we can get down to that, we can build something up from it, but without coming right at the question, we're going to stir the same old stew we always do."

"Right, but what about the. . . "

Ethan interrupts, "Start with this. Are you, I mean you and no one else. . .are you religious?" He reaches across the booth and pokes his finger in my chest to emphasize how direct he intends the question to be. Before I can answer, he continues. "Ya' see, the problem with every attempt to understand religion by walking around it and jabbing at it. The problem with that is that it takes the life right out of the whole subject. It kills the patient in order to study it." When I try to object, he waves me aside. "I know all the arguments about being objective. . .about getting at the evidence." He says this with a smirk, then adds, "And that's a good thing in its place, but religion's more nearly like something we are already wrapped in. We start inside it. Or it's inside us. Words are such bastards when it comes to what I'm thinkin' right now. That friggin' dream undid me, I tell ya'."

I know Ethan's words name what I've really wanted to do on this pilgrimage, but I've hidden in the thicket of my own rational quandary. Rather than move into the subject, I've moved around it and away from it in order to *gain perspective* or something of the sort. But religion is somehow a peculiar subject that can never be adequately understood by making it purely an object and *investigating* it like a geologist might study a volcano. Thinking this way, I know, will drive my academic and scholarly colleagues to distraction, but I'm not here to satisfy them. . .or myself, really.

As we leave the café, I say to Ethan's back, "All right. Yes. I am religious, and I've been saturated with it since I first peeped over the bassinet. It's been a convoluted journey, but my most intellectual attempts to understand religion are all driven by my own lifelong participation in it. So, what're we to make of that? I mean, how does that help us kick this thing off?"

As we approach the room to retrieve our gear, Ethan turns. "Why?" he asks.

"Why what?" I counter.

"Why are you religious? Do you have a choice, actually? Have you been had by religion?" He pauses. "Or, is it the result of being born into that pious clan, your family?"

I ponder this question as I brush my teeth and gather my few things for our departure. Ethan follows suit, and we're inside the truck in minutes. We leave Santa Rosa at last, leave the interstate and head across the prairie toward yet another interstate and then on to Pecos. We should make it probably by around noon.

"I could say," I begin, "that I haven't been able to find a way out of religion. But that sounds feeble, and it doesn't say much."

"I noticed," Ethan responds with his first grin of the day. "But you really haven't tried to get away from it. You're hooked."

Am I? Hooked, I mean? I think to myself. *Am I addicted... caught.* I continue musing as I stare through the windshield at the pinion and sage whizzing past.

Standard answers to Ethan's penetrating question, such as the fear of death, have never been sufficient to explain why I'm religious. At best that's only part of the picture. There's something deeper, more foundational, a kind of primordial intuition close to instinct. Although I've thought about what it might be, I seek it like a blind man searches in a well lit room. The best I've found so far has to do with a sort of preconscious experience, if that makes sense. The only language that works to take me further is to describe the experience as a *finite encounter with the infinite*. I know this sounds abstract and goes right by most people, but it speaks to me.

****

Saturday, a free day to be fleshed out. Nothing spectacular. "A movie," she suggests. They examine offerings. Equus. The advertisement spreads large across the page.

> Alex is an adolescent with a troubled soul. He has finally been noticed by a young woman at the stables where they work. She draws him to her. They rendezvous for an evening.
> After awkward, tentative adventures into the town and into the night, she boldly lures him back to the stables. Seduction unfolds in the loft, but abruptly Alex flees her. He descends to the floor of the stable, where six magnificent equine beasts stand tethered for the night. Alex ceremoniously removes a scythe from the wall and stabs each horse through both eyes.
> On the psychiatric ward, Alex gradually reveals himself to and through a priest of the mind. The young man worships horses! They are his gods, and he lives his passion through them. His daily work is his life. Horses! But they are gods, and they dare not be allowed to see him with the woman in the loft. He must, in the presence of the woman, hide from the gods. Or hide the gods from himself.
> But the priest of the mind sees more. He sees something missing in himself: the absence of passion, of encounter with the gods. The priest can "heal" Alex, but what will be lost? The passion of dwelling among

the gods will be removed, and...what? What will be left for Alex? The priest's own drab existence stands exposed. Despite the horror of the sightless horses, he envies the patient!

The man and woman leave the theater. He is troubled, but the disturbance lies in the depths, where he cannot reach. He tries to speak, but he is in a stupor. He asks for solitude, and she encourages him into it. He drives to his solitary dwelling, where he lies sleepless into the night. He knows the film, Alex, the priest are addressing him.

Starkly awake and restless to exorcise his bewilderment, the man sits on the edge of his bed. As if a door had opened to his trove of memories, he sees himself. He is a young child. He is in the yard. A train whistle sounds in the distance. He shudders with terror, and flees behind the house to crouch near the back door, where the mother putters with her day. He is safe there. The train...and especially the locomotive...cannot see him hiding.

Transported back to his original god, the man finds himself adrift in the elemental moment of recognition. For Alex horses serve, but for the man it is the locomotive. This distinction makes no difference. They are both gods, and, as with Alex, he knows again the first moment of divine intrusion, where the overwhelming Other engulfed and left him trembling.

The man identifies with Alex. But what about the priest? Two forces present themselves: the initial passion of the primordial god-encounter, and the propensity to domesticate the revelation! Alex and the priest of the mind dwell in the man. They are at odds, but intimately so. The sophistication—that is, the sophistry—of growing up steals the passion of the first brush with the infinite. Its allure recedes into the background, and the throbbing dynamic is tamed with the halter of "decency and order." The alternative? Madness! Or, can the child persist in the man?

Breakthrough is never enough. It only leaves the door ajar.

****

Long before we can possibly be *aware* of the dilemma of our existence, we experience it obliquely, shrouded by the clouds of our budding consciousness. We sense the abyss, the possibility of endlessness, indeed, of nothing. Death and our fear of it is only a crucial shock that brings this more elemental intuition to our conscious attention, and this consciousness usually comes later.

The religion of our birth-family does not *cause* this...how can I put it, this *shock of infinity*. At best, our familial religion only brings the experience into a kind of formal focus, but this process is complicated, because religion as we experience it through family and culture can actually distract us from this most elemental *knowing*. Damn. That's not really it.

"See what I mean," Ethan says. "Language can't get at what we're talkin' about."

"Then what would you call it?" I insist.

Ethan, now warming to the subject, grins as he proposes, "We'll need to make it up."

This is right. What I'm trying to dig into is so far below the surface of ordinary conscious experience, so far below our memory of the thing itself, that I need some way of indicating it. After a bit I suggest this perhaps awkward phrase, the *Primary Impulse*. Yes, the elemental instinctive intuition of my finitude caught in the thrall of the infinite is the Primary Impulse.

I call it *primary* because it grounds and undergirds our very awakening to existence as human beings. We "fall" into our humanity through the crucible of this moment of our finitude's encounter with the infinite. We *participate* it. I call it an *impulse*, because it's not actually consciously and readily available to us. It more nearly wells up and claims us as terror and ecstasy.

"I notice," Ethan interrupts, "that you sometimes use 'participation' without putting the preposition *"in"* after it. Why?"

"Yeah, I do," I admit. "It's because I'm using 'participation' in a special, sort of technical sense. The way I use it stresses that we are more or less defined and shaped by our participation. It constitutes us... .I. . ."

Before I can say more, Ethan points. In the distance ahead of us, the first long gray line of horizon hints of the high country. I continue.

"Maybe this'll help me make it a little clearer," and I proceed to tell the story of the birth of my son, the first child. He was only about two or three weeks old, and we had the habit of placing him in the middle of the bed on his back. I noticed that periodically, as his arms and legs flailed, he suddenly jerked and a momentary fear seemed to register on his face. This kept happening to him, and it bothered me. He was the first kid, and I wanted everything to be perfect. I worried that he might be spastic.

When we visited the pediatrician, I asked her about these jerks. She asked questions about exactly when and how he did this. Then she said, "Oh, he's jerking because he can't find the edge."

"Edge? Edge of what?" I asked.

"The womb." she responded. "He's been closely confined there for nine months, and he's seeking some limit, because he can't really imagine where he is without it." She went on to talk to us about swaddling him or putting pillows on each side of him.

Ethan's taken with my story. "That's right. When nothin's defined and bounded, we're lost. I remember when I started writing poetry, and I was experimenting with blank verse. Then one day I read Robert Frost's criticism of blank verse. He said it was like playing tennis without a net. That cured me. I knew almost immediately that what I needed was a limit, a barrier to allow my poetry to. . .to come forth, poetically. Otherwise, it'd be so much spilt water."

"But then," I counter, "there's the boundless. . .you know, the space where there's no edge, or in your case, the sea of words and silences with no prescribed order. When my son couldn't find the edge, he was. . .and of course this is way too sophisticated to be exact, I'm probably over interpreting. . .lost in the potency of infinity. I remember how startled he'd look to me. He was flabbergasted by the nothingness of his new habitat. He feared free fall."

That's how basic this idea of our finite encounter with infinity is. It belongs to what the philosopher Martin Heidegger calls our "throwness." We're cast into the abyss of human existence, and we must find our way within the conditions available. This is our foundational double bind. We are terrified by the lack of edges, the threat to our finite condition, but we're at the same time fascinated and drawn beyond the edge. We suffer the urge to enter infinite possibility and at the same time to confine it and bind it to the limitations of our own finitude. We lust for infinity, but we become lost in the details of our finitude. This is the thrall and thrill of existence.

As a result of the double bind inherent in the Primary Impulse, our earliest inclination is to flee from infinity, and we have an impressive arsenal of protections from pursuing what the Primary Impulse has to teach us. Through my own self-examination and listening to and observing other people, I've distinguished three strategies most commonly used to escape the implications of the Primary Impulse.

"Lay 'em out," Ethan says, but then he abruptly pulls off the road and into a scenic overlook. We step out of the truck and walk to a low retaining wall. We're looking east into the mid-morning light. A panel is provided to describe the history of the area we're viewing. First, the Native peoples, then the Spanish, then the western trekkers, and now us! One bit of information especially impresses us. The prairie tall grass was so high when the first Spanish explorers ventured here, that they had to have poles held up with little flags on them to keep up with each other. And they were riding horses! Now the grass is barely ankle high, worn down by the tread of our kind and over grazing of our livestock. "Still," Ethan concludes, "It's ravishing country. I could stay right here 'til dark."

We return to the truck, and Ethan asks me to drive for a while. He wants to, as he says, "watch the land unfold." Once we're on the road, he says, "You said something about the ways people keep tryin' to side step their fear of infinity," and this gives me a cue to go back to our discussion.

First, and probably the basis for the rest is downright *denial*. We cut ourselves off from the threat of infinity. It's too much for us, because it reveals our definitive condition: *vulnerability*. This vulnerability is why we flee to whatever security we can muster, first our parents, then our local world, and finally the great cultural cocoon. Through all of this we join with others like ourselves to provide ourselves with a *world*. That is, we replace the threat of infinity with a large, perhaps expanding, but contained order.

Second, we carry out our denial by *deviation*. I mean deviation from infinity-as-infinity. We conjure what might be called more *manageable infinities*. Of course, these are not infinity at all but fancied schemes for projecting a sense of totality or of the whole onto our range of comprehension. This strategy is more nearly an effort to trap infinity in the interest of mastery and accounts in part for the Promethean projects of our kind. We simply cannot abide infinity-as-infinity, as the formless abyss. It's horrifying! And religion itself can be perhaps the most definitive deviation of all.

Or, third, we are even less astute, when we pursue our denial by *distraction*. This is by far the most common strategy of all. We simply become preoccupied with whatever is immediately at hand. We entangle ourselves in the details of *everydayness* as though it were an end in itself. We don't live *in* the moment; we live *for* the moment. Indeed, not a few of us assume that our moments are ends in themselves, and we are left with the question framed in a popular song of some years ago: *Is that all there is?*

"I think there's a fourth possibility," Ethan interjects.

"Like what?" I want to know.

"Uh, not sure how to put it, especially if you're using alliteration like you do, but . . .well here's a go at it. It's the strategy of 'diving in.'" He uses his signature air quotes. Some people actually evade by overdoing in some way the very thing they would otherwise evade. They dive into infinity so obsessively that they miss the everydayness that might otherwise temporize their passion. You know, allow it to be more nearly related to the everyday." He looks away before adding, "They're addicted to infinity as an effort to deny finitude. Yeah, that's it."

"What troubles you about that?" I ask.

"Mostly what gets to me is that they think, because they've crossed the threshold of . . .of. . .let's call it *'the divine encounter,'* they've arrived. They confuse the first step with the destination. They forget what Merton put so brilliantly, 'In the spiritual life every step is the first step.'"

"Are you saying that such an option does the opposite of denying or avoiding the infinite by simply plunging into it and thus avoiding finitude itself?"

"Right. Something like that," Ethan agrees. "It's like denial, deviation, and distraction in reverse. Instead of running from the infinite, the trick is to hide away from life in some version of the infinite. . .It's a denial of finitude itself." He looks at me with a sort of puzzled glee, one of his favorite facial poses, but he makes a certain sense to me.

While these games of finitude—however many there might be—come to dominate consciousness, the Primary Impulse persists. In fact, it goads the strategies of denial, deviation, distraction, and perhaps diving in aimed at repressing it. Thus, the Primary Impulse remains submerged, as it were, and below the surface that occupies so much of our attention. Yet, like the hound of heaven, it pursues us. Only when the surface of our condition is disrupted by some significant crisis that undermines our projects and preoccupations may the Primary Impulse break through our endless facades and grasp us once again with its starkness, its intimidation and its promise. In brief, the Primary Impulse is there all along, the lust at the core of every act, every urge, all of our reaching.

"Okay, okay," Ethan interjects, "but we've not even begun to relate this whole business to religion, and. . ."

"It has everything to do with religion, or at least with the founding sensibility of religion," I continue, sensing that we're finally on a roll in getting at the thing we're here to understand.

To the extent that we take seriously the Primary Impulse and cannot find ourselves living in perpetual forgetfulness of it, we become therewith religious. This is what we called the other day the *religious sensibility*. And this sensibility is why I'm religious, or at least it's the first movement of it in my own life. At this point it is little more than a kind of primal awareness and attitude toward the whole of things. We know and take seriously that we—including our entire species, our habitat, and our world—are somehow *contained and sustained*.

To put it simply, we are not the origins of ourselves and we are not the end of ourselves. In terms of the basic structure of existence—birth, life with joy and suffering, and death, we are *fated* from beginning to end, and all of our possibilities, no matter how expansive, take place within our fated condition. Further, we must in some sense *find ourselves*, meaning ourselves as bounded within finitude, in response and relation to that which contains and sustains us. In so far as we entertain this *sense* of things, we are religious. This is all I mean by the religious sensibility, but it, in turn, is the ground for all that we consider as religion. The religious sensibility is the potentiality of religion itself.

"'And thereby hangs a tale,' as the saying goes," Ethan says with a grin. He wants me to interpret his dream based on what we've discussed, but I insist that it's his dream. He needs to find the point of it. Besides, I'm no dream analyst.

I know what he's doing. He can never stand what he takes as over seriousness. So, we revel briefly in the delight of that proverbial American lure, the open road. Our chariot slices through the rising terrain, bearing us toward the beloved heights.

While reveling in it all—the hum of the motor, the curves of the road, the rising, undulating landscape, the piercing blue of the high country sky—Ethan begins to decipher his dream. "All right, then, I'm runnin' from the worst sort of finitude you can experience: war. To say that it's hell is to trivialize it. But I'm runnin' with superhuman speed, tryin' my best to reach something, but I don't know what it is. Maybe it's the infinite itself, but whatever it is, it is 'the unknown.'" He makes his invisible quotation marks in the air.

"But what I don't get is that voice, sayin' that I'm not goin' to die but I'll wish I had. That's the shits!"

I want to tell him that the voice is saying he's making a mess of his life now by his obsession with his past, that he's being so ridiculous it makes the voice laugh. But I want him to figure it out on his own. As I say, it's his dream.

I return to our thoughts about the Primary Impulse and its realization in the religious sensibility. This is the bedrock, I believe, of religion...of my own religiousness. I realize that none of this can be "proven," not in any ordinary way. It is more like something that happens to us, or rises as an undifferentiated awareness. It "wounds us from behind," as Kierkegaard puts it. It is unrelated to any sort of calculation or deliberation but comes unbidden. To sense it, we move beyond ordinary knowing to recognition, even if only as a shadow passing over us. My language here is deliberately imprecise and imagistic. I had rather elicit recognition than provide an explanation. As the ancient voice said, "Who has ears to hear, let them hear."

But how does religion, as we ordinarily think of it, relate to this religious sensibility? This question circumscribes our pilgrimage into the mountains. To answer this very query is why we, or at least I, came here. What happens to our religious sensibility as our human condition unfolds? I have a host of thoughts waiting to yield insight, but I'm fatigued enough to give the project a rest.

I spot a clump of trees off to the west with boulders tossed nearby. We have a lunch packed away that we prepared yesterday in Santa Rosa, and I point to the trees and suggest we go over and sit awhile.

"How much farther is it?" Ethan asks, childlike.

"Not more than an hour or so," I reassure him. "We have plenty of time. Besides, I'm hungry."

"Yeah, me too," Ethan confesses.

We take the sack of food and a couple of bottles of water, holding the barbed wire up for each other, and hike to the trees. It's not as idyllic as it seemed from a distance. Lumps of cow dung everywhere, but we find a relatively flat boulder and take up our perch. We munch on slightly soggy sandwiches and graze over chips, while staring southeast from where we've come. The land drops and flattens as it recedes. The silence between us echoes across the landscape and returns as a sigh.

Second Movement: Exploration

Five

> Divinity lies all around us, but society remains too hidebound to accept that fact.
>
> William James

∽

The road to Pecos angles off to the northwest from Interstate 25. We listen to Leonard Cohen rasp out one of his stunning visionary ballads. We continue past the Pecos National Monument on the left. Ethan wonders what it is, and when I explain that it's a partly restored native ruin, he wants to take a look. But it's mid-afternoon, and I promise we can come back tomorrow.

In Pecos we stop at the general store for a break. The stock intrigues us. Cultural dissonance abounds, including clever, though antiquated, devices for a more basic way of surviving. We stare at things hanging on walls and from the ceiling: single trees, push plows, apple peelers. . .you name it. We examine some of them to determine their use.

Ethan picks up a Budweiser, and I take a root beer. We leave and begin the snaking narrow passage up the Pecos River canyon, past an active Benedictine monastery. Again, we decide not to stop. Maybe on our way back.

The cluster of houses in the village gives way to scattered homesteads strewn mostly along the river. The hairpin bends in the road slow our progress. We do not care because the unfolding display of the good earth rising to distant heights entertains us.

Eight miles later I instruct Ethan to slow, and we turn right into a barely visible drive. Down and through a rickety gate, standing open to greet us, we bounce along for a hundred yards. Abruptly, as if by magic, a log house appears on our left. Two rangy dogs, a border collie and a golden retriever, stretch and saunter out to welcome us.

"This it?" Ethan asks, and I nod. He has never been here and he doesn't know Collins.

We hear a voice behind us. "Yo!" That's Collins' universal greeting. He comes to the pickup and says simply, "Get out." We go through the ritual of introductions with me serving as master of ceremonies. Collins invites us into his studio, and we gawk at his work: sandstone etchings composed of Native symbols and cut to every shape and size we can imagine, along with paper art framed elegantly to honor the traditions of America's first peoples. The clutter in the studio threatens to overwhelm the beauty of the art. I remember that I had not warned Ethan about this. Ethan, in a word, is fastidious with his surroundings. Odd for a plumber and poet.

Collins is not Native. He could pass for one, but he objects to the very idea. Claims it dishonors Native people. He stands solemn while we cast our eyes about his barely ordered chaos. He is lean, not especially tall, and wears a ponytail reaching far down his back. I've known him for years, at least twenty, and we're close. But, as I was careful to warn Ethan, Collins does not talk. Only rarely does he hold forth for more than a sentence or two. He once said to me, "I don't speak, I show." Words of an artist!

In the house we encounter the same clutter, modified only slightly for convenience and probably for visitors. Collins dismisses himself to feed some stock for a neighbor and check on the dogs. Ethan sits grinning, and I can tell that Collins pleases him. Still, he says, "Man, why does he want to live in this mess. He could throw shit away for weeks and still have some left." He waves his hand to dismiss the clutter.

We need to stretch after so much sitting. We adjust our bodies, go outside, and stroll along the road until it dissolves into a pasture high on a hillside. In the late afternoon sun we are satisfied to trudge and take in vistas and horizons. When we walk down by the Pecos, I notice a sweat lodge Collins has constructed. It rests solemn and mysterious in a flat space among cottonwoods near the river. The fire pit lies to the east and the wood in it is stacked, ready to burn.

"Like to do a sweat tonight?" Collins asks as we enter the kitchen. I look at Ethan.

"Well, there's a first time for everything," Ethan responds, and that seems to settle the matter.

"We'll eat later," Collins announces and goes to the telephone. He negotiates with someone about the sweat, but, as usual, he doesn't explain.

Half an hour later a tractor fusses its way up to the house. On it is a burly man in his fifties or sixties and a young boy, a teenager, wearing no shirt and holding on to the tractor seat from behind. The older man appears to be Native. Collins introduces the man as Peck and the boy as Jack. As the sun sets somewhat early behind the surrounding ridges, we stroll single file toward the sweat.

We sit in lawn chairs watching the fire heat the rocks stashed inside a cone of wood. It becomes a silent vigil. Collins brings out a cooler and we pass around drinks. The rocks eventually begin to glow, and Collins walks to a bush on the other side of the lodge where he undresses and then returns, naked. The older man, then the boy stand and strip. I follow suit. Ethan, seeing the process, joins it.

We line up in single file, the older man Peck at the front, then Collins, me, Ethan, and Jack. At the entrance of the lodge the flap is raised and the older man kneels to crawl inside. I notice that our identification with other animals is more vivid without clothes. We follow, crawling around from left to right, clockwise. When we're all inside, except for the boy, the older man moves a bucket of water to his side, and the boy begins to bring in large fiery stones from the fire. He balances them on a shovel and with some effort drops them into a pit in the center of the lodge. He delivers four of them before entering the lodge and dropping the flap behind him. I look up and recognize the familiar bending willow branches framing the turtle-like structure. They are covered with a combination of old blankets, pieces of carpet, and some plastic.

Inside, darkness reigns, and we sit cross-legged in a circle of silence for some minutes, until the older man speaks. He welcomes us and tells us that we are here to pray and to share with each other as the heat and moisture purify our bodies. Presently he scatters a dipper of water from the bucket onto the stones. They sizzle and spark. Moments later the heat drops as from above and engulfs our upper bodies.

The older man begins to chant in another tongue. At first we listen, but when Collins joins him, we follow, awkward at first, but eventually the space is filled with our five voices blending into shared rhythm. More water is transformed into steam, and the chanting continues. Then the older man pauses and begins a prayer of gratitude to the universe for our lives and for this opportunity we have. Collins follows with his own brief words and then each of us in turn. The space is close and the heat increases with every splash of water from the dipper.

Fifteen or so minutes later the flap abruptly opens, and the boy slips outside. More stones are brought from the fire and dropped into the pit. With the flap open, the heat at first diminishes, but the fresh stones increase the temperature again. I can see Ethan. He's quiet, concentrating. The flap drops once again.

During this round we are each invited to name some problem or crisis in our lives that we wish the others to bear along with us. Collins speaks spare words about his mother's death. The older man worries for a daughter who has lost her job. I am about to speak, when Ethan says he longs for the gift of forgetting, that his memories bear far too much weight within him. I say a sentence or two about the lingering grief of divorce, and finally the boy says he must learn to read better. At the end of each statement we voice a common response: "I hear your need and bear it in my breast."

****

The marriage is disturbed from the beginning. Too young, too naive, too pious. The man is distracted by the passion to know. The woman is distracted by unfinished childhood. The man and the woman grow apart and back together in ceaseless clumsy rhythm.

Then children! A consolation without measure to assuage the anguish of the troubled bond. Innocent and intent on life itself, they both remind the man and the woman of the stuff of the bonding. Amid the striving and contending, the marriage, still troubled, persists.

How long, the man asks, should a marriage last that is not lasting? He does not know. No one in his clan has taken the course of severance, and the religious tradition forbids it. He has left the tradition, but its echo remains. He struggles but endures, until the struggle eats away the endurance and he moves out and away.

Contention changes but does not end. Guilt! The children! The future! The cost! The man's days are marked with these forces impinging. He manages to teach and read and write, to meet the steady duties as they come, but a fog of bewilderment hovers about him in the midst of all of it. He discovers a different order of endurance, but the scheme of former expectations lie shattered in his psyche.

But the human spirit is fathomless in its complexity. The gift of liberation beckons to him but is slow in coming. The man must wrench himself free from much more than unrealized wedding promises. He must become single! He was never single before. Yes, there is liberation, but it comes more as threat than gift. He grows wary of the open door, of being "that solitary individual." The calling to stand forth as himself takes three years to answer, and the call continues still.

When one life is exchanged, in the midst of it, for another, a death precedes rebirth. Rebirth breaks forth from death, and death is defeat before it is liberation.

****

By now the misty heat is serious, with drops of moisture falling on our heads from above. The flap opens. A brief reprieve. More stones, still hotter than the last. The flap comes down once again, and we turn to statements of gratitude. I privately wish for less steam, but the older man increases the doses. The heat reaches down to the ground around us.

Ethan, to my surprise, speaks first. Soft, almost tearfully, he gives thanks for the occasion and its cleansing gift. The boy says he is pleased to be going soon to Arizona, where he will spend time with an older brother in the San Francisco Mountains. The older man is grateful for his health and that of his family. He concludes, "There is no thing better than health." I can sense that he speaks from a reservoir of experience. Collins is grateful for the chance to make beautiful things that other people find pleasing. By this time I am so moved by these simple words of this odd collection of humanity that I can do nothing but give thanks for them, for their presence and their voices. Suddenly, I sense that there is nothing more fundamentally important than this time, this place, and these people. Everything else seems to have dissolved.

When the boy raises the flap this time, I wonder whether I can make the fourth round. I look toward Ethan with some anxiety. After all, this is his first sweat. I see that he is already curled on the ground, seeking the coolest place he can find. When Collins asks if he's all right, Ethan assures us that he is. The routine repeats itself, and in this final round we sing and chant songs of joy to prepare us once again for the world. They are simple sounds from another language, but we can sense their spirit. Near the end Collins asks us to do the Ohm. I note to myself this seemingly natural blending of Eastern and Western ritual. We repeat the Ohm seven times, each time becoming more harmonious and resonant. At the end the older man offers a brief prayer that we join at the end by saying, "And all my relations."

Collins, the older man, and the boy crawl outside, stand and walk steadily to the Pecos River, where they plunge into water of that I know is frigid in the early summer. Ethan and I stagger to our feet, then sit and stand again. We wobble to the bank and scoot into the water. I've done this before, but I'm prepared to shudder. The water, though cool, soothes every pore, as I lie back and allow the current to do its work. I look upward at a spangled night, and the vastness swallows me.

Collins has towels. We dry, dress, and walk to the cabin. Unknown to us, Collins has prepared red beans and rice. We only need to wait for the cornbread. I stare at this concoction of humanity, gathered around this table as if at a sacred meal. It is a sacred meal. Conversation is minimal, a circumstance unusual for both Ethan and me, but here it is more than fitting. It is like a grace itself.

We go to the porch and stand. Conversation is still minimal. Abruptly, the older man prepares to leave, the boy moving beside him. Perfunctory farewells are muttered, and they depart into the night. Only the disruptive cough and rumble of the tractor breaks the silence.

Ethan takes the bed, this being one of his last opportunities for some days, and I climb into a small loft to sleep on an aging and somewhat lumpy futon. Yet, I prefer it, because a few feet above me is a skylight through which the splendorous night will send me to sleep with its light show. As I climb toward bed, Ethan says, as if to himself, "This is my best day in months. I feel like I've worshiped in the right place."

In the stillness I muse to myself, Was this itself a religious event? It seems to fit, but it has no context or point of reference, except our common humanity and our use of an ancient ritual. Then I realize that I don't care how it is taken. If it isn't a "proper" religious gesture, it should be. It is enough that I feel renewed and cradled in an unfathomable harmony with...well...*everything*.

Six

A finite cause cannot have an infinite effect.

Yogananda

~

A country breakfast launches us into a turnaround day, between driving out here and heading into the mountains.

We load into Collins' van and follow the curves back into and through Pecos to the entrance of the Pecos Monument. It has just opened, and we begin to walk leisurely along the marked trail, guide pamphlets in hand. A glimpse of history reveals itself through broken down and partly restored walls. The highest walls are part of the central feature of the site, the ruins of a Catholic Church, established in the seventeenth century.

"Devoted to saving the 'heathen' from themselves," Ethan declares. "Religion and arrogance once again meet head on." Collins nods decisively. He always defends and supports everything Native at the expense of everything not Native.

"Everybody does it, I suppose," I offer, "Tryin' to convince other people that our way's the best way, but when it comes to religion. . ."

"Those people didn't," Collins says, startling us with a rare comment as he gestures broadly to the rows of small squares that were once homes for Native people. I register some confusion, and he adds, "Native people don't need to make other people see things their way. Maybe we could learn somethin' from 'em."

After reading the plaques placed around the adobe walls of the church, we follow a trail west along a ridge. In the distance rise the mountains we'll soon enter. They are placid and inviting in the brilliance of the New Mexico morning. When we reach a kiva that has been restored, we pause, and then one by one we descend the log ladder into the cool, hushed dimness.

We stare at the fire pit. I point out the *sipapu* slightly off to one side and explain its symbolism. A small six-inch hole in the earth, it represents the source from which all life comes. We sit and lean ourselves against the wall. The lure of stillness wins out for several minutes as we study the interior architecture, logs crisscrossing above us, the rectangular opening with the ladder leaning into it, the plastered walls, and most of all, the circular shape.

"I could live in here," Ethan confesses. "A safe place."

"It's the Mother's womb," Collins responds. "Everybody's safe there."

"The people who used these places," I note, "were more connected than we are. I believe they knew things we need to relearn."

"Too bad we can't go back to the early beginnings, before things went haywire," Ethan says, as if to no one. "But then again, I wonder whether things were all that pure then. Was there ever a beginning in the first place, I mean a crisp starting point, pure and uncontaminated?"

"We're so charmed by beginnings," I suggest, "by any sort of idealized past, but I seriously doubt there ever was such a thing. Like a pure religion, for instance." Collins' head turns abruptly toward me at the mention of "religion." He knows that Ethan and I are in the process of examining religion, but Collins earlier told me on the phone that he thinks it's a waste. He insists that Native people did not have a religion. What looks to us like a religion was simply a highly integrated way of living in connection with everything around them. He said, "Hell, tribal people didn't even have a word for religion. It was too much a part of them to separate out. That's how it ought to be."

For a while I sit in silence, thinking about our much more personal and intense consideration of religion yesterday. I want to discuss this with Ethan, but I know that Collins has no interest. It dawns on me that, before we can take up the religious sensibility as we did yesterday, we must first clear away some debris in how we think about religion today, especially those who seek to comprehend it most fully.

Sitting in this space, once devoted to sacred acts of communal life, I begin musing over Collins' comments. Almost every person I know, who is devoted to the study of religion, thinks it best to begin by looking at its beginnings. If they can get back to its origins, they imagine, they will know what it is in its most pristine form. They'll capture its pure expression. But is this process the best way to get at religion? Is it actually possible to do more than guess or speculate, no matter how much we learn, at the origins of religion?

Early attempts at a "science of religion" all began with origins, and most attempts rested on confidence that the origins could be readily uncovered. Mostly, contemporary societies of primitive people—in the early days of studying them sometimes still called *savages*—became the source of theories about origins. I'm thinking particularly of E. B. Tylor or James Frazer, but there were others such as Max Mueller, the father of a "science of religion." What impresses me now is how confident they were that they could recover the "facts" and that their "scientific" interpretations were actually scientific. Although we've moved well beyond those attempts to account for religion, this business of origins and source continues to haunt the subject.

I must admit I'm as drawn as the next person to the idea of origins and how religion may have emerged. The quest for the murky past, if nothing else, intrigues me. At the same time, I'm suspicious of the whole enterprise. When we try to move back behind written history, everything we say is conjectural, taken from secondary evidences such as scrapings on rocks and other bits of residue. There is far too much "reading into" the slender evidence to produce confidence in our speculations on how religion came into existence.

To turn attention to contemporary expressions of religion among living indigenous groups is not much better because we too readily take for granted that they've remained pretty much the same as their forbears. They likely have some continuity with their distant past, but all the way back to beginnings? The long and the short of the matter is this: we cannot base an adequate understanding of religion on finding its historical origins. We simply cannot know enough to make more than educated guesses. This speculation may be fun and perhaps in some sense even helpful, but it's not enough to make a fitting case for the beginnings of religion.

Anyway, the idea of religion as a specific and distinct human phenomenon comes relatively late in history. With the introduction of written languages, we humans began a long and increasingly intricate process of making distinctions. Among these distinctions was the separating out of religion and the gradual demarcations of its character and then its limits. This process took place, it seems, alongside the recognition of at least more than one particular religion and the differences between and among them.

In addition, William Irwin Thompson may be right in claiming that, with the rise of civilization, there was a substantial breaking away from the sense of elementary connection with the order of things—a kind of "fall," which then required that religion stand forth as an antidote to the break. Thompson leaves the impression that religion may have been created at just that point. Prior to that, he proposes, what might now pass for religion was unconsciously imbedded in what he calls a sense of "the ecstatic Oneness" of ancient peoples. Thompson, too, is making conjecture, but it may be worth noting, if we are to specify how religion has actually come to be employed as a distinct phenomenon. It also leads to the conclusion that the sacred was by no means absent before religion became distinct. On the contrary, what we now call religion was, as Collins insists, so pervasive and integrated in primal cultures that naming it was unnecessary. It was simply a lived sense of the sacred, as Ethan and I discussed earlier.

Religion may have come with the emergence of humanity itself, but the recognition of it as a specific thing came more gradually. That's my point. Furthermore, attempts to actually understand religion as a whole are even more recent. Use of the word itself—*religion*—may be quite modern, and surely the way it is now applied may be. Once we began isolating religion as a behavior for conceptual consideration, and with the attempts to understand it by means of scientific investigation, the very idea of *religion* underwent a major mutation, namely, an *objectification*. It became a "thing" to be studied, probed, and assessed for its meaning and merit. And this kind of study is exactly what Ethan and I have pledged not to do with the subject. Religion's about us, here and now.

With objectification two questions especially came into play. First, what is the unique character of religion? Repeated attempts have been made to address this question, and this present pilgrimage is in some ways yet another effort to respond to it. Second, what is the status of religion in terms of its bearing on human existence and destiny? Many modern interpreters consider it as secondary or derivative, as I noted earlier. They contend that it is better explained by other features of the human condition, such as politics, social order, or economics. Other voices, however, insist that religion is a primary and separable expression of our humanity and is not reducible to anything else. If properly understood, I hold to this latter position. What I'm contending is that religion arises from that Primary Impulse belonging to our very humanity.

Let me put this discussion another way: religion and religions have histories. I have already mentioned this, but it needs emphasizing here. What this amounts to, as noted earlier, is that religions change over time, and, I believe, the very character of religion undergoes change. This tendency to change would not be especially interesting, except, as stated earlier, that one role of religion is to resist change by providing maximum stability and continuity in response to the flux and uncertainty of human existence. Religions strive to provide the fixed center around which everything else revolves, so they gravitate toward order and forms that are fixed and repetitious.

This is also the reason tradition bears such weight within religions. Whether religions are or can be successful at providing this stability is another question, but in persons and communal contexts where religion is taken to provide such stability, it appears to work for practitioners. Well, it works until such pressures come to bear that it must change in order to continue. Ordinarily, the changes are sufficiently gradual as to go largely unnoticed within a given generation.

To understand better the dynamics of change in religion, I want to offer some comments on what I mean by it. A physicist friend once told me that in his field there are three "orders of change," as he called them: second-order change, first-order change, and zero-order change. These orders, I find, can be applied to any kind of change, including religious change.

Second-order change is change within a given system, change that allows the system to continue functioning. Within any given religious system there are endless minor, and occasionally major, shifts, but they do not challenge the system itself. Over generations these changes may alter the religious system significantly, but on the whole, the religion continues to be experienced as the same.

First-order change occurs when the system itself is challenged and there is a change in that system itself. In religion this kind of change can be illustrated by the rise of Buddhism within Hinduism. While there are continuities between them, they are now two distinct religions with different histories and dynamics. A similar case can be made for the emergence of Christianity within and then out of Judaism. In both cases we have the introduction of new religions, new systems.

Zero-order change is more radical. It is change in the phenomenon itself, in its very character. The religions of hunter-gatherers are not the same as religions of agrarian peoples. Different foci, different needs, different forms prevail. More dramatically, when agrarian religions give way to more complex forms arising from equally complex civilizations, the very character of religion again changes. Written language, for instance, makes forms of religion possible that an oral culture does not entertain. Or again, once the very idea of one world appears, some religions—most notably Islam and Christianity and to a lesser degree, Buddhism—become seriously cross-cultural and strive to become universal. This zero order of change might be called, in the cultural and not the biological sense, *evolutionary*.

Today, I propose, we find ourselves at the center of still another culturally evolutionary mutation in the character of religion. It could be a matter of zero-order change. It is prompted by the sheer number of religions around the world, with new forms continuing to emerge, and the increasing proximity of these religions to each other. The universalist claims of both Christianity and Islam bind them to the inevitable conflict that such claims produce as they strive to occupy the same space at the same time. Two universal religions, each claiming exclusive finality, cannot prevail *together*. A new way of construing the limitation of any and every religion, including Christianity and Islam, is being called into consideration. The array of religions moving ever closer to each other under the coercive force of econocentric and technological globalization requires that differences among these religions be addressed and new ways be discovered for relating them to each other and to our postmodern setting. Hence, another kind of inquiry into religion is in order, and the pilgrimage Ethan and I have set out on is to some extent devoted to that end, namely, the prospects for religion as it undergoes elementary mutation.

Two heads appear in the opening of the kiva. We stir, realizing that in our relaxed reveries we've lost track of time. With visitors upon us, we climb the log ladder and squint our way back into daylight.

On our way back to Collins' cabin we stop at the Benedictine monastery, and a cherub-faced brother meets us at the door. We can see books and pamphlets displayed on tables, surrounded by typically Catholic trappings. I pick up a tract entitled *The Charismatic Catholic*, and presently I notice that all of the materials share a flavor: popular spirituality laced with the somewhat more zealous concentration on pious vigor and vitality. Yes indeed, I say to myself, the blending and separating of religious motifs never ceases. Ethan looks knowingly my way.

The diminutive brother says effusively, "We have plenty of food and several guests. Please join us."

Ethan exudes, "Ah, Benedictine hospitality. It never fails." And following the brother's lead we traipse off to a bustling dining hall. After we're seated and a prayer is offered, we turn to our lentil soup, salad greens, and bread. Before we can begin talking with the monk who has joined us, a voice at the other end of the hall sounds forth and a reading begins of an O'Henry story, of all things. And true to form, the story ends with a twist.

We hang around for afternoon prayers before leaving. Our monk, Brother Xavier, seems to be assigned to us. He asks questions about what we're doing, where we're going. "I always ask that," he adds, "because then I can then travel vicariously with our guests." He laughs broadly, and we join him.

When Ethan says, "We're headed into the wilderness to think about religion," Brother Xavier springs from his chair and warns, "Very dangerous subject. I try to stay clear of it." He says it with his faint Irish flavor and a playful gleam in his eye.

"What do you mean?," Ethan retorts. "You're saturated with religion in this place."

"It's my cover," Brother Xavier confides. "I use it to allow time for the spiritual life, don't ya' know. Religion's a fine masquerade for exactly that." Then he launches into a lengthy explanation, maintaining that religion, while it's supposed to facilitate the spiritual life, more often than not gets in the way of it. "At its best," he concludes, "religion is a vehicle, don't ya' know, for lettin' the power through. The power of the Holy Ghost, that is. I became a Benedictine to make sure I'd practice my religion, but it drove me into my own wilderness, where the Spirit dwells. That's the charismatic part of the trip. . . the lively part. Catholics, ya' know, have trouble bein' properly lively. Not me. I broke free of it while I was in the middle of it."

"Why don't you leave the monastery?" I pose.

"Couldn't do that. I'm a Benedictine, I tell ya', and I wouldn't change it for the world. Besides that, who'd have me out there," and his arm swung broadly to indicate the world outside the monastery. "This is the only place I can find to let spirit run free."

I'm on the verge of further inquiries, when the bell tolls for the next round of afternoon prayers. We walk across the foyer and into the tiny chapel. Twenty or so people fill the space, and we stand, chant, bow, kneel, and recite. Ancient. Persistent. Lovely.

We are barely out the door when Ethan pipes up, "These monks' ancestors were probably the ones who tormented those Native folk. But, what the hey, they may be making reparations with soup and spirit talk." Our conversation dissolves from there and into the bliss of evening on Collins' porch.

Seven

To breathe is to risk. Only in its cessation is there final safety.

Anon.

~

Dawn comes before I'm ready, but at the sound of Collins' gravelly voice, I awaken. Today we begin our venture into the mountains. Ethan's not enthusiastic but stumbles his way into the kitchen. He sleeps in the buff and makes no attempt to dress, until he has sufficiently warmed himself by the kitchen stove.

We heave our packs out of Ethan's truck and into Collins'. He'll drive us to the edge of the wilderness. Ethan moves his truck to the back of the cabin and out of the way. Before the sun crests the surrounding heights, we're jolting our way up the drive and turning right onto the narrow pavement tracing the flow of the Pecos. We're driving against the flow of the river. I sit in the truck bed, watching light edge into the still-dark forests moving past us. We have more than twenty miles to ride, with every turn of the wheels taking us further from civilization. Over the last few miles we drop onto an unpaved washboard road, which becomes ever more resistant to our passage. The last mile is all bounce and recover.

"This is it," Collins announces as we pull into a circle drive with picnic tables and rude campsites strewn along it. "Looks like you won't have a lot of company. Too early. We're just past the spring thaw." I see two cars and a large pickup with a horse trailer attached. "Might have to deal with horses now and then." He helps hoist my pack out of the back of his truck, and we lay both of them on the ground. He leads us up a rise, past an official Forest Service outhouse, and to a gate. "That's Iron Gate. You start there." I've been here before, but I know Collins. He's always thorough about packing.

We discuss the food drops. Collins will meet us in a week with food supplies and fresh clothes. Then a week later he'll pack into a site near the base of Santa Fe Baldy. He'll bring enough food for all of us. He swears he can do it. He waves and drives away unceremoniously.

I assume we'll don our packs, pick up our hiking sticks, and head for the gate, but the next thing I know Ethan's unloading his pack. "What in blazes are you doin'?" I ask.

"Never go into the bush without checkin' everything out," he says as he spreads a light blanket and begins to lay out the pack's contents.

"Well, if you did leave somethin' out, there's not much you can do about it," I insist.

"All the same. . . " is his only response.

In self-defense I go through the same procedure, and it turns out to be helpful. I find a couple of things I can leave out, but the drill also helps me remember where things are located. Packing is itself something of an art, if not a science. Some state-of-the-art packers bring every latest gadget to insure their comfort. Others are so Spartan that the weight of their packs is minimal. These are seasoned back-country people, who mostly look down their noses at the rest of us. Packing for them is their way of going native.

Ethan and I are somewhere in the middle. He goes for comfort, and I go for a light pack. Both of us end with pretty much the same weight except he carries that infernal 357 magnum between his pack and its webbing. Where we're headed, the Pecos Wilderness, is not really deep wilderness. If necessary, a person could hike out of it in a long day's trekking from almost anywhere, but even at that, we'll be remote and don't want to be without the necessities.

If a person is packing, there are endless books with endless lists on what to take, what not to take, and how to load and carry a pack. We keep it simple. There are basically three sorts of things we need: clothing suitable for the high country, enough food to make it to the drop or make it back, and shelter to protect from the elements. Oh yes, and some system for purifying water. Don't want to drink bad water up here. I know this list sounds too general, but it's roughly the necessities. The differences come with how much clothing a person wants to haul, what kind of food and what tents and sleeping bags serve the purpose without weighing down the pack. Beyond that, it's mostly little necessities such as a good knife, flashlight, and rain gear. The rain can be furious up here. I won't go into our actual list, but it's enough to say we're particular and know what we'll most likely need. A few shakedown trips can teach anyone that.

One thing more. Everyone decides what to bring for entertainment. I always bring along a journal and at least one small reading book. The book is usually a meditative piece that can be read and reread to inspire reflection. Thoreau's *Walden* used to be my favorite. It goes well with packing. I notice that Ethan has two substantial novels. That'll add some weight, but I say nothing. He knows. I bring a camera. Ethan makes fun of that. He brings a couple of small bottles of Jack Daniels and a mysterious package. I wonder about both. Since Vietnam he's had some bouts of trying to drown out the memories. We'll see.

Packing the gear is as important as what we pack. Balance! That's the trick. We want the load to ride cleanly, since we're the pack mules. Ethan is more meticulous than I am, but we both take care to place things precisely and to check the balance before we depart.

Aside from casual banter, we say little. We're concentrating. When I've finished loading, I take the three items I want to leave behind and place them in the fork of a tree: a flannel shirt, a largish candle, and an extra metal bowl. We'll come back for them at the end. If not, they're there for some other wayfarer. I fuss at myself for not making this decision earlier.

We shift the packs from the ground to our backs. Ethan groans, while I concentrate on finding the comfort zone of these 45 pounds. Straps are loosened, others cinched. Shoulders flex. I tighten the waist belt, shake my body like a horse dismissing flies, and go to a nearby tree to retrieve my hiking pole. Ethan leads the way, and presently we open Iron Gate into the wilderness. It's still fairly early morning, but we're not sure of the time, because we left our watches behind in the truck. Chronos is somehow irrelevant out here.

Within a quarter of a mile we find our pace. This is always important. Modern packers tend to bring the pace of civilization with them, and it requires some attention to find the rhythm that fits more directly with nature. A pilgrimage cannot be hurried. I have been on trips, especially after following a harried schedule, when it took as much as two to three days to find the pace. It can take that long to arrive and to *be there*! This shows how contaminated we are by the contrived world, and until we try something like this trek, we aren't even aware of it.

As we hike, I find myself musing about the word *wilderness*, a place of *wildness*. At a museum in Florence, Italy, I once saw a display of late Medieval and early modern maps. In certain regions of some maps, namely, areas that had not yet been plotted, the early cartographers drew dragons. As I stared at these antiquarian pieces, the museum guide said that the dragons represented the danger of the unknown. They were something of a warning against venturing too far into unmapped terrain. See, I think to myself, the hint of infinity haunts the edge of the known.

Although this present wilderness is relatively tame and certainly has been mapped—we're carrying some topographical versions with us—the lure and even the threat of wilderness, however muted, remains. This threat is why so many people respond to my passion for backpacking by confessing, "My idea of camping is the Holiday Inn." I grow sad for them.

One of the ways religion is sometimes described is that it serves to provide both order and meaning for its practitioners against the tide of untamed force and chaotic randomness that comes with immediate experience. In other words, we could say that religion itself tames the "wilderness" by bringing order out of what appears to be chaos. This is certainly true of what I call *formal religion* and insofar as it is true, then religion itself, like the trappings of culture, is contrived, or so it seems. Ethan and I will need to examine whether and how religion is contrived. Consider these two descriptors of religion: contrivance and taming. Together they remind me of a process that is at once artificial and potentially dulling in its effect. Is this the character of religion?

We must admit that the chaotic and unknown domains are threatening, and they threaten because they powerfully encroach on us and are beyond our control. An encounter with the unknown can be overwhelming to us. There is in us, therefore, an urge to order, similar to "the urge to form" that Ethan mentioned earlier. It is evident in art, in the complexities of culture, in the very routines by which we order everyday life. If so, then why not understand religion as perhaps the ultimate effort to wrest order from the chaos of immediate experience? I say "ultimate" because religion reaches for the cosmic in relation to the most intimately personal and communal conditions we encounter. Religion leans toward the whole and offers us a place within the whole. That may be its work.

Having said this, I'm still troubled by this image of religion as contrived taming. What awakens and invigorates our existence is not the contrived and the tame, but the wild and the uncontrolled—the thrall and thrill of *possibility*! Here we're back to what I've claimed to be the *existential* origins of religion: the Primary Impulse and its offspring, the religious sensibility. But the sensibility in itself is generalized and only vaguely articulated. We might say it is preformal or informal.

When the religious sensibility becomes contrived and tamed, it provides a sort of cocoon of perpetual assurance against the *tremendum* of infinity. Yet, in our vulnerable finitude we reach for assurance. Without some measure of ordered life and its consolation, we fall into maddening disorientation. Is there any way between the horns of this dilemma?

Some years ago I found myself simply declaring that there are two kinds of religion—or better, two ways of being religious: the way of *security* and the way of *risk*. I've been unable to shake this perhaps simplistic understanding of people's attitudes toward their own religions. Furthermore, by far the majority appear to opt for security over risk and to see risk as nothing but foolhardy. A longing for eternal security drives the religious sensibilities of millions to create our endless forms of ordered piety. Pay close attention and observe how the religious life expresses itself, and this phenomenon will become evident. I'm willing to concede that security is a real and present need for all of us. Without some modicum of security, I would hardly enter this mountain wilderness. At the same time, if the drive to security overwhelms the longing—the lusting—for something beyond the assured, then isn't our security little more than our imprisonment? The religious sensibility itself stands forth out of the most definitive insecurity we can imagine, the Primary Impulse.

Let's begin here: religion has its origins and promptings in the wilderness, in the wildness. Without the encounter with the edge of order and the threat and promise—the beckoning—it affords, we would likely not entertain religion at all. This is perhaps the first paradox of religion. It thrives on engagement with the wildness and the outrageous reach of possibility, while at the same time it drives toward the conquest of that wildness. It strives to tame the wildness. When I read of the elemental experiences of the religious, I am struck by the marginal boundaries they stalk. This risk taking is most dramatic among the prophets and mystics, but it applies to all definitively religious experience. Great religious experience is not safe or predictable. It shakes all order, all security, and casts us into the wilderness that shifts our very ground. In brief, it transcends all form! This is the inner depth of religion's *transformative* force. Wild!

Here's the issue: How do we exist in the risk of such a transformation and at the same time find forms that provide security without canceling the risk? We may long to live fully in the wildness, but we can never totally achieve such a life. Forms are inevitable, but they can be soft ones. That is what our present pilgrimage into this wilderness, modest though the present risk is, seeks to examine. Thus, our pilgrimage here becomes a symbolic gesture toward risk and toward religion itself understood as risk. Religion, I want to argue, is risk itself in the most profound sense of the word. We go out on the proverbial limb! We find ourselves suspended over "twenty thousand fathoms," as the philosopher Kierkegaard puts it. Or, as Pascal famously contends, we make an ultimate wager. Whatever security may be gleaned, it cannot set aside or even diminish this risk. It can only sustain the risk.

Our contemporary social orientation is so committed to security that what I've just said sounds foolish. "Why take a risk unless forced into it?" But then there's that contrary cliché, "Nothing ventured, nothing gained." We're caught between these two. We know that risk is constant and unavoidable, but we spend most of our energy minimizing or denying risks and building security to thwart, or at least ward off, risk.

With religion, when taken seriously, the risk is particularly acute. It involves our whole existence and the rest of our lives. Religion is not an achievement, something we can finish in order to move on to other things. It permeates the whole thing, our existence that is, and it does so all of the time. Anything less is really only a facsimile of religion, a "nod to God" we might say. Even if conventional and popular religion modifies or undermines this uncertainty with forms and routines, the underlying ferment which prompts these practices remains foundationally RISK! Religion which offers security easily degenerates into one version or another of fixated pious presumption.

To grasp this better, an analogy might be helpful. In the world of modern American romance we speak of *falling in love*. This phrase has long occupied me. Why would we use *falling* as a description of the immediate passion that overtakes us, when we are smitten? Actually, it is a most apt way of putting the case, because in such instances we do fall under the spell of the "other" as one who invades us, unmasks us, and invites us, literally, *beyond ourselves*! We are taken over by the presence of this other, and we are out of control. We are in the wilderness of the greatest of all unknowns, namely the vital mystery of another human being who, at least for the moment, undoes us and redefines us. This experience is existential—that is, total and inward—risk at its most vulnerable, and we really cannot stand it for long, that is, we seek to stop the falling.

If a sustained relationship follows from our falling, we begin to organize it. In other words, we *interpret* the experience. I will go so far as to say that an uninterpreted experience is not worth having. At the same time, all interpretation modifies and may distort or, in the end, overwhelm our experience. Still, we want to order the possibilities the experience and its attendant feelings offer us, and we do this by generating shared expectations. We schedule our encounters, decide to make the relationship exclusive, make plans for coming occasions. All of this is to check or take charge of the drama and trauma of our falling. We strive by these means to shift from risk toward security. This process usually includes some version of challenge and response, seeking to stake out our personal sense of ourselves so we do not become entirely swallowed and lost under the spell of the other. It often begins by claiming a boundary for ourselves, as in "I love you, but. . ." Here the falling abruptly halts and the call to order takes over.

One common outcome of our organization of falling in love is to standardize the relationship. This usually involves a decision to live together on a sustained basis or marry or both. Not only does this ordering seem inevitable, if a couple sustains their relationship it is considered desirable and good. The good lies in the increased security and the diminished risk. Of course, as the relationship deepens, it elicits a different depth of risk, the risk of self-revelation.

But here's the rub: something is gained by organizing our relationship, and something is also lost—or at least diminished. The risk that sprang forth from the passion of our falling in love may decline and even disappear within the web of our ordered lives. The question facing anyone in this situation is whether and how the security of ordered life and the passion of risk in loving can be simultaneously maintained.

If this analogy holds, religion involves something of the same process. Even if a person begins with an orientation to conventional religion—as when we are born into it— an awakening to the vitality and passion at the heart of religion is a kind of falling. If and when this takes place, the risk of religion becomes more than evident, and the challenge becomes much the same the challenge associated with falling in love: how to maintain and nurture the vitality and dynamism—the risk—of the awakening within the forms and practices by which we express and sustain it.

****

A religion of intense piety and moral stricture has marked the boy-man's life from infancy. His feelings about the religion vacillate between a sense of being distinct and a sense of social alienation. He is alternately proud and embarrassed, comfortable and unsettled. The ambivalence haunts him, and his double life leaves him restive.

One week each year the tables are turned and the girl-women at school are allowed to ask the boy-men for dates. A quaint practice! To the boy-man's astonishment a sophisticated "worldly" girl-woman a class ahead of him asks him for a date. He is more astonished than enthusiastic, but not knowing what else to say, he accepts.

The boy-man arrives at the girl-woman's home. Two other couples appear. The girl-woman proposes they go to a movie. The boy-man has never attended a movie. Too much a part of the world! What is he now to do? Reluctantly he confesses, "We. . .I do not go to movies."

The others, surprised but accommodating, consider alternatives. Hil-

degard offers another option: "We can stay at my house and play cards." The boy-man, more painfully this time, adds to his confession. "I do not play cards." Now he is shrinking into a pervasive sense of isolation, of extravagant peculiarity.

Again the others take this dilemma in stride. Soon they hit on an option the boy-man can accept. They spend the evening playing miniature golf. The evening goes well, but after that the girl-woman only smiles and waves at him in the school halls.

The boy-man is somehow pleased. He has staked out the territory of his peculiarity. He feels committed to this moral terrain, and his feelings of ambivalence recede. But what is he to make of this tiny domain of his family faith? It engulfs him. He inhabits it quite like a fish inhabits water. He can occasionally see beyond it, but the domain is safe and precise. In this domain he knows the boundaries, and the possibilities are within his imagined anticipation. Gradually he allows this faith to become his.

Worship in the modest church of the boy-man's youth is always informal and emotionally charged. Leaders know how to trigger emotion and to encourage its expression. A particular service in the evening becomes especially intense. Others of his own age are openly confessing faith and demonstratively emoting in response. A great release of fervor and energy sweeps through the cluster gathered at the front of the sanctuary. Suddenly the boy-man is beside himself. His center dissolves into a wider center beyond his control. He is "caught up" within a felt "Presence."

The Moment passes soon enough, but the boy-man is no longer the same. He finds himself on the other side of an interior and invisible divide. He has touched the ecstatic dimension, if only briefly and prematurely. The occasion is interpreted to him by other voices, but they cannot encompass the Moment itself or its implications. He has passed over a threshold and is committed to what grasps him, though he cannot grasp it.

****

Thus, Ethan and I take this pilgrimage into, of all places, the wilderness. This is the kind of pilgrimage it is: We do not make our way toward a shrine, a temple, a sacred ground—nothing secure. We move into and through the wild places, the places that resist taming and contrivance. Only by not being tamed and predominantly subject to human contrivance and convention does it remain wilderness, does it draw us to carry our survival on our backs into and through it. To face, as it were, the dragons at the edge of the map! A lovely and dear woman, my wife, once described a mountain wilderness of massive pines as "the cathedral of the green steeples." This is the cathedral we're entering.

But then, the very idea of religion as wilderness and risk contains another paradox. It is found in the word *sanctuary*. A sanctuary is at once a sacred space, a symbolic meeting place between humanity and divinity, and a safe place. In earlier times, in some cultures, a person who had violated some serious taboo could be safe from retribution if they could make it to a sanctuary. This notion of sanctuary suggests something about the sort of risk religion invites: it calls us to risk being secure or safe only in the milieu of the divine. That's where the "leap" or the "wager" centers. In this respect, religion is sheer courage or daring.

Ethan spots a rock jutting out over an expanse and calls for a break. We suspend our conversation, drop our packs, and dangle legs over the cliff's edge. Ethan offers me trail mix. I offer him water.

"That's what Brother Xavier was trying to say," I realize abruptly.

"Explain," Ethan insists.

"Well, he sees religion as a dangerous thing, because it threatens the liveliness—the spirit. . .which is the very basis of religion in the first place."

"Danglin' over the abyss, whatever else it is, ain't boring," Ethan notes, then says nothing for a long time. I continue to muse on the convergence of what Brother Xavier said and what we've discussed about security and risk.

I find myself muttering, "Religion is every bit as dangerous as it is inevitable. . ." More silence from Ethan.

"See that expanse," he finally says. "It must be close to five, maybe six hundred feet to the bottom of this cliff. See those ridges and peaks over there, probably a mile away. When I think of religion, I mean the real stuff we're tryin' to get at, I think of that expanse in relation to your stupid little camera trying to take a picture of it. They never turn out." After a pause, "They're downright pitiful. But we keep trying to capture the panorama, get the picture that reveals what we're seeing. Never works, but we keep at it anyway."

Now it's my turn to ponder in silence. Then I find myself blurting, "It's about experience and memory. That little camera tries to substitute for memory, but it can't do it. Memory, like the camera, retains our experience but only as a distillation of it. We can't simply rely on the memory, as important as it is. We're obliged to return to the directness and power of the experience itself." I say this as if something startling has shown itself. Then I add, "Somewhere in the mix of experience and memory *meaning* arises."

All of a sudden, I feel a rush of momentary despair about a subject that has so marked my life and my vocation and that I continue to try to plumb. The photograph in relation to the thing pictured is absurdly disproportionate, tiny, and at best vaguely representative—a reminder. I want to do more than stare at photographs. I want to enter the thing photographed, its smells and taste and all of the emotional timbre it includes. I want to engage the panorama as a living habitat, a larger-than-life dwelling. And I believe this desire is the drive behind religion, but we keep losing the drive in the photograph—in the details. Is memory nothing more than an internalized camera, constantly snapping pictures, some foggy and others vivid? If so, we either continually return to the experience or we settle for a nostalgic longing for the original encounter. Or, for a new encounter yet to come! Problem is, we can be as lost in the future as in the past, let alone in the web of current structures we build to house ourselves.

Ethan stands and lifts his pack. I give it a boost onto his back. He does the same for me, and we hike upward from the cliff and into afternoon sun, slanting through the timber to light our way.

Eight

> Like a single flame vanishing into a raging inferno, the absorption of our finitude into the infinity of God can be terrifying.
>
> Rabbi Niles Goldstein

~

In the late afternoon we locate our first night's campsite. We're not that tired but want enough time to set up, eat, and relax before dark. This particular location pleases us. It's atop a long slightly rounded open stretch known as Hamilton Mesa. What a vista! Off to the west the rounded tops of Pecos Baldy and Santa Fe Baldy rise to sketch a horizon, and to the east the range ripples away into oblivion. We stare at the expanse, squinting to capture its reach until our eyes ache.

The first night on the trail is always a shakedown of sorts. Remembering exactly where the gear is stashed in the pack, unfolding the tent, setting it up, releasing sleeping bags from their confines and dropping them into the tent, inflating mattresses. The chores go on. Camping is high maintenance. I've done all these things many times before, but recovering the rhythm takes a while.

We pitch separate tents on opposite sides of the site. Why? Ethan snores.

"Let's pull that log over here by the fire pit," Ethan proposes, and we tug, lift, and heave it into place. Behind it a flat rock suggests our kitchen. It appears to have been scrounged by some previous wayfarer. We accept the gesture, but our practice is to refrain from moving stones any more than necessary.

After dinner I wash dishes, using water Ethan purified at a nearby spring. He walks off with the food bag to hang it on a tree limb. Bear-proofing. It's early in the season, but when it comes to creatures, you never quite know. Twilight settles around us as we complete our tasks and perch on the log near the small fire.

At this time of day there's a brief period of utter stillness when nothing—not even the wind—seems to stir. I have long noted this time and call it the *changing of the guard*. Creatures of the day retreat before their nocturnal replacements claim the night. This is my favorite interlude in the wilderness, and I comment on it.

"Hear the silence?" I barely break the silence.

"Loud, huh?" Ethan responds.

The hush is penetrated by a family of coyotes raising their evening cry down to the west toward the Pecos River. We look at each other but say nothing. The feeling tone of these moments is *reverence*. No other word conveys it better, and I say as much.

"Yeah," Ethan agrees. "Some of my best memories of Nam, despite everything else goin' on, sometimes came just after sundown in the bush. If we felt safe enough, we'd relax and wait for night. Just like here, the jungle would shut down. Not for long, but it was precious.

"Once I mentioned it to my patrol and said somethin' about it making me feel protected. The rest of our patrol, mostly grunts, nodded, but this one corporal, huge and rough but always reliable, stood and said, 'Hell, the whole thing's a pure accident and so are we. I'm gonna take a leak.' He walked off muttering, 'A really bad accident.' We called the guy Pepper. Can't remember why. "Two minutes later this awful roar shook us all to attention. A scream followed. He'd tripped some booby trap... Lost a leg." Ethan says it in a matter-of-fact way. Then he adds, "Moments of reverence in the bush didn't last long."

Once the stars take over I find my head drooping. The cool of the night invites sleep. Without discussing it, we move to our tents with minimum ceremony.

Well into the night, I awaken to the racket of pans and plates rattling. Before I can unzip my tent flap, I hear Ethan yelling, "Get out of here! I'm comin' after you right now, you son of a bitch! Scat!" I peer out to see him standing naked and waving that 357 in the air.

"What is it?" I ask.

"Damn bear. It ran over my tent ropes. Nearly knocked the whole thing down." Ethan finds a rope, pulls it taut, and pushes the stake back into the earth.

"Did it scare you?" I want to know.

"Well, yeah. That's why I went for this equalizer."

"A big 'un, I guess?"

"Big enough, I reckon." Then he laughs. "You hear me sayin' scat'? What a thing to say to a bear. . .Scat!"

The intrusion gives me permission to sleep until the sun strikes the tent. When I come out, Ethan is already standing by the tiny fire drinking coffee. We watch the sun's beams light up Santa Fe Baldy until it appears to glow. "What a fine accident," Ethan says. "Can you believe that guy, Pepper, makin' such. . .an uh. . .ontological declaration and walkin' straight into the jungle to have his leg blown to kingdom come? I woke up thinkin' about that. Wonder if it changed his mind about accidents. Probably not."

"Well, it was an accident, wasn't it?" I ask.

"Then again, it could've been a message. Like the universe sayin' 'Hello, Pepper!' All I can tell you is that he was scared shitless, and so were the rest of us. If 'it's all an accident' like he said, I do wonder why he was so terrified. Legs come and legs go, if you get my drift. One accident's about like another, when they're all accidents." He stretched the word *all* to the breaking point. "I'll say this much: fear and 'it's all an accident' do not match up. Fear reveals this hidden possibility that somethin' might, after all, matter."

I recall a famous aphorism, I think it was by the Greek dramatist Aeschylus: "Fear created the gods." I mention it to Ethan, and he says, "Exactly. If there's no God, fear'll generate one."

Is this true? It seems to say that the real source of religion is fear. This conclusion is entirely too glib for me, but so many people have taken it to be true that it deserves at least a response.

The question Aeschylus' saying raises involves the whole business of origins that we've already discussed: How did religion start? We'll never find the answer, but the question won't go away. To me there appear to be two ways of understanding the question. It can be a *historical* question like When, how, and why did religion came into existence? Or, it can be an *existential* question, such as What in the human condition accounts for religion?

Most attempts to get at origins go primarily for the historical approach. By looking at primal—or archaic, or oral—societies, attempts are made to discover how religion arose. Some of these attempts are made by conducting research such as archeology, but more often contemporary examples of primal religion—an increasingly rare phenomenon today—become objects of study in order to find an answer to the origins question. Although these projects can be intriguing, I don't find them really answering the question of the origins of religion, at least not at the necessary depth. These approaches only explain how religion took shape among people as they sought to express their religious sensibility.

Besides, contemporary primal people cannot simply be assumed to be updated versions of the "original" humans. After all, they're actually our contemporaries, only a different version of the times, and no matter how much they may represent continuity with the earlier forms of human existence, they are not the originators of human society or of religion. I'm not saying we should not learn from them. Actually, we may have much to learn from them, but we cannot assume they bear the stamp of original—or pure—religion.

Beyond that, when we try to conjure the origins of religion by chasing after the roots of hominization, that is exactly what we are doing, conjuring. Even if we are faithful to the evidence available, it's not sufficient to do more than offer informed conjectures—hunches. Most such efforts are a combination of fancy and of "reading back" more nearly our own biases regarding religion.

I question the motives of many such efforts. The hidden assumption often at play is the belief that religion itself is an archaic throwback now in the process of decline and disappearance. As we've noted, early theories about religious origins certainly made this assumption. Granted, others have tried to give religion a legitimate place in the human enterprise. Many sociologists, for example, grant religion a crucial function in maintaining social solidarity. Still others propose that it provides moral grounding for life together in the human community.

In the end I find all these efforts unfruitful in capturing the depth and vitality religion represents. When I observe people decisively engaged in their religions, I sense much more taking place than archaic practices or efforts at social and moral solidarity. I readily confess, of course, that religion does these things and that much of it is at most conventional and often only nominal, but to concentrate on this obvious fact misses the more profound pervasiveness and persistence of the religious sensibility in human experience. To put the matter bluntly, I want to understand religion at its best, at its most definitive and profound. I want to consider whether and how it may be a decisive, sui generis, dimension of our humanity. Admittedly, this interest is not popular in the contemporary study of religion, but I hold that to disregard this possibility bleeds religion of its richness and force in human experience.

If I have not heretofore shown my colors, they are now flapping in the wind! The academic study of religion to which I'm referring here operates on two broad assumptions. First, it assumes we can properly and sufficiently account for religion by studying it *from the outside*. In text after text on the subject readers are invited to engage religion as a phenomenon like any other and to apply to it all the intellectual resources necessary for understanding it. Let's examine this idea before raising a second related issue.

I do not oppose thinking about religion from the outside. On the contrary, I practice it myself. But here's my question: To what extent can such study ever hope to adequately grasp its subject? This question may be asked of any scholarly effort to understand things closely associated with human existence, but in the case of religion, the problem is especially pointed. After all, religion makes astonishing claims about humanity and its relation to ultimacy—to the infinite. How dare we set aside this fact as beyond our interest or capacity to address! Yet, as theorists of religion we set it aside incessantly. When we do so, I believe we may sacrifice the very core of religion qua religion on the altar of human analysis and comprehension.

With this assessment I'm on even more treacherous ground. On the one hand, if I assume the outsider approach to religion, I miss something of its true character. On the other hand, if I posture myself as an insider, I threaten to overwhelm all consideration of the subject with a narrow and subjectivist perspective. I believe there is a middle way, which I will only note here and further develop as our pilgrimage continues.

Earlier I mentioned that authentic knowing may be best understood as *participatory*. That is, we actually know only what we consciously engage through the very way we live. Unfortunately, the activity of knowing, especially scholarly efforts at knowing, is too often isolated from living. To consider knowledge as a form of participation in what is known changes this. Knowledge, or understanding and the way we live, become two sides of the proverbial coin, each informing or transforming the other. The mode of participation I have in mind here is what I've been calling the religious sensibility itself.

An example may be helpful. I'm thinking of a colleague at the university. He is an anthropologist who teaches courses on religion. One of his most common comments assures people that he is not himself religious but is interested in the study of it as a feature of human culture. In other words, he wants it to be known that he teaches from the outside. I applaud his claim to be objective in that I admire his effort not to "contaminate" his study with a particular religious bias. But still, this *is* his bias! There's no escaping it. (This very discussion is, for good or ill, from my bias.) Further, this particular bias may itself entail a severe limitation on my colleague's comprehension of the subject he wishes to study: religion. In other words, such a study may become, in a significant sense, self defeating; the subject to be understood cannot be understood from the perspective assumed. Something foundational is left out of account: What does it actually mean to *be* and to *act* religiously? That's what Ethan had in mind, when he asked me if I were religious.

But what if there is a more basic way of knowing and understanding, what I am calling *participatory*? Another way of describing it might be as *empathetic engagement*. I find two ways of entering into the study of religion by this means. We can study all religion through our particular participation in one or another form of religion. This approach might be called *confessional-observational*, and the limitations of it should be obvious. The particular religion almost inevitably becomes the standard for what counts as an adequate religion. We may resist this standardization, but it remains always a threat to intellectual integrity.

Or, we might engage a more foundational appreciation for religion as such, one in which critical understanding is under-girded by empathetically embracing religion as a fundamental expression of human existence, that is, as the religious sensibility. We need not be participant in a particular form of religion to do this. Simply put, we're only asked to be open toward religion as an aspect of human potentiality while striving to understand it manifestations.

One kind of example of this participatory attitude is found in a volume by Catholic priest John Dunne. In *The Way of All the Earth*, he reports on his five-year stint as an actively participating Buddhist. He did not surrender his commitment to his Catholic Christianity but placed it in suspension while "being" a Buddhist. He calls this process "passing over," and he contends that this deliberate form of *participation* did not undermine his other faith schema but actually enhanced and deepened it. This experience is not quite the same as the participatory *teaching* of religion, but it is related in this way: By exercising his ability to suspend, or bracket, his particular religious tradition and enter intentionally into another, he shows a more universal participative sensibility toward religion as such. It is this empathetic engagement that, to a notable degree, anyone seeking to understand and appreciate religion may employ with greater success than a strictly outsider posture allows.

Second, what I am suggesting here is only possible if another common assumption among those who study religion is challenged. As already mentioned, religion today, and since the eighteenth century, is widely assumed to be a secondary, derivative, or extraneously conditioned expression of human existence. Some go beyond this assumption to assert more: that religion is in principle misguided or pathological. That is, religion is dependent upon some other aspect of the human enterprise for its explanation and for any justification it might have. In short, religion can best be explained by its connection to something other than religion. Karl Marx explains religion economically. For Freud it is a misplaced father fixation. For Durkheim, a resource for social solidarity within societies. For Nietzsche, a misguided effort to deny our own existence and "the will to power."

Back at the turn into the nineteenth century this attitude toward religion had just begun to find its voice in Europe, and the religious world was fumbling for a response. Into this situation entered a young twenty-nine year old hospital chaplain in Berlin. He wrote a book with an intriguing title: *Speeches on Religion to Its Cultured Despisers*. In it he boldly proposed three things: (1) Religion is not secondary to anything else in human experience but is a singular feature of what it means to be human; (2) Religion is not an abstraction but always takes a particular form based on particular experiences, because human beings are "particular," that is, circumscribed by their finite existence in specific times and places; (3) In every particular expression, however, religion is fundamentally and universally experiential and therefore inherently subjective. This is its character as religion. He defines religion as "the feeling of absolute dependence on God."

Friedrich Schleiermacher's argument is important for two reasons. The first is that he dramatically challenges the popular notion that religion is a secondary—and therefore dispensable—feature of human existence. The second is that he begins a process of redefining religion as most basically an interior orientation of the self in relation to itself, to the world, and to God. I wish in this pilgrimage to pick up Schleiermacher's thread, especially his insistence that religion is not secondary and derivative but at its core is a unique irreducible dimension of human existence. This is a large claim and by no means popular today, but as our conversation continues, I hope to show it is plausible.

"Man, we've wandered all over the place," Ethan blurts out and breaks my concentration.

"Want to go back?" I ask. We've been walking for a couple of hours, exploring the mesa.

"I'm not talkin' about our walk. I'm talkin' about our talk. You started off with that quotation from Aeschylus and then we've run away with the subject of how religion got started and how we can and cannot study the subject. I'm in brain warp!"

"Me to," I admit, and we stop at an unnamed creek, take off our hiking boots and wade. The water is icy but soothing. We stand in the water until our feet go numb, staring at the transparent bed of the creek in search of small stones that take our fancy.

Our plan for this whole trip is to break camp only every two or three days. We're in no hurry, and the distance we plan to cover up to Highway 518 is not all that far. That's where Collins will meet us for the first food drop. When we're not on the move, we'll take day hikes, lounge around, read, and make notes. Since every turn along our trail will be a picture postcard, there can be no boredom.

Nine

What is man in the infinite?

> Pascal

~

Finitude is the very structure of the human mind.

> Paul Tillich

~

Wilderness packing took my fancy long ago and still intrigues me, probably for the standard reasons. Most alluring is the opportunity to engage what I keep calling *uncontrived nature*. No. It is more like being claimed by nature. But something more attracts me. When I go into these spaces, I strip down the excess. What I aim for is a balanced *simplicity*. What I need becomes far more crucial than what I want. To carry the resources for my own sustenance on my own back is both sobering—I don't want to forget anything crucial—and satisfying.

When I mention these musings to Ethan, he at first dismisses them with a complaint about the sacrifice of sleeping on the "cold, cold ground" only to please me. I make no apology but persist in my conviction that the simplicity of concentrating on things and tasks more nearly fundamental to living revitalizes me.

"Guess you're right, but it's damn un-American!" Ethan declares. "We're supposed to be devoted to acquiring as much plastic junk as our plastic cards will allow, to impress people we don't even know. And we throw in the endless purchase of entertainment to make sure that we somehow, by magic, find happiness." His cynical voice is at sinister pitch. "Who wants simplicity?"

"I do," I confess.

"You're a freak," Ethan announces, as if reminding me of something.

"But there's this stripping away of the unnecessary in order to find. . .I'm not sure how to say it. . .The Way?"

"Sounds too pious for me. Besides, when all the stripping's finished, what if there's nothing left. . .no 'Way'? Or, more likely something we all make up to fill the void at the end of the stripping."

"It's a risk, like I said the other day. And that's what being religious, at its best, is all about." I'm emphatic, as if convincing myself by saying it.

"You sound like an ascetic-come-lately," Ethan accuses with a smirk.

"You know better than that, but you've got a point." As I say this, Ethan begins making our evening chocolate. A crisp still coolness enters with nightfall and calls for the drink's sweet warmth. "If you want to call it *asceticism*, I'll allow it to stand, as long as you agree that there're all kinds of asceticisms, some of them being either pathological or perverse. . .or both. . .but not all of 'em. What I'm talking about, as I said, is a stripping away of the unnecessary. . .the excess."

Ethan turns from the camp stove to insist, "I really don't like *unnecessary*. I don't want to live only by what's necessary. It reminds me of those biologists who insist that everything we do is for survival and the continuation of the gene pool. Sounds utterly fatiguing and absolutely boring! And it's absurd. There's gotta be more to it than that."

"All right, then, what if I replace *unnecessary* with, say, *unfruitful*. I mean, getting rid of whatever doesn't contribute to. . .uh. . .living well." I know I'm reaching here and not being all that articulate. Ethan will probably come after me, but I'm also chasing a truth about life and about its relation to religion.

"That's how we always wind up. You go for 'stripping things away.'" As he says this he puts down his mug of chocolate and once again makes his infamous quotation marks in the air. "And I go for. . .plentitude. . .or abundance. You're always the ascetic and I'm the glutton."

"Or worse," I retort. "Maybe it's more of a trade-off. I strip away some things so that I can enjoy abundance in others." I reflect, then add, "Perhaps this is more nearly a psychological predilection than it is a matter of religion as such."

Ethan hands me an aluminum mug of chocolate. Its steam rises to join the early evening air, and we sit on the log, sipping. We allow nightfall to take over before either of us speaks again. Then he says, "Well, if that's the way it is, then I have some serious decisions to make."

"Like what?" I ask.

"Like what do I want an abundance of and what am I willin' to give up for it?"

I ponder before responding. I realize that something about this whole pilgrimage may be at stake in Ethan's question. There is this elemental orienting decision we make—or at least face—and it relates to that religious sensibility I insist on defending. Maybe this decision is why so many seriously religious people are drawn to asceticism, to some great stripping away. It's like getting rid of distraction. Scholars studying religion these days speak of its close relation or identification with *sacrifice*. This much is becoming clearer to me, the decision between abundance and stripping away Ethan calls for might be the more *existential origin* of religion itself that we talked about earlier.

I will say this: I cannot be or have everything that I might wish. Learning this truth is a huge advancement, because it confronts me with a fundamental decisiveness about what goes and what remains, what contributes to life and what detracts. It appears that we can't really get on with living unless we face and respond to this challenge. We all encounter it in one way or another, and we encounter it over and over. My question is whether this fact might relate to the origin of this marvelous and awful dimension of our humanity we call religion.

Or, perhaps the origin lies still deeper. To summarize what I've been thinking, the issue Ethan raises might be boiled down to the more commonly stated query, What makes life "worth living?" If so, this question is more general than strictly religious, although religion may offer at least one possible answer to it. It may be more helpful to examine the anxiety or the attitude this line of questioning raises.

Two candidates present themselves: *fear* and *wonder*. These words are used here to refer to what might be the most elemental tension human beings face: aversion and attraction. Fear is the basis for aversion, and wonder is primordial attraction. Human beings live suspended between these two poles of the existential dilemma.

In chasing after the origins of religion, more attention has been paid to fear than to wonder, as we've noted. One of the most common assumptions is that the basis of fear is the unknown. That is, insecurity and uncertainty over what cannot be determined and mastered dominate human life, while the obligation to decide and act in the world continues relentlessly. If this tension does not produce anxiety, what does?

"We've already agreed that the basis for the religious sensibility goes deeper than the fear of death, but maybe we should dig into that fear somewhat," I propose.

"Right," Ethan agrees, "but there's bound to be fear in confronting the infinite itself. It'd be like vertigo from staring into a bottomless pit with no hooks to hold you back from fallin' forever."

"But for now," I ask, "what're we goin' to say about death itself? Isn't it a kind of. . .well, finger pointing toward the abyss of infinity?"

The idea that this sort of fear, fear of the unknown, is the proper origin of religion does often become fixated on that one fear: *death*. Let's admit that much. Because death is at once inevitable and yet uncertain, and because it marks the termination beyond which only the play of imagination ventures, it marks the crisis over whether and how life can be worth living at all. Tolstoy addresses this anxiety boldly in his little book, *My Confession*. He asks this question repeatedly: If we all die in the end, then what is the point of living, indeed of doing anything in the hope that it might make a difference?

Only a few possibilities, if any, are available in the face of death. First, people can and do simply ignore death beyond the ordinary recognition of the fact of it. Death in the abstract may be acknowledged, but a presumption of indefinite postponement dismisses its bearing on personal life. A dramatic account of just this way of addressing death is captured in Tolstoy's short story, "The Death of Ivan Illych."

A second option, related to the first but more aggressive and subtle, is to deny death itself. Ernest Becker has gone so far as to claim that being in denial about death is the universal condition of all human beings. Humanity cannot accept death and face the demands and challenges of life. Thus, we generate endless "immortality projects," as he calls them, to pretend *to ourselves* that we can thereby trick our way out of death. He goes so far as to say that this approach is the proper source of all human violence and that it produces the very condition that makes religion necessary.

In the third place, death may be addressed by imaginatively anticipating a continued existence of one sort or another after death. While this strategy is not confined to religions, most of them include a version of this possibility. Indeed, arguments can be found that insist that a belief in life after death as the only, or certainly the primary, reason for religion and that without this expectation, neither life nor religion makes sense. In other words, religion gives the answer to fear of death by taking away its finality.

And of course there are those who insist that death be affirmed and embraced as final—nothing beyond the grave—while believing that this life itself is quite enough and well worth living.

"So, then there are two ways out of this death fear," Ethan proposes. "You can take the coward's way or th' way of courage."

"What are you sayin'?" I want to know.

"Or maybe a third option. If you ignore death, you're stupid. Whistlin' in the dark! If you deny it, you're a coward. It takes courage to dare livin' on the promise of something after death and maybe even more courage to put all your eggs in the basket of this life."

"Or you could say that the life after death option is itself cowardly, because it's a way of not taking death seriously or of seeing it as some sort of advancement. Another sort of denial!"

"Could be," Ethan admits, "but it does show imagination. That's a sort of courage, I think."

****

The child, born into a strict piety belonging to the "holiness movement," goes with his family to church, and they go often. During special seasons comes the Revival, a protracted sequence of nightly services of evangelistic preaching. That means preaching to address and reach the "lost" for their salvation. Visiting itinerant preachers, especially given to the style of preaching appropriate to confronting sin and sinners, are invited to lead.

Now that the child is old enough to pay attention, he listens especially for the stories. They intrigue him and provide a peculiar entertainment in the otherwise weighty confines of the services. On the last night, the evangelist—that is, the visiting preacher—presents an especially charged message centered on the pending "days of tribulation" and the horror of being unprepared for them.

The message is graphic in the extreme, yet as intriguing as a horror movie—which of course the child has never seen because movies are forbidden. In this imagined future great surges of plague will undo the populace. People will flee to the hills for safety but will find none. All water will be changed into undrinkable blood, and in their hunger people will turn to eating the flesh of their neighbors and family.

The child, for the first time in church, sits riveted. The most memorable description has to do with the inability of people to die. They will cry out for death, asking the very rocks to fall upon them, but when they do, the people will be crushed and left palpitating in agonized pools of flesh and blood. Still they will not be able to die. This image is so stark that the child has one of his earliest remembered thoughts about death and the possibility that it could be a good thing. The idea of being unable to die paralyzes him with its possibility.

After drawing this unearthly picture of the future, stalking the front of the church as he shouts his declamation, the evangelist's voice dramatically softens. He turns to the images of the promise offered only to those who are prepared for the End. They will escape this devastation and be wafted away to unimaginable raptures of fulfillment. This promise is offered much like a hearty meal to the starving, and people are moved to affirm it or to embrace it. The child, shaking from the baldness of the mental images assailing him, considers moving down to the front during the invitation, but he cannot move. He remains anchored to the spot.

The same night a feverish dream enters the child's sleeping mind. He stands, with the entire congregation and his family, in front of their church. It is a basement church, unfinished and sitting on a bluff near the river. He looks up and presently sees other people rising and wafting away into the heavens. The image is vivid. When his father, standing nearby, begins ascending, the child realizes he, too, must seek to rise.

The child begins to float upward with surprising ease, but slowly. He rises until he is above the telephone poles and wires. He sees them barely below him. But he can climb no further. He strains but begins a slow descent. Back on the ground, he makes repeated leaps to launch himself but to no avail. The rest of his family rise and depart. Even his dog lifts smoothly from the earth and disappears into the ether. The child wakes up.

This dream is the earliest and most memorable dream of his childhood.

****

I throw more wood on the fire to stem the night chill settling around us. "One thing this conversation helps me see is that we humans don't necessarily turn to religion because of the fear of death. There's nothing automatic about the relation between them. Here's a test. Suppose we could eliminate death." Ethan throws up his hands at the proposed fantasy. "I know that's farfetched, but use your imagination. Besides, you know that there are all of these 'immortalist' societies that either believe it's possible or that immortality is already the case.

"Anyway, if there were no death for us to fear, would religion still exist? I once had a student who asked me about this, and I wonder what you'd say."

Ethan stands and stretches, reaching skyward. He says, "Yep, I believe there'd still be religion around and the reason is that it's about more than death or the fear of it."

"Yeah, that sounds right. It's more about life than about death, but death is a sort of wake-up call to living. Like Woody Allen says, 'Death is nature's way of saying howdy.' Or something like that. The ancient Israelites, for example, may not have had any serious notion of personal life after death, and yet they still had a thriving religion. So maybe the better question is not to start with the idea of no death but to consider whether there can be a religion without a concept of personal survival beyond death. If so, then religion can't be tied to death or the fear of it as much as might be assumed."

Ethan adds, "But there's that other primary motivator. I mean the idea of wonder that you mentioned. I wonder what you mean?" he adds mischievously.

Wonder, not in the ordinary way we use it, such as "I wonder what time it is," but in its foundational meaning as something closer to amazement, has to do with attraction. We're drawn to the world, to its cosmic reach, to the promise and demands of living, to other people. Wonder, however, is complex. It also includes a sense of distance, of our being "under the spell" or caught up in that which draws us and may even take us up into itself. This means that attraction includes both a sense of connection or longing for connection as well as difference and a respect for whatever draws us. This respect is not fear as we discussed it earlier, but it does include an aspect of fear. It might best be understood as our awareness that we cannot reduce what attracts us to ourselves. Another word for wonder in this sense could be *reverence*.

Fear of the unknown, and specifically of death may be a kind of prompter in the wings that nudges toward religion, but religion itself is not about escaping or conquering death. It's more nearly about the possibilities that belong to our human existence and especially about our connection with the whole of things, our profoundest sense of *belonging*. Wonder is the awareness that opens these possibilities and draws us to them.

When I think of wonder in this way, the great cosmological-yet-personal questions come to mind: What is the source and nature of all things? How are we related to all of it? How did we get here? Why are we here? What are we to do? As imperative and inevitable as these questions are, however, they still do not reach the core of wonder. They are the way wonder expresses itself as we interrogate our world and ourselves in relation to it.

Thus, even this profound way of thinking leaves me to ponder whether wonder, the sort of wonder that belongs to reverence or awe, necessarily forms the basis of religion. In other words, could we have religion without wonder? Seems doubtful in the extreme. I'm thinking that wonder may be the first blush of the religious sensibility.

As fundamental as fear and wonder may be to our struggle for the worth of life, they still do not appear to me to be sufficient in themselves to explain the origin of religion. They simply do not provide the primary foundation on which religion arises and builds. An even better architectural metaphor might be "bedrock." It comes closer to the image I wish to convey. I seek the most likely ground for the possibility of religion in the character of human existence itself. No doubt some will say that this question is not the proper one, that there is no such thing as human existence itself, or that we cannot determine it, but I cannot be satisfied without seeking it. Thinkers like Jean Paul Sartre argue that there is no "human nature" because human existence is forever unfinished and open ended…free! That is like saying, "There is no human nature, but I will now explain what it is, namely, open-ended potentiality."

What kind of creatures are we? Yes, we are capable of fear and wonder, but is this capability sufficient? Such questions are among those perennial and gnawing queries that will never leave us alone. Candidates for answers to these questions reach from Aristotle's "rational man" to Mark Twain's "the only creature that blushes...or needs to." Yet, if religion is unique to our species, and this itself must remain an open question, might it not be the case that a clearer comprehension of our *kind* could provide a clue to the roots of religion? A large order indeed, and one on which we are not likely to find consensus.

Granting the treachery of trying to identify the specific quality or qualities that make us human, I propose at least this much: to be human is to be possessed of a certain consciousness in relation to ourselves and to everything other than ourselves and we are conscious of that! I will break this statement down for further clarification. First, humans are conscious. This statement does not say nearly enough, because it seems obvious enough that other sentient creatures are, to one extent or another, also conscious.

My point is that we humans are conscious in a certain way. It may well be that the entire universe is conscious and arises through a universal consciousness. This idea is attractive, and by no means novel. But I will not pursue it here. All I wish to note is that whatever the reach of consciousness might be, human beings participate it in a particular way.

This leads to a second element in my proposal: human consciousness relates itself to itself—or *finds itself* in relation to itself. We are not only conscious but conscious of ourselves being conscious. We can and do relate to ourselves. This capacity might be called *self-consciousness*. Without it, we could not be, for instance, persons, if we take person to mean the self relating to itself in its relation to other selves. Now there's a mouthful, but think about it. Moreover, because of this capacity, we may further characterize our humanity as fundamentally *relational*.

Obviously, our relation to ourselves does not end with ourselves but as the self-relation relates to everything else of which we are or might be conscious: the world around us, other human beings, and possibly something like a cosmic or universal whole. We are the creature constituted through, made for, and perhaps made *of* relationships, and because relationships are essential to who we are, we live and find ourselves in and through *participation*.

Other relevant issues, such as whether we human beings have an essential fixed nature, or whether we are more constituted by relationships than we are the source of them, or again, whether and to what extent we are agents of our own decisions and actions, we do not need to pursue here. Perhaps as they become pertinent to our discussion, we will address them.

This sketch of who we humans are is skeletal in the extreme. It can surely be expanded greatly, and it can surely be challenged. It is certainly not offered as the only possibility. Still, it is one legitimate way of characterizing our kind, and I believe it is adequate for our present purpose. All I want to do is outline a way of thinking about our humanity sufficient for stalking the elusive question of the origin of religion as such. If I am right, that the source of religion is best found in the existential condition of our humanity—specifically in the finite encounter with the infinite—and not by investigating the historical origins of humanity, then some brief account of what I mean by *humanity* is at stake.

"Talkin' about ourselves is a bottomless pit anyway," Ethan says in revolt. "It's all our kind seems to do, if you ask me. I don't see the need for a lot more of it." He tosses the last dregs of chocolate from his mug and announces that he's ready for bed. I rise with him, take one last look at the spectacle of the spangled sky above us, stir the fire with a stick, and pour water on the coals.

Ten

> This world of imagination is Infinite and Eternal whereas the world of Generation or Vegetation is Finite and Temporal.
>
> William Blake

～

There are different styles of backpacking. Packers sometimes hike into a site, make camp, and stay there for a week or so. Others break camp and hike every day. This style is more goal oriented, an effort to move from here to there. Ethan and I have decided on a compromise. We'll stay at a location for a couple, or at most three, days before moving further. This plan gives us time to explore as we go, while carrying lighter day-packs. It also allows us time to read, muse, and relax for extended periods.

Today we move north toward Pecos Falls. We're up earlier, making a fire and cobbling together a breakfast. We eat more heartily because we're traveling. Neither of us speaks. Ethan says he's a morning person, but he believes it's indecent to speak before ten o'clock. I'm a chatterbox, but I refrain. This is how friendships work.

We hear noises down toward the trail. Horse packers! A low-grade hostility prevails between backpackers and horses packers. The horses muck up the trails with deep tracks—especially when the trail's wet—and dung. Besides, most of the horse packers are what we call *mountain tourists*, trying to visit the wilderness without participating in the challenge of it. And their horses can carry much more gear, often leaving campsites with clutter. Our view is that we should walk through the wilderness leaving as few tracks as possible. Basically, it's one more version of elitism—both ways.

Still, we wave at the riders. There are four, and we'll soon follow them up the trail. One horseman leaves the others to ask if we've seen another group come through. When we say we haven't, he wonders aloud whether they could've gone to Moira Flats. We both shrug, and he bids us a good day. When they're out of earshot, we find pleasure in the silence.

Repacking, especially the first time, requires close attention. Everything that has come out of the packs, including what is now refuse, goes back into the packs. It's best to take our time, and we do. Time's our friend here, because those sundials we ordinarily wear on our wrists are not with us, and deadlines are distant memories.

"Shit!" Ethan's monosyllable punctuates the air. He's forgotten something that should have already gone into the pack, and he must partially unpack. I chuckle, and he throws a clod at me.

"Ah, I see you're ready to talk."

"Not quite."

We finish our tasks at about the same time, lean the packs against the sitting log, and take a substantial drink before lifting the gear onto our backs. "Everything's about rhythm," I muse out loud but to myself.

"Don't go musical on me," Ethan insists.

"But that's the trick. The whole thing's musical. Can't do anything well until you catch the rhythm of it." I'm thinking about the process of loading a pack. About halfway through loading, I find the groove of doing it. After that, it was effortless, efficient, and I felt that it was doing itself through me, not by me. It's what the Taoists call *wu wie*. Sounds odd, but I do believe we're always seeking that feeling. Psychologist Mihaly Czikszentmahalyi calls it flow. In a sense Taoism, Buddhism, and other traditions are basically about seeking the *flow*. Confucius provided a methodological scheme for life to follow in order to achieve the flow.

We lift our packs, swing them into place, and cinch the straps. I continue thinking about this notion of rhythm. It happens in whatever we do, within ourselves, between people, between ourselves and the entire world. This pilgrimage requires a whole scheme of rhythms: walking, resting, and through it all paying attention to each moment and also to the whole venture. Waking, eating, loading, lifting, walking. All of it forms a pattern. It's a holograph in which each element reflects the whole, and when I can keep that in mind, the rhythm takes over. It's like reading a novel. The story is the whole thing, but every word, sentence, paragraph, and chapter makes the whole thing possible. It forms a circle, or maybe a spiral, in which the pieces turn back to reveal the whole story.

"Why do you always talk in circles like that? It can be annoyin', you know," Ethan announces, and I grin. He's ready to talk.

We take up hiking sticks and drop down the hill to the trail. Ethan leads. The trail runs along the western edge of Hamilton Mesa. It is relatively flat and the hiking is relaxed. We find our gait.

Thinking is the hidden center of this pilgrimage, the thread holding the rhythm together. I love thinking. Even when it's work, it's more like play than labor. But I feel that today I might turn off the demands of my own relentless flow of thoughts and put myself on cruise control. We came here to explore this one subject, but I want to step back from it and let it lie fallow for a while.

Stopping the flow of thought is not easy for people who think. When I say *think*, I don't mean having little petty obsessions or "melodramatic ponderations" over people, problems, or plans. That's just the ego screaming at itself.

What I have in mind is a devotion to making sense of what I experience and of lacing it together into a workable image of the big picture—or at least the bigger picture. This is sometimes called a *worldview*, but I don't need to be quite that grand about it.

I remember the title of a book by the popular mythologist Joseph Campbell: *Myths to Live By*. That may be closer to what I'm thinking about thinking. It has to do with thinking mythically, thinking through to the story that rings true. Later, as I told Ethan before we left Oklahoma, we do need to think through how myth expresses itself in religion. But here I go again, thinking.

T. E. Lawrence, popularly known as Lawrence of Arabia, wrote in his journal something like this: "I had a good morning. I was able to go for several hours without thinking." He was an obsessive thinker. He couldn't easily turn off his thinking.

A friend of mine who teaches an Eastern style of meditation says that our minds are munchy. We are forever stewing in thoughts about this and that. True, but it's not the same as the problem Lawrence had. He thought big thoughts, mythic thoughts, but at times he felt he was not in control of thinking. His thinking took him over.

And it is clear enough that I'm having the same difficulty on this trail. Here I am, thinking about how I can turn off the faucet of thinking. At least for a while! But that's still thinking. Mercy!

"Must be after ten," Ethan turns as he speaks. I note in my mind that he's not fully here yet. He's still tied to the clock. We stop, drop our packs, and snack on dried fruit. Then he asks a truly astounding question: "What you been thinkin'?"

Ethan can be uncanny, but asking this question, even if it's as commonplace as questions come, stuns me. I stare into the distance until he looks at me. He expects a response. I start to say "Nothin'," but decide against the adolescent option. "You really want to know?"

"Let's hear what you say before I answer that."

"To tell the truth, I was thinkin' about thinking."

"Good God! Give it a break."

"That's what I was thinkin' about, how hard it is to stop thinking."

"It's easy as pie. I've spent this whole mornin' not thinkin'."

"How?"

"Mostly I notice. That's the best way. When I notice what's actually going on and then notice the next thing, thinkin' takes a back seat. It sounds corny as a pop self-help book, but if I can find the moments and actually hang with each one as it comes, the mental drill sergeant quits yelling in my ear. Thinkin' can be a distraction sometimes."

"I'm not very good at that. How'd you learn to do it?" I ask. "We've talked about everything under the sun over the past four years, but we never actually discussed this."

"It started in Nam with smokin' grass. We'd stoke up, even in the bush, when we thought it was safe. And we'd 'find the zone,' as we called it. I would've gone stark ravin' mad, if I hadn't discovered that zone. What it taught me after a while, especially when the supply of weed was scarce, is that I could find the zone without the stuff. It was harder and I could be distracted easier, but I did find it. . .sometimes for a whole day. It might've saved my life a couple of times. Noticin' was basic in that place. . .But even when I came home and started plumbin' with Dad, I could work under a house for hours and hardly realize the time. I just kept noticin'."

"Yeah," I agree, "I've found it occasionally, but only in fits and starts. I can't keep it for long." I start to say it has to do with rhythm, but Ethan picks up his pack. I follow.

We walk. He says, "The only real help I've found, besides weed. . .and that doesn't always work, I can tell you. . .is mystics and shamans. They think, but thinkin' doesn't overwhelm them. What takes them out of themselves is a sort of receptivity to what's going on. It's what I mean by 'lettin' instead of 'makin.' You can do that when you take notice. It's a way of payin' attention without bein' separated from what you're payin' attention to."

I immediately recall this notion that constantly occupies me: *participation*. We can be mindful, as the Buddhists keep insisting, without the separation that thinking imposes between itself and whatever we are thinking about. In some way, although I'm not sure how, this relates to the whole subject of this pilgrimage. Religion, if it means anything, is about a "binding back," making connection beyond our estrangements and isolation. It is connection! Or *re*-connection!

If thinking involves separation, and if religion is connection, then what good does thinking do when it comes to religion? Here we are in these mountains, bathed in the elegance of nature, and we're spending most of the time thinking about something that maybe we cannot really, and certainly not fully, engage by thinking about it. I wonder whether we can think religion without thinking *about* it.

All I can say at this point is that thinking—at its best—belongs to our existence as human beings. To be our kind of creature entails, among other things, thinking. It's a key manifestation of consciousness. And in a way, thinking is not just one thing among others. I might even propose that thinking is consciousness organized and focused upon that of which we are conscious.

****

When the man is a boy, he dreams. He dreams more when awake than asleep. He dreams so incessantly that school disrupts his dreaming. He does not do well in school, preferring to act out dreams in the simulated world of play. This is his art.

Exactly how this dream life changes lies in the murky reaches of memory. A high school teacher has the temerity to ask him to write for the student paper. But he does not write. He dreams. She insists, and day by day, line by line, she monitors his words on paper. He learns, though slow-

ly and fitfully, and in learning he discovers that he can learn and that he imagines much but knows nothing!

And so, to college! The first of his family to venture there. Driven by knowing his ignorance and drawn to its surcease, he stalks the halls where knowing resides. Blundering into the unknown, he studies philosophy, never having heard of it and not knowing exactly how to spell it. (Filosofy, his first try!) So bewildering are the words, the ideas, the movement of thought that he discovers more than his ignorance. He senses that he is cut off from coming to know.

Ah, then he makes a discovery. This subject, of all subjects, is not exactly about knowing, not directly or primarily. It is about thinking. His perplexity plunges deeper. Learning and knowing are not enough. Thinking supersedes both and makes them worthwhile. But his thoughts, while many, have birthed from his imagination—from dreaming. They have little order, and they can never check each other. One thought, if it satisfies his dreaming, is as good as another.

But wait! The laws of thinking laid bare in the endless squiggles of logic, and more generally, the "canons of reason" that challenge thoughts and force them to the test, all of these grand arts harking to antiquity, disturb his dreams. He must bring his mind to heel so it can yield its fruit. This is the gift of philosophy, and he finds liberation there, the liberation into thinking.

Thinking is dangerous. It is dangerous to the thinker because it pushes the thinker outside the zone of what is taken for granted and into the limitless reach of the possible. It is dangerous to the world because it encourages the rebellion of another possibility besides the one belonging to common sense. Thinking, done faithfully, inspires an "uncommon sense," and dictators hate this. Dictators are everywhere, even benevolent ones.

More ominous, thinking has its limit. Thinking is not living, not the full-blooded passionate surge of being alive. Yet, living is not thoughtless. Now that the boy has become the man, this is his soul's dilemma. He lives beyond dreams toward something more—stable, more abiding. Yet, he lives! And anyone who lives continues only through the dream and through the passion of deciding and acting, a domain only observed by thinking.

The man awakens, but does he awaken from his dreams or in them?

****

When I mentioned consciousness earlier, I really didn't go much beyond the idea that it is the quality that relates us to ourselves and to everything else. But consciousness is complex, to make the understatement of the year. It includes all the elements within our psyche available to us. I include the affections (emotion, feeling), and conation (willing, deciding), cogitation (reason, imagination, intuition), to say nothing of embodiment itself. All of these elements, and more perhaps, constitute the perpetual activity of consciousness within the human psyche. I could go on to mention others, such as language, the unconscious, and so forth. Here's my point. All of this, I'll call it the *consciousness complex*, constantly mixes and interrelates as consciousness responds to all that comes before it. Thinking is the organizing thread through all of this. It is both one of the elements and the way we organize and hold all the elements together. So, if we're conscious—and I believe that consciousness is us—thinking is serious business. It's how consciousness puts its world together.

One problem with all of this is that we keep dividing these elements into bits and pieces. We split emotion away from thinking, willing and deciding away from feeling, and so forth. We even study ourselves by concentrating on one or another of these elements or some cluster of them. We compartmentalize consciousness, sometimes to the point of fragmentation. We compartmentalize so much that we lose track of the consciousness complex itself. In a sense, we become lost in the fragments, as it were, but if we pay close attention, we know better. Consciousness reaches its fullest realization, not in splitting and fragmenting, but in connecting!

To make matters more difficult, there is bad thinking, thinking that is fractured, filled with idle fantasy, or poorly organized and out of focus, or deluded, to say nothing of devious. This may not be an adequate way to put it, but it will do for starters. I grew up with adults warning me through this cliché: "An idle mind is the devil's workshop." Maybe there's some truth in it, give or take blaming it on the devil.

Thinking is not everything by any means, and under some conditions it's not even the main thing. Still, if we're going to appreciate its place, we need to explore how it works for us. (Isn't this amazing: I'm suggesting that we think about thinking itself? Most of us most of the time simply think, whether poorly or well, but we seldom double back and pay attention to our thinking itself and its limits.)

Beyond idle thinking, a kind of stream of consciousness, or immediate problem solving, or worrying, we might inquire into the purpose of thinking. Consider these three concepts in relation to thinking: information, knowledge, and understanding.

The first two, information and knowledge, do separate us from the "stuff" of our thinking, that is, what we think *about*. By these means we apply our thinking to mastery of ourselves and our world. Science has this genius. Information, for instance, provides thinking with its raw material. When we strive to overcome ignorance or solve problems through thinking, we are using more directly the *rational* capacity within thinking. We receive and collect facts, or at least what we take to be facts, and we try to find associations among the facts. This capacity is very basic. Consider the word *inform* as to *in-form*, to place the raw material of our experience into *form*. Quite literally this means to give form or perhaps to discover form within the flow of our ongoing experience. This is no small ability, although it is a fairly elementary level of organized thinking. Much more is required.

We seek a unity and comprehensiveness that goes beyond filtering facts or claimed facts. We seek knowledge. While we can say that we "know" facts, they do not make up serious knowledge. Knowledge in the full-blown sense of the word is more than facts or their mere organization. Knowledge entails the *interpretation* of facts in relation to each other and their relation to ourselves in such a way that we *comprehend a world*! Or at least some part of a world we deem significant. Thinking is the primary activity in achieving this knowledge.

But information and knowledge are not enough to account for the place of thinking in human existence. A third dimension, *understanding*, is a more fulfilling aim of thinking. Understanding is closer to ideas like discernment or vision but still distinct from them. To "stand under" is to be on the inside of more than knowledge. We are on the inside of being human and of living our humanity through the best we know but also beyond the best we know through the audacity and risk of living.

Understanding has to do with comprehensiveness. Here we live as in the *presence* of what we know. When thinking moves through and beyond what we know to how all that engages our consciousness interrelates, we enter the domain of understanding.

Understanding moves quite beyond in-formation and interpretation to integration. When the philosopher Martin Heidegger distinguishes two kinds of thinking, calculative and meditative, he has this in mind. Calculative thinking has the aim of knowledge, while meditative thinking is in the service of understanding. And understanding responds to living. It serves living.

Most of our thinking stalls out, at best, at knowledge. To think beyond knowledge to understanding, however, may allow for a thinking that overcomes its own separation from what we think about or what we claim to know. At the level of understanding, our thinking may, and I believe does, become *participatory*. It moves in this direction, when we begin to insist that thinking serves our actual existence, and we embrace it as a resource for living—not as a form of mastery *over* the world.

This brief excursus into thinking—after I have decided to spend the day not thinking—has this purpose: it calls for a way of thinking about thinking that penetrates the separation of thought from life. A common name for this separation is intellectualism, that is, the attempt to reduce understanding to knowledge for the purpose of dominance rather than participation. This is why religion is often perceived by intellectuals as anti-intellectual, also why some religious practitioners, especially when challenged by the canons of reason—that is, disciplined and sustained systematic thinking—take refuge in anti-intellectualism.

Understanding, while it is necessary to religion or to any dimension of life as a whole, is not all there is to religion. If, as I suggested quite early in this pilgrimage, religion is our *connection to a higher order of things*, then it surely includes our very sense of who we are as well as our ultimate orientation. This orientation, however, is participated as i, or I might say, a way of being in relation to ourselves and to the whole of things. Understanding does not cause this participation but arises in actually living our orientation. It is the "thinking element" in this process.

The reason I keep digging for the origin or basis of religion is to unveil its relation to life itself and thus to our most profound depths of understanding.

"Sounds right, but I thought you were tryin' to stop thinkin'," Ethan chides. "You're on a worse binge than usual." He stops on the trail and leans against his stick.

"The best way, I guess, is to stop before I get started," I suggest.

"Right. Once you're on a roll, what're you gonna' do?" Ethan sympathizes and then adds, "Now that you're sailin' let me add a wrinkle. I don't believe your little scheme is complete. There's something beyond understanding."

"And what might that be?" I challenge with mock confidence that I've nailed the business of thinking.

"Not sure how to put it best, but I'll call it *vision*. Thinkin' seems to me to include somethin' more than a process like you've laid out. It has a receptive side. I could call it *insight* or maybe *discernment*, but no one word fits exactly. That's why, when I have a really tough idea I'm tryin' to express, I use what I call the *shotgun approach*. I find a cluster of words that point toward what I'm aimin' for.

"It may be closer to a kind of *unveiling* or a life-shattering 'Aha'! I've had these from time to time, when I'm noticin'. What I actually mean is that something *intrudes* on our thinking, takes it over. Thinkin' can help prepare the way for it, but thinkin' can't cause it. You have to wait. Receive. Thinkin' is transformed by this in-breaking."

"I see...right," I respond, stirred by Ethan's recitation. His proposal opens a window in my understanding. I add, "Maybe something closer to *intuition*. I do like that word. Or, I wonder about an old word from the dictionary of religion: *revelation*."

"Or maybe the mystical," Ethan adds. "We keep reaching for words, but that's because what...we're...tryin' to say is not ordinarily acknowledged or talked about, especially these days. Then again it may not be as rare as we assume. People just don't have a vocabulary for it, and anyway, it runs deeper than words."

"I like the word *deeper*," I chime in. "I remember a statement by Paul Tillich that illuminated my..."

"There's another word," Ethan interjects. " *Illumination* is another way to point out this fourth dimension of thinking. Or, *enlightenment* is another one... But, as you were saying..."

I continue. "Tillich said something about religion that I still ponder. He said, 'Religion is the depth dimension in human existence.' I'm not sure what to do with a metaphor like 'depth.' It's really not very precise, but it clarifies something about religion. . .and probably about all truly profound thinking and living. I might say that a painting, a piece of music, or a poem is *beautiful* or *elegant* or *brilliant*, but those words are not like *deep*. When I use it, I think of a well or the *deeps* of the ocean. It's about what lies at the bottom of things, like when we say we need to get to the bottom of some problem. And when I keep chasing after the origin or basis of religion, what I'm really seeking is its depth."

"Know what comes to my mind?" Ethan doesn't wait for me to guess. He stops and turns around for emphasis. "It reminds me of somethin' that either has no bottom, or if it does, we can never reach it. *Deep* means you can keep on probing and playing with it, because it always allows for more. It lures toward. . .infinity! Using your image of the sea, it's quite literally unfathomable."

I add, "And that's exactly how I think about the sacred. It's what calls us through and beyond ourselves into…what? The *boundless*!"

As we begin walking again, I'm struck by how far we've moved from my original subject: thinking. Yet, not all that far because actually we're getting at an intrusive experiential encounter that bears thinking away into the deeps! And it is visionary! I still like that image. I'm talking about the breakthrough into thinking that shapes and claims consciousness itself, an encounter of consciousness with or in Consciousness. The reasoning aspect of thinking isn't undermined, but it is transcended as insight, discernment, or, to use another metaphor, seeing. I think of a seer, one who sees further and deeper into things. Such people are truly see-ers. Wisdom, in its profound meaning, not the more casual and trivial ways we use it, is about this seeing. The wise ones go beyond and return to us with sight—*in-sight*. Understanding itself is not merely extended. It is lifted to a new dimension of unconditional participation.

As I ponder these notions of depth, in-sight, and sight, another metaphor leaps to mind: *heart*. We use this word to refer to deeply felt thoughts and responses, as when Mary, the Mother of Jesus, "pondered these things in her heart." Heart is usually taken as "the seat of affections" or emotions, but it is also more than that. When we say we want to "get to the heart" of some problem or interest, we are talking about something quite close to depth. Metaphorically speaking, we want to "see"—that is, *discern*—the depths.

I have the image of burrowing down into the matter. The word *core*, which derives from the Latin for "heart," carries the same weight. The core of anything is its vital center, literally what makes it tick. When Pascal makes his famous statement, "The heart has reasons that reason knows not of," he is speaking of this transformed depth of thinking, in which the entire consciousness is melded and caught up in participatory in-sight.

To push further, "heart" connotes also a union of reason with *will*, with our intentions and orientation toward action. This union is beautifully captured in the title of one of Kierkegaard's books: *Purity of Heart Is to Will One Thing*. Thinking with heart binds our understanding with our willed intentions. I sometimes sense that the notion of the heart is most nearly a locus of the harmonic convergence of thinking, affection, and intention.

As I marvel at all of this and the possibilities this cluster of metaphors suggests, the word *image*, then *imagination* comes to mind. Thinking, almost all of it beyond the most rudimentary levels, is borne in and through the image. Thus, the capacity for imagination—image making—is absolutely primary to thinking and especially crucial for these more profound reaches of thinking. Without it there is little to move our thinking beyond the confines of organizing immediate sensory experience and making up theories about it.

Abruptly I have a memory:

> *The man teaches a course in the philosophy of religion fairly early in my career. A notably bright student takes the course, as he later confesses, in order to make fun of religion. He proudly declares that his major is biochemistry, and that his scientific prowess is his pretext for declaring war on religion. Religion is not, as he keeps saying, 'rational.'*
>
> *The student sits on the front row and frequently asks questions; and questions most claims about religion. He is especially exercised over the word 'transcendence.' The teacher shows him the various ways it is used and offers an account of its uses in religious discourse, but the student will have none of it. He is intense and persistent, something professors should*

applaud and celebrate, but he could be distracting for other students, especially ones who neither know nor care about his concerns. To facilitate their conversations, the teacher suggests he drop by the office.

In one conversation the teacher begins to sense that, despite the student's considerable intelligence, he is somewhat dense about religion. The teacher confesses that he believes the student may not be capable of religion. The teacher proposes that the student may suffer from a sort of religious idiocy. The teacher is not proud of this judgment but needs to have the student's close attention.

The student justifiably bristles at the idea of his being incapable of anything.

He asks, "Why would you say such a thing?"

The teacher responds, "Because you have no imagination!"

"That's just what I thought," the student retorts exultantly. "The whole thing's about nothing but imagination! It's pure fantasy!"

Before the teacher can monitor my words, he finds himself replying, "Yes, religion is very much about imagination. But so is science, and because you lack imagination, you will not make a good scientist, nor will you ever understand religion."

The teacher intentionally wants to challenge the student's intellectual presumption.

The cluster of concepts and images I introduce to comprehend this fourth dimension of thinking—that is, vision or whatever word we select to describe it—may seem overdone, but there is a reason. We either seldom reach the fourth dimension, or if we do, we find it generally discounted and not encouraged in our culture. It is too mysterious, too ethereal, too unwieldy. This fourth dimension is left to the labyrinth of our inner subjectivity, a dark box about which little can be said. This much is certain: the academy—the citadel of higher learning—gives the fourth dimension little play. I grant that in the Humanities and the Arts, it may receive some attention, but even there it is seldom central. We don't know how to *test* it!

I won't try to argue this in general, but if we're to come to grips with religion, I believe we must grapple with this fourth dimension, the depth of a participative consciousness, and...

"Would you look at that? I'm stoppin' right here," Ethan declares from up ahead on the trail.

I join him, stare at an Elysian meadow dropping off to the East into a grove of aspen, and remind him, "But we've been walkin' so slow and we're not even close to the Falls."

He stares at me, as if to remind me that distance is irrelevant and that perhaps even I am irrelevant. I realize my outburst is nothing more than the residue of the contrived world, where achievement is measured by getting somewhere. The *where* is simply made up. Shortly we're making camp in an open space beneath towering ponderosas. The site has been used before, and we're soon at ease with tents pitched and gear stashed.

Ethan strolls into the open meadow and says, "Only problem is that we can't see sunsets here. We'll have to settle for sunrises."

Thinking slows and dissolves into slumber.

Eleven

No loneliness is as severe as the awareness of finitude afloat in the sea of infinity.

Anon.

∼

Sunrise expands to daylight brilliance before we peer out of our tents and join it. I trek down to a bog near the aspens, where there's a tiny spring. It takes a while to pump enough water through the purifier to fill our bottles. By the time I'm back, Ethan has oatmeal bubbling.

Today will be a solitary one for each of us. We have not negotiated this, but we know we need it. I need to do what I promised to do yesterday but failed: not spend the whole day thinking. After breakfast and cleaning our dishes, I take my hiking stick, a small journal, a flask of water, and saunter toward the grove below. Ethan waves and soon disappears into the timber on the other side of our campsite.

After wandering for a while, smelling the morning and feeling the sun penetrating my light shirt, I locate my spot. It is slightly dished out, and from the way the grass lies flat, it must've been a bed for deer or elk, maybe last night. I sit in the bowl, barely in the shade, and for half an hour I stare at the shifting grass and the dancing aspen leaves. I do nothing, nothing at all. I am there.

I move into a modified Lotus position and breathe deeply, noticing the movement of air into my lungs and out. This exchange connects me in another way to all that surrounds me. Eyes closed, I enter a more tranquil state and begin meditating. Time dissolves, the present expands. All thought drops away, and I'm suspended as in a womb. The Nothing and the All merge.

How long I remain in this state I do not know, and without a watch I can only read the fact that I now sit in a splash of sunlight.

The surroundings are vivid and aglow with color. I'm refreshed as though I had entered REM sleep. Best of all, I feel utterly alone but not isolated. I revel in this solitary state.

While my mind rummages within all of this, I feel a slight movement on my right arm. I look down to see a tiny ant plying its course through the hair, and before I know it I'm remarking aloud, "Hello there. I'm not alone at all. Look at you."

Presently I recall a conversation with one of my daughters, a practicing Buddhist. She once told me that her Rinpoche had reminded her that she is never alone because all things are connected. We are especially intimate with all living things, what she called "sentient beings."

I find myself infatuated with the early summer wildflowers and listening to the distant call of birds. I'm aware that I am indeed part of this tableau of nature, and I attend this truth by watching the diminutive creature on my arm find its way to the back of my hand. I look up to see a white butterfly flutter past me and disappear into the trees. I notice.

But I'm a Westerner, caught in the tangle of our human constructs. Perhaps this state is ubiquitous for humankind. It is difficult to maintain my fix on this wider connection with the throbbing world all around me, engulfing me and holding me there. There are some people even in our hemisphere who stress this wider connection.

I recall Henry David Thoreau's discussion in *Walden* of the universe of ants and how intriguing he found them. This discussion is important and partly explains why I'm in these mountains, but somehow it is not quite the focus of my sense of connectedness yet aloneness. When I experience this sense, I experience a peculiarly *human* absence. Even though I'm connected to the dynamic of nature as well as, perhaps, to a transcendent dimension, I also sense myself standing apart and over against my kind.

In the West we do emphasize how every human being is notably distinct and separate from every other human being. This view is not a curse or necessarily a burden, just how I experience myself, and I want to pay attention to it. It may well be that the awareness of connection and of isolation are companions, a psychic dynamic that belongs to the way we are.

I munch on chunks of a granola bar and drink water retrieved from the spring this morning. This idea of being alone continues to claim my attention. The immediate sense of my present isolation comforts me, but I wonder whether this would be the case if I were lost or if I were cut off from possible human contact. Would all of these presences of nature be sufficient for me and for how long?

All of the great stories of people being marooned come to mind. Why are they always on islands? I suppose islands represent contained and circumscribed space from which there is no easy escape. Islands are like extensions of ourselves in our separateness, which is why they make such great settings for stories of isolation. Yet, the words of John Donne echo in my mind: "No man is an island entire of itself."

We are drawn to stories of isolation. I wonder why? Perhaps we are lured by the challenge and ordeal of having to go it on our own. Or, these stories remind us not to venture too far from the security and consolation of society. In America, I suspect, these stories reinforce our presumption—or delusion—that we are utterly self-reliant.

A professor friend assigned students to spend an entire day completely alone. They were not only to be without other people, but they were not to read, listen to music, or have any other distraction from their aloneness. The students were then to write responses to their experience. Most of them found they simply could not do it, certainly not for an entire day. Some only endured for a couple of hours. When my friend told me of the experiment, I was not surprised.

He asked me what I thought about why the students had such difficulty being by themselves, and I conjectured that we live in a stimulus-dominated world where we are attracted, confronted, mesmerized, goaded, invaded, teased, lured, bombarded, seduced, or distracted by a ceaseless barrage of external attractions. Our constant challenge is to sort out the information from the noise or titillation supposedly imbedded in the racket. Little wonder that being alone is so utterly rare, frustrating, and—to give it the name of the one true curse word of our time—boring!

For most of us, being alone is a test or a comfort, depending on our temperament and past experience—that is, how we have been programmed. Yet, there is a qualitative aloneness that comes only through deliberate cultivation until it becomes an art. By means of this sort of aloneness, we discover our center and ground for life in the world. Not everyone necessarily uses this means, but I find it to be a compelling resource.

These reflections arouse two images. First, among some Native American tribes the "Vision Quest" serves as a time of testing and of crying for a vision. The subject is taken or goes into an isolated place, follows traditional rituals, and waits alone until receiving a vision or message. The waiting may take days before the breakthrough comes.

Second, among monastic traditions the hermit takes on something of a similar discipline but in a more sustained way. The discipline becomes a lifestyle. Some are attached to a monastic community while others live in more constant isolation. Their calling is to pray for the world and in some instances to also perform acts of service from time to time.

In both of these cases, among others, aloneness becomes a medium of spiritual fulfillment, but fulfillment is not always the outcome. I think of people who endure solitary confinement for sustained periods. Why do prisons use this as special punishment? The assumption seems to be that severe isolation and deprivation of such resources as light and sometimes sufficient food is punishment in itself. And it is. Being forced into isolation that is entirely different from entering isolation on purpose.

My own aloneness on this mountain is by no means forced. I came here, in part, to flourish through being alone. Furthermore, I can walk away from this aloneness easily enough.

Whether the aloneness is inflicted on us or chosen by us, its value is this: in aloneness I am most likely to encounter myself. I am forced back on myself. This concept may have the ring of pop psychology, but it has a far deeper resonance in human experience. The deliberate practices of aloneness, which I've mentioned, speak of the merit of it, and at the core of their merit is the depth, complexity, and worth of self as such.

We have been reminded *ad nauseam* of the words emblazoned above the door to the Temple of Delphi: "Know thyself." Placed where these words were placed and stated as starkly as they were, their implication is that knowing ourselves is a challenging and ceaseless mission. It comes only through the demands of introspection, and to be introspective in any sustained way, we had best embrace aloneness as a serious medium.

Some years ago I began reflecting on aloneness and deliberately practicing it, and I gradually gained insight into its potential. Isolation—and I mean utter isolation, as in marooned on an island—is a curse. The word *idiot*, which we take from Greek, literally means "to be totally alone, isolated and incapable of connection." I long ago watched the movie of Helen Keller's life, *The Miracle Worker*. What struck me most was her profound isolation—her idiocy—as a result of being unable to hear or see and thus unable to communicate and relate. Then came the miracle! Her sensory limitations were breached and she made connection with the world. Astonishing!

Despite the threat of isolation, however, we are always to a significant degree alone. I mean by this that we experience ourselves as here and everything other than ourselves as there. Even in the most intimate moments of human relationship, as when "two become one," this sense of distinction remains or quickly returns. I keep calling on words like *connection, participation, presence* to underscore the primacy of relationship, but in our concrete experience we still and always harbor *difference* and with it, separation and isolation.

In part this tension between relation and isolation is determined by culture. Some cultures emphasize one, some the other. At root, however, the tension belongs to human existence itself. We live suspended between our separateness and our connectedness. We are both and cannot be utterly reduced to either.

****

The boy is thirteen and a scout. He goes to summer camp with his troop, encouraged by parents. He is away from home by himself for the first time. The separation feels alien but enticing. He fights a dim loneliness in himself

The camp has a sizable lake, and in the center of the lake stands a tower with platforms at various levels. It is known as the Forty-Foot Tower. The challenge is to dive or leap from the top of the tower at least once during the week. Everyone who makes the jump receives a badge to decorate their sash.

The scouts follow a buddy system. Everyone has a partner, and the partners are always together, checking on each other. Safety! The boy and his partner take a canoe from the shore and push it into the lake. Flailing and unsteady, they make their way toward the tower. When they reach it, they tie up and carefully but enthusiastically climb the ladder. At the ten foot level, they easily plunge into the water and swim back to the ladder. Buoyed by their success, they even more carefully make their way to the twenty-five foot level. They do not jump but watch others, even younger and scrawnier than they go off the platform. They wait.

By Wednesday so many other scouts have made the leap from the twenty-five foot level that the two buddies pledge themselves to follow suit. Mixing terror with temerity, they reach the tower, climb to the designated level and, with suicidal intensity, make the leap. Their masculinity is affirmed.

On Thursday morning the number who have gone off the forty-foot level is announced at breakfast. The list is intimidating. The two buddies have not even climbed to the top, let alone jumped. Time is growing short, and they decide to act. Once again they are back at the tower, climbing onto the ladder and heading to the top. As they pass the twenty-five-foot level, the boy becomes increasingly anguished. He climbs slowly, holding on to the ladder has his tether to life itself. When they reach the top, there is no rail, and the platform is some eight feet across. The boy cannot stand. He is on hands and knees, quaking. He dare not peer over the edge into the abyss below. As he stares across the tiny platform, he abruptly notices movement beside him. His buddy is standing and beginning to move. Presently, with a horrific cry, the buddy is off the edge. Seconds later, a distant splash. The boy, overwhelmed, retreats down the ladder and into the canoe.

Plying his way across the lake, the boy is silent in his utter isolation, betrayed even by his closest companion. The next day, even his best friend—a runt and wimp—dares to make the coveted leap. The boy is more alone than he has ever felt. What is he to do?

It is Saturday morning. The bus is to leave for home after lunch, and still the boy has not plucked up the courage to jump. By late morning he realizes his last opportunity has passed. Everyone is moving toward the dining hall. Indescribable desperation consumes the boy. He decides he cannot go home without making the leap. He'd rather die. Running alone to the dock, he locates a canoe and begins paddling solo for the tower.

He looks back to make sure he is not seen. When he reaches the tower, he quickly moves upward on the ladder. Despite his terror, he moves with dispatch until he reaches the top. Undeterred, he stands at the back edge of the platform and, knowing he will die, rushes across the few feet and hurls himself into the air. He drops and plunges, striking the water in ungainly disarray.

Back on shore, the boy rushes headlong into the dining room, seeking out his scoutmaster. Breathlessly, he tells the man of his achievement, expecting that at last he will receive his patch.

"When did you jump?"
"Just now."
"Who saw you?"
"No one. I did it by myself."
"You mean your buddy was not with you?"

With this query the boy realizes he has violated a crucial prohibition. His feat will not be acknowledged, and he will receive ten demerits—the largest one can receive for a single infraction.

Stunned and devastated, the boy does not eat lunch but waits for the bus—alone. When it comes, he slouches on board and into the back, where he sits in bitter silence. On the ride he cries more than once but watches to make sure no one sees him. For the first time in his brief life, he knows abandonment, and with his self-incrimination added to it, he cannot imagine ever recovering and returning to his troop.

When the boy reaches home, he bursts through the kitchen door, falls into the arms of the mother, and sobs out his pitiful story. It takes the mother a while to piece together the account and understand. After listening patiently, the mother kneels in front of the boy and asks, "Son, did you go off of that tower?"

The boy responds emphatically, "Yes ma'am, I did."

The mother concludes, "Then you actually did it, and whether anyone else knows it, you know it."

Gradually the boy finds peace with himself.

****

We best confront our isolation, not by hiding from it in "the madding crowd," but by embracing the domain of our aloneness. This means we engage two threats: lonesomeness and loneliness. When

I am lonesome, I suffer the specific absence of a particular person or other specific persons with whom I am in relationship. It may be a friend, a mate, a group. It doesn't matter which. What does matter is that lonesomeness has a remedy, at least in principal: we can reunite. When we are together, I'm no longer lonesome. Death and distance, of course, are the two great barriers to overcoming our lonesome states.

Loneliness is another matter. It does not have to do with any other particular person, persons, or group. Loneliness is existential, that is, a foundational sense of standing apart and of not being able to overcome that sense through contact with others. In other words, no contact with other persons solves this riddle of our sense of isolation. Loneliness is a persistent feeling of separation and isolation even in the face of our ostensible relationships.

We can be lonely in a crowd, perhaps especially in a crowd, and we can be lonely among our closest associates. Most often the prospect of this more profound isolation so threatens us, that we rush headlong into "the group" or into any version of relational life in order to avoid it. Rather than hide from it, however, this loneliness is the locus of the most fundamental demand that we engage ourselves and probe deeper into ourselves in order to come to terms with this very condition of loneliness.

The promise of genuine self-knowledge lies in the movement through loneliness and beyond it into *solitude*. To put the case simply, solitude is the transformation of our loneliness into the dwelling place of our selves. We come to ourselves, so to speak and find ourselves at home within ourselves. This process, as arduous as any we can undertake, is the very reverse of anything like egocentrism or selfishness.

Theologian Paul Tillich puts it brilliantly: "We overcome self-centeredness by becoming centered selves." Without this center we cannot relate. His statement itself hints at the tie between this entire conversation about aloneness and our larger subject, religion.

Philosopher Alfred North Whitehead defines religion in a curious way: "Religion is what the individual does with his own solitariness." When I first read this statement, I found it far more puzzling than informative. It seemed not only far too spare, but also more nearly a poetic expression, something close to Coleridge's proposal, "Religion is morality touched with emotion." But Whitehead is quite serious. He finds that we encounter the *heart* or *core* of religion only in an interiority that grows out of our sense of aloneness, understood as solitude. He even goes so far as to say, "Thus religion is solitariness; and if you are never solitary, you are never religious."

Does Whitehead go too far in his emphasis on the solitary—and thus individual—character of religion? I will put it this way: he utters at least a partial truth, but what he says is out of balance with the whole understanding necessary to account for religion. His partial truth is that, if we probe our aloneness to its roots, we discover our most elemental connection, namely, our connection with whatever grounds and sustains us. To unveil this connection *is* religion. In this way, solitariness ceases altogether to be isolation. It becomes the dwelling place of ultimate connectivity itself.

But, as I say, Whitehead's emphasis on the solitariness of religion requires balance with religion's inherent relational quality. On the one hand, we are to some extent drawn—if not driven—toward solitary life in response to our encounter with, and the threats of, other people. On the other hand, when we strive to express what our solitude unveils, we do so within a human community.

In this way, the solitary aspect of religion is always couched within our quite ordinary human relationships. While the vital core of religion may well lie within the solitary, it cannot become articulate and overcome the threat of isolation except within a community and through forms of expressive connection that give it voice.

Robinson Crusoe became quite religious during his isolation on the island. It was the means by which he achieved solitude. Yet, he did this by reading a Bible he had retrieved from the wrecked ship. But the scripture he read was provided not only through a community but by a long tradition of shared practices and convictions that conveyed those writings to his generation. His solitude, while as acutely tested and laboriously achieved as we can imagine, is still made possible by an *invisible community* made present through the sacred writings that came to nurture him.

All of this is to say that religion itself arises in the nexus where our aloneness and our connectedness meet. This place is solitude, the very opposite of the idiocy of separation and isolation. Yet, the experience of separation and isolation urge us to that solitude!

The sun is in full heat. I've been watching the changes in the slant of its beams through the aspen and onto the slight rolling of tall grasses. Presently I hear a distant commotion in the direction of camp. When I sit up and look in that direction, I see Ethan standing in the trail with his arm up as if in greeting. I cannot see anyone else, but when I stand, I spot a slight movement through the trees. It looks like a horse. I pick up my gear and saunter toward camp.

By the time I reach the trail, I can see Ethan speaking with a man leading a burro. The man is enormous and burly with a copious beard. He appears as if a character in some old western, perhaps a prospector. The burro, a black creature with enormous ears and tan markings down near the edge of its white belly, leans down to graze. It shakes its head as if trying to gain slack in the rope tethering it. The gear on its back shifts and creaks.

"This is my friend," Ethan gestures toward me as I approach.

The burly prospector—or whatever he is—shoves a beefy hand my way, and we greet. "I'm Marvin Holt. . .just say 'Holt,' if ya' will." He looks around as if seeking something and then asks, "Ya'll mind if I set camp around here? There's not much place else for another mile or so."

Ethan blurts," Man, it's a free country. . .or so they say. Pick a spot." He gestures at the expanse around us. Then he adds, "When you're set up, come over there." He points toward our campsite, "and we'll visit."

Holt nods his agreement and turns down toward a small clump of trees across the trail from our camp. He walks as if he's familiar with where he's headed. He disappears into the trees with his obedient beast following behind him. We meander toward our camp.

We stir about the site, casually preparing an early dinner. Ethan asks, "What'd you do?"

"Mostly I sat this livelong day. It was a glorious thing to let the day show itself."

Ethan nods, "Yeah, that's as good a day as you're gonna have. I read a while, but mostly I walked. The timber's thick down that way, but I made it all the way to the river. I even sat in it for a while, until I couldn't feel my own body. . .talk about out of body. . ."

We had just finished eating, when we hear grass swishing and twigs breaking. I look up to see Holt lumbering toward us with a pan in his hand. Steam rises from it. "Hey, ya want some blackberry cobbler? It's fresh-made."

By now the aroma has captured us and we're not inclined to turn down Holt's offer. Three metal bowls appear, and we sit on the ground imbibing in concert. Conversation comes in short bursts, punctuated with laughter. We're finding our way further into this encounter, the dance of meeting.

As talk relaxes, we take the measure of each other, and Marvin Holt takes on more dimensions. He runs a water treatment facility in a small town in northwestern New Mexico. The facility has problems with arsenic in the water. We discuss the water issues of the high desert, where more and more people are drawing on the supply. He then describes himself as a "weekend mountain man." I tell him that, when I first saw him, I thought I had walked into the set of *Jeremiah Johnson,* and he responds, "Could be, pilgrim."

He takes to the mountains once every month, winter and summer, to keep alive his love affair with these heights. Also, he says, that's as often as his woman'll tolerate. He used to pack, but with a bum back, after effects of war injuries, he leaves the hauling to Mercury. It takes me a moment to realize he's referring to his burro.

"Why do you call him Mercury?" I wonder.

"After a buddy in Vietnam…" Holt responds, and I immediately glance at Ethan. He leans forward, and I know the shape of the evening to come. War stories! They fall into the when and where of their tours, and the ritual is launched. I've been here before, but since I'm not a vet, I know that I'll be an observer.

Stories ranging from play to pain mark their shared memories. I even hear accounts from Ethan that he's never mentioned before. In the midst of the lively exchange, Holt stands and walks off without a word. Minutes later he's back, holding up a small plastic bag and grinning.

"Now I know you're the genuine article," Ethan declares, as Holt tosses the stash of weed in his lap. Without ceremony Ethan takes out the book of papers in the bag, places a pinch of marijuana on a sheet, and expertly rolls it into a smoke. He lights it and hands it to Holt. Then Holt passes the joint to me. I take one draw and immediately begin a fit of coughing.

Ethan observes, "He wasn't there," as if this explained the coughing. It doesn't. I never smoked and can't seem to get the hang of it. So, I take one more sputtering draw and sit back to listen and watch. Within half an hour the stories are more flamboyant and the laughter more ecstatic. By the time the sun sets they're bosom buddies in the fellowship of shared pain and collective memory.

A quiet interlude allows the three of us to muse and to stare into the fire in front of us. The sparks are intriguing. They rise as if escaping to some other world. Then abruptly Holt asks, "What're you guys doin' up here?"

Ethan says, "Smokin' with some groovy bastard who wandered into camp," and they're off into peals of hysteria.

Then Holt, in feigned solemnity, says, "No, I mean what're you really doin'?" Then gesturing broadly, "Cause I ain't doin' nothin'!" More riotous laughter.

Ethan sits up and says with a slight slur, "We're up here figurin' out religion."

"Religion?" Holt almost shouts. "Hell, it's not up here, is it? Or maybe it is," and he's immediately serious, his eyes suggesting he has taken a trip to some other time and place. He takes another draw and stands unsteadily. "If you really wanna know about religion, look no further. Look no damn further! I'm the man you're lookin' for.

"I was raised a Catholic, I mean really raised in the stuff. Schools, nuns, confession, confirmation, altar boy, the whole screwball thing. And it took. I was what you could call a gooood Catholic. Paid all the dues you can pay. Then, because I blew off college, my ass was drafted and on a plane to the jungle. I had my Saint Christopher round my neck janglin' with my dog tags. I even had this rosary in my pocket." He pulls it out. "I still carry it. Security, ya know." *Slim security in that risky place*, I think to myself but do not say.

He sits down and stares into the fire so long I think he's forgotten the whole subject, but then he says, loud and strident, "But all that stuff 's bullshit. The bush teaches you that. There you are, duckin' and dodgin' for your very next breath, and everything you ever thought would save you just plain goes out the window. Then you find out about true religion. Ya' wanna know what it is? True religion, I mean?"

"Preach on, brother," Ethan encourages.

"True religion happens when you're on your belly, still as death and listenin' to these sons of bitches walkin' past you an' searching for you to kill your ass. Then you pray for the first time while you're shittin' yourself, and you are not kiddin' about it either. You're torn up over bein' so far away from God and wantin' to hug up close. Now that's religion, pure as puddin' and without any damn decorations on it. All this fine soft stuff that goes on in mumbles at the altar. . .know what I mean? That's not it, I tell ya'.

"Religion, if it's worth a good goddamn, is in the ditches, where people are desperate and know what they've got need of. That's what that stupid war taught me, and it's about the only thing I can appreciate about it. Religion is about desperation." and after an extended pause, "and we're all fuckin' desperate. We just don't like to face it." Another long silence, then, "We spend our whole cotton pickin' lives pretendin' we're not desperate, that we have it covered."

Holt sags back against a stump, sweating as if he's tried to give birth. I want to respond, to offer some consolation or suggest an exception, but I know better. This is a solemn moment in which a scream has been heard from the primal condition we all share, with or without Vietnam.

Ethan weeps. Holt looks over at him and tears trickle into his beard. They connect around haunted memories not available to me. No one speaks after this. We all sit until one by one we slip away and into our sleeping bags. But I can't sleep. This idea of desperation and religion keeps me staring at the canopy of my tent.

Does Holt have it right? Is authentic religion a response to our desperation? Are we only truly religious when we're desperate? Or do we hide from our desperation to avoid religion? Or again, do we use religion as a hideout from our desperation? Maybe religion isn't a solution to desperation but our attempt to escape from it. And all of this seems connected back to our old topic of fear and that quotation from Aeschylus, "Fear created the gods."

I recall Thoreau's truism, "The mass of men lead lives of quiet desperation," and wonder exactly what constitutes human desperation in the first place. I wonder whether *everyone* is desperate or only certain troubled souls. Or, everyone may actually be desperate all the time, but desperation is so fearsome and fatiguing that we construct endless devices to deny or ignore it. That seems to be Holt's take on it.

Many of the modern thinkers who try to reduce religion to something else or give it secondary significance—I'm thinking at the moment once again of Marx, Freud, Durkheim, and their cohorts—like the idea that religion is nothing but human desperation and thus, in the end, delusional. But I don't believe that's what Holt means. He makes desperation more basic, something like this: to be a living human being is to be desperate whether we recognize it or not, and only when we realize this condition, are we genuinely religious.

If this is true, I need to penetrate to the core of desperation itself. But fatigue intrudes, and gradually the puzzle over desperation dissolves into sleep and fitful inchoate dreams.

Twelve

There is a crack in everything;
That's how the light gets in.

Leonard Cohen

~

Rain!

It doesn't begin slowly and build but assaults my tent canopy. Afternoon showers are common in the mountains, especially later in the summer, but when the day begins with such a deluge, it's likely to continue for some time.

After listening to the torrent for half an hour, I unzip the fly and look out to see what I fully expect: a drenched world. I zip back up and roll over trying to recover sleep, but it's no use. I sit up, shake myself awake, and wrestle into a pullover. Mornings are always chilly, but rain adds to it.

I write in my journal for another half hour and am about to reach for a book, when Ethan calls out, "Is it rainin' over there?"

"Appears so," I shout back above the noise.

"Got anything over there to eat?"

"Nope," I acknowledge. "Never keep food in my tent."

"What a good little scout you are! Plan on starvin'?"

"Not if you fix somethin'."

After a considerable pause, Ethan conspires, "My tent's bigger'n yours. You come over here." More silence. "Oh yeah, grab some food on the way."

I peer outside again, standing on my knees to inspect the sky. It's all gray, socked in. No promise on the horizon of eventual relief. I duck back inside, wipe rain off my head, and dress. With a poncho draping me like Count Dracula, I step outside and decide simply to ignore the rain. I retrieve the food bag and call out to Ethan as I approach his tent. He opens the flap, and I stuff the bag, then myself, inside. Any camper knows that this cannot be achieved without wetting things down in the tent. The trick is to minimize it.

Ethan complains just for the joy of it. We scrounge in the food bag and find enough to keep hunger at bay. We sit cross-legged beside each other. The effort to talk louder than the clatter of rain on the tent invites silence, but shortly we hear movement outside. Before I can rise to look, the voice of Holt grunts at us, "Got anything to eat in there?" We stare at each other, realizing that the tent's about to become much more cozy.

I unzip and Holt thrusts his bare shaggy head inside. For emphasis he shakes it like a drenched dog and raindrops swirl through the tent. He invades us with his bulk, grunting and puffing as he makes his way inside. Oblivious to everything but escaping the torrent outside, he finally makes himself comfortable. We are all together, cheek to jowl, as the saying goes.

"Man alive, it's socked in far as the eye can see," Holt reports. "I've seen these things go for three days or more. Hope you're friendly." He grins and a large stuff bag materializes. "Brought my own victuals." He asks if we want anything.

Ethan points to our food bag and says he needs to add to the moisture outside. We bend, reach, and stir for the next five minutes, until he returns. "Know what?" he asks. We wait for his answer. "Can't do a blamed thing about it, rain or shine. It's fate, and the only thing I know to do with that monster is dance through it."

"And most everything is fate, if you ask me," Holt volunteers. "Hell, maybe all of it." Ethan agrees.

I remember Holt's comment last night, that he thinks religion's about desperation. I had gone to sleep thinking about that. I didn't take him to mean fear. Desperation is somehow stronger, more basic. It rests more nearly on some vague hope than on raw fear. Desperation's earnestly trying to reach some goal and being perpetually frustrated and confronted with impossibilities.

So, you cry out against the rough edges of those impossibilities. It doesn't much .birth of religion—or at least one way it comes to birth.

I continue to wonder about all of this while Holt digs for beef jerky. He passes it around. I ask, "If it's all fate, is that what makes life so desperate?"

Holt looks at me like I'm an extraterrestrial. "What're you talkin' about?"

"Last night you said desperation is the basis of religion, and I wondered. . ."

"You can't hold me responsible for what I said last night. I was stoned." Then he ponders. "No. That's not right. When I'm stoned, I most nearly tell the truth, if you will. So, what did I say?"

I report Holt's comments from last night. I add that his idea of desperation may be related to his notion that everything is a matter of fate. He stares at me for an uncomfortably long time.

"My God, you're probably right, but you actually want me to talk about such things in daylight, just after breakfast, when I'm more or less sober?" He grins, rips off a strip of jerky, and is about to say more.

Ethan interjects, "Nam made a lot of people into fatalists. That's how they handled their desperation. Fate became their religion."

Holt whirls toward Ethan. "That's some deep shit, brother. But you're probably right. I've got a good dose of this fatalism myself. You know, this huge whatever-will-be-will be attitude, but then again, I keep wonderin' if it's not a cop out, a way of blowin' everything off with a 'who gives a damn.' He paused. "But I don't think that's a religion worth havin'. It's like cavin' in, more depressin' than anything else."

"Or liberating!" Ethan ventures. "What if fatalism is a way of escaping or gettin' over religion. . .an alternative to it."

I'm so enthralled by this line of conversation that I want to take notes, but I find myself asserting, "What if fatalism is not an escape or substitute but the edge or threshold of religion, so to speak. We become desperate and settle for fate as a stalling action to keep from becoming religious?" I may not agree with this, but the thought intrigues me.

Earlier I distinguished between fate and freedom, but I didn't examine fate and its role in actually forming the religious sensibility. For the ancient Olympian religion of the Greeks, fate is the final wall against which everything founders, even the gods. No one can resist or even negotiate with fate. To challenge it is to enter the domain of tragedy. We can only cooperate with it or illustrate it.

Fate appears to function as the boundary beyond which neither humans nor gods can venture. It is the realm of *necessity* or *inevitability*. No matter how we try to plot a course that appears to be of our own making, in the end we're subject to this impersonal web of necessity. I suspect that rats in a maze could assume that they are somehow in control of their world, but actually they are chasing about within confines they cannot imagine. I do wonder whether we humans may not simply inhabit a much more complex maze. A case can be made.

To be caught up in this way of thinking, to be a *determinist*, has been a key concern of religion. The Olympian religion is based on it. In Islam there is that graphic saying, "It is written," the common recognition that Allah is the determining basis for what happens to human beings. In Judaism and Christianity, this same line of thinking lies hidden in such notions as election or divine predestination, but for the most part fatalism is transmuted into Providence. That is, a *personal* God, while ultimately in charge of all that happens, nevertheless softens the hard boundary of fate by a compassionate—and sometimes judgmental—engagement with and care for humanity. Ordinarily, this providence "allows" for some significant form of human autonomy. Even here, however, in the end this personal God still *determines*.

Even the Eastern religions negotiate a similar terrain with the inevitability imbedded in *karma* and in the process of reincarnation. Human autonomy is actually illusory and becomes perpetual delusion, until one recognizes its illusion and refuses to desire human fulfillment within the maze of *samsara*.

All of these religions, of course, have a variety of interpretations, and none can be reduced to such a simplistic explanation as I offer. My point is this: they are formed around a response to fate. That is, fate—and thus determinism—shape the religious response. Religion is about surrendering to fate, finding our way through it, or transforming it into destiny. If fate itself is not finally adequate to account for religion, and if it is not itself a proper religion, it may nevertheless serve as a point of departure for an adequate understanding of the origin, or source, of the religious sensibility, the heartbeat of religion.

By examining fate not as a theory but as part of our lived experience, an opening into the religious sensibility may be discovered. Let's take a commonplace type of human experience.

I have a friend who has unexpectedly collapsed and fallen into a coma. Doctors not only cannot bring her out of the coma, they cannot find any reasonable cause for the coma. All they know is that she is virtually brain dead. A team of competent specialists converge on the patient and, after careful examination over days, conclude, "We can do nothing. She can be kept artificially alive, but we recommend the removal of life supports." With that admission, we can do nothing, fate as the boundary of the presently possible enters the picture. We might plead, "if we only knew more" or "if we had more time" or "aren't there more tests?" but our pleading does nothing to sidestep the fact that, as things stand, my friend is fated to die shortly.

People may begin at this point to urge us to pray for a miracle. They may utter a variety of well-rehearsed euphemisms, such as "God has a higher purpose" or "the ways of God are unfathomable" or again, "all we can do now is hope." All of these appeals, regardless of how well intended, are simply ways of softening fate. Even if my friend should somehow recover, she is still bound to die, and thus fate is only temporarily postponed, and we are, at best, temporarily assuaged.

****

Pressures from all sides close upon the man. None of them are unusual or unpredictable. In fact, the pressures are of the most ordinary variety: relationships, time, and money! No training prepares him for these pressures. They are simply there, and they persist. At home it is relationships, time, and money. In the congregation it is relationships, time, and money. In graduate school it is relationships, time, and money. Within this thralldom the man can no longer clearly locate himself. He is swallowed by the forces he has welcomed.

But the man knows better. From the deeper soundings of what he teaches, what he preaches, what he studies, come the resonant assurances of something more, something at the edge of knowing. Yet, he is blocked from it by—what? He cannot make out the passageway to that something more. Tension builds within him.

He goes to the bank near the end of the month, only to learn that once again he is overdrawn. Expenses exceed income. That is the story, and it appears to be the end of the story. The banker insists that the man do something about it, but what? He's reduced expenses to the bone, and there's no additional income to be imagined.

The man leaves the bank and makes his way, for no reason other than frustration, to the church. He has no office there. The building is too small. He walks through the sanctuary slowly, as if longing for the space to speak to him, looking at the refracted glints of color through the stained-glass windows. He moves into other rooms, where classes meet on Sundays. Each is decorated to fit the age that gathers there, and the typical artifacts lie strewn around. He finds himself sitting on a tiny chair designed for five-year-olds. He taught here last summer during day school, and he can still see the writhing, sweating little ones reaching for attention and for life.

After sitting in the chair so long he loses track of time—another pressure point. The man finds himself moaning. At first the moans are punctuated with silence. Then they become longer and more dominant. Moans become groans. His stomach tightens with each utterance of guttural growls. His voice becomes alien to himself, as if another were crying out within him and using him.

Gradually the man slumps from the little chair and melts onto the rag rug beneath him. He curls into a fetal ball. The sounds, now unearthly, continue and grow deeper and louder. He is about to cease when unexpectedly the voice within him cries with a more urgent energy until it rises to a scream. The scream is no longer reluctant but insistent. It pours forth much like stupendous vomiting. Everything packed down and held within him escapes in a mighty rush. The scream reaches the apogee of his body's capacity, but it continues with a desperation the man has not known. Something must be exorcised, whatever "it" might be. It is beyond naming.

The voice, no longer able to sustain the volume, dies away into silence. He lies still, sweating, hyperventilating. He regresses back toward himself and finally into himself. He continues to lie stupefied with wonder at what has taken him over. He does not sleep, but he is at rest. When he sits up, he begins to monitor his own moment of madness, wondering who might have heard him raging in the dim light of that little room. He considers whether he might have made a foray into temporary insanity. But is it temporary? Yet, he knows down deep, where he has not ventured for some time, if ever, that he has touched something within. At last he stands and, wobbling, finds his way to his car.

On the Sunday following, the man departs from the Lectionary to preach from a particular text:

> Likewise the Spirit helps us in our weakness; for we do not know how to pray as we ought, but that very Spirit intercedes with sighs too deep for words.

He strives passionately to convey the weight of those words and the force of his own screaming. The congregation stares back blankly at him, with only a rare countenance registering recognition. On the way home the wife wonders what in the world he was trying to say. This thought emerges: there is no way to say the thing that most needs to be said. Words! The vehicles we keep using but which fail at the crucial point!

****

Endless stories of "the fell clutch of circumstance," as the poem *Invictus* states it, could be multiplied. They all conspire to reveal that we human beings—despite every effort to maintain our sovereign will or any such claims to autonomy and endless possibility—are children of fate. If this is the case, then my most basic question, the one that has prompted this pilgrimage, is this: Is religion nothing other than desperation over fate and masquerading as a way to human fulfillment? Put more precisely, is religion grounded in the effort to breach the definitive wall of human boundedness, that is, fate? I propose that religion is indeed devoted to penetrating fate and transforming its desperation into self-transcending meaning despite our fated condition. In brief, religion strives to transform fate into destiny.

To make this case is a large order, and for several years Ethan and I, along with other friends, have sought for a proper point of departure. And this subject of fate and religion takes us back to that earlier discussion of human finitude and its encounter with the infinite. I need to review and further examine these ideas.

My first breakthrough regarding the finite and infinite came while reading in *Ecclesiastes*, that singular text in the Hebrew Scripture revealing the depths of the human condition. I had planned to use the text to discuss the historical roots of existentialism. I wanted to show that, even in the midst of the sacred literature of Judaism—and later of Christianity—the fundamental anxiety regarding life's meaning is recorded. Koheleth, the speaker in that book, spends great effort declaring that for "everything under the sun"—that is, everything within the scope of human comprehension, in other words, the *bounded* or finite—"all is vanity of vanities." The *vanity* lies in the transitory and ultimately unsatisfactory character of all human desire, aspiration, and fulfillment.

In the midst of this striking discourse, the author observes once again that all toil, that is, human effort, is vain. Then he imports God into the discussion. This move is important, because Koheleth does not use God often and never as an escape from the "vanity of vanities." But in Chapter 3 God is said to have done a strange thing: "He has made everything beautiful in its time. He has also set eternity in the hearts of men; yet they cannot fathom what God has done from beginning to end." Other translations differ, but most of them are generally consistent.

What struck me in this statement is the image of humanity as somehow caught in the middle. On the one hand, we have "eternity" in our hearts. On the other hand, this gift does not allow us to find out "what God has done from beginning to end." What a bind! We are able to imagine the eternal—or the whole, or the infinite, or simply the big picture— but we cannot comprehend it, let alone master it. Koheleth then goes on to propose that, "there is nothing better for them to do than be happy and enjoy themselves as long as they live; moreover, it is God's gift that all should eat and drink and take pleasure in all their toil." Thus, the author's resolution of the human dilemma appears to be *resignation*. We can do nothing about the eternal, and meanwhile, "under the sun. . .all is vanity of vanities." The one thing left to us is to *enjoy* the situation while we live. The only way out offered by Koheleth is this sort of fatalistic hedonism.

I must confess that this solution to the human situation is attractive to many of us. In a culture of immediate gratification and preoccupation with ourselves, it can be alluring to actually dismiss the larger issues of human existence—matters having to do with eternity—and, as one commercial put it some years ago, "go for the gusto." The problem with this way of responding to life is that, sooner or later, the inevitability of circumstance and consequence—fate—overwhelms or undermines the efforts to "be happy and enjoy" ourselves.

Holt insists, "I'd like to be...what did you say...a..."

"A fatalistic hedonist," I repeat.

"Right," Holt agrees, "but, like you say, the hedonistic part does not work out for long. And besides, my wife won't cooperate."

His levity breaks our concentration, and he decides to look outside. Still raining, but not as furiously. We stir around to find more comfortable positions. Ethan dozes. Holt stares. I muse.

That word *eternity* entices me. I reflect on the unfortunate fact that most people think of eternity as endless time, but although it is related to temporality, it actually refers to non-time or to the idea of not being subject to time. It's more nearly the time-transcending *Now*. If so, what does it mean to say that God has "set eternity in the hearts of men?" Perhaps it means that, while I cannot escape time, I can imagine the alternative to it. Could this mean that, in at least one respect, we participate in *the mind of God*?

Rather than pursue this line of thinking here, I want to examine another term often tied to eternity, one that I used in earlier discussions: *the infinite*. I have a hunch that these two terms are yoked together because we humans are bound—fated?—by the conditions of time and space—or better, of time-space. Of course, we are bound in other ways, but the philosopher Immanuel Kant is right that we are virtually constituted by the categories of time and space. The very possibility of human experience rests on time and space. If eternity is the alternative to time, the not-temporal, then infinity is the alternative to space, the non-finite. It is not measureless space so much as non-space and thus parallel to eternity or non-time. As difficult to comprehend as this is, we can hold these ideas in our imaginations, as Koheleth says.

Eternity or *the eternal* and *infinity* or *the infinite* are persistent terms hovering around discussions of religion. Why is this the case? Could it be that religion is as such *about* the eternal in relation to the boundedness of our temporal existence and *about* the infinite in relation to the boundedness of spatial existence? In exploring this question I will focus on the latter term, *infinity* or the *infinite*.

With this subject we are potentially on very confusing ground.

The very idea of infinity has been questioned from the dawn of Western thought, and wherever it is entertained, there is perpetual controversy. To help us avoid a number of pitfalls, I want to make a simple distinction between two ways of considering infinity or the infinite: the *mathematical scientific*—or perhaps *cosmic*— and the *personal existential*. These ways are not mutually exclusive, but they are quite distinct.

For instance, here's how I personally first encountered the infinite. I was a child sitting at the kitchen table, when I noticed that the little girl in the yellow dress holding an umbrella on the Morton Salt box had another Morton Salt box under her arm. I looked closely at the box she held to see if there was another picture of the little girl on *that* box. I could not really make it out, but I had this thought: if there is a picture on the second box exactly like the picture on the box I held, then there must be another picture on the yet smaller box. This would mean that the boxes and the pictures on the boxes could go on forever. With that childhood experience I discovered the basic problem of infinity. Can things go on forever? This did not terrify me but puzzled me.

I suspect that human beings have been perplexed by the *possible infinite* since the dawn of conceptual thinking, if not before. And in religion, particularly the monotheisms, the cosmos is considered finite and limited. Only God is infinite, eternal, unbounded. But the possibility of infinity must have arisen as a problem to which these theisms offered an answer. The anxiety over the infinite likely began straightforwardly with such encounters and reflections as the one I had as a child. But if there is *actually* infinity, it can be profoundly unsettling. How can we possibly comprehend the world or ourselves, if the world is unbounded? And who am I as a bounded creature in relation to infinity to dare trying to comprehend it?

To indicate the disturbance this thought can stir, consider the ancient Greeks. Their word for infinite was *apieron*. It meant infinite but it also meant more: undefined, indefinite or chaotic. Thus, they tended to use the word in a negative way to refer to what has no order. For something to have order or form, it must be bounded or limited, literally *de-fined*. Because of this, *apieron* was more nearly a threat to order and comprehension. Even the *cosmos*, the whole of things, was considered finite, because it is ordered and has comprehendible form.

Much Western thought since then, especially mathematical scientific thought, has engaged the question as to whether there is an infinite, and if so, how we might begin to understand it or represent it. With increased knowledge of our world, infinity, at least as a plausible explanation beyond the boundaries of what we know, continues to be posited. But infinity is often taken to be vacuous, a kind of abstraction or cipher. The subject and the questions it raises remain open and controversial.

Although our very attempt to make sense of words like *infinity* and the *infinite* must begin with concrete encounters with our physical world, these encounters are not where I wish to focus. Rather, I want to address the *disturbance* such ideas generate for us human beings. I will occasionally refer to the problem of infinity as expressed in mathematical scientific thinking, but my interest lies in the human concern—the anguish and trepidation—over the possibility of ontological infinity and our existential encounter with it.

Let's begin by relating the infinite back to our starting point: *fate*. We do not actually *experience* fate. What happens is that we experience limitation or "the wall," the boundary beyond which we cannot penetrate. This boundary defines, delimits, and in the end, controls us. Fate is the name we give to the boundary itself. But the very idea of boundary or edge implies something on the other side of the boundary. While we cannot penetrate the boundary, we can imagine something beyond it. The principal name for this beyond is *the infinite* (or *the eternal*). If this is the case, then the infinite is fundamentally *the unbounded*! This unbounded, as such, lies beyond our comprehension, but at the same time it affects us. We feel we are *contained* within and by it!

The very thought of the Infinite as the unbounded encountered through our lived experience can be terrifying. An historical reference may help to show this. The eccentric genius Giordano Bruno lived in the last half of the sixteenth century. Among his profoundly disturbing claims was that the universe is infinite. While Galileo left the sun in the center of our planetary system, Bruno held that the universe has no center, that we live in an acentric universe. Stated otherwise, the center is everywhere and the circumference (the boundary) is nowhere. He even proposed that there are multiple universes.

The Roman Catholic Church of the day held firmly to the notion that only God is infinite or eternal and that everything else—the entire universe over which God reigns—is finite and temporal. Given the power of the church at that time—and its fear lest infinity get out of hand, Bruno did not last long. His ideas were too threatening because he unleashed—among other revolutionary possibilities—the idea of an infinite universe. He was burned at the stake early in 1600 at the Roman Piazza Campo di Fiori.

The church, in other words, was intensely interested in the infinite, and they wanted to keep it "in place," as it were, by ensconcing the infinite solely in God. Bruno, by the way, confessed to being a faithful son of the church, just as Galileo would do throughout his own life during the next half century. These scientists did not see themselves as undermining faith. They sought knowledge of the world around them, and both were convinced that knowledge can only enrich faith—or at least that genuine faith can never be undermined by the increase of knowledge. This conviction sounds right.

"Man, I gotta get out for a while. This stuff's too deep for the likes of me," Holt announces as he moves up on his knees. "Besides, I got cramps." He opens the tent fly and inspects his world.

Rain still falls but only lightly. He steps out and reports that he can see blue sky off to the northwest. I climb out awkwardly, and Ethan eventually emerges. We gaze at a drenched campsite and stand mute in the drizzle, beginning to organize the rest of the day.

Mercury brays in the distance, and Holt looks up. As he walks toward his camp, he turns back. "After a while, ya'll come over. I'm gonna make dinner." He does not wait for confirmation, but he knows we'll come because he has what we like to call "real food" as opposed to our freeze-dried fare.

Thirteen

Secularism distracts us from the infinite by offering us a throbbing immediacy, but the infinite continues to haunt the edges of existence, at the threshold between forgetting and remembering.

Anon.

～

Holt feeds us a stew he prepared before his trip. This is the advantage of having a burro to haul the gear, and for us it is a considerable advantage—home cooking, so to speak. We sit in the evaporating dampness with the twilight sun shafting its way through pines. Steam rises along the beams. All is well. We dine in silence.

I'm tired from the day's inactivity and decide to take a walk along the trail. Ethan and Holt stare at me but do not move. I wave back at them. What a pair!

When I return an hour later, it's dusky dark. Holt has lit a lantern and hung it in a nearby tree. They are sitting in his two small camp chairs; between them, on a pan turned upside down, a bottle perches. They have glasses and are sipping. I don't like this because I know of Ethan's problem with "spirits," as he calls them. He becomes alternately exhilarated and morose, and the more he drinks, the more dramatic is the swing between these poles. He becomes a temporary manic-depressive. And always, with enough of the drink inside him, the darker side appears.

I sit across from them on a rock. Eventually I spot a steel cup and pour myself a drink. Why not? But they are downing two or three to my one. The conversation, at first random and sporadic, gradually becomes louder and more focused. I can see them picking up speed as thoughts and memories race along synapses. It won't be long—this I know from much experience—before Ethan is telling the stories that belong to the curse of that damn war. At first they will be graphic but more or less "normal" accounts from those days. They are etched in his psyche, and he never forgets. I wonder if Holt is like that.

Conversation is now more animated, and the downward spiral into memory begins. "I once killed one of my own men," Ethan begins. Holt does not so much as blink at this startling statement. They only stare at each other, and there's something between them, peeping from their rumpled faces and rumbling depths.

"Did it on purpose," he adds.

All Holt says is, "Well, there are times. . ."

"He was one of my closest buddies," Ethan continues. "A royal fuck-up but always enthusiastic and ready to go. We'd been humping along this road, but I didn't think it was safe to be out in the open like that. I gave an order for us to hit the weeds. I always kept my patrols spread out so we couldn't all be hit at once. I could see them on each side of me, moving steadily ahead like a wave. All at once we heard a clicking sound up ahead, and I gave the signal to hit the ground."

"We laid there, still as. . ."

"Yeah, but never still enough," Holt interjects. "Your heart's makin' too much noise."

Ethan nods and continues. "Then this kid. . .he couldn't be more'n nineteen. . .just erupts on my left perimeter. We all look up, and the medic runs across to him. I follow. Everybody else crouches around us searching for movement, but there's not a stir. After a blast, you know, it can be deadly quiet for a few minutes. Hell, it even scares the birds, monkeys, and whatever else is around. They shut up too."

Holt pours another round, but I decline. Ethan says nothing for some time, as if he's forgotten the story.

"Are you rememberin'?" Holt asks.

Ethan glares at him. "My problem is I can't forget. I remember too damn much. . . everything. There are two kinds of vets: those that can't forget and those that can't remember."

"There's another bunch," Holt maintains "the ones that hide it all away and pretend not to remember. They're the ones that chap my butt. 'Memory cowards,' that's what I call 'em."

"True, true, true," Ethan repeats, "but it's a far sight safer on your mind." He puts his glass down and grabs his head in both hands.

Holt insists, "But they don't have the guts. . ."

I can see a challenge brewing, and I'm about to intercede when Ethan says, "Let me tell you about guts. This kid I'm talkin' about. . .his name was Randy Caldwell. . ." At the voicing of his name Ethan breaks and looks away into the night, tears dropping on his arm.

"Anyway, what this kid had done was crawl on his belly and trip a mine. Why he was crawlin' and why there was a mine in the middle of nowhere, I'll never know. 'Course they were anywhere and everywhere, like Johnson grass in Texas. But when the medic cuts his shirt away, this boy. . .Randy. . .has his whole midsection blown away. His guts are spillin' out, and the medic is holdin' on to them and tryin' to poke 'em back.

"I can tell it's no use, and the kid is screaming for somebody to do somethin'. I try to get his attention, but he's like a dog I saw once caught in a steel trap. He's raging at everything that moves. Finally, I get him to look at me, and he turns dead serious, almost calm. He looks right at me, and says, 'For goodness sake, shoot me. Anything's better'n this.'

"We discussed medivac and any other options we could think of, but the medic says we're too far out, and nothing can be done. He asks if he should give the kid a lethal dose…you know, of morphine. Then the kid, fading slowly says again, in an amazingly stern voice, 'I said shoot me. Can't you do that for me?'

"Now what're you gonna' do in a situation like that? I pull out my side arm without another thought, tell him he's my best buddy, and shoot. After the ringin' everything is again quiet as death. Death is like that. That's why we say, 'Silent as a tomb.'" Ethan leans back, takes a sip of bourbon, and looks as though he's undergone surgery without an anesthetic.

"They bring you up for it?" Holt asked with a knowing glance.

"I volunteered. Told 'em exactly what happened. And when this major asked me why I did it, I said, 'cause I loved him.' The guy looked like I'd slapped him, but he didn't ask me any more questions. Once they interviewed the whole patrol, they dropped it."

I had heard this story before, but I concentrate on the way he repeats it now. Like a litany, but I can tell he finds release in the telling, at least momentarily. Alcohol drives him back to it as though reliving the moment. But he doesn't seem to get beyond it. The recitation repeats itself every time he's drunk. Ethan's memory has become a prison.

Holt stands and walks into the trees. He returns and checks on Mercury before sitting down. He shakes his head and mutters, "Awful...Lord Almighty...awful stuff we haul around." They both stare into empty space. I sense they are about to end the evening, but almost immediately Holt enters into a childhood story about finding his grandfather hanging in the family's barn. "Until Nam that was the worst day of my life. A little kid shouldn't see such stuff, and grown men shouldn't see things like we saw either."

They are now locked into a spiral of memories, and knowing Ethan, it will continue to the point of exhaustion. I decide to slip away and into sleep. They do not notice.

Later in the night I awaken to raucous voices. They are not arguing but celebrating something. No sooner do I lie back down than I'm shaken by the report of a pistol firing. Once, twice, then a cluster of cracks. I wonder whether I should go over and rescue them from themselves but decide against it. Corralling drunks is like herding ants.

I awaken in the early morning to the muted sounds of a new day. What I dread is that Ethan is always impossible after drinking the way he did last night. He'll likely be at best mute or more likely brooding and raging against the way things are in the world. These cynical-cum-nihilistic interludes always follow his trek through the inferno of his war memories. Once he told me it is these sinister forbidding images that goad him to understand and pursue religion. He said, "When you hit bottom, I mean really hit it, you have to face up to what's there and what can be done about it. That's where religion has its chance, if it has any at all."

Here we are, back at desperation, I think. Then I sit up in the tent and ask myself how many days we've been on the trail. When I count up, I realize we're supposed to meet Collins in two days. We can make it in one if we're forced, but trooping along that fast is not our style. I exit the tent with the intention of waking Ethan. Outside, however, everything is placid, and I don't want to break the spell. I pick up three empty water bottles and head for the spring.

While pumping, I again find myself puzzling over memory. Ethan is trapped in a memory grid, but aren't we all trapped in memories? Once again, memory is like every other human capacity: it is a necessary medium and at the same time a limitation. With regard to memory, to escape it we must be, in the true sense of the word, out of our minds. But some of us allow memory to guide us without being reduced to it or overwhelmed by it. Ethan's obsessive archeological digs into his past keep him tethered to his past.

I wonder whether and how this business of memory relates to that discussion of infinity yesterday. At first I make no connection, but then this thought comes to mind: *infinity cannot be thought of in isolation from finitude.* The *in* tacked onto *in-finity* means "not." So, it may be understood as "not finite." Thus, it cannot really begin to be comprehended without some prior understanding of *finite* or *finitude*.

Once the bottles are filled with fresh water, I set them aside and walk into the trees. A limb hits me in the eye, and while rubbing it, I say aloud, "Now there's finitude." I chuckle to myself.

Most of us understand finitude by continually running up against limits. That's what finitude is, limits. We encounter these boundaries first in our bodies, but that's only the beginning. The more impressive and disturbing limits show up in the tangle of our minds. This attempt to gain a better understanding of religion is an example. A canyon could be filled with books trying to make sense of religion. So, why, I keep asking myself, do I think I can break the boundaries of this subject? Like every other significant line of thinking, it can tie me in brain knots.

But we—I—keep on chasing through the labyrinth of thoughts in ceaseless attempts to...to do what? Well, I'll damn sure never break free of my finitude with regard to this subject. No matter what I think, say, or write, it will and should be challenged by showing its limitations. I even do that to my own thoughts! So, why shouldn't someone else join the fun?

I believe it's the very experience of finitude itself that drives me to continue. Back to that statement in *Ecclesiastes*: "God has placed eternity in their minds but not so they can understand what God is doing from beginning to end." We have just enough of a glimpse into *possibility* that it goads us to push against the limits of the finitude.

We generally handle finitude through organization. That is, we try to find out how much can be grasped even though it'll never be enough. By making sense and measuring limits, by insisting on *this* and not *that*, we stake out sufficient understanding to encourage us to continue. So, infinity is like the proverbial carrot and stick. It lures us to imagine beyond the limits. In fact, I believe this imagining is the basis for our life passion. It is our *lust* for infinity.

But I don't want to be grandiose about it. Finitude remains the ever-present condition within which we actually exist. We start and end there. Our finitude is complicated by something more than *limits*. Our boundaries are constantly in our faces, but it is the mind, where we imagine infinity, that makes finitude so disturbing. Ethan is stuck in memory. His mind has him cornered. Sometimes I want to scream at him, "Damn it! Quit living in yesterday. Come back to here and now and take a look at the future!" When I say something like this, he rails about how I have no experience like his and that I cannot possibly understand what he's gone through.

Still, I want to go back there with him, find the snare that holds him and release it. But I'm his friend, not his therapist. He hates therapists anyway. The ones at the VA hospital drove him wild. He said, "They take sane people and drive 'em wacky." So, I don't suggest therapy, but he needs someone who can unhook him from his obsessive fixation on those grim memories. Or more likely, he's got to do it for himself—even if someone helps out.

Ethan's memory trap is part of his finitude, and I must confess it has been part of my own. When I was going through the divorce, I went over and over my whole marriage and where it went wrong. I couldn't talk to anybody personally without going there. My fixation continued for at least three years, and when I reread my journals from that period, I wonder how anyone put up with me. So, I can't really judge Ethan, but he does remind me of my own finitude. William Blake calls this finitude our "mind-forged manacles." Now there's a graphic image.

How did I break out of my memory trap? Probably like anyone else does. I found a future. Possibilities began to distract me from my fixation on the past. It didn't happen all at once, but in hindsight it was a recognizable process of recovering my passion for what might be. In that sense it was the *presence of infinity* as open possibility that lured me beyond the trap of memory.

To be released from the memory trap is not to forget. Forgetting is itself another trap. I found a fresh context for remembering, and I could integrate my past into the domain of unfolding possibility. I had to embrace my condition as a divorced man, while not allowing that fact to define what could be. In that sense, it's a kind of forgiveness, a release from the past in favor of the future.

****

The man visits Turkey, taking students to study Islam. They are in Istanbul. The guide asks whether they would like to go to the mosque for early morning prayers. The man and several students meet the guide at 5:00 am and they walk to the mosque. To their profound shock, they see more than two thousand men—along with several women taking another entrance—enter the mosque, spill out onto the portico, down the steps and into the street. They were kneeling en masse in prayer.

Following this striking spectacle, the man asks the guide, "Why do Muslims pray five times each day." The guide thought for a few moments and replied, "The most important thing for a Muslim is to remember God, but that is also one of the most difficult things to do. We keep forgetting. By praying five times each day we are reminded."

The man listens in stunned silence. He remembers that in early Christianity one common way to describe worship was to speak of it as the practice of anamnesis. Amnesis, the Greek word for forgetting, becomes the word for unforgetting or remembering when the prefix is added. Worship, then, is unforgetting or remembering God. Same purpose the guide ascribed to Muslims praying five times each day.

The man ponders this insight for several days, writing notes in his travel journal about the centrality of memory in the practice of religion itself. Such remembrance, he finds is not bondage but liberation for those who practice their religion.

****

All of this may sound rather like a lay version of self-analysis, but I'm reflecting on it to make a specific point. Finitude, whether in the form of limitation or fixation, would be a sheer trap—the *end* of creative imagination and possibility—without infinity and our lust for it. In other words, we live our finitude only as we live it on the cusp of infinity.

My thesis on the existential origin of the religious sensibility comes at this point: *with the encounter of finitude with the infinite—and I mean our sense of it, whether conscious or unconscious—the religious sensibility is seeded.* The driver behind the multifarious faces of what we commonly call *religion* lies in the consciousness of our finitude in the presence of the infinite. This infinity is no doubt inchoate and nebulous—even chaotic—in the extreme. Indeed, it cannot be otherwise. It is more nearly as echo is to sound or shadow to substance. It haunts and hovers long before it becomes the articulate awareness I'm now discussing.

And every concept of the infinite, including this one, is itself infinitely less than the infinite, our finitude reaching beyond itself but always from within itself. All we need do is listen to mathematicians or physicists try to comprehend and explain the infinite. In the process they become more nearly poets than analysts. Or, in the language of anthropologist Ernest Becker, "we are the creatures who write poetry and shit." The former reaches for infinity, and the latter assures our finite grounding. This is our singular human condition and the birthplace of all religion.

My lone reverie is interrupted by distant noise up the hill. I can see Holt leading Mercury. The burro is loaded with Holt's gear. He seems to be leaving, and I rush to give him a send off. He sees me coming, stops, and waves.

"Where's Ethan?" Holt asks.

"Not sure. I think maybe he's still asleep." I look over at the tent in time to see it shake with internal disturbance.

Ethan pokes his head out. "What time is it? Oh, man!" And he disappears, falling back inside.

"Hell, it's daytime. Raise your butt from the dead," Holt insists.

"Hang on. I'm comin'," Ethan promises, and in moments he's out of the tent, half dressed, and offering a mock salute. He walks over to Holt and embraces him. "Always a pleasure to run into my kind. . .and thanks for the hooch. . . Where you headed?"

"Just up the way to Beatty's Falls and then down into the Moira Flats. Think I'll spend a day down there before headin' back. It's a peaceful place. . .as long as boy scouts aren't there whoopin' it up."

"Well brother, I hate to see you go. What're we gonna' eat tonight?" Ethan chides.

"Nuts and berries I guess. When're you leavin'?"

I respond, "We should'a left today. We're supposed to get to St. Barbara's Trailhead by tomorrow. Guess we'll be humpin' it."

I can see Ethan frown. He hates to do anything in a hurry, especially backpacking. When we finish our farewells to Holt and he hikes off to the trail, Ethan asks, "What'll happen if we don't show tomorrow?" I don't want to answer this because it'll make him want to stall even more. I feel an obligation to Collins. I stall.

"He'll probably just leave the food there for us," Ethan ventures.

"No, he won't do that," I retort. Then I say what I know is true. "He'll camp there at least for a couple of days and wait on us. After that, if he has time, he'll come in here lookin' for us."

"No kiddin? Man, that's all right!" Ethan is impressed. "You put it that way, I sure don't want to disappoint him. A fellow like that comes along in a blue moon. Maybe we can take two more days, but no more than that. Whatta you think?" He turns directly toward me, and I agree.

We're low key through the evening. Ethan is trying to regain his sobriety. At least he's not on one of his grievous binges about the whole world and all that's in it, but he is somber through dinner. I think about telling him of my thoughts of the day on the origin of religion, but I can tell it's not the time.

We sit up late, staring into the fire. My last thought before retiring is about the mystery of flames, how they're both there and not there, dancing on the disintegration of their host. I sneak into my tent early enough to make a few hasty notes by flashlight.

Fourteen

...cradling our infinite on the finite seas

                        Baudelaire

∼

Less than All cannot satisfy man.

                        William Blake

∼

We're on the trail early. The sun hangs barely above the trees as we leave camp. Ethan awoke with a demon, saying only that we needed to move today so we can meet Collins on time. Good news for me, but I can tell a dark mood grips Ethan. He's like this after drinking, but usually only for a day. I don't ask any of those inane questions, like, "Somethin' wrong?" or "What's the matter?" He'll say when he's ready. For now I wait him out.

Ethan leads, head bent forward, at a quicker pace than usual. Only our feet scuffing the earth report our presence as we enter a dense stand of ponderosa. I embrace the quiet, barely noticing a breeze disturbing the foliage. We've been out here long enough for the wilderness to engulf and inhabit me. I move within it as one might walk through a cathedral or mosque. When this sense arises in me, I no longer need to be anywhere else or do any other thing than this. Rediscovering this sense is what repeatedly beckons me back to the wilderness. I've come home.

The breakthrough from yesterday comes to mind, and I muse on it as we hike. Religion has its birth at the juncture where consciousness—or for most, the unconscious—recognizes infinity in the context of lived finitude. I already started discussing this earlier, before we took to the trail. *Good enough*, I mutter to myself, but I'm not sure where this leaves me. All I've achieved is a pinpointing of the existential ground of the religious sensibility, and I cannot prove or demonstrate it. I can only claim that it seems to fit our elementary human condition, the minimum necessary for religion to take form.

To put it rudely, I might ask what any person is actually doing when acting religiously. The answer appears to be something like this: *a person is acting religiously when he or she is aware, through the act, of the need to connect with a larger whole, a One or an All—the infinite—in such a way that the person is fulfilled or in some respect completed.* The primordial sense of the infinite from within the confines of finitude prompts exactly this way of responding and acting, and without this sense I cannot imagine why or how the religious dimension kicks in and can begin to be expressed. This sense is prior to every other candidate for the origin of religion, whether it be Durkheim's sense of social solidarity, Eliade's urge to the sacred, the encounter with and fear of death, or any other possibility.

I'm by no means the first or only one to come up with the centrality of this finite-infinite polarity. These words of ancient Israel's prophet Isaiah, for instance, appear to capture the idea: "For my thoughts are not your thoughts, nor are your ways my ways, says the Lord. For as the heavens are higher than the earth, so are my ways higher than your ways and my thoughts than your thoughts." Passages such as this speak of the unbridgeable chasm between the infinite (God, in this case) and the finite (Israel).

Nevertheless, those ancient peoples experienced and claimed a vital and immediate relationship between the two.

An insight of Pascal's found in his *Pensees* has long impressed me. We can hear the mathematician in him as he describes not *the* infinite but *two* infinities. Under the heading, "Disproportion of Man," he notes that human beings are middle-range creatures, suspended between the infinitely large and the infinitely small. Ordinary observation of nature and of our place in nature is enough to humble us with this truth.

First, he describes the infinitely large, so unbounded that even our entire visible universe becomes "an imperceptible dot." As if that weren't enough to dwarf us, Pascal then proceeds to describe the tiniest things, showing how these things are made up of increasingly minute "universes" and parts within those universes. We human beings are sandwiched between these two immeasurable immensities.

Where does this situation leave us? Pascal describes our situation graphically: "Anyone who considers himself in this way will be terrified at himself, and, seeing his mass, as given him by nature, supporting him between these two abysses of infinity and nothingness, will tremble at these marvels. I believe that with his curiosity into wonder he will be more disposed to contemplate them in silence than investigate them with presumption."

Pascal then concludes with a soul-stirring question: "For, after all, what is man in nature? A nothing compared to the infinite, a whole compared to the nothing, a middle point between all and nothing, infinitely remote from an understanding of the extremes; the end of things and their principles are unattainably hidden from him in impenetrable secrecy."

Thus, like Koheleth in *Ecclesiastes*, we are seen to be at once drawn toward the infinite and yet utterly incapable of understanding, let alone mastering, it. This includes an inability to understand with any finality even ourselves. Pascal continues to lay out the implications of this human suspension between All and Nothing, noting how our persistent arrogance insists on reaching for the "absolute" truth belonging solely to the infinite. And we are all in exactly the same boat. When it comes to the infinite, no one of us and no group of us has any advantage whatsoever.

Near the end of this discussion Pascal utters one of his most famous, oft-quoted comments. I have carried this statement, and several others, with me when traveling, and periodically I read through them to help me maintain perspective. Here is his remarkable conclusion:

> Man is only a reed, the weakest in nature, but he is a thinking reed. There is no need for the whole universe to take up arms to crush him; a vapour, a drop of water is enough to kill him. But even if the universe were to crush him, man would still be nobler than his slayer, because he knows that he is dying and the advantage the universe has over him. The universe knows nothing of this.

In thought—the mind, or what I have more broadly called *consciousness*—lies the greatest gift humanity possesses: we can discern our suspended condition between the two infinities. Thus,

Pascal urges us to "strive to think well." We do this adequately only when we know our thinking, our consciousness, remains always suspended between All and Nothing. This suspension and our consciousness of it, I claim, is the cradle—nay, the womb—of the religious sensibility.

Ethan virtually plunges along the trail in grim determination, a drill sergeant oblivious to his troops. He pauses at one point, but only long enough to drink water. I have been lost in my reveries, and before I catch up with him, he strides away. *This day is probably not going to be dull,* I think to myself. The only advantage of this somber march is that it affords me opportunity to press ahead with my thoughts. I do believe I've hit bedrock in my attempt to probe for the existential origins of religion, and I want to insure greater clarity by persisting and further examining the insight.

My mind drifts back to another voice, writing almost two hundred years after Pascal. He influenced me profoundly in my young adult studies. His name is Soren Kierkegaard, the Danish intellectual genius. In a little text on the fundamental human dilemma entitled *The Sickness unto Death*, Kierkegaard begins with these striking words:

> The human being is spirit. But what is spirit? Spirit is the self. But what is the self? The self is a relation which relates to itself, or that in the relation which is its relating to itself. A human being is a synthesis of the infinite and the finite, of the temporal and the eternal, of freedom and necessity. In short, a synthesis. A synthesis is a relation between two terms. Looked at in this way a human being is not yet a self.

What a mouthful!

Kierkegaard, regardless of what one might think, is not trying to bamboozle the reader. He is describing the utter complexity of the human condition. We are, he insists, a *synthesis* and a most special one: a synthesis of the finite and the infinite. This is yet another statement of what I've been urging.

But what Kierkegaard does to help move the matter further is to show us that human selfhood is not automatically granted with the fact of the synthesis. Rather, we are obliged to *relate* to the relation constituted by the synthesis. Only then, in that synthetic intimacy, does the self emerge, and this process is arduous indeed. Only by beginning at the point of *despair* and moving through its darkest regions can we hope to become constituted as the self. Herein resides the religious struggle itself, the process set in motion by the synthesis of the finite and the infinite.

All of this is more than arduous. It's *impossible*, as impossible as Pascal has already indicated. Elsewhere Kierkegaard states the impossibility in stark language: "There is an infinite qualitative difference between the finite and the infinite." He describes an unbridgeable chasm yawning between the finite and the infinite, and it is more than a matter of quantitative *distance*, as in mathematical and scientific discussions of infinity. It is qualitative. It has to do with significance! Our mere finitude is truncated, tenuous, and trifling over against the infinite.

Yet, we are a synthesis of the two. We are that trifle which *participates* unconditional significance. This mind-bending way of putting it may be more than we are prepared to engage, but when pressed to its depths, this synthesis is where the religious sensibility takes breath. This is why Kierkegaard winds up describing the resolution of the synthesis in terms of "the Leap," and he means by this phrase to describe the subjective experiential case of faith itself.

To help me nail down this *idée fixe* regarding our "fix"—that is, our suspension within the finite-infinite synthesis—I want to consider one more approach. In a much more recent book, *Finite and Infinite Games*, James Carse invites us into the subject by using game theory in a novel way.

He says, "There are at least two kinds of games. One could be called finite, the other infinite. A finite game is played for the purpose of winning, an infinite game for the purpose of continuing the play." We humans, Carse shows, live constantly in reference to both of these games, but they are utterly different.

When we do anything whatever, we are most often doing what we do as a finite game that we seek to win, but, ironically, we can do the same things as an infinite engagement with life itself as the game. Finite games are games of conquest, and they dominate most of our waking hours. The infinite game—and there is only one such game—is perpetually played for no other purpose than to *participate* in the play. The infinite game is not about us, but we can be about the game.

To grasp fully Carse's vision of these two games requires a careful reading—and rereading—of his book. What surprised me about it was that it does not mention religion at all, and yet the entire book is about the religious attitude within and toward life. I was so impressed by this that after reading *Finite and Infinite Games* I wrote Carse.

I pointed out a possible problem for religion, if we agree with his book. I said that, on the one hand, religion is *not* the infinite game. In a sense it is only one more finite game, often confusedly masquerading as the infinite game. On the other hand, religion, when being properly religious, seeks to do honor to the infinite game by providing a location for its acknowledgment in the midst of our many finite games. Religion, when truly religious, *points*! Religion refers to the infinite but never is, in itself, the infinite game. Carse responded to my suggestion with affirmation.

Gratifying!

What did I mean by this? I meant that religion does have a peculiar relation to the infinite game from within our myriad finite games. Religion honors and *intends* the infinite game, the game to be freely and playfully engaged as life itself. But religion cannot, in the very nature of the case, capture—let alone confine—the infinite game. The *temptation* of religion, of course, is to claim the infinite which it can never possess, and this pathological possibility must be examined during our pilgrimage.

Admittedly this discussion of games may sound complex and perhaps bewildering—or frivolous, but when we're down at the nub of the encounter of finitude with the infinite, matters are no longer at the surface of our existence. We plumb our depths—remember that metaphor?—and the depths of existence itself. So, we stay with the challenge.

At the very end of Carse's book, he concludes in a way that may help keep an awareness of the infinite game alive for anyone who can grasp it:

> It is not necessary for infinite players to be Christians; indeed it is not possible for them to be Christians—seriously. Neither is it possible for them to be Buddhists, or Muslims, or atheists, or New York-

ers—seriously. All such titles can only be playful abstractions, mere performances for the sake of laughter. Infinite players are not serious actors in any story, but the joyful poets of a story that continues to originate what they cannot finish. There is but one infinite game.

All of the voices I have used here to help me express this finite-infinite tension within us are only representative of how this way of understanding the origin of religion might be recognized. One flaw in my use of them is that they are all *Western* voices.

Religion as such is planetary in scope, not only, or even primarily, Western. I do find, however, that if we probe the great *Eastern* traditions, the problem of the finite and infinite is quite as embedded or implicit within them. The finite trap of *karma* and reincarnation, whether in Hinduism, Buddhism or another tradition, stands against the infinite release from the cycles of life. Hinduism further sees universes rising and coming to full flower only to dissolve and become replaced by succeeding universes—infinitely. Or, if one reads only the initial passage of the *Dao de Ching*, the infinite lies implicit in the "unnamable" Dao:

> The dao that can be told
> is not the eternal Tao.
> The name that can be named
> is not the eternal Name.
>
> The unnamable is the eternally real.
> Naming is the origin
> of all particular things.

Indeed, I will risk overstatement by proposing that the Eastern religions may well be far more attentive to, and respectful of, the infinite than the Abrahamic monotheisms. I will not argue this, but do think about it.

Ahead of us I hear voices and laughter. I look up but see only Ethan standing at the brow of a rise, staring. We have arrived at Pecos Falls, a destination for some packers and occasionally for hardy day hikers. The Falls are not especially dramatic, more like a "slide" of water over boulders and into the escaping stream below.

An Asian family made up of parents and a cluster of gleeful children splash in the stream. They climb up moss-covered stone faces and slide down repeatedly. I wonder how on earth they made it this far into the wilderness, but I do not ask. They notice us only briefly, pausing to look us over before returning to their familial delights. Ethan moves above the falls, locates a crossing, and sits on a prominence to watch. I join him. He takes out dried fruit. Our food supply is dwindling.

Still he remains lost in silence. I wait for an opening to enter with him into his turmoil. I know it's stirring within him. I've seen it before. The only question is when and how it will manifest: in outrage or whimpers. Presently I hear him weeping. Tears drop on his khaki pants. He appears absorbed in the playing family below.

Then I realize: they are Asian! Probably not Vietnamese. They are more likely Korean, and when I listen to their chatter more carefully, it sounds Korean. Ethan, I can tell, has made them into a Vietnamese family, remembering. It's always the same story. He doesn't even need to tell it.

The patrol approaches a village, bent on pacification. He always says that word with a tone of weighty irony. A child comes down the lane toward them, smiling, and as the patrol starts to relax, one of them spots the grenade the child carries behind his back. Immediately, "all hell breaks loose." That's Ethan's stock phrase. Shooting erupts. The child lies bleeding in the lane. Men in black dress pour out of the village, and in the horrendous melee that follows, most of them lie dead, along with families unable to escape fast enough into the jungle. Ethan almost always says, "I think I got the kid." And he adds, "How can you shoot a kid like that, such a tiny warrior...probably forced into it."

"There's no absolution for killin' children," he at last states emphatically. "So, what's the good of religion? If it can't give some relief to the soul, what's the point?"

"Ethan, you know damn good and well that religion can't give absolution if you can't receive it." My frustration is at the edge of anger.

"Is that all you've got to say?"

"Know what? I think you've been at this so long you downright enjoy leaving everybody speechless. What can anybody say? You've decided to make your case the impossible one. No matter who else receives forgiveness—or absolution—you are beyond the pale."

I almost add that this is the greatest ego trip of all, *not that you're the grandest of them all but that you're the single most incorrigible case in human history.* But I refrain, not wanting to bait him.

"Tell you what," Ethan mutters after a long while. "This wilderness reminds me too much of that place. . .especially that," and he points to the waterfall and the family cavorting below. "And some perverse demon sends a family up here to add drama to it all. . .God!"

"It's all inside yourself, not over there." Before I can say more, he cuts me off and stands.

"When we meet up with Collins tomorrow," he virtually explodes, "I'm leavin' with him. You can stay up here if you want, but this place spooks me out like it's haunted." With that declaration he stalks away toward the trail, giving me no chance for rebuttal.

I'm livid. Ethan has done this twice before and always when we're in some remote place that makes everything complicated and turbulent. Anger is not common for me, but he can draw it out like no one else. Not since the divorce have I experienced such rage. It gives me energy to march behind him, following paradoxically in defiance. I tell myself I should be more patient, that he's struggling to break out of a terrible self-constructed prison. That does no good.

I fume my away along the trail for half an hour, stewing about how I'm going to handle the situation. Eventually I recall a conversation with a Tibetan monk, a lama, at a monastery in Scotland.

I asked him what he thought the greatest difference was between the western way of solving problems and his way. He said something like this. When people are angry, only two choices are possible for westerners: they can either express their anger or they can hide their anger. Most often, he hides it at first, and then when he finally expresses it, the anger has control of him.

"My tradition," he said, "gives a third way." When the lama said this, I immediately thought of the description of Buddhism as "the middle way."

The lama continued by describing this third option. He said that people could simply *pay attention* to the anger and try to learn what it has to teach them, especially about themselves. If they do this carefully, two things happen: they discover that the anger is entirely theirs and belongs to no one else, and examination of this truth causes the anger to simply go away or dissolve into insight. He went on to say that all human emotions can be instructive if taken in this way.

I found the lama's observation intriguing at the time, but I had not experienced sufficient anger since then to test it. So, as we hike in haste, I decide to address my own anger.

Why am I in such a rage at Ethan? After all, he's my closest friend and one who has taught me so much. Am I disappointed that he threatens to ruin our trip, our pilgrimage? I decide this isn't it, although if he decides to leave I'll need to make some adjustments or leave with him.

It takes me some time to locate the culprit within. My anger, I finally recognize, is only a cover for something more basic: *frustration*. And my frustration is not at him but at myself for not being able to say or do the thing that releases him. I'm actually chasing around with my best friend trying to play God, if you will, by *saving* him. What insanity! I'm nobody's savior, not even my own.

Then I have an even stranger thought: this anger is really about yet another attempt to overwhelm finitude and deliver the infinite gesture. Granted, it is rooted in *goodwill* toward my friend. But it's still my own rescue and deliverance compulsion. If I'm going to be Ethan's friend, I must *join* his process and walk along with him rather than try to dictate his way out or short circuit the whole business. I keep trying to pacify him—or is it myself?

The relief that comes with my discovery is immediate and spectacular. After a while I inwardly thank that lama for his gift, and by the time we reach a campsite that will work for the night, I'm almost giddy. Here's what it has boiled down to for me: I've realized I must quit trying to carry both Ethan and me up these mountains. His "prison" has imprisoned me, and I really cannot support him or be of any assistance by clanging the door closed on both of us. I have my own prisons, my own burdens of finitude. That ought to allow me some sense of sympathy, if not actual empathy.

Ethan remains morose but cooperative through our meager dinner. Sleep comes before twilight fully fades.

Fifteen

If the many become the same as the few when possess'd, More!
More! Is the cry of a mistaken soul: less than All cannot satisfy Man.

William Blake

~

The wood is damp, but I scrounge enough twigs to start a fire. Breakfast will be spare today: coffee, granola bars, and the last fragments of our dried fruit. We sit on a damp log sipping and munching.

"Damn!" Ethan's first words of the day. "You can't expect to win a war like that. It was the dumbest and worst thing this country's ever done. When you've got people who'll crawl on their bellies all day long and through the night to fight you, you're not gonna' whip 'em. That's for sure. And it doesn't make any difference that you've got all those fancy weapons." Silence, then, "Hell, I admire 'em for what they did. . .passion and determination. . .protecting home turf. Can't beat it."

I wonder where he's going with all of this, but he doesn't go anywhere. He looks off into nothing. Something has changed. He has obsessed on the war from the time I first met him, but he usually only makes random comments, until he drinks or stokes.

"Wish I could go back over there. Maybe I could do somethin'." Ethan says this as though I'm not present and he's discussing with himself. "Gotta' do somethin' for heaven's sake. . .or it'll drive me over the cliff."

"Yep. You do whatever you need to do, and I'll. . ."

"I intend to, but I don't know what that is just yet," Ethan confesses. "All I really know is this: I cannot go on discussing religion like we've been doin' because religion's a crutch. It's like a damn escape clause in life's contract."

"You think that's all it is, a way to sidestep life?" I ask, thinking maybe I can draw him into a serious discussion so he can shift his thinking.

"Don't get me started," he blurts back. "I'm not talking in general terms here. I'm sayin' that it has not done me any good since Nam. And God knows, I've given it more than one shot. But the beast won't leave, and I can't tame it. Whatever religion's supposed to do, it's not doin' it for me, right in here," and he ends by pressing an index finger into his chest like a revolver.

"And that's what counts in the end," he says with finality, throwing out the dregs of his coffee and stalking off toward his tent.

In less than an hour we're on the march again. Today we'll reach the St. Barbara's Trailhead, and we're both ready for it.

The only thing I can seriously admire about Ethan's entanglement with that war is his tenacity. It may be a pathological obsession, but he's not about to let go of it. I think of the ancient patriarch Jacob and his great all-night wrestling match with his God, or an angel, and his walking with a limp the rest of his life. At least, I conclude to myself, he hasn't lost his passion, even if it's mad.

Ethan's two favorite words are *passion* and *imagination*. He uses them as verbal icons for his way of taking on life. I once asked him if he couldn't use his own imagination to move past Vietnam, and he shot back that it was the power of imagination that kept him engaged with it.

"Most of my buddies," he said, "lost the images, and that made 'em lose the memories. Imagination! That's the blessing and the curse of my life. It lets me remember but it won't let me forget. Forgettin's unimaginative!"

As I dredge up these past conversations, my mind eventually rummages its way back to the notion of finitude and infinity and how they merge in our very existence. And when they do, sparks fly. Or, to put it another way, the *passion* for life lies exactly at this juncture. Here we humans are, couched in the bounded nest of finitude, crying out from within it for, dare I say it, everything! A lot of the crying is nothing but our cupidity, our desire to suck everything up into ourselves. And that makes the passion as dangerous as it is promising.

I began to sense this danger not long ago when I read this question in Georges Bataille's *Inner Experience*: "To ask oneself before another: by what means does he calm within himself the desire to be everything?" For Bataille, to admit to the desire for everything is the foundational confession of human existence. He, and we, know this longing is impossible, outrageously so, but the propensity—the passion—remains. We are the creatures able to imagine "everything," the infinite, and we long to possess it.

The capacity comes with the harsh fact that we are utterly finite as we labor under the lure of the infinite, while constantly lost in the details. Bataille says that if this passion is lost and we become "disintoxicated" by the sinister temptation to domesticate ourselves, everything is thrown into question, and we lose our elemental orientation.

When I probe human existence in this way, the one word that keeps coming to mind for how we actually live in response to the urge to encompass everything is, as I've said, *lust*. To be humanly alive in a qualitative sense is to *lust for infinity*, that is, for "everything."

I choose the word *lust* deliberately, knowing it is laden with sexual connotation and is almost always used negatively. Lust has been heavily moralized in our common lexicon as inordinate sexual desire. Mercy! It's even one of the seven deadly sins. Lust is immediate, uncontrolled passion for the other in the interest of one's own gratification, and as such, it may so depersonalize the other and reduce them to object that we can understand why the term is used to describe morally objectionable sexual desire.

Yet, without such passionate desire as lust implies, the human race might wither at its source. Why can't a culturally acceptable relationship still include lust?

I speak here simply of intense and concentrated desire. If we hark back to this desire itself, in its raw urge and urgency, we may learn something about it in relation to our lust for infinity. Thereby, I hope further to grasp and appreciate the religious sensibility at its source.

Our primary organismic desires, those we share with other creatures, are not summoned by a deliberative process. They simply manifest themselves. They break forth. We're hard wired with them, and we must contend with them. Other species are controlled by such things as periodicity and the rhythms of estrus, but we find controls in the taboos and permissions of sociocultural life and our internalization of them.

These boundaries and the vigor used to enforce them speak loudly of the primacy and power of these urges, even as we are compelled to control them. They must be carefully directed because they are so necessary to personal and cultural life and yet also dangerous in their potency.

The Greek term for this vital capacity in humans is *eros*, but for the Greeks, *eros* means more than sexual desire. It has to do with the urge originating beyond us and moving through us toward completion of our very being (and not entirely unlike Bataille's desire for everything.) The sexual erotic is only the first and primary manifestation of eros.

The Greeks know that this force must be guided toward human fullness in some way, and they argue over how best to harness eros. The one thing they never do is try to deny or squelch this force, because it permeates human vitality from its sexual grounding to the most profound reaches of human possibility. In this way the Greeks honor eros—or what I shall insist on calling it here, *lust*—while insisting that it be so directed that it allows humans to flourish. Read Plato's *Symposium*. It gives the full sweep of eros for the Greeks. Or better, read *Zorba the Greek* or watch the movie version for a glimpse of the masculine version of eros.

This is the way I'm using *lust*, because I want to emphasize its primal immediacy, vitality and power—indeed, its necessity—in forming our humanity. Its sexual expression is not lower in the sense of inferior. On the contrary, sexuality forms the *base* of the urge to life and therefore of the lure of infinity itself.

Sigmund Freud, despite his numerous follies, is addressing an important truth in his insistence that sexuality is at the core of human motivation. Had he pursued the full implications of his claim, he might have discovered that sexuality is actually a primordial manifestation of "the desire for everything," that is, the *lust for infinity*.

To put it bluntly, sexuality may well be implicitly religious or at least a precursor to religion. Otherwise, how do we explain the intense entanglement of sexual prohibitions and taboos within the moral stipulations of religions? Or, on the contrary, consider those religions that welcome the close interface between human sexuality and the sacred.

I have in mind particularly some Eastern forms such as Tantric Hinduism and Buddhism, but these are only the more obvious examples. If religion is not simply reduced to a part of life but is the inner urge that steers the whole of life in response to the infinite, then sexuality is obviously as important an ingredient in religion as any other dimension of existence.

When religion is addressed experientially as something that actually arises within our psycho-spiritual and emotive capacities, one word is frequently used to describe its most intense expressions: *ecstasy*. Meaning literally "to be beside one's self," ecstasy suggests an intense form of self-transcendence, one in which we are taken, even if only momentarily, beyond the confines of our finitude and into a boundless emptiness. This kind of experience may be rare and brief, but given the fact of it and its continuing possibility, we may further discern the close affinity between sexuality and the most intense religious experiences. In both we can become *beside ourselves*.

Given our contemporary penchant for scientific explanations and justifications, we should not be surprised that scientific evidence for religious experiential states is being sought. In a movement currently labeled *neurotheology* scientists studying the activity of the brain during religious practices such as prayer and meditation claim that responses in the brain indicate that such practices are hard wired into the brain's potential.

While this does not provide any evidence whatever for the truth of religious claims, it does suggest that such religious processes are more than fitting to human beings. This is another way of saying that people who act religiously are not necessarily crazy!

Many questions and criticisms can be and are being raised in response to this sort of scientific inquiry, but I'm not especially interested in those here. What I want to underscore is that one discovery made by some researchers is the close association in the brain of the sexual urge and the religious urge to the ecstatic.

Here is only one statement of the case. In a book popularizing the implications of brain research for religion, *Why God Won't Go Away*, Andrew Newberg, et al. assert:

We believe, in fact, that the neurological machinery of transcendence may have arisen from the neural circuitry that evolved for mating and sexual experience. The language of mysticism hints at this connection. Mystics of all times and cultures have used the same expressive terms to describe their ineffable experiences: *bliss, rapture, ecstasy,* and *exaltation*. They speak of losing themselves in a sublime sense of union, of melting into elation, and of the total satisfaction of desires.

The researchers go on to say that sexual and mystical ecstasies use the same neural pathways. They are quick to urge, however, that this does not mean sexual and mystical experiences are the same thing, only that they have an affinity in the context of brain function. Further, people who report high states of religious experience tend to describe them by resorting to sexual language.

While these reports are not proof of the close connection I'm proposing, it is highly suggestive.

****

The boy lives in Texas. He lives at the edge of the country. His friends inhabit the country, and the country dwells in them. The boy's friend Gene is one of them. He invites the boy to his home far from town. The boy is drawn to this home. Smells are novel and the pace is steady but has a languid texture. Most sounds, especially at night, are not made by humans. The boy goes to Gene's home repeatedly, once in a while for the entire weekend.

The boy and his friend Gene sleep on the screen porch. It feels as though they are sleeping outside. The porch is distinct from the house, and the boy feels separated from everyone except his friend. He can see into the night and sometimes watch the day take shape.

It is Saturday morning. Gene and the boy have the day to explore. They do, ranging along the Colorado River for miles, chasing turtles, watching armadillos and jack rabbits scurry about when disturbed. A rattler fusses at them with its tail. They chatter about boy things. They sweat. They produce appetites. They fall into the kitchen, bearing their steaming bodies into the steamy room. They assault dinner and then leave for the cooler breeze outside.

The boy and Gene sit on a fallen log beneath an aging mesquite. Abrupt-

ly Gene asks, "You wanna see my sister take a bath?" The boy is surprised but ready for any adventure. He says, "Yes. . .but how do we do that." Gene points to a smokehouse out back. "Saturday nights she takes her bath in there." In the fading light of dusk they watch the mother and the daughter. They carry buckets of water, some hot and some cold. After several trips the girl-daughter returns once more with clothes over her arm. Gene and the boy wait, and soon they see splinters of light coming from the inside. Gene says, "She's lit the lantern. Come on."

The boy follows Gene in a wide loop through the brush behind the house, using the smokehouse for cover. As they approach, Gene motions the boy to move quietly. They sneak into position between two bushes directly behind the ancient structure. They sit on the ground. Gene points to a fairly large knothole just above them, and he rises on his knees, peering into the room. The boy fears being caught and wants to retreat, but Gene holds him by the arm. Gene motions for the boy to look.

The boy, shaking, rises to his knees and squints at the light through the opening. At first he sees nothing but movement and light steam rising in the center of the room. Then, stunned, he spots her. The girl-daughter stands in the midst of the slight swirl of fog, a statue not moving. The boy stares so long that Gene pulls at him, and the boy crouches back down. While Gene looks again, the boy wanders in his mind between exhilaration and embarrassment. How can he ever look at the girl-daughter again?

The boy has never seen, or thought of seeing, a naked girl. He thinks she looks almost like any typical boy who's naked. Then Gene nudges for him to rise again. Once his eye adjusts, he sees the girl-daughter covering herself with soap. When she turns to place the soap on a table, she faces directly toward him. She appears to stare at the boy, and he almost lurches back. Then he sees a strange darkness near her lower body, small but distinct. A wedge! He drops to the ground.

Gene wants to leave and motions that somebody might come. The boy remains seated. He is transfixed by what he has witnessed. He knows that this glimpse is somehow momentous, and he stares at the ground to seal it in his mind. The two boys slip away into the night. They never mention their experience, but the boy remembers.

****

I find myself wishing I could talk with Ethan about this connection between spiritual experience and sexual language, but he plods ahead, bent on our destination. He has said more than once that sex and sexuality are far more complex matters than we recognize.

He found in Vietnam, for instance, that he and his comrades would be sexually ravenous after returning from the heat of violence. He swears that the violence itself somehow triggers a blind eroticism. He said once, "It's like the urge to death and the gore of killing are crying out for the urge to life, and we go screaming toward any kind of sexual union. Or maybe all of it's tied into death. Beats me, but I'll say this much: it's powerful stuff."

Somehow—and I do not know exactly how—sexual eroticism, *violence*, and our sense of the sacred are connected. When we throw violence into the mix, things become complicated in a hurry. The best explanation I can muster comes, again, from Georges Bataille. He insists over and over that religion is rooted in the idea and practice of *sacrifice*, that sacrifice is inherently violent, and that violence is associated with the erotic. When we examine erotic factors related to sacrifice, as Bataille does, the association of the three categories appears to fit. I mentioned sacrifice earlier, but it deserves further attention in relation to violence and the erotic.

If we seek the origins of religion or the sacred in the human past, Bataille may be right about sacrifice being the origin of religion, but I'm seeking its source not in human history but in the constitution of our human existence. The existential origin, I hold, lies in the awareness of our finitude and the imagination of infinity, what I've called the *Primary Impulse*.

In light of my contention, what is to be made of sacrifice—and by implication, violence—in religion? And why are they tied up with the erotic?

I once heard a Quaker speaker explaining the peculiarities of the Quaker version of Christianity, and he did so by showing how the idea of sacrifice changes in the history of Judeo-Christian development. He pointed out that Abraham's aborted sacrifice of Isaac marks the end, at least in principle, of human sacrifice. After that, animal sacrifice becomes the symbolic substitute expressing sacrifice. Then along come the ancient prophets, who decry the use of ritual sacrifice as an adequate expression of Israel's religion. The people, they urge, must express their religion by obedient action and an interior change of heart. (The Jews gave up the practice of animal sacrifice after the destruction of the second temple in 70 c.e.)

When Christianity comes on the scene, the Quaker speaker insisted, it rests its message on one single sacrifice: the sacrifice of an innocent representative of God, a last human sacrifice aimed at ending the need for sacrifice. In this situation, sacrifice dramatically shifts. With St. Paul, the followers of Jesus are to *become* "living sacrifices." This understanding enters into the church's symbolic character in the form of the Eucharist, in which Christ's sacrifice continues to be relived through the eucharistic elements and within those who receive them.

Protestants virtually eliminate even the symbolic notion of sacrifice by turning the Eucharist into a banquet feast that uses both Word and Sacrament as nourishment for life. Then come the Quakers. They are among the more radical reformers of sectarian Protestantism. They arise in the seventeenth century and declare that all the symbolism and all notions of sacrifice are dissolved into an inner transfiguration that comes when people receive and become *living participants* in and with the Incarnate Christ.

This process is entirely *internal* and needs none of the external gestures of sacrifice, either actual or symbolic. Hence, the Quaker speaker concluded, sacrifice is no longer necessary or even desirable within religion.

Whether this Quaker has the history and its interpretation exactly right, he does offer a helpful proposal: while sacrifice may have belonged to the historical origins of religion, particularly Western Judeo-Christian religion, sacrifice is not necessary to religion.

Perhaps this is one reason the Quakers, among a few other religious groups, are such ardent advocates of nonviolence. That is to say, if sacrifice is tied to violence as well as to religion, as Bataille holds, then the end of sacrifice must mean the end of violence. It does not follow that the end of sacrifice is the end of religion, however, only that the character of religion changes fundamentally.

This discussion of sacrifice is limited to the history of two religious traditions, but I wonder whether sacrifice is nearly as central to most Asian religions. While it is a factor in some of them, Eastern religions do not appear to dwell on the subject or make it nearly as basic as the Western monotheistic religions have done. Granted, I'm not sufficiently expert here to register more than an impression about the Eastern *emphasis* on sacrifice. I do note all of the more primal indigenous or oral religions tend to use sacrifice in their practices, but again, I can argue that this belongs to their historical and cultural formation, not to the character of religion as such.

Despite this extended argument against Bataille's idea that religion or the sacred is inherently bound to sacrifice and violence, I remain perplexed as to why sacrifice has had such an important function within religion. Here's a hypothesis more in line with my position that the proper locus of the religious sensibility lies in the existential engagement of finitude with the infinite, the Primary Impulse. It could be that the dramatic cleavage between finitude and the infinite prompts a radical act to bridge the abyss. John Lame Deer's description of the Sun Dance comes to mind here. When the dancer is suspended between heaven and earth, as it were, with piercings through muscles, that's dramatic enough to suggest my point.

Given the lust for infinity and the *impossibility* of bridging the abyss, sacrifice could have arisen as an attempt to do the utmost to achieve the impossible, to give up whatever is required to make the connection. If this is the case, then sacrifice is our expression of perpetual frustration over our situation vis-a-vis the infinite. This possibility does not justify our making sacrifice central to religion, but it may help explain it.

None of this discussion resolves the relation between sexuality and the sacred or religious. Nor do we need to resolve it. We need rather to acknowledge this relation and to see sexuality as the primordial passion associated with our *lust* for the infinite.

This strong proposal challenges both popular religious moralism in many quarters as well as more secular analyses, such as that of Ernest Becker. He says our sexuality, along with our embodied life, is a source of shame to our "higher" sensibilities.

The sexual force reminds us too much of our mortality or, I suggest, simply our finitude. This is, as a matter of fact, probably true and may explain why popular piety is so disturbed by the least sexual deviation from fixed sacred laws of conduct.

At the same time, this truth further makes my point. In our lust for infinity, we are disturbed by our finitude. We long to deny it or to minimize its bearing on our more elevated spiritual aspirations.

The denial of our finitude fostered by efforts to achieve the infinite through the denial—and specifically the denial of our sexuality through suppression and repression—spawns *false infinites*. Not all asceticism is necessarily guilty of this profound error, but ascetic practices are often inspired by the illusion that a minimization of attention to finitude will ensure proximity, if not closure, with the infinite.

Following a trip to Italy, where I read extensively on the life of St. Francis while visiting Assisi, I found myself both admiring and chiding him. There is no doubt but that he is one of the great spiritual voices of Western Christendom, sometimes referred to as "the second Christ." But he was an ascetic who severely constricted attention to his bodily life in terms of food, shelter, and any amenities. Further, he was a zealous celibate.

I read an account of doctors examining his bones during the transfer of his body to the chapel crypt where it now lies. They found that he likely died of malnutrition. What troubled me at the time was my realization that while he honored the sensual world through his relation to nature and as expressed it in his "Canticle to the Sun," his asceticism also denied the significance of the sensual.

By the time I reached home in Oklahoma, I had filled a journal with notes on the bond between sensuality and spirituality and the need to recognize their harmony. My reason for taking this position—which I continue to maintain—is that the root response to our lust for infinity lies in the very stuff of embodied existence itself, in our finitude, and we do ill to ourselves and our spiritual potential when we deny or dismiss this truth. I am an embodied self. As has been observed, we do not *have* bodies; we *are* embodied. Whatever means we may find to pursue our lust for infinity, they must include this most immediate and inescapable resource: embodied existence, sensuality, including our sexuality.

"Eureka!" I hear Ethan shout up ahead. He's out of sight, and I pick up the pace. He has reached a clearing and dropped his pack by the time I arrive. We look around and see a pickup and further down, sure enough, we spot Collins' van. I call for him. No response. I wait, then call out louder. A head appears above the hood of the vehicle. Collins waves to us and beckons. We lean our packs against a tree and join him.

Collins has a tent set up nearby in a grove of aspen. A stew brews on his cook-stove. We're famished and grateful.

"You gonna stay the night?" Ethan asks.

"Stayed last night. Thought you might come in," Collins responds.

I know Collins. He's always on time or early, and he'd wait here a week if he had to. Or he'd come looking for us. "Man, I can sure use some of that stew in my midsection," I confess.

"Who said it's for you?" Collins smirks as he reaches for metal bowls resting on a much-used rag of a towel beside him.

We squat and eat lustily and soon take a second helping. When we finish, I head over to a narrow stream for water to wash the dishes. When I return, Ethan and Collins are talking.

"I told Collins that I think I'm gonna go back with him tomorrow," Ethan reports.

"Huh," Collins grunts. "I thought I'd hike with you guys this week."

This proposal clearly stalls Ethan's plan of escape, and he sits for some time pondering his predicament. Finally, he asks, "What about the next food drop? How'll you get more food?"

"I already hung it in a tree down by a trailhead at Santa Fe Basin. I'll hike out and haul it in next weekend." Collins is always meticulous with such details. "There'll be plenty of food."

Ethan stands and starts to walk off. I know he's brooding over what to do, and I say, "Collins, here's the problem. Ethan wants to leave, but now there's no way for him to do it."

Collins sits up, always challenged by such perplexities. He points to the van. "He can take her. I don't want to come back up here anyway."

Within a few sentences Collins has worked out a plan for Ethan to take the van, go back to the cabin and either stay there or leave. I wonder how we'll reach Collins' cabin in two weeks, but he says that Ethan can stop by and tell Peck to meet us back at the Holy Ghost trailhead.

Ethan visibly relaxes, reaches down for a rock, and slings it into the trees down the hill. For the first time in three days he's himself again, and before we pitch our tents and settle for the night, we're engrossed in idle conversation about things that do not matter but console us with distraction. Laughter marks the end of the day.

Third Movement: Formation

Sixteen

Man is a stream whose source is hidden. Our being is descending into us from we know not whence. The most exact calculator has no prescience that somewhat incalculable, may not balk the very next moment. I am constrained every moment to acknowledge a higher origin of events than the will I call mine.

Ralph Waldo Emerson

∼

Ethan swings his backpack into the rear of the truck and swings himself into the front seat. He has said little, and although I wonder where he'll actually go, I stifle the inclination to inquire. Collins steps to the window, gives Ethan instructions about the drive back, and waves him out. As the truck turns west, Ethan's arm comes out of the window flashing a farewell, the only serious effort to communicate since last night.

I'm still puzzled by his departure. Ethan's unpredictable sometimes, but this is a new wrinkle in the saga of our friendship. Of course, Collins and I have packed together many times, and we're comfortable. My only regret is that he doesn't say much, is not especially interested in my pilgrimage, and is most especially hostile to the subject of religion.

We're both partly packed, and we turn to finish and be on our way. We'll be retracing part of yesterday's trail before veering off toward Lake Katherine. We won't make it there today, but maybe by tomorrow.

While Collins cleans some spilled honey out of his pack so we won't be bear bait tonight, I sit on a rock and make notes in my journal.

"You're always scribblin'," He says over his shoulder.

"I've got things to remember," I fire back. He's baiting like he often does.

"Try rememberin' what I'm tellin' you: there's no need for writin' everything down...or anything!"

"Hard to do when it's heavy stuff like this."

He doesn't answer but wears his famous I-know-more-than-you smirk. He has always scoffed at what he calls "high learning." Thinks it's a waste of time because nobody's ever going to come close to making sense of things, at least not by that means. I've agreed with him but insist that just because a question has no clear or final answer doesn't mean asking it is useless or unimportant. I realize how odd this sounds, and I can't explain it. Even so, I find that the uncertainty regarding the truly basic and perennial questions is precisely their allure. They keep us engaged in what Carse calls "the infinite game."

Collins hikes like a mountain goat. He goes fast, especially uphill, and he sometimes leaves the trail and takes off. "Bushwhacking," he calls it. I go at my own pace, but when he hikes freelance, it can be a challenge. I settle for trying to keep him in sight. I like to walk at a relaxed pace so I can think.

This thought came to me early this morning, and since Ethan's not here to discuss it, I jotted it in my notebook. I wrote, *Infinity is impossible but we can experience it as open possibility*. I like that paradox. I went on to note, *This is the bind in lusting for infinity, and it forms the key problem for the religious sensibility. The sensibility struggles at this point in giving birth to religion. That is, the religious sensibility does not necessarily produce religion, at least not in the way we ordinarily think of religion, but we are drawn through the sensibility into giving it form.*

I continue pondering the paradox. When I say that infinity is impossible, I mean it cannot be encompassed or comprehended. Otherwise, it wouldn't be infinite! This seems straightforward enough to anyone who understands the concept at all. When we dare to traffic in the infinite, as I believe we all do, we engage the impossible. To understand this within actual religions, a useful example might be the Jewish tradition of not speaking or writing the Hebrew name for God. Rather, because the name is so sacred (another way of saying *infinite*) they substitute another word, *adonai* or "Lord." They do this to honor the fact that, when they attempt to *name* the infinite, they are venturing into the region of the impossible. This is part of the foundational commitment within Judaism to "fear the Lord."

The idea of mystery, as used in religious discourse, also speaks to the infinite as the impossible. Mystery, contrary to popular usage, is not a synonym for problem. Problems are, at least in principle, capable of being solved, but we do not *solve* a mystery. We live in an ongoing relation to mystery as that which both involves us, and which, by its nature, remains beyond our measure and control. We do not solve a mystery; we *participate* it. Problems belong to the finite domain; mystery belongs to the infinite.

If the infinite is, for us and for everything finite, the impossible, then how do we presume to participate it? We participate the infinite by anticipating it. As Koheleth puts it, "God has put eternity in our minds." It functions like a dark echo whispering to us and luring us into a lust for it. Yet, we do not and cannot comprehend its impossibility. What we can and do experience is the infinite as *open possibility*. This is, as it were, how infinity comes upon us. By open possibility I refer to the fact that we can always anticipate—if only by sheer imagination—things being or coming to be other than they are and being *more* than they ever are. Hope itself participates in this way of ceaselessly orienting ourselves toward what is not here and not yet, but hovers in anticipatory imagination as the promise of possibility.

But open possibility is also more. Imagination allows us to play in the field of possibility even if any serious hope—understood as expectation or actual anticipation—has dissipated. This is the grand gift that keeps our lust for infinity alive. As a passage in the New Testament puts it, "With us this is impossible, but with God all things are possible." To sustain this perspective is to keep possibility alive against the tide of the impossible, and this hope becomes fertile spawning ground for religion. It allows the incomprehensible infinity to come alive within the fields of finitude.

Yet, open possibility remains fraught with dark temptation. We easily latch on to it as sufficient to override the impossibility inherent in the infinite. The ego and its attendant overreaching easily falls prey to presumption at this point. Hence, the great temptation, cupidity, from the Latin cupiditas, referring to the basic desire to take everything up into ourselves. Because we can imagine open possibility, we become smug and grandiose in our reach for mastery of the impossible. Much of the reach for the stars hype constantly pushed through the media, especially in America, often and easily degenerates into the folly of imagining that our possibilities actually conquer the realm of the impossible. This belongs to the desire for everything!

One of the more common and utterly misleading clichés of our time is this: "You can be or do anything you want to be or do." This mindless overreaching is by no means limited to cultural extravagance. Religion itself can and does succumb to exactly this nonsense. For instance, any religious form that presents itself as containing "the absolute," whatever that can possibly mean, has already succumbed to the fatefully self-deluding temptation. Indeed, this may be religion's temptation without peer, religion's own cupidity, that is to say, the *sin* of religion.

All of this is to suggest that, as the religious sensibility comes into play through the encounter of our finitude with imagined infinity, the lust for infinity can abort or suffer misdirection in the attempt to articulate itself as religion. Another way of saying this is that, given the religious sensibility, it does not necessarily follow that everyone will express the sensibility in ways we commonly construe as religion.

A common argument holds that every human being is religious but that religion expresses itself in endlessly diverse ways that may not include what we usually take religion to be. Paul Tillich, the noted twentieth-century theologian, comes close to this position. His famous general definition of religion is this: "Religion is a state of being ultimately concerned." This definition is surely broad enough to cover a multitude of options. In fact, the only time I heard Tillich speak, he used this very phrase. During discussion afterward someone asked him to give an example of what he called an "ultimate concern." Tillich turned and looked out a window behind him, where he could see a tennis court. He turned back and said, "Tennis will do." This shocked most of our fledgling minds. Tennis! A Religion? He proceeded to add that tennis is a very poor choice for one's ultimate concern but that it still could be for some people.

Anyone who has observed a sports fanatic can hardly argue with

Tillich. His point is that anything whatsoever can be taken as an ultimate concern, but the test is to orient one's self to a concern that is genuinely *ultimate*. (Based on years of reading Tillich, I find that *ultimate* could easily be replaced with *infinite*.)

Implicit in Tillich's view is the idea that the religious sensibility of which I am speaking may not issue in a developed or formal religion as it is generally understood. If an atheist's atheism can be her ultimate concern and therefore her religion, then we have a broad definition indeed. Further implied, however, is the idea that the religious sensibility is still alive among those who boldly reject or resist any manifest religion whatsoever. It remains alive to the extent that they continue to lust for infinity by reaching for the impossible, the ultimate, as though it were possible.

It might be helpful here to examine the three most basic strategies we may use to try to come to terms with the pressure of our lust for infinity and the religious sensibility. The first strategy is the denial or rejection of infinity altogether. Many voices in the modern world, dating from the Enlightenment, find it sufficient to draw limits around the finite possibilities and deny or reject that there is anything more. A common name for this strategy is *reductionism*. Simply stated, the reductionist takes any claim regarding the infinite and reduces it to a finite claim. When Freud, for instance, claims that belief in a "heavenly Father" is *only* a misguided projection of our need for the security of our human father onto the fictitious heavenly substitute, he is offering a classic case of reductionism. Numerous other examples could be given. I might add that a careful reading of Freud's life and career, and especially his drive for "immortal greatness," may suggest that the lust for infinity was still very much upon him.

This modern attempt to reject religion by subverting the lure of the infinite characterizes the age of secularization. The word *secular* derives from the Latin *saeculum*, meaning "this present age" or, implicitly, "this present world." The idea is to confine the realm of human interest to the world that is in principle available to human experience, inquiry, and understanding. If there is any consideration of infinity in this context, it is the quantitative notion of infinity found in mathematics. There is no qualitative infinity, or if there is, we have no way of making it available to us, much less participating in it. Therefore, we can safely neutralize or dismiss it. This way of thinking, obviously, undercuts the very core of religion as an expression of the human condition.

No doubt the *spirit of secularization* has dominated Euro-American culture increasingly since the eighteenth century, and vast numbers of people affected by it live as though the religious dimension of existence is obsolete and moot, or, at most, tangential. Nevertheless, people continue to express one or another sort of *ultimacy*, such as the variety of ideologies arising in the twentieth century. Nationalism comes to mind. These ideologies are sometimes even called *quasireligions* or *surrogate religions*, because they function or behave as though driven by the lust for infinity. This fact supports the conviction that this primordial religious sensibility has not been eliminated even in this age devoted to swallowing up infinity into itself.

Recent trends in thinking, usually under the vague and often abused term postmodern, challenge the excesses of extreme secularization. There are signs of a rather nebulous resurgence of trafficking in the sacred under such slippery terms as *spirituality*, which we discussed earlier. Predictions of a process of resacralization or re-enchantment are evident, and insofar as this is the case, it speaks to the tenacity of the religious sensibility, even in the most cultured reaches of modernity.

Still, if we granted that secularization is being challenged, it does not mean that secularization is near the brink of its demise. Too many contemporaries continue to live boldly within the confines of immediate this worldly boundaries to contend otherwise. The strategy of denying, or at least ignoring, the infinite continues to prevail for many people today and still dominates in Western civilization.

A second strategy for coming to terms with the pressure of our lust for infinity is more peculiar. It entails the denial or rejection of our finitude. At first blush this denial seems absurd, but consider some instances. In the ancient world, and continuing into the present, a movement—or general attitude—known as *Gnosticism* holds one or another version of the idea that this world—the domain of finitude—is illusory. If we find the secret or *gnosis* of life, we can rise above or escape the bondage of our finitude. This way of thinking takes on endless variations. I have in mind Christian Science as one modern example. When its teachings include a rejection of the reality of the body and bodily conditions, it is being Gnostic. Likewise in the popular New Age movement when Shirley McClain and many others declare, "I am God," they seek to sidestep or minimize the hard demands of finitude by dissolving it into a presumed easy identification with the infinite. I find that Hinduism and Buddhism, when they insist that all (finite) existence is illusory and trapped in *samsara* or *maya*, they appear to be offering their own version of the Western Gnostic story-line.

The strategy of diminishing finitude often finds expression in numerous spiritual, as opposed to religious, movements or orientations. Indeed, many such advocates are deliberately striving to bypass the religious dimension altogether by dissolving the need for it. They do so by eliminating or depreciating finitude as decisive to the human condition. They consider themselves to be going beyond religion and any need to mediate or at least contend with the tension between finitude and the infinite. Thus, they triumphantly declare that they have overcome religion through spirituality and the discovery of this or that *wholeness* or *oneness*.

While this current trend began on the fringes of popular culture through the New Age Movement, the thinking associated with spirituality has broken out of these confines and appears in the general populous. Such topics of discussion as Spirituality and Business Leadership are enough to illustrate this. Further, this way of thinking has filtered into the more traditional forms of institutional religion and appears in one or another muted expression. This process may not be exactly deviant, but its capacity to address the actual conditions of human existence remains to be shown, especially where the condition includes severe suffering and other forms of human fragility.

To summarize, I have mentioned two ways of striving to overcome the dialectical tension of our finitude as we imagine and lust for infinity or the impossible. One denies the infinite, or at least our association with it, and the other denies our finitude or diminishes it to a nuisance. The former tries to diminish the need for religion by reducing it to something strictly within the bounds of finitude, such as serving a social need or as a psychological crutch. The latter tries to rise above religion by arriving at the infinite through *gnosis* or some version of enlightenment.

A third strategy is more common and in the end becomes a temptation integral to every attempt to *translate* the religious sensibility into an actual religion. This strategy is more complex and requires greater detailed attention. Here we move from the existential origin of religion in the Primary Impulse to its historical origins, where the religious sensibility takes explicit *form*.

I discussed the concept of form earlier, and here I want to apply the idea more directly to how the religious sensibility becomes translated into the actual religions we encounter in the world. As noted before, we have an inherent urge to form. This is the way we strive to *manage* the buzzing confusion of our finitude. Or, to say it differently, we have difficulty enough entertaining open possibility, let alone the infinite. The complexity and the threat of boundlessness are simply too much for us in our finitude. As a result, our lust for infinity and the religious sensibility strive to take form. Another way of saying the same thing is that we have a penchant for confining and controlling the infinite. Or at least vainly trying!

It could be said that the religious sensibility itself, as we become conscious of it, is in-formal or perhaps pre-formal religion already. Any articulation of the sensibility, which seeks to express our lust for infinity, no matter how preliminary, ill conceived, or perverse, is already part of the process of translating the sensibility into a religious form. As noted earlier, Georges Bataille seeks to capture this passionate basis for existence in his work *Inner Experience*. Likewise, in Carl Jung's autobiography, *Memories, Dreams, and Reflections*, he emphasizes his conviction that religion is experience. What can this mean but that religion begins to take form in the crucible of fundamental human experience? In a more systematically developed way, William James makes the same point most forcibly in *The Varieties of Religious Experience*.

All these thinkers concentrate on experience. Nothing is more concrete and vital than experience. As consciousness in its most immediate expression, experience is the grounding nexus of everything human. Little wonder, then, that the religious sensibility is said to stir itself toward the formation of religion and the religions through the stuff of experience.

But experience is not the *source* or origin of religion but the necessary medium through which religion takes form. (The source, I keep insisting, is the Primary Impulse itself as it comes to expression in the religious sensibility, which grounds any experiential expression of it.) Peter Berger warns in *The Heretical Imperative* that experience, while crucial to the formation of religion, is also a threat to the form religion takes. The reason is that experience as such cannot be controlled or managed. It cannot be brought directly into form but remains personal and inward, as well as dynamic and open-ended.

This is why formal religion waffles between honoring experience and striving to control or direct it, if not quash it. William James tries to solve the relation of religion as experience and as form by holding formal religion suspect. He sees it as a "second hand" manifestation of what properly belongs to religion: experience itself.

To appreciate the inevitability of formal religion and its worth, James, along with others who stress the primacy of experience, must be challenged. He draws too sharp a line between the personal experiential and the formal structured character of religion. Our finitude entails a drive to form, and form gives order and stability to our finitude, including the dynamics of our experience. The form need not *necessarily* or *inevitably* undermine the dynamic, although there is a perpetual tension between them and a corresponding temptation to reduce the dynamic of experiential religion to form. At its best, formal religion provides the dwelling for sacral experience while guiding and encouraging experience. This, I admit, is an ideal statement and not easily realized or maintained, but it remains the *intent* of formal religion.

To establish and sustain this line of thinking, I must introduce a decisive factor into our discussion. All that has been said thus far leaves the implication that religion is primarily, if not exhaustively, a *personal* matter—private business, as it were. And it is personal, profoundly so, but we do well to consider what *personal* means. As has often been noted, that word derives from *persona* in Latin and *prosopon* in Greek. These words originally referred to masks that actors wear on a stage to impersonate different characters. These masks, in other words, provide the actors with an identity for the purpose of relating to other characters on the stage and indirectly with the audience. Thus understood, *person* never means anything approximating "private."

To be a person is to stand forth and take on *identity* by means of relation and relation by means of identity. To be a person is to live suspended in this reciprocal process. In other words, personhood arises and expresses itself only in and through relationship. What has been missing in our pilgrimage up to this point is the full acknowledgment that there is no such thing as an isolated free-standing human being as *self* or *person*. Person or self arises within the nexus of community, that is, within relational schemes that allow the person to *come into being*, that is, to stand forth.

I insist on this point because discussions of *experience* commonly presuppose, especially in the West—and most decisively in America—that experience is a strictly private and internal matter. This view becomes clear when we recognize that no one can have anyone else's experience. In this sense, experience is private and internal. It is mine and not yours. No matter how much we share of our experiences and how *communal* they feel, no level of intimacy can overcome the fact that experiences remain distinctively *inward*.

Having admitted this, however, experience arises always in the context of relational interactions. This elemental dynamic of self-and-other lies at the core of our human condition and the very possibility of experience. This is so much the case that, among our primal experiences, we experience the other as other. It is also the source of our ability to imagine the point of view of the other and thus to stand outside of ourselves.

This brief excursus is taken to stress this truth: the translation of the religious sensibility into a formal religion with its schemes, institutions, and practices can only take place in the nexus of community. In short, the *historical origin* of religious forms is communal, while the *existential origin* rests in the quite personal, but never purely private, lust for infinity. The lust for infinity takes form communally. These two rivers, the existential and the historical, converge to articulate religion as we know it.

Collins stops at a fork in the trail and points to the right. I nod, and we pause to drink water. The day has flown by with my mind in pursuit of the murky bedrock of religion. Within an hour we're walking in the premature twilight cast by ridges and peaks to the west. Collins stops, drops his pack, and scampers off the trail and uphill. When he returns, he swings his minimalist pack onto his back and simply says, "Come on."

Some fifty yards above the trail we enter a tiny glen of soft grass surrounded by moderate boulders. Campers have been here before, but the place remains hidden and seldom used. Although it's a bit of a hike to water, I could stay here indefinitely. A soothing place tucked away, lying fallow and inviting!

We set camp quickly, pitching tents at some distance across a fire ring from each other. The trick is always to find level ground. That's where we place our tiny domiciles. I look up to find that Collins has disappeared. That's his way. What a peculiar man! He's totally unlike Ethan, but they're both peculiar. My wife observed, shortly after we married a few years ago, that I had the largest collection of weird friends she had ever known. I had to concur, but I took it as a compliment. "Orthodox" friends are seldom as stimulating.

Collins returns with three bottles of fresh water, and we cook early because we had bypassed lunch, settling for energy bars. Steaming coffee wards off the creeping chill of early evening, and we sit on convenient boulders dragging on our drinks in silence.

"Not supposed to think or talk about religion," Collins declares in a low tone. I stare at him. "It's somethin' you do right along with everything else." He says nothing for a while, then adds, "It's who you are. Native people know this. That's why their religion's pure."

From many previous conversations, always in bits and pieces, I know he does not plan to pursue this. It's his way of declaring himself on the whole subject of my pilgrimage. I'm left pondering his words. Of course, I know what he means. I've read enough writing by Native people on the way they see the world to know that Collins is simply taking their side in the matter.

Collins is not a Native American, and he never pretends to be. But he's more Indian than anything else. About fifteen years ago he married a Navajo woman. Her family objected in every way they knew how, virtually closing her off from the clan. But, as Collins put it, if a person remains faithful to who they are, Navajos will respect that.

Eventually he and his wife went deep into the reservation to visit her clan. For a long while the clan barely tolerated him. He told me they were never rude, but they practiced an uncanny silence of distance and separation. "Very effective," he said. He kept going but he also kept his mouth shut, something whites can seldom do. When her father became ill, Collins and his wife went there to help. Collins took care of the sheep.

When the father recovered, another relative, an uncle, came to Collins and asked if he would be smoked and become a member of the clan. Collins told me he was flabbergasted, but that's how the Natives do things. Their decisions seemed to come out of the blue. Collins went through the smoking ceremony and received a set of Navajo clothes and some blankets, along with a name. After his wife died from diphtheria—which she caught in Albuquerque—Collins continued to live with the clan. He lived there until he had learned to carve art in sandstone and decided to market his work. He continues to return to that region of desolate beauty when he needs, as he puts it, *uplifting*.

Collins once told me that the greatest gift he'd ever received came from his Navajo family: *the gift of silence*. I can say this much: he learned it well, and in a sense he teaches it wherever he goes. He teaches silence with silence. More than once, he's said to me, "Silence is the primary form of communication. You learn to listen." When we're together for very long, I have the feeling that he knows something unspeakable but compelling.

Religion is something you do, I say to myself as we crouch in the darkness and stare into the fire's slender rising flame.

Seventeen

> The task of (religion)...that of providing opportunities for people to touch the infinite center of all things and to grow into all that they are destined to be.
>
> John Shelby Spong

∼

I wake up to find a cup of coffee resting on a flat stone outside my tent. It has a plate over it to retain the heat. I reach out, look around for Collins, and see that he's nowhere in sight. I take the cup inside and let it prod me awake.

The first feel and sights of early morning in the wilderness are more delicious than the most body-warming drink. The sun has not yet breached the eastern horizon, but its foretaste glows along the gray-black ridge. Below, in the deep and distant valley, a cloud hides the earth in a snug protective cover. I quote Sandburg's poem, "Fog," to myself:

> The fog comes
> on little cat feet.
>
> It sits looking
> over harbor and city
> on silent haunches
> and then moves on.

Sometimes the only worthy words come from poets. I think of Ethan.

The day creatures have not yet assumed command, but a lone raven stands sentinel atop a gaunt dead pine. I raise my cup in greeting.

A twig cracks behind me, and I turn to see Collins with an armload of dry wood. He drops it, sinks to his knees, and prepares a morning blaze. I watch him move with ease and studied care to lay the wood. He is a priest at worship, setting out the elements for a liturgy to the new day. I stand stark still, in reverence for the simplicity of the sacred process. If I spoke of it, he'd pretend to be insulted or snicker at my metaphoric excess, but he'd understand.

After breakfast I assume we'll pack and hike, but Collins only squats against an aspen stump and watches the fire. I wash dishes and walk downhill for water. It takes a while, and when I return, Collins is gone. Another one of his magical disappearing acts!

Uncertain about the day, I walk aimlessly around our hideaway. I keep looking out to see if he's coming. I find myself fretting about what to do—waiting for Godot? It's amazing how we—or at least I—take cues from other people. I keep wondering what Collins wants or expects. In my frustration I'm tempted to complain about his disappearances, but then I catch myself. I don't agree with Sartre that "Hell is other people," but they are a test for us. He's not even here, and I still feel his absence as a palpable presence, testing.

My thoughts again spin away toward Ethan, and I conjure images of where he might be and what he could be doing this morning. He and Collins merge in my mind to become tiny lively clowns, tricksters dancing around the fire and taunting my restless presumption. "Friends!" I mutter aloud. "The first sign of infinity." The words burst forth from somewhere below consciousness. Then I think, *they're the thing most immediately irreducible to me or my wishes. They're always beyond. . .*

This thought transforms my ill-conceived anxiety into reflection and before I know what I'm doing, I've retrieved my journal from the tent and begun jotting notes. Thoughts of other people, of Martin Buber's immortal "Thou," and the whole business of coming to ourselves through meeting and being met, spin themselves through my notations. When Buber declares "All real living is meeting," he captures this most astounding truth: *other people are our most direct and immediate encounter with the infinite*. Not that other people *are* the infinite, but they stand in for it by refusing to be a function or extension of me while at the same time making claim upon me by merely do so—I practice the most fundamental and universal form of *idolatry*. I become God.

If and when, on the contrary, I allow other people to lay claim to me, to bind me with them in my own finitude, they become proxies for the infinite or windows into the infinite. This is another way of saying that transcendence begins with other people, and when I experience transcendence in this way, I participate *presence*.

To oversimplify somewhat, it boils down to this: through presence I am first claimed from beyond myself by another of my kind, a person, a member of my species! Whatever else the infinite includes, it rises to consciousness here.

This insight takes me back to thoughts from yesterday about how religion takes form in and through human community. Community is not its origin. That's where I break with Emile Durkheim and the social theorists who ground religion in society and human solidarity. They may be right in a historical sense, but the origin of this very capacity to form religion in and through our common life lies in the existential impulse that grounds religion, and that impulse in turn rests on our finitude as it encounters infinity.

I speak here of *formal religion*, that is, religion as we commonly think of it in the world: Hinduism, Buddhism, Taoism, Confucianism, Sikhism, Shintoism, Islam, Christianity, Judaism, and others, to say nothing of the array of indigenous forms—and the list continues indefinitely. All of these religions *take form* in the matrix of human community, at least, in part because our first encounter with the infinite other is the human other. When human beings conspire—literally "breathe together"—for survival and flourishing in the world, the religious interest is already in play, and religion becomes articulate in this setting. Thus, the foundational lust for infinity takes shape in and through community.

I find myself thinking about my remarriage a few years ago: a dynamic still taking form.

****

Exploration into the unknown marks the man's life. He has seen beyond the veil, and he knows there is more, endlessly more. Every avenue of adventure invites him. Experience from the most intimate encounters to the far reaches of speculation into possibility draw him beyond the confines of his former life. The man knows nothing, and the not-knowing is his promise of the future.

A spinning cascade of days, weeks, months, and years yields a gracious chaos. The man barely keeps his equilibrium, inward within himself and outward with the world. He is carefully careless about everything except his involvement. In the deep of night he wonders, and occasionally trembles, at what unfolds, as he follows after—what?

But with his fall into life's abyss comes the inevitable landing. It does not come with a crash but with a noticeable touchdown. The man finds the woman. No! The woman finds the man. Nothing sudden. Only the rising to consciousness of her presence, her being there! Young. Zesty. Intense. Spirited. Reaching for life, for meaning, for a doorway barely ajar. Intelligent. Devoted. Restless. Daring. Willing to blunder without backing away. Peeling away her weighty childhood in favor of something yet to reveal itself. Passion wed to compassion and unafraid to name injustice. Never interested in perfection but committed to doing, feeling, thinking—and always, always breathing.

The lover-mate does not catch the man, for she is no trapper. She releases him even further. With her he finds himself unleashed, but he cannot fathom his good fortune. He casts about to find a center, to locate himself in this new constellation. It does take time, for the man is slow. The mystery of bonding comes to birth, and writhes and cries its way to life. The force of womanhood, disclosed once in hallucinogenic visions, becomes palpable.

The lover-mate and the man wed in a fit of expectancy. They begin giving form to their passion. The tiny cabin, the children, the moves, ever striving to be themselves with each other, turning solitary adventures into solidarity. All of the strains of merged lives surface, rise to crisis, and yield imprints that make the twining fuller.

The lover-mate is unfettered by the world of orthodoxies that have marked the man's past. He waits. She, at once drawn and repelled by religion, enters upon discovery by a different avenue. The era of spiritual quest, spawned in bewildering variety, offers promise, and she pursues it, drawing the man with her. Together, they take the dare to explore the inner mindscapes and terrain of greater spiritual promise. They expose themselves and probe the possibilities with abandon. For a time the man and the lover-mate release themselves from the confines of spiritual prohibition and prescribed expression. They taste from various wells of insight until they discern the boundaries of this option. They recognize the propensity of spiritual life to be captured by ego and turned to self-serving adventures into ephemeral clouds of presumption.

Disillusionment dawns gradually at first, and then with bold awakening they turn away. Too many pitfalls of self-indulgence lie in wait. The excursus has not been in vain. Much has been gleaned about the possibilities and demands of an interior orientation. This interior awareness is not lost, but prepares them for the return to the harder course of life " in this present age."

Promise marks a fresh venture. What have the great traditions of Western faith to offer here and now "in this present age?" The man once again explores the faith once delivered, and the lover-mate enters seminary. Together they plot a course within but at the edge of the Great Tradition. They are able to participate and honor the magnificent symbols that undergird their past and offer continuing spiritual sustenance. Yet, all the while, the man and the lover-mate remain free to examine, interrogate, and hold all of it under suspicion. A novel place to dwell! They live at once "inside" and also "outside." They are committed but live in freedom through and beyond commitment. The measureless "something more" lures them beyond the given. They do not know what it is, but they feel its pull.

****

What drives religious formation is the dynamism of our lust for infinity. Without that spiritual force, religion would not emerge to give order and direction to the dynamism—and often to limit, control, and stifle it!

Collins materializes and finds me pouring over notations. He has a limp rabbit's carcass in his left hand. I stare at it, and he says, "Didn't bring enough meat, so I set a little trap up the hill last night." With experienced hands he proceeds to skin and gut our dinner. When he finishes cutting the meat into pieces, he places them in a plastic container and then into a covered pan, and walks toward the stream below. He'll put it in the water to keep it cool for tonight.

He returns. "Hey," he says jauntily, "The Great Spirit provides! Write that in your little book."

I break out some lunch snacks and spread them on one of the boulders. We eat. Collins' hands still show traces of the rabbit's blood. Life taken—or is it given?—for life. What an uncanny scheme! Watching him squat in that Navajo way he learned on the reservation, I see him morph into the *original man*, blood on his hands from administering death so he can live. He represents the first signs of the formation of religion: the sacrificial kill in honor of continued living. Could this have been the initial mystery that pressed primal humanity toward the religious form with its rituals and tales reaching to engage the mystery, to penetrate it? Who knows?

My mind sweeps along this thought trajectory all the way to human sacrifice and cannibalism. For only the flash of a moment I can see, as through a thin veil, the passionate attempt of earliest humanity to literally swallow the infinite as it manifests in the other human being. Is this how it all started? Even the most learned and careful scholars can only offer informed conjectures. Hunches! The origins of our kind and of our religions remain, and will remain, hidden in the murky fog of a receding antiquity. Yet, my momentary hallucinatory glimpse, through Collins, in quest of origins, speaks to—the possibility.

What we can know is that, regardless of historical origin, the phenomenon of religion has emerged from our primeval roots to take form in the religions we now recognize in such vast array. With this truth in mind we return to the innate human urge to give experience meaning through form. Hence, the world's religions!

Collins breaks my concentration by standing and saying—or rather announcing—"We'll stay here today and head for Lake Katherine tomorrow." With that, he vanishes once again. Nothing loathe, I make my way south toward an outcropping of boulders, always my favorite perch. It has to do with vista!

When I arrive, I find it more massive than I had expected. It takes me a while to pick my way to its face and to rock climb to the top. I sit with my legs dangling and allow the vista of the now fog-lifted valley below to engulf me. The vastness!

For some time I sit meditatively, allowing the expanse around and below to engulf me. Without warning, my eye catches a stirring in the underbrush below me on the trail. As I stare, a mountain lion materializes as if by magic. He saunters onto the trail with a regal calm as though he—or is it a she, I can't tell—reigned without peer. Checking the direction of the wind, I am pleased to note that I am upwind of the creature.

As I watch the beast, barely breathing, he (she?) takes on the aura of a vision, capturing the inner vitality of the wilderness. It is as though we become a distillation of the vitality and spiritual force of the wilderness itself. I find myself whispering Blake's magnificent peon to the tiger:

> Tyger, tyger, burning bright
> In the forests of the night,
> What immortal hand or eye
> Could frame thy fearful symmetry?

Then I recall the fifth stanza, my favorite:

> When the stars threw down their spears,
> And watered heaven with their tears,
> Did he smile his work to see?
> Did he who made the Lamb make thee?

The holy, it seems, unveils itself in the most unexpected places. This mountain lion, unbidden, manifests the sacrality of these high places. As the creature walks down the trail for perhaps a hundred feet, then veers off and away, my reverie continues for some time. I realize anew that this vast clime is exactly the proper locus for attending the religious sensibility.

Where was I? I ask myself; then I remember.

With our growing sensitivity to the planetary scope of diversity in culture and religion, a new line of questioning about religion has gradually emerged. If there are so many religions, how can any one of them claim finality to the exclusion of all others? Among these many expressions are there perhaps underlying patterns that unite all religions? Or, is each religion so unique it can only be understood from within its own history and cultural context? How can religions positively engage each other, or are they hopelessly at odds? What may we learn from comparing religions with each other? These are only a few key queries in the current effort to make sense of the convoluted and entangled mass we broadly designate as *religion*.

In recent years, this line of questioning has inspired a new phenomenon among colleges and universities in America: religious studies. Scholars from different fields seek to wrest from the phenomenon of religious multiplicity some degree of coherence. As always, these scholars are divided over whether and how this might be achieved. I participate in this current process, but a perpetual question haunts me as I teach and pursue my studies: *What does the intense study of religion do to religion?* In fact, this question is one that compelled me to undertake a pilgrimage in these mountains.

I'll state my problem in a different way. People practicing their religion in community do so with a different understanding of the religion from observers of their religion who do not practice it. In Religious Studies, this has come to be known as the *insider-outsider problem*. On the one hand, insiders are hopelessly biased in their interpretation and understanding of their own religion, or so we generally assume. On the other hand, outsiders can never grasp the vitality, the passionate dynamism of the insider's religious participation. This is a dilemma indeed.

Here is how I come to terms with this dilemma, at least for the present. First, I find people who participate in no formal religion at all to be at a singular disadvantage. Even if they are broadly sympathetic toward religion or toward a given religion, they do not adequately grasp what is taking place. Only through participation can they *understand* or *discern* the throb and thrust of actual religious life. Outsiders may somewhat assuage this disadvantage by an awareness of their own more fundamental, religion-like commitments, but their perspective remains limited by observing from outside.

Second, this point of view does not mean that outsiders have nothing to contribute to understanding religion. On the contrary, they may, to some extent, have greater comprehension, that is, broader *perspective* on the religion under consideration. They can certainly more often ask penetrating questions. Furthermore, if they seek to understand a number of religions, they may discover threads of commonality that suggest something about the very core of the formal religions which insider practitioners may miss.

Third, while insiders know best what their religion means for them, their failure of distance limits their ability to interpret their own participation. This limitation may be modified for some practitioners in this way: Theologian Paul Tillich speaks of "the circle of faith" and of people entering that circle through "the shock of recognition." This is another way of describing what happens when one moves from outsider to insider.

Then he proceeds to discuss a special capacity for at least some insiders. They are "theologians," and to serve this role for fellow insiders, they learn to live both "inside" the circle of faith and "outside" of it. That is, they serve the insider's interest by cultivating the capacity to make excursions outside the circle. In this way, insiders may learn how their own faith orientation relates to the larger "outside" frame, to the world. Admittedly, this is a relatively sophisticated role for any insider, and not many insiders appear capable of it or even interested in it. But it is possible!

To make this discussion more personal, I am a religious insider who participates in a particular formal religion. This participation, in part, drives my effort to understand religion. In a sense, I'm striving to understand myself as a religious person. I've never been able to shake religion, even though I can be highly critical of it and of my own form of it. This critical capacity is what has allowed me to stand both inside and outside the circle of faith. Although I have some advantage by standing, as we might put it, in the borderland of faith, it has a notable limitation. I can only be most fully inside my own faith.

When I address another religion, I am simply one more outsider and suffer from all of the associated limitations, with one modest exception! As an insider in one specific formal religion, I enjoy a general sensitivity to religion in principle that outsiders not associated with any formal religion do not often possess. Beyond that, I remain an outsider to other forms of religion and must recognize the way this outsider status circumscribes the extent of my understanding of them.

Finally, what all of this leads me to conclude is that we need profound empathy and endless collaboration in the effort to comprehend more adequately the phenomenon of religion. This is true for understanding my own religion as an insider. To use a cliché, outsider perspectives help me "see myself as others see me." Or, to summarize, movement toward a more adequate understanding and appreciation of religion requires the whole community of those who attempt to do so, and they include both insiders and outsiders. Not that the effort will ever fully grasp what we seek. Religion entails, as already noted, engagement with mystery. Furthermore, it is historically dynamic and subject to change. To grasp its depth and its shifts remains an ongoing, a living process.

Granting all I've just noted about insider and outsider approaches to religion, I do have a fundamental view of how best to examine formal religion in relation to its array of expressions. If we're going to allow the one word *religion* to serve as our umbrella term, it must have a sufficiently comprehensive and unifying use to serve that purpose.

I realize, of course, that a number of scholars are now saying that the word itself is a modern—and potentially misleading—invention, largely driven by Western colonial experiences of alien religions. Some even recommend that *religion* be dropped altogether and that we settle for the study of specific traditions in their historical and cultural contexts. This attitude tends to arise where there is suspicion or rejection of any such notion as a universal religious sensibility.

Clearly I reject this view. I hold that *existentially speaking*, human beings are inherently driven by their finite engagement with the infinite, what I keep designating as the Primary Impulse. Existential attempts to address this tension constitute the religious sensibility. Formal religions arise within primary communities in attempts to give order and form to the Primary Impulse and its consequent religious sensibility.

Several years ago I taught an interdisciplinary course with a professor of sociology. One day in class he asserted that religion cannot be defined. Immediately I challenged his claim. I agreed that there are many attempts to define religion. In fact, at the time I had a five-page collection of definitions. I also agreed that no definition is final or fully adequate, and I agreed that definitions differ according to the purposes of the person generating the definition. Nevertheless, I insisted that religion can be defined if we sufficiently recognize these limits of the definition.

My own boundary is this: I do not seek to define religion as such but only its *formal* character as it takes shape in historical communities of people. In addition, I take religion to be endlessly varied in terms of its *content*, so varied that no definition can possibly cover the actual substance of all religious forms.

Some religions are closely associated in history and substance, such as Judaism and Christianity or Hinduism and Buddhism, but even they are decisively distinct in content, that is, in conceptualization and expression. Over time their differences become even more accentuated. But if we consider the *form* of religion rather than the content, we can readily recognize "family resemblances" among virtually all religions. If this were not the case, we could hardly use the same umbrella term, religion, to designate them.

In response to my sociology colleague, I went home and worked out a definition of religion. Although I have refined it over time, I still use it in my own reflections on the formal mode of religion. It may sound stuffy and stilted on the surface, but I'm trying to be as precise as possible, as anyone should be with a definition. Here is the definition:

> Religion is a mytho-symbolic system of convictions and practices, grounded in experience and expressing communal and personal fulfillment through an unconditional transcendent orientation.

I admit that this statement is loaded, but I want to use it to make sense of religion as we see it practiced by people around the world, that is, as it takes observable form.

This definition belongs to a class known as *cluster definitions*. It offers a series of characteristics to be found in any religion, and the definition attempts to connect those characteristics in a coherent scheme by relating them to each other. Not all religions necessarily have all these characteristics, but religions tend to have most of them in one expression or another. Particular religions also tend to emphasize some characteristics and treat others as secondary or even trivial.

Finally, I confess that I do believe at least one of these characteristics is utterly necessary for a formal religion. Without it we have only a religion-like phenomenon, what I've called a *quasi* or *surrogate* religion. I have already discussed this idea, and here I wish to make clear that I intend only what is most decisively a religion, not like a religion. I will indicate the one *necessary* characteristic later. If we keep these qualifications in mind, I believe my definition can be helpful in framing what I mean by formal religion.

Let's pause again to consider the use of religion as I've employed it. I agree that the word itself and its current use derives from modern conditions. When religions were sufficiently isolated and more integrated into the dynamics of entire communities, especially tightly knit tribal communities, there was little, if any, need for the word itself. Only with the discovery of so many and such varied forms of religion did the word come into currency. This fact, however, makes little difference to my discussion of religion on this pilgrimage. Whatever has been the case, we now face a multiplicity of communal forms that express themselves in sufficiently similar ways to all be included under this one umbrella term.

It has been noted ad nauseam that religion derives from the Latin *religare*, meaning "to bind back," or some variation of that idea. If this is the case, then religion appears to presuppose that humanity has broken away, fallen away, or in some sense finds itself separated from that to which it fundamentally belongs. In short, we humans need "binding back" to some condition from which we are now alienated.

Based on my analysis of the existential basis for religion, this sense of separation can be said to rest in the tension between our finitude and the lure of the infinite. We strive to overcome the gulf we encounter between ourselves and the infinite possibility ever before us. We seek a binding to and within the infinite. This is the way I construe the "binding back" character in the word *religion*.

Looking down from my perch on these boulders, I see Collins walking below. He is following the trail we will take tomorrow. He walks along rather like the beast that recently preceded him. I cannot make out what he's carrying, but whatever it is, it's sizable and slung across his back.

The bare edge of a dark cloud appears behind me over the western mountain ridge. I turn and watch it creep into view. I can already smell rain and decide to climb down and return to camp.

Collins sits cross-legged with a large weathered grayish backpack in front of him. He's just opened it.

"Where'd you find that?" I ask.

"Up on the hill." Collins gestures back over his shoulder toward the southwest.

"Whose is it?"

"Some dead guy."

"Dead!" I spring to rapt attention.

Collins says nothing but retrieves a sheet of wrinkled paper from the top of the pack. He reads it to himself, staring at it for some time before passing it to me. I can barely make out the scribbling on it. I don't actually read it but ask, "What do you mean, 'dead guy'?"

"Well, I didn't actually find a body," Collins explains, "just some scattered clothing and a few bones. Not sure they're human, but it looks like they are. No tellin' how long he's been up there."

Stunned by Collins' matter-of-fact report, I press. "Well then, what happened to him?"

"Read the note," Collins says, pointing to the paper in my hand.

I sit on the ground near him and try to decipher the scrawl on the paper. It is scribbled in dim pencil and appears to have been written hurriedly and with a hand barely under control. I finally make out enough to ask, "Did he kill himself?"

"Looks that way to me," Collins agrees. "Must 'a been two, maybe three years ago. Not much left but this pack."

I turn back to the note and begin translating aloud: "This world's for shit. My life's for shit. Only this mountain re. . ." and I cannot make out the rest of the sentence. "I like trees and. . ." The next word might be "animals," but I can't be sure. Then the scrawling becomes larger, and I make out the rest: "Hey, mother, if you're out there and sober enough to read this, I'm supposed to say that I love you and its not your fault. But that is not true! I won't have to think about you any more and I won't have to hunt for you. I hope nobody every finds me. Nobody's ever found me so far. To hell with life!" The note is signed "*A.*"

I look up at Collins. His eyes are glassy with moisture. He once said to me, "I don't say much. I mostly feel." And he does.

After rereading the note to myself, trying to let the grim facts settle into my mind, I say, "What're we gonna do about this?"

"Grant his last wish," Collins says softly.

"What's that?"

"That nobody ever finds him. A person ought to have final wishes granted." Collins ponders before adding, "We found him, but we know how to keep silence." There's that silence again, defining the moment.

Collins begins to unload the pack. He does it as though taking inventory. Neither he nor I will keep anything. It would be disrespectful. We find a few clothes, a dead flashlight, small cookstove, a bedroll, a large piece of plastic, hunting knife, a small book that turns out to be, of all things, *Catcher in the Rye*. A map of the region is stuck between pages of the book. There's no tent, no food.

We look at the pitiful stock from the pack, and Collins concludes, "He didn't come up here to camp." He begins replacing the items in the pack, handling them with an uncommonly gentle hand as though this action were part of last rites.

When the pack is refilled and zipped, I ask, "What will we do with that?"

"Bury it," Collins says firmly. "Don't want somebody or some creature carryin' it off. Looks like they carried him away." He stands, retrieves a folding shovel he always carries on the outside of his pack, and begins walking toward the trail. I know what he's doing, and I follow.

We move briskly for almost a mile. Rain, the light afternoon kind, pelts us. Abruptly, Collins turns to the right, and we ascend a steep incline. We walk for another half hour, until he stops and points up ahead. "It's there, under that tree." An enormous lone spruce stands in an open meadow, its limbs unusually low and near the ground.

When we reach the tree and duck under a low limb, and after my eyes adjust, I spot pieces of faded reddish cloth scattered about under the spread of tree limbs. Collins points out where he found the pack leaning against the tree. Then he points to a bone on the ground, and presently I can see others. Some are broken, and most are relatively small.

"Either bear or coyote, not sure which. Maybe ravens too. Looks like they tore him up and carried most of him off." We can see a few bits and pieces of bone and clothing trailing to the south beyond the tree's cover. The scene is at once vivid and stark but also fantastic and not quite graspable.

We continue walking around the tree and, widening our circling each time around it. Collins goes back to the spot where he assumes this unknown man or boy had ended his life. He leans down and picks up a small rusted revolver lying almost invisible in the, but. . ." He leaves the sentence dangling to suggest that, even so, the little weapon had done its work.

Without saying more, we begin to pick up pieces of cloth and fragments of bone, anything we consider to have been part of him.

The slight drizzle passes away to the east and leaves a chill in its wake. Collins locates a place downhill from the tree and begins to dig with his shovel. The process is arduous, and we spell each other. By the end we've dug a hole about three feet into the earth. Our fingers are covered with the soft loam, and we're sweating.

We take the residue of the man's life, wrap it in a worn flannel shirt from his pack, and take the bundle and pack to the grave. Collins places the pack in the hole, and I add the bundle. Covering the hole takes far less time than digging it, and when we finish, the mound of dirt has a miniature grave-like appearance. Collins walks away unceremoniously, and I assume our work is finished until I see him carrying two rocks toward the grave. We sit on the ground while he takes an all-purpose tool from its sheath on his belt and begins to etch the stone. He works for several minutes before I see what he's creating: the letter A.

The larger stone serves as a support for the smaller flat one with the solitary letter displayed for the world. We stand in solemn recognition of a human life. Collins says something about honoring all life, even the anonymous ones that pass our way, and he then says some sing-song things in Navajo, looking up to the sky a couple of times. When he finishes, I repeat the Our Father, and we stand motionless.

As we make our way down the ridge in the twilight, I ask, as much to myself as to Collins, "I wonder whether we should report this to someone, maybe at the ranger station."

"None of their business," Collins quickly insists. "A man has the right to die unnoticed, even if I have the obligation to acknowledge him. I did not seek him. He came to me as I walked. So, I acknowledge him and also his request not to be found. Both." He speaks calmly but emphatically. An addendum to the benediction.

We walk to camp. I sit on a stump thinking. It dawns on me that death is the definitive anonymity, final and eternal.

Eighteen

The Divine was expansive, but religion was reductive. Religion attempted to reduce the Divine to a knowable quantity with which mortals might efficiently deal, to pigeonhole it once and for all so that we never had to reevaluate it. With hammers of cant and spikes of dogmas, we crucified and crucified again, trying to nail to our stationary altars the migratory light of the world.

Tom Robbins

~

"Where is he now?" Collins asks the question out of the blue after an hour's silence. We're chewing away on fresh fried rabbit and nibbling at steaming vegetables from a freeze-dry pouch.

"Who? Ethan?" I want to know.

"No," Collins states. "Him," and he nods to the south toward the grave.

"Oh, A," I acknowledge. "Well, he's dead. That's where he *is*!" I emphasize the last word.

"Is that all there is to it?" Collins asks with interest, seeming strangely animated by the discovery of the afternoon. He looks at me as if expecting a revelation.

"Do you mean to ask if there's any continuing existence for him?" I ask.

"Somethin' like that. You're forever pokin' and frettin' over religion, but it seems to me, in the end, to come down to that question: where is A now?"

I suspect a trap but I'm so pleased that Collins wants to talk that I rise to the bait. "Yeah, religion is about destiny. Fate is there for everyone to experience, but destiny's about whether fate makes some ultimate sense. . .I mean, whether it's going somewhere. At the same time, destiny doesn't necessarily mean something like, say, personal immortality. It could mean something el. . ."

"Don't lay out theories. I know those. And I can make more up, if I need to. Do you believe that man up there, whoever he was, is somewhere, anywhere, right now, and if he is somewhere, where is he?"

"I don't know, and no one else knows either. Religions propose different answers, and followers usually accept them, but no one actually knows, nobody's been there, so to speak."

Collins obviously has something more to say in response to my stumbling effort to appreciate the complexity...the impossibility, of the question. "It has to do with 'invisibility'," he begins. "Things that cannot be seen but are real...maybe more real than what we do see."

"What do. . ." I try to interrupt.

"Let me finish," Collins insists, raising his hand like a school child. "Life itself's not visible, but we still believe it's real. Living things are different from dead things, and the difference is life. Or, as Native people usually speak of it, *spirit*. But spirit, like life, is invisible. It's like the wind. You can't see it. You can only see how it moves things. . . trees, grass and such. Life's the same way. You can see the body move and all of that, but you don't really see the life itself. Even when you're alive, where exactly is the life?" He looks off in the distance for about a minute. "And what happens to it when what was alive is dead?"

"Maybe," I retort, "the life simply went out of him like a fire goes out when the fuel's spent."

"But where did it go when it *went out*?" Collins comes down hard on the last words. "Did it just disappear? That's really peculiar for something that seems as real. . .as full of vinegar. . .as life."

"I heard a physicist say that nothing that exists in nature ever disappears, but it may change forms so much that we no longer recognize it. That's an educated guess, of course, but it makes sense to me." I see Collins nod in response, and I continue. "So, with A it could be something like this. Maybe the very specific characteristics that made A exactly who he was. . .his personality I suppose. . .might no longer exist. That's what I believe. And his body simply takes on other forms, 'dust to dust' as it's commonly put. But the life—or maybe it should be called something else, like *consciousness*—is the mystery for me."

"Like I said, Native peoples usually call it *spirit*, and it's taken to be more real than anything else, only it belongs to the invisible world and not the physical world. It's sometimes called the *dream world*. That man we buried today is somewhere, maybe not in his. . .like you said. . .'personality,' but his life-stuff or spirit continues. Maybe it's resting in the dream world. A tribal elder once told me he visited that world every night and sometimes he hated to come back."

Collins' last words drift off, and the conversation ends as bluntly as it began. He's back into the realm of that silence he inhabits. It's as though he makes occasional raids into communication and then goes away, where talk evaporates. The night and lure of sleep hide everything, and we drift off to our tents.

The next morning breakfast over, we begin packing up, our movements deft and mechanical. We're loaded and hiking within less than an hour, but not before carefully policing the site. As I keep stressing, "Leave it as though you were never there." That's our motto. It's disgusting the way some of these momentary habitats are trashed by campers, and we've always been zealous about honoring every place we dwell, no matter how briefly. It's a kind of obsession with our breed of packers.

Single file, moving briskly, we make our way toward Lake Katherine, our next destination. Presently, Collins veers off and up to the right. At first I think he's decided to bushwhack, but shortly I realize he is walking toward the grave. When we arrive, we approach the earthen mound slowly, with a sort of solemnity. We stand before the tiny grave for several minutes before Collins turns, and I follow him back to the trail. I can tell from his brief loquacious outburst last night and this visit to the grave that Collins is moved by his discovery of A's remains. He may never speak of it again, but he knows something, perhaps unfathomable, as a result.

The easy rhythm of our gradually climbing hike frees my mind to plunder afresh the perennial topic of this pilgrimage. At first I ruminate on last night's conversation about death and destiny, but what intrigues me about Collins' comments is that one word, *invisibility*. Somehow it relates to the word that has dominated my thinking about the Primal Impulse and religious sensibility: *infinity*. Could it be that invisibility is the edge of infinity, where it begins?

Yesterday, when I considered how human beings seem to represent the infinite, it had to do with something intangible—and therefore invisible—a kind of underlying force, elusive but revealed in and through the face that stares at us. I can only experience another person externally. What goes on *within* the other remains always invisible to me, tucked away in personal interiority. I can only guess at what might hide there, and even if the other reveals some inner workings to me, I can only receive its external form in words and gestures. No matter how much intimacy or empathy I have for another, their inner life remains, yes, *invisible*. To engage this invisibility is to touch the edge of infinity.

A fragment of poetry from Rilke's *Ninth Elegy* comes to mind, unbidden:

> Earth, isn't this what you want: an invisible
> re-arising in us? Is it not your dream
> to be one day invisible? Earth! Invisible!

Religion, it occurs to me, arises as the attempt to render the invisible infinity visible. In other words, to give it form. Hence, formal religion as I've been thinking of it. Since specific formal religions are what almost always come to mind when the word *religion* is used, I want to examine further and in some detail, not the endless external variety of religious forms, but something more akin to the *underlying form* that allows us to speak of any and all religious forms with the one word, *religion*. I indicated this idea of a kind of universal form yesterday. Now, to examine the idea further I want to return to that definition I worked out some years ago. To restate it:

> Religion is a mytho-symbolic system of convictions and practices, grounded in experience and expressing communal and personal fulfillment through an unconditional transcendent orientation.
> As I admit, this statement is dense, but if it's unpacked, element by element, I believe it articulates the underlying form of formal religion in a helpful way.

As I admit, this statement is dense, but if it's unpacked, element by element, I believe it articulates the underlying form of formal religion in a helpful way.

****

When I say that religion is mytho-symbolic, I combine two intimately connected ideas. As mentioned earlier in this pilgrimage, symbols and the symbolic are decisive for human understanding. The moment we move from the immediate rush of experience to any attempt to grasp the experience and render it understandable, we do so by means of imagination and through the genius of the symbol. Symbols are the gift of imagination and the medium of *meaning* and of *valuation*. Insofar as we seek to make sense of our existence, we humans indwell the domain of symbols. In religion, this is most acutely the case for at least one reason, if for no other: If religion seeks to make the invisible visible, how else might it occur but through symbol? To render the invisible *there*, we must generate symbols to unveil it.

In my defining concept, the symbolic is hyphenated with *mythic*. Symbols are not free-standing isolated bearers of meaning. Symbols tend to blend toward an overarching symbolic unity, and when the symbols are taken together, they cluster to generate something like a vision, a whole-life perspective, what in a more rationalized way we call a *worldview*. Myth is a way of comprehending and engaging the whole of what makes sense to us. Myth is the ancient—and also very current—means of bearing this unitive scheme of symbols.

The most foundational and ready expression of myth is the *story*, but not just any story. Mythic stories intend to articulate the unity of symbolic meaning so that we are assured of the big picture or some significant portion of it, and our place in relation to it. Not all mythic stories are necessarily, and certainly not explicitly, religious, but all religions take form and are borne by means of myth as I use it here. Myth is not only inevitable but of immeasurable worth to the integrity of formal religion.

I am tempted to pause here and defend myth, but this is not my purpose. I am not saying whether myth is a good thing or a bad thing but only attempting to describe its inevitable role in religion, as well as in meaningful life in general. I could extend the discussion to show how most of the dimensions of human understanding—including science, believe it or not—participate in myth, but I need not go there.

Suffice to say, since the eighteenth century, myth has suffered by being reduced to a synonym for *false* or *fiction*. This association is unfortunate, because myth, at root, is always about truth, not about factual or literal truth, but about the comprehensive sense one has of how things hang together. In other words, myth is about *meaningful truth*, the way a people—or a person—construes itself in relation to its *world*.

****

My definition includes an even stuffier and more loaded word: *system*. I use it to refer to something already stated more than once. Human beings have the urge to give form to things. This propensity belongs to the human condition of finitude because otherwise we become lost in the uncertainty and insecurity of impinging infinity. Here I suggest that we express form by forming systems, complex organizations by which we can comprehend particulars in relation to wholes. Religion, no less than any other dimension of human existence, does this, and its specific way of doing so is by the network of symbols held in mythic unity. Moreover, systems seek closure or completeness or perhaps comprehensiveness. Systems aim at tying a bow around the otherwise chaotic flow of lived experience and the stream of consciousness.

****

But more must be included, if we are to grasp the mytho-symbolic system that constitutes religion. For example, this system articulates itself through *convictions*. I use this word deliberately to avoid more religiously loaded terms like *beliefs* or *doctrines*. As I use the word, *conviction* may include these aspects of religion, but it is also a more inclusive word. It includes both cognitive and affective features. Granted, the cognitive relates to beliefs and doctrine. Adherents to religions, either explicitly or implicitly, tend to believe things and to order their beliefs in something like a system of doctrines imbedded in myth. We might even say these systems of belief and doctrine are rationalized mythology. Some religions, of course, emphasize belief more strongly than others. For instance, Western Christianity has given special emphasis to belief and doctrine, while Hinduism or Taoism holds beliefs more implicitly and less central.

I use *convictions* to include affective or emotive aspects of religion as well. I refer here to experiences of *felt commitment and devotion*. Feeling a sense of total immersion in one's religion is common to religions, but again, some religions—and some versions of given religions—stress this emotive immediacy more than others. To state the case more generally, religion tends to *move* its practitioners one way or another and some more than others. In this sense religion bears within its practitioners a passionate devotion.

****

Religion is always about *doing* something. What a given religion may consider appropriate *practice* differs notably from what another religion may expect. Yet, participants are expected to be practitioners, usually in at least three respects. First, religions express their mytho-symbolic system through *ritual* and *ceremony*. Even the least liturgical religions have some minimal communal practices that identify the participants and express the mythic truth held by them. Other religions may concentrate more centrally on the role of ritual and ceremony to establish and maintain their form.

Second, religions require or encourage a particular *way of life*, including habits of dress and other common gestures that demonstrate one's identification with, and loyalty to, the religion. Again, some religions minimize such practices, while others may deem them as evidences of commitment to the religion and of the sanctity of participants. Hasidic Jews dress and behave in distinctive ways that identify them, but a Baptist Christian may be indistinguishable in daily life from anyone else in a society.

Third, followers of most religions are expected to practice *moral precepts*. That is, they are to act toward others in a moral way by following whatever precepts their religion may dictate. Moral practices may focus on the religious community itself, the larger world, or both. Some religions are more morally focused than others. In Judaism and Islam moral practices are more overtly central, while in some versions of Buddhism, they are more muted and implicit or may center in a certain attitude, such as compassion, more than in specific moral precepts. Still, morality has historically been closely tied to religion, and people in general tend to expect religiously committed people to behave with some sort of moral rectitude. Although this expectation may have been frequently, unfulfilled, it nevertheless persists.

****

The idea that religion is *grounded in experience* has become more central to Western thinking in the twentieth century. In Britain and America this idea's roots reach even further back to what was called *enthusiasm* in eighteenth-century England. Not only is the affective and emotive quality stressed, but there is an emphasis on direct, immediate, and highly personal encounter between the person and the Divine—or whatever comprehensive symbols of infinity are embraced. From this stress, for instance, grew the American revival movement with its emphasis on the conversion experience. Later, experiential stress came to include demonstrative practices and led to what became known as the Charismatic Movement, especially in American Pentecostalism. Such "enthusiasm" is not the exclusive property of Western Christianity. It is actually prevalent in ecstatic expressions within many other traditions, including Hasidism in Judaism, Hinduism, and Primal religions. As I've watched Whirling Dervishes in Turkey, I have been struck by the experiential depth of their purpose in this practice.

Nor does experience always take an overt demonstrative expression. Experience may be mostly, if not entirely, *interior*, and many liturgical and devotional practices aim, not at demonstrative experience, but more nearly to guide one into a stillness in which one's inner orientation is central.

If we focus on America, this appreciation of direct religious experience as the source or core of religion began early. Jonathan Edwards, in response to the early sweep of revival across the eastern American seaboard in the 1740s, wrote a dramatic defense of emotive religious experience: *Treatise Concerning Religious Affections*. With William James' classic, *The Varieties of Religious Experience* a century and a half later, the emphasis on experience in Western interpretations of religion was established. James goes so far as to contend that religion is primarily, and above all else, about experience. He largely dismisses much of what I'm calling here formal religion. He identifies formal religion with its institutional expressions, and he does not much like it. He calls it "second hand," by which he means secondary and inferior to religion as experienced. He insists that *formal religion* tends to undermine the passion and immediacy of religion by controlling and delimiting its experiential force.

Certainly some religions concentrate on experience more than others, but I cannot think of any religion that does not give it some place in its scheme which makes sense. Otherwise, how does a person actually engage the religion and *participate* it? Experience is often circumscribed and shaped—indeed limited and controlled—by the other elements of religious form I have mentioned, but experience remains a vital center of manifestation for the religious sensibility. For this reason, religions—especially the more rigidly formal—have a love-hate relation to religious experience. It is difficult for any system to *control* experience, and the formality of religion tends toward at least some measure of control over the dynamism of immediate experience. This tension, which William James does not appear to understand or appreciate, may be more or less inevitable in any formal religion. More emotive religious forms control by *directing* experience and providing a mythic framework for understanding it, but this, too, is a way of constraining experience.

****

Formal religions are at once *communal and personal*. This is, I realize, true of every dimension of human existence. To be human is to dwell within the perpetual tension of self and other. It is fruitless to debate the primacy of one over the other, because they mutually entail each other. There is no human community without persons, and persons become and express personhood in and through community.

In religion, this particular tension is especially focal and often controversial. Some religions stress the personal or individual aspect over the communal or group aspect, while others do the reverse. In some respects, Buddhism is intensely personal in terms of meditation, but the tradition still stresses the sangha, the community of monks. In still other religious traditions—and especially in some sects within them—the communal is even more pronounced, such as orders of intense communal asceticism. The ancient Essenes or various forms of monasticism come to mind.

In America, with its long tradition of celebrating individuality and the worth of persons, the tension between the communal and personal aspects of religion is especially marked. Although religion remains corporate and formal to a notable extent, the way individuals relate to it is increasingly arbitrary, that is, voluntary—and *personal*. Individuals feel free to belong or not belong to the community, to change communities when one group doesn't meet their personal preferences, or to withdraw from community altogether, while insisting they are still ostensibly associated with the community and in some vague way guided by the community.

The faith of which they speak remains the one generally associated with the great communal forms of their given religious tradition. Explanations might be the popular "I am spiritual but not religious," usually meaning not interested in formal—and especially institutional—religion. Or, some may insist they do not need to practice a formal religion to be religious. Such explanations express this growing tendency to see religion as a private matter, that is, a personal or individual commitment distinct from external forms.

I cannot help but notice that, when individuals practice their more personal and private religious orientations, they continue to borrow heavily from the larger communal traditions around them. This borrowing suggests that it is difficult, perhaps in the end impossible, to have a purely private religion. If religion is about binding together rather than splitting and isolating, then it is inherently resistant to making sharp demarcations between the communal and personal aspects of religion.

Religion, like all of life, requires specific communities to sustain itself. A purely *private* religion seems to me rather like schizophrenic behavior, in which a person creates such a private and distinct reality that no one else can share it. As a result, communication with other persons breaks down. This danger of privatizing religion is one reason why I insist that formal religion is at once communal and personal.

****

If we ask what the end or aim of religion might be, from its informal manifestation in the religious sensibility to its most formal articulation, I propose that it aims at communal and personal *fulfillment*. I choose this word as an umbrella to include a variety of ways people and communities strive for one or another kind of fulfillment. Traditional religious language includes a variety of terms: *salvation*, *redemption, enlightenment, illumination, liberation,* and *self-realization,* among others. In some religions the language referring to the fulfillment promised is quite explicit and technical. In other traditions it may be more flexible and provisional.

In all cases, however, the language of fulfillment promises a better state of existence now, in the future, and ultimately for those who follow the religion. Broadly speaking, religious fulfillment is of two kinds: the ultimate fulfillment of one's destiny and the more this worldly or mundane fulfillment of wellbeing in this life. The role of destiny, either for a group or for individuals, looms large in most religions, but again, more intensely in some than in others. The destiny promised ranges from the promise of a salutary life following death, arrival at some ideal personal state in this life, or a utopian fulfillment of a whole people, if not the whole universe. Not all religions emphasize destiny to the same extent, but all religions address it in some fashion.

Fulfillment also includes the promise of well-being in the face of the common challenges of life. Thus, religions offer ways of facing and overcoming suffering, fear, and loss, along with the threats of evil, sin, illusion, and inadequacy. Most religions do not promise avoidance of these darker conditions (although there are exceptions), but they tend to provide ways of responding and coping with them. Moreover, many religions offer ways of *rising above* the threatening conditions of existence and of affirming, if not celebrating, life in the face of them.

****

Hiking at this height and climbing steadily as we go is both exhilarating and tiring. We've stopped repeatedly to view the vastness spreading before us and to drink and snack. Although I become lost in these demanding thoughts about religion, I "surface" at every breathtaking panorama offered. My experience becomes antiphonal between the splendor of this setting and the reflective mission of pilgrimage. They answer each other.

Collins points ahead and up the mountain to the west. "I think Lake Kathrine's up there. Not far. We should be there in half an hour." He turns and hikes off. I swing my pack onto my back for the last push of the day.

We break out of the timber and into a small open meadow. The lake, little more than a slight pond, lies in the midst of an open space. Almost immediately we hear voices, and Collins turns to me with obvious disappointment. He is, as I keep noting, a solitary man. When we discover that voices come from a cluster of campers to the west toward Pecos Baldy, we start scouting for a place at some distance from them. A small site across the trail from the lake welcomes us. From there, we can barely hear the chatter.

Our routine, now so familiar, unfolds seamlessly. Tents pitched, mattresses inflated, gear stowed, water located, fire-pit cleaned and prepared, wood gathered, stove filled with fuel and set up, food pouches chosen.

Before preparing our meal, we decide, without discussion, to walk back to the lake. The lake is shallow and tiny, but the water has that pristine, inviting transparency that somehow speaks of tranquility. We squat and stare. Collins looks up toward the group of campers. They have become abruptly quiet, and we stand to see what's happened.

The group is now sitting in a circle. One of them, a big man, stands inside the circle. We can hear his voice but cannot make out his words. Then one lone word, loud and clear, wafts to us: "Lord."

"Ah," says Collins with a knowing nod, "A gaggle of piety up there. Wanna' join 'em?" His question seems half serious. I shake my head. "Why not? They're doin' it, the very thing you keep thinkin' about."

"I never liked goin' to church late," I explain.

"But you could make a study up there. Ask some questions. Maybe interrogate 'em."

"About what?" I want to know.

"About what they're doing...tryin' to achieve with all that religious jabber." He looks down and shakes his head. "I'll tell you this much, Navajos don't chatter about such things. I keep tryin' to tell you, they don't do religion at all. It's somethin' they are, if you get my point."

I ponder Collins' comment for a while. "People are different. Religions are different because people are different. There's no one way, no final right way."

"You reckon they'd agree with you?" Collins nods his head toward the worshiping group.

"Probably not. Most folk just draw a circle around their way of doin' religion . . . or doin' anything. . .and stop at the edge of it." I add, "Nothing especially wrong with that, except when people interfere with other people's way of doing it."

"But couldn't they learn something from another way of doing it?" Collins asks and then adds, "Like, what if some old Indian walked into the middle of their circle and started dancin' or chantin'? What do you think would happen?"

"They might freak but probably not. They might even want to. . ."

"We ought to get naked, maybe a loin cloth of some kind, and walk right up there. It'd be a religious encounter like they've never seen and likely never will." He laughs so loud that some of the group turn heads toward us. With that, we head back to camp.

Nineteen

> All religions, including Christianity, are demonically distorted because they elevate their finite reality to the ultimate. It is true that they stand for the ultimate. . . .But if they do more than stand for the ultimate—if they divinize themselves—then they become demonic.
>
> Paul Tillich

∼

F^{og!}

I peer out and can barely see Collins' tent twenty feet away. We're in the clouds! I keep staring out, as if trying to penetrate the density around me. Then I see her, a deer and her fawn standing statuesque at the edge of our campsite. She appears puzzled by our tents. Her stillness is contagious and the fawn mimics her. So do I. Only when she satisfies herself that she's secure, does she proceed through our camp and past me so close I could reach out and touch her. I can smell her animal scent. I feel cozy in the fog, closed in and swaddled. But who is the mother? Ah, I know.

I'm outside before Collins and have coffee brewing. I hand him a cup through his tent flap. Sitting on a rock and staring into nothing, I'm engulfed in a sense of profound mystery. Where it originates or what it means is beyond me. It wells up and becomes articulate as a sense of being in the place where I most belong, included in this "cloud of unknowing." I've been in these wilds for ten days, and at last I'm coming to be here. Without deliberately meditating, I'm in a state, only rarely realized, of deep mindfulness.

"We ought to try for Lake Katherine today," Collins declares unceremoniously as he emerges from his cocoon. "I'll check the map, but by the time we reach Arrowhead, I'll need to hike out for the food." "Arrowhead" is what my wife and I called a small meadow lying under Santa Fe Baldy to the southwest. It is a Shangri La we shared with Collins and his wife on an earlier expedition.

Collins sits on a stump, still sampling his coffee, and stares at the map. "It'll be a decent hike, but we can do it with plenty of daylight to spare. I wanna get there in time to hike around without the gear."

I nod agreement. We hear our pious friends on the other side of the lake complaining their way into the day. Noise travels on the fog, and I hear one of them rail at the fog: "It's blinding me! We're gonna be the blind leading. . . " I can't hear the rest, but there's no need.

Fifteen minutes before we're ready to hike away, the fog thins, then, as if by decree, lifts. By the time we're ready to leave we can see the sun rise and splash against Pecos Baldy. We can even see part of Santa Fe Baldy in the distance to the southwest. We've thrown off the cover of night, and the day radiates and claims command of the wilderness.

As usual we start with Collins in the lead and me following in our silent solemn pilgrimage. For a while I allow my mind to free float as I watch the trail reveal itself ahead of me. Amazing, I find, how the mind can take its own course when we relieve it of fixed concentration. Momentarily I'm back home telling my wife about this adventure. Then I go searching for Ethan, wondering where he is and how he's resolving things. Or whether he is! Only gradually do these rambling thoughts dissolve into the landscape, and I continue, as they say, "in the zone."

We pause to take a drink and stand aside to let horse packers pass. As usual, they muck up the trail with horse manure and deep tracks in the soft earth. Collins stares at them and barely nods to the lead rider. We return to the trail.

Thoughts stir, but I cannot remember exactly where I was. I know I was working yesterday on my defining concept of formal religion, but where was I? I'm not sure and stop to pull my journal from an outside pocket. Every day, sometimes at night and sometimes in the morning, I jot notes to keep me focused and for later reference. I turn to last night's entry and remember.

It's a good thing that I didn't try to finish my definition yesterday because I'm now at the most important part. My mind needs to be fresh. The very last phrase of my working definition is made up of the most definitive element in my defining concept: *fulfill-*

ment...through an unconditional transcendent orientation. Those last three words portend the heart of the matter. They address the very core of my definition. Whatever else formal religion entails—all of those aspects already discussed—they all depend on these last three terms, if religion is to be *religion* and not something else, something less.

I want to pick these three terms apart with care. To speak of the *unconditional* is to refer to a conviction that is not simply one among other commitments but the one conviction that grounds all others. I readily admit that many people who are conventionally religious or religious in name do not treat religion with this depth and force. This superficial religion is indeed "second-hand," and abundant examples can be offered of this attitude. But for people who take their religion, their faith, as decisive for their lives as a whole—and this kind of commitment is the intent of religion—their conviction is unconditional. To put it crassly, they cannot imagine abandoning it or not living according to it. It guides every aspect of their existence. Religion becomes the prism through which they understand and live. Examples of this, though perhaps less common, are also rife among religions.

I choose this word *unconditional* over certain others. We could use *absolute*, but I find that word singularly unhelpful. It remains the favorite of people who are devoted to their religion as "the truth" to the exclusion of all other claims. And they often like to juxtapose, as the contradiction of *absolute* truth, the epithet relativism. I reject these terms and this distinction and could give several reasons, but I will offer only one. The word *absolute* most nearly means something like "without exception" or "exclusively," or worse, "unquestionable." This simply will not do for at least one reason: religion engages and is engaged with the infinite, and no human claim, however dearly held, can presume to have captured the infinite. Thus, *absolute* is deviant, a case of what Rene Girard calls "deviated transcendence," another way of saying *idolatry*.

Other words have been used to speak of what I call the *unconditional*. The two most common are i and *ultimate*. Either of these would be of service, but they are often used in so many other contexts that I shy away from their connotations. *Universal* refers to the whole of things, maximum inclusion, and it implicitly includes infinity in its embrace. At the same time, universal seems simply to refer to everyone and all things, while I want to emphasize the subjective engagement of religious people in their religion with its depth and intensity. Such people do likely see their religion as reaching to embrace the whole or the universal, but I want a word that stresses a certain intensity of devotion. The word *unconditional* better connotes that quality.

As for *ultimate*, I could use that word in my definition. It suggests that our religion entails the highest and final reach of our devotion. But again, it does not quite convey the subjective, dare I say it, passion, of profoundly religious conviction. Thus, I will stick with *unconditional* and propose that the way decisively religious conviction works *for the religious person* is simply without conditions. Or, without reservation! It is a convictional plunge, a *leap*.

If the notion of unconditional conviction appears weighty—and it is—the word *transcendent* can be overwhelming. During my graduate school days I took a course entitled Naturalism and Mysticism. The professor gave us one assignment for the semester, namely to write a five-page essay on transcendence. We repeatedly submitted our efforts, only to have them rejected. Our assignment was to continue rewriting until we met the standards of the professor. Mine was accepted on the sixth attempt. Since that time I have always approached this word with profound respect and always a twinge of trepidation.

This word *transcendent* is the lynchpin of religion as I understand it and try here to define it. Once, when I used this word in a class, a precocious student shot back, "What do you mean by *transcendence*?" Before I could fully gather my wits, I found myself responding with equal vigor, "I mean *you*!"

The student's face screwed into bewilderment, and I knew I had to explain further. I said, "You are not me. Is that right?" He nodded. "And I am not you," I continued. "Nor are we either one reducible to the other. In this rather everyday sense you are *beyond me*, that is, you transcend me.

"But transcendence may be even closer to us than that. We might be said to transcend ourselves. The philosopher Jean Paul Sartre, for instance, maintains we are more than what we are or appear to be at any given moment. We are also the possibilities implied in our own freedom toward the future." I went on to speak with the students about various ways we might speak of *self-transcendence*.

By then my students' eyes began to glaze over, and I paused to note that the idea of transcendence is truly complex and many splendored. It begins with a propensity of our species to go beyond itself and its boundaries. I believe it belongs to that primordial encounter I have returned to repeatedly between our finitude and the infinite. The infinite lures us beyond our confines and thus begins within us and in our most immediate encounters with the world, most especially our encounters with other people. All of it *transcends* us, beginning with our very selves. To be conscious is to be engaged in this reaching or going beyond.

In this regard I am repeatedly drawn to the most intense and intimate experience of transcendence in ordinary human existence: falling in love. I have gone back to that key drama before, but it is most acutely pertinent here. To fall in love is to fall under the spell of another, to be overtaken, and in especially intense cases, to experience a certain self-dissolution into the other. We are beyond ourselves. This encounter is at once exhilarating and threatening to our very stability as persons. With respect to our commonplace sense of order and boundaries, we find ourselves *out of control*. I mentioned all of this earlier. And of course, this falling does not and cannot last long. It is far too devastating to our sense of self-continuity. We seek once again the safe confines of a more familiar boundedness and the sense of the other as a more acceptable, if commonplace, transcendent. We might speak of this encounter with another as a singular instance of the *power of transcendence*.

When I use transcendence as part of my understanding of religion, however, I am pressing it beyond all of the more ordinary occasions of its use. In this context, transcendence is the encounter with the infinite as presence. The infinite ceases to be an *idea*, let alone a mathematical referent. Nor is it reduced to the subconscious dread and fascination of the Primary Impulse. It is at once the other, that which cannot cease to be other, and also that by which I am utterly contained and sustained. I use presence to give this transcendence the texture of intimacy and to suggest that I am, as it were, aware of being constituted by and within it. When earlier speaking of knowledge as *participation*, this is what I had in mind. It arises only as encounter, a merging without loss of distinction. Transcendence lies at the edge of human comprehension, because we dare to participate the infinite from within the confines of finitude. This participative awareness is so peculiar to modernity that, as Owen Barfield notes in *Saving the Appearances*, "Since participation is a *way* of experiencing the world in immediacy, and not a system of ideas about experience, or about the world, we obviously shall not find any contemporary *description* of it." This observation is exactly right. What I'm saying cannot be said straightforwardly. It can only be experienced. We are had by it!

At this juncture in my pilgrimage through these heights I am at the apex of focal concentration. This insight into transcendence is what I have long sought in my sense of what religion strives to manifest. Take all the other elements in my concept of religion, and religion is still not decisively *religion* without this openness toward encounter with transcendent presence. This is why all candidates for religion that remain within the mundane order of things, from *nationalism* to *football*, are not religions. They may masquerade as religions, but they are cases of deviated transcendence, only pitiful surrogates. Religion, whatever else it includes, is about the infinite as transcendent presence.

Formal religion, what we are currently discussing, devotes itself to the articulation and ordering of this transcendent presence into form through the elements of religion already discussed. It does so in myriad ways, but most Westerners readily assume that I am speaking of, ah yes, God. I agree that God is one way of speaking of transcendent presence, and the dominant way among theistic religions, but God is by no means the only way, nor necessarily the best way. The very locution threatens to *reduce* the infinite to something less than—well, the infinite—to contain and bind it within this or that contained understanding. This is why I find the phrase, "the *existence* of God" so nonsensical and misleading. It "thingafies" God, as a friend has put it.

Before I dare address this awesome and convoluted idea of God in order to place it in this conversation, I need a break. Collins has stopped ahead of me, having looked back and seen me falling behind. I pick up my pace and approach him, dropping my pack beside his. He has found a prominence from which we can view the rippling mountain spines to the east. We break out snacks and water bottles and sit astraddle a log.

"You tired?" Collins wants to know.

"No, not at all," I insist.

"Well, you got so far back I thought maybe I was humping too hard. I just want to make sure we reach Katherine with plenty of daylight."

"I'm really fine," I assure him. "It's just the usual, you know. . .thinking."

"What about this time?"

"God."

"Good God! You're impossible!" Collins grabs a stray stone and hurls it into the void below.

"What's wrong with thinkin' about God?" I want to know.

"Nothin', nothin' at all. . .except you can get lost in that canyon and never come out. That's all I say." He's emphatic.

"Yep," I admit, realizing that thinking about God is like *getting lost* deliberately. "Sometimes," I add, "I guess I like bein' lost. Never know what might turn up if you really get lost." Collins stares at me with half a granola bar in his mouth. Then he grins as if he understands what I've said better than I do.

We don our packs and turn uptrail. Collins says over his shoulder, "You just go ahead and lose yourself. I'll be the bell sheep."

The ascent becomes steeper, and for a while I devote myself to breathing and walking. Just as we level out I mutter under my breath, "God," as if I'm summoning. The years of reading about that word and discussing it ad infinitum swirl in my mind. All of the popular chatter about God, and the anger it stirs, along with the soothing reactions, at least in America, to any political leader invoking the name, come to mind. How can I utter anything truly intelligible, let alone novel, in the great wake of the history that word leaves behind it?

****

The man and the woman, husband and wife, are in Wisconsin. A church retreat, part of their work. The man shares his story of the childhood fear of locomotives to describe the primal religious impulse in its early childhood origins.

Following the session, a woman in the retreat rushes up to the man and breathlessly explains that a notorious eccentric English professor at Madison wrote a book entitled The Locomotive God many years earlier. She cannot remember the author's name or the contents of the book, but she encourages the man to find it.

The man begins a search for the book. The university library yields no hint. He reviews the holdings more than once. When he goes to a librarian, she suggests that he put a hyphen between locomotive and God. Immediately the book title appears on screen. The man enthusiastically chases through the stacks to the shelf where numbers have led him. There it is: The Locomotive-God!

Pulling the book from the shelf, the man checks it out. Avidly he reads through the substantial text, noting the peculiarities of the writer and his style, as well as his obsession with a Freudian analysis of his early childhood experience.

> The author is two years old. His mother takes him to meet a sister arriving by train. He has never seen a train. When the gigantic locomotive appears with its grinding rush, panting and bellowing steam, the child is devastated by its massive invasion. He stands trembling and screaming on the platform, much to his mother's consternation. This moment, the author insists, shapes the rest of his life around the strange god.

The man is moved to tears by the author's confession, as by a confirmation. His own story is corroborated. Why does he need this affirmation? He does not know, but he finds consolation in the book. He is puzzled by the author's need to make sense of the experience through Freud until he recalls when it was written: 1928, as Freud was being discovered in America.

But Freud, the man believes, has the weakest of understandings of the way religion arises. Freud, as with so many modern thinkers, has no insight into the possibility of the infinite or transcendence or how early in childhood it presents itself to experience. What difference might it have made to the author if he had refused to shrink the locomotive-God down to the size of the Oedipal struggle?

It is one thing, the man decides, to have experience, and it is another to understand the experience. In fact, he had only found his experience of the locomotive-God revelatory long afterward the experience, as a man alone in his room in the late night, and his insight had to be triggered for him by the story of a child whose gods were horses. What else lies entombed far below the surface of consciousness, waiting for a window of escape into comprehension? The terrifying tremor of the infinite, he senses, prompts the rush into forgetfulness. Or, it inspires life-long attempts to tame its monstrosity.

****

I'll begin here. Whether we speak of God, gods, or the goddess, we inevitably enter the "cloud of unknowing." I ruminate on that image for a while, remembering the fog this morning and sensing the genius of that phrase. How dare we claim to know anything of the great unknowing from within the fog of finitude? Yet we try, and here I am, trying again. Perhaps I can at least lay out some of the near terrain necessary to any useful consideration of God.

All "God talk" intends the infinite and strives to give shape to it in some way. My earlier reference to transcendent presence already begins this process, but when God, gods, or goddess is invoked, the drive toward specification of the infinite becomes more intentional. If, however, none of these efforts can hope to *capture* the infinite, our first confession must be this: the infinite, because it is infinite, cannot be grasped by any delimiting formulation. And all formulations are delimiting. Whether we speak of transcendent presence, God, or any related cognates, we are already quite literally out of our depth and reach. We are shrouded in "the cloud of unknowing."

This means, if nothing else, that all talk of God must begin and end in *mystery*. This word, already considered, comes most pointedly into play at the intersection of our finitude with infinity. By using mystery here we do not attempt to avoid the process of trying to make sense of God. Rather, we simply admit our boundedness in even broaching the name. In brief, God is not a problem or puzzle to be solved but a mystery to be lived. If we take this condition seriously, then our talk of God may be sufficiently modest and provisional to be of some use to us. Mystery, I like to stress, is knowing as much as we do and yet living in amazement at the knowing as well as at the as yet unknown.

Why, then, do we speak of God at all? Speaking of God, or even of what I'm calling transcendent presence, is an inevitable concession to our need. As noted repeatedly, we are finite and bounded, and in the face of the infinite we strive to give it form in order to engage and traffic in the infinite. No matter how inadequate the effort may be, we are obliged to undertake it. We find ourselves engulfed in the whole, the all, the one, the boundless, the eternal, the ultimate, the absolute, and on and on. All such language reaches into the great cloud to feel blindly after the infinite.

The inevitable lust for infinity begins with our primordial sense of the infinite, the Primary Impulse, but we are at once threatened by the infinite. Accordingly, we turn to language to grasp, if not to gain some measure of control over, the infinite. God is the most common locution to serve this need because it moves in the direction of rendering the infinite most like us: *personal*! Let me hasten to clarify. Not all concepts of God are personal. The Hindu idea of Brahman-Atman, for instance, is usually described as *non-personal*, and while there are Hindu notions of a more personal deity, at the core of that religious complex, the mystery of which I speak is honored by leaving the infinite at once beyond and also inclusive of the personal (This is the reason for the word *Atman* attached to *Brahman* with a hyphen.)

Granting all of this, those religions which emphasize God and its cognates tend to render God personal. In cruder uses, God is construed as virtually a person, a specific deity with traits something like our own. The traits may be infinitely grander than ours, but they somehow parallel ours, at least *by analogy*, as St. Thomas maintained. This elementary objectification of God, that is, making God an object among the elements and features of the universe, inherently fails in the intention of the very idea of God. It reduces the infinite to one or a cluster of finite features of the infinite. It may be the greatest of all objects, but it remains an object.

If we are more sophisticated, we may consider God not as *a person* but as *personal*. This way of putting it at least honors the infinite by taking up the personal into the boundless whole without reducing God to person. But why *personal*? I've given this question much thought and have come to this conclusion: we make God personal because personhood is the highest quality we know or can imagine. In the movie *Fiddler on the Roof*, when Goldie wants to compliment her son-in-law for being able to purchase a sewing machine, she says, "Now you are a person." This captures the timbre of the idea of personhood. It is our highest realization.

For this same reason, when we are elevating some aspect of nature, especially in poetry, we often do so by personifying, by giving it the qualities of person. Although using the personal to express our use of God is blatant anthropomorphism cum anthropocentrism, it is understandable. We reach for the highest expression of finitude within our experience as the best analogue for comprehending God, and, as I've contended, the other person awakens in us the potential of infinity itself. As long as we realize what we're doing, this metaphorical process may be sanctioned. The problem begins when we forget that this is what we're doing, and we begin to reify God as personal. In formal religion, especially the theistic ones, we succumb to this temptation far more than we resist it.

We long for and need an intimacy with the infinite because we actually already participate it. Herein, the religious sensibility itself begins. The use of anthropomorphisms serves to express this intimacy, to aid us in drawing close to God as the infinite. In this respect, personalizing language about God may be a resource for us to give form to what is forever formless. It may serve us in our finitude. It serves only so long as we discern that this language is solely for our benefit and that the language remains couched within the great cloud, the mystery, of unknowing. The best we can declare is that God is our most focal pointing gesture toward the mystery of the infinite as Transcendence. Hence, my descriptive addition of *presence*.

This lengthy digression on the one word, God, is offered, because this term remains the most common one for addressing the transcendent presence, and it is usually fraught with as much confusion as clarification. I now hasten to add that transcendence, as the most decisive element in my concept of religion, does not require belief in God. Transcendence, understood here as transcendent presence, may find expression in various ways. For example, in Buddhism, which for the most part offers no concept of God, transcendent presence remains. Perhaps the nearest equivalent to God in Buddhism is *Nirvana*, which is more nearly "space" or spacelessness, what might be described as the divine abyss. It means quite literally "no-thing," or "no place," beyond the division between what is and what is not. Admittedly, this concept is difficult, largely because its referent is vacuity or formlessness.

As I have indicated, transcendence is the one element in an adequate concept of formal religion most necessary to it. Other elements may be more or less present, but without transcendence—that is, without *intending* the infinite—we do not have religion. At best we only have some aspect of life projected as religion.

The last term in my defining concept of formal religion, *orientation*, is crucial. I maintain that the principal interest and aim of religion is for us to discover or receive a sense of who we are and how we relate to the whole of things. This is orientation in the most fundamental sense. We discern ourselves, our finitude and boundedness, in relation to the infinite, the boundless. The inner lust for infinity, the religious sensibility, takes form around this singular urgency. We strive for and thrive on this orientation. This is the grand paradox of religion: to be lost in the infinite is to be found.

As these last thoughts swirl through my mind, leaving me exuberantly exhausted, Collins calls out, "Behold! We're here!" He always wants to set camp with plenty of daylight, mostly so he can scout around afterwards. It is only mid-afternoon.

Collins drops his pack at the edge of a clearing and I follow suit. We walk toward the lake across an open expanse. He points back to our packs and says, "We'll camp back down there. Rangers don't want us close to the lake. Too much traffic."

We notice two lumps near the lake. When we move closer, we realize they are two people sitting on a blanket. Then we hear a whimper and realize that they have a little child or infant between them. Collins whispers, "How in hell did they come all this way with a baby." I shrug, and we walk toward them, talking so they'll know we're approaching. One of them turns, dreadlocks whirling about the head. He stands.

Then he calls out, "Hey!" and waves to us. We wave back and continue toward them. The woman then rises, leaving the infant on a blanket. We offer friendly greetings, the usual ritual exchanges. The man sticks out his hand and says, "I'm Frank, and this is Liz. The baby's Delilah." They both wear dreadlocks and clothing that has been worn more than once. Liz reaches down and picks up Delilah, showing the baby to us. The infant can't be more than a few months old.

After brief halting exchanges, Collins points back downhill toward our packs. "We'll be camping down there. If you need anything..."

"Well," Frank volunteers, "we're pretty hungry. We're almost out of food."

"Huh," Collins mutters in astonishment. But as usual, he doesn't ask questions. "Tell you what," he adds, "we'll go back and set camp. Then we'll fix some food for everybody. You come over, and we'll eat."

The couple nods and we wave ourselves away toward the lake. After standing at the water's edge for a few minutes, Collins wonders aloud, "What are they doin' up here without enough food? This is just the sort of thing that gets people in all kinds of trouble. You just don't come up here like that, on some kind of lark." I can tell he's exercised at the couple. We turn to look back at them, but they're already headed away and to the south of where we'll make camp.

We scout around for the best site, performing our nesting rituals, and begin poking through our diminishing cache of food. We have a couple of days, maybe three, left before Collins plans to hike out and bring in fresh supplies, but we may not make it, if we feed all of us. "What the hell," Collins concludes. "If necessary, I can go on out tomorrow. It won't be that much further." We decide to make it a feast, mixing a couple of compatible freeze-dried packages. Afterward we'll have pastry dessert. I go for water and return about the time the dinner is coming together.

We lay out some dishes, hoping they bring their own. I throw down a much-used beach towel to serve as our table on the ground. Then I walk up to a rise and look in the direction the couple took earlier. At first I see no one, but soon they come into view, walking in a tight little wad, like a moving blob. I wave several times until they see me. Liz points and Frank waves.

The couple, effusive in their gratitude, eat voraciously. Delilah leans against her mother, watching. Liz slips her a small piece of carrot mashed in a spoon, and the child devours it. Collins and I dig through our food to find more carrots for the child. At first there is little conversation, only grunts of satisfaction. When Collins delivers the pastry, the aroma is enough to raise a chorus of delight.

When Collins cannot stand it any longer, he asks, "How'd you get up here and come without enough food?"

"It's kinda' embarrassing, I guess," Frank admits. "This other couple came in with us, but they were goin' back out. They brought a lot of our food. Their plan was to hike out after a couple of days and then come back with more food. They shoulda' been here two days ago."

Liz interjects, "They're not the most responsible people, and I didn't like the idea that much, but then. . ."

Frank interrupts, "Our plan's to stay here for the summer. They're supposed to bring in several loads of stuff for us. We've made up a nice camp back there, lean-to and a tent and everything."

"Why do you want to stay for the summer?" I want to know. I'm thinking of the baby and the vast list of things they need and what can happen to people out here.

"Well, we don't really have a place to stay right now," Liz explains, "and we thought we could stay out here and not need a place. . .but then, we've gotta have food at least."

Before I can respond, Collins says emphatically, "I'm not sure that's such a good idea. I can tell you stories that'll curl your toes. If it was just you two," he says, pointing to them, "that's one thing. But that baby. . .well, too much can happen."

The couple listens in a stupor of dumbfounded innocence, as though they'd never imagined any possible danger in their adventure. Frank responds, "Then I'm not sure just what to do. Unless Bennie comes back, we don't have transportation back at the basin, and. . ."

"Don't worry about all that," Collins declares with a wave of his arm. "The most important thing is to go out of here. Even if your friends show up, they'll have to bring a good bit of food to make it through the summer. . .several trips." He's fuming, but I can tell that he intends for them to leave, probably with him in the morning.

Conversation continues as though a decision has been made. Frank and Liz tell us they are Rastafarians and that they've moved here from California to help set up a truck farm next year. I shake my head at their unfailing confidence and unthinking optimism. We discuss their religion a while, and I gain a bit more insight into what motivates them. When Delilah begins to fret, Liz says they should leave. She stands and we all join her. We invite them back for breakfast in the morning. They are lavish in their thanks for the food and the visit.

When they're gone, Collins says, "We're gonna take them out of here. I think I'll walk out for our food stash in the morning, and they can go with me."

"But what can they do without transportation down the mountain," I want to know.

"There should be a phone at the ski basin, Collins surmises. "If they can't reach anybody, I'll call Peck. He can come and take 'em somewhere. It's a mess, but then, that's life." He shakes his head in disbelief. "White people!" he blurts out in mock despair, and it becomes his benediction on the day.

Twenty

> The decisive question for man is: Is he related to something infinite or not? that is the telling question of his life. Only if we know that thing which truly matters is the infinite can we avoid fixing our interest upon futilities, and upon all kinds of goals which are not of real importance.
>
> Carl Jung

~

"Want me to go with you?" I ask as I watch Collins strap on his empty pack. It's barely daylight.

"No," he answers emphatically. "I can make better time by myself, and I wanna' get back before dark."

"So you're not takin' 'em with you?" I ask.

"Nah. I decided we can do that later, after we've talked with 'em about their plans. They seem lost to me.

He picks up a small package of trail mix, drops two bottles of water into outside pouches of the pack, and munches on yet another granola bar. As he's about to leave, he turns back and asks, "You gonna' feed that brood?" He nods toward the other camp.

"Sure," I insist. "If they're awake when you pass, tell 'em to come up. I'll do the last of the powdered eggs."

Collins waves over his shoulder and disappears into a cluster of pines at the top of a rise. If there was ever a lone wolf, he's it. I don't really understand how we've stayed connected all these years. I must've met him the year his wife died. I was single then and stayed with him for over a month. More silence than any monastery.

By the time I've stirred and dressed, I see Frank and Ivy coming down the trail in silhouette against a gray sky. Actually, I hear Delilah before that and turn to see the three of them. They cluster around the tiny fire that's just coming to life, and I hand around dried pears. "The appetizers of the house," I announce. They grin and gnaw away, a ragged little crew. They're all hair and wilted clothes, but they're mild and peaceable, without evidence of the slightest anxiety. Talk about living in the moment.

"Eggs all right?" I ask, and they both nod enthusiastically. Ivy is busy with Delilah, and I ask Frank to stir up some pan bread as I hand him the package. He reads the directions and tears open the pouch. We prepare the bread first, and I dig around for some liquid butter and a small jar of strawberry jam. In the wilderness, I've long since learned, food is not based primarily on exotic culinary or nutritional interests. We could haul all sorts of unprocessed food up here, but it would be heavier than anyone wants to carry. Only if we have a llama or burro, like Holt had, can we manage healthier organic food. But this much I can say: almost anything we cook on the trail, including food we wouldn't touch back home, tastes delicious. And camp food is much more nutritional, to say nothing of more tasty, than it was when I first began these wilderness treks.

We sit around the beach towel again, and I serve the plates. I hand hot tea to Ivy and Frank, and Ivy pulls out a small nippled bottle for Delilah. The child takes it with the same relish we show for our plates.

"I don't know what we'd of done if you hadn't come along," Ivy says.

"Well, we'd be hiking out today. That's what we'd of done," Frank assures her.

"Yeah, I know, but then what?" She shrugs as she asks.

"Now you don't have to worry about any of that," I assure them. "Collins is bringin' in enough for at least five, maybe six days, and we can give you a ride back at the trailhead." They seem utterly satisfied with this plan, and as we visit further I realize this couple takes playing it by ear to a new level, an art form. Eventually Frank concludes that he believes that, if a person lives with a positive outlook, things work out. He punctuates this brief litany of American positive thinking by gesturing broadly and saying, "See!"

Of course, I muse to myself, it always works out if someone else appears to rescue us at the right time, but I keep this to myself. And who knows? Perhaps I am supposed to be the reason it works out.

Ivy picks up the dishes and begins cleaning them before I notice.

So, I grab our containers and the water pump and go for more water, and Frank walks the baby. While pumping water through the filter and purifier, I stare into the limpid pool and see myself, shaggy beard and all. I'm aware that I actually look about as unkempt as Frank and Ivy. It somehow makes me feel at home, as though I'm with kindred.

"How long are you up here?" Frank asks as I walk into camp.

"It's supposed to be about three weeks in all, but we'll probably cut it a little short."

"Is it the food?" he asks.

"Partly, but that doesn't matter. I'm fairly close to getting what I came for," I confess.

"What's that?" Frank wants to know, and we sit down on a fallen log downhill from the campsite. He places Delilah on a small worn blanket near his feet.

"Frank, you ask too many questions, like always," Ivy chides from near the campfire.

"Nah, I don't mind," I interject. "Actually I came up here on a kind of pilgrimage, tryin' to figure things out. You know, the big picture." I sweep my arms broadly with this confession.

"Well, that can take more'n three weeks, I'd say," Frank responds with a chuckle.

"Probably," I admit, "but I did a great deal of preparation before I came."

"Like what?" Frank continues his interrogation.

"About twenty years of thinking, reading, and discussing."

"That might just do it," he admits. "I really like to think about things, but it's hard to keep it all straight. What've you found out so far?"

"Mostly I'm concentrating on religion," I report.

"A huge subject!" Frank says. "A jungle. I've given it lots of thought myself, especially since we became Rastas."

Ivy hangs two small frayed hand towels on a bush and joins us. She shows interest and asks, "Okay, so what've you found out about religion?"

"Now you're askin' the questions," Frank observes.

Ivy stares at him in that a way that turns him mute and continues, "I mean, not everybody's that interested in, you know, religion and all."

"Why are you interested?" I ask, turning the interrogation around.

She points to Delilah. "When she came along, it blew both of us away. We knew we had to answer some serious questions and make a place for her to be safe and happy." After a pause, she adds, "We were already Rastas, but it hadn't really taken hold yet."

"And you think religion can help make Delilah safe and happy?" I continue.

"Right. You can settle for money or for some place in this world, but if you don't have any of that—which we don't and don't want it—then religion's the best angle."

Religion as angle, I think to myself and wonder whether religion is perhaps nothing more than a strategy for survival or for thriving. I realize that running into Ivy and Frank may be more intriguing than I'd thought at first. At least they're verbal.

Rather than try to set out my own point of view, I decide to find out how they see things. We don't have anything else to do all day. So, why not?

"How long have you been Rastafarians?" I ask.

Ivy is about to speak when Frank says, "Four years next month."

"That long?" Ivy wonders.

"Yep, it was when Pendleton came to stay with us, remember, and we asked him about his hair and all." Frank warms to the subject. "I really liked what he had to say, and we went to this festival up in the mountains by Taos. They were dancin' and singin' like mad. All that reggae gets in your blood. And if you add ganja to the mix, you can downright leave the planet. . ." His words drift into silence, as if he's been transported somewhere else by the memory.

"I'm surprised you'd be interested in a Jamaican religion having to do with the repatriation of blacks back to Ethiopia." My remark is casual and not designed to probe, but Frank is primed for it as though he's heard it before.

"At first I joined just to piss my father off. I loved takin' my hip Afros to his place. He about flipped out the first time, especially with all the jivin' and easy way they talked. He couldn't understand shit, but he wanted to pretend he was tolerant."

Ivy interjects, "But it wasn't just that. What about the movement and Africa?"

"Well, that came later. You remember when we heard that great speech on Marcus Garvey and decided it's our duty to return Africa and Africans back to their former glory."

As we chat I keep wondering whether religion can get any stranger than this. People, it seems, can take up almost any religion based on any motive. In earlier generations, religions came from inside one's own group or culture. Now it's so random and unpredictable. Or is it?

It's not as though there were no provocations in Jamaica. Here's a new religion, rising from the cultural ashes of Jamaica's Kingston slums and devoted to the cause of alienated African blacks. And these two barely adult whites in the middle of America come along and join the movement. Oppression, I recall thinking over the years, breeds religion as the ultimate form of rebellion. In fact, one of the tougher ways religion works for people is to give them a *higher* justification for rebellion. When people hurt enough, they bypass the power of their oppressors by connecting with a power that trumps the enemy, their devil.

But what starts out as a movement, dynamic and protean, takes on form. It always does. Definite beliefs, specific rituals, identifying symbols, all of it. That's what I've been thinking through for the past two days. I've wanted to plot the schema of religion. Abruptly, I find myself asking, "Do you believe Haile Selassie is a living God?"

"We're not exactly sure about that," Ivy volunteers, "but he is a revealer of God...Or somethin' like that. We've heard it discussed over and over, but the important thing is that through him we can see liberation coming."

"Isn't it liberation for blacks? You're supposed to be inferior, maybe even the devil, according to their teachings." I'm probing to find out what can possibly attract them to this religion that should be alien to them. I want to know how much of it they swallow and how they swallow it.

"Well, the ordinary whites are inferior," Frank adds. They belong to Babylon. But the whites that are alienated themselves and can see the problem, they're welcome... they can be added to the New Israel. It's like we're adopted."

That's how it is with a religion, I think to myself. Once you're on the inside, you make it into a system. Every question has an answer. Immediately I can see what Frank and Ivy have done. They belong to an alienated fringe of American whites, for whatever reason, and they need to have a home. More importantly, it needs to be a home as different from the one they've left as they can find. In other words, they want it to be strange, an alien religion for the alienated. It makes a kind of sense.

"About two years ago we saved up and went down there for Nyabingi." Frank reports.

"Yeah, down to Jamaica," Ivy adds.

"It's different down there," Frank admits. "They were so suspicious of us. It took a while to be included...but I really understand that. I'm not the enemy but I represent Babylon in their minds because I wear the face of the enemy."

Their explanations—or rationalizations—intrigue me. I find myself wondering aloud, "It seems to me you've gone out of your way to follow this movement."

"It's not all that different," Frank insists. "We have our own messiah, and we use the Bible. It's read at nearly every meeting. Reminds me of the Episcopal church where they dragged me when I was a kid. At the meetings I heard nearly the same thing, only then it was *The Book of Common Prayer* along with the Bible. It was all read over and over. Rastas are pretty much like the same thing, only with a different messiah, and they're more sincere and serious about it."

Delilah whines and Ivy picks her up, raises her blouse, and begins nursing. The shade retreats from our campsite, and the day warms. Ivy shades Delilah's face. I feel stiff from sitting and decide to stretch by taking a walk. The little holy family, illumined by the sun, wave as I retreat.

I walk back up toward the lake, pondering the appearance of this motley young couple and their religious zeal and easy confidence. I can't decide what puzzles me most, their religion or their audacity at thinking they could live out here for the summer with so little support. They're either blissfully oblivious or daringly courageous. Probably some of both.

What interests me most is how this new Rastafarian religion is not all that new, at least in its basic structure. It unabashedly takes much of its character from classical Western religion and mixes it with an amalgamation of rituals, symbols, and beliefs right out of the African experience of living as aliens in an alien land. Once again, they're able to give form to chaos, and the form sustains them and grants them a future. Repatriation to Ethiopia is heaven for them Rastafarians, and they await its promise just as practitioners of other religions live in expectation of some form of completion or fulfillment. It's only more intense and dramatic because of the desperate situation many Rastas, especially in the early years, faced. . .and still face.

From what I know of this religion, it remains lively, in particular through its rituals and music: Reggae began with their musical prophet, Bob Marley, and continues to invigorate practitioners. The music has even bled into American popular culture. As long as its people experience or perceive their oppression, they'll be passionate in their response. It is, after all, a rebellion through symbolic form against the order imposed upon them by the dominant cultures around them. But I wonder what will happen as the oppressive conditions change—if they do change! Will the form overwhelm the vitality and dynamism of the movement? Perhaps it already has to some degree. I just don't know. What fascinates me is that in less than a seventy-five years, the Rastafarians have become a more or less formal religion with so many of the associated trappings. They're not yet an institution and may never become that organized, but the movement, like all movements, gradually evolves toward more structure. It's really necessary for their survival and continuation, as predictable as night follows day.

I wonder to what extent other religions in general take form, or at least have their original impetus, in a sense of oppression or some such sense of pronounced perplexity and vulnerability. Since religion inevitably addresses human finitude with its frailty, fallibility, and faults, the actual experience of boundary and threat surely contributes to its formation. If this is so, it could be that the fault line between religious dynamism and religious formalism lies in human success in resolving the major boundary threats of finitude. As we create humanly contrived solutions to our problems, as has developed apace in the West since the Enlightenment, the passion of religion appears to recede and the formality of it dominates. Where this process takes place, religion itself comes under threat from what we've come to call the *secular spirit*, and we move toward the reduction, if not the elimination, of the role of religion in our personal lives and in society itself. It becomes akin to window dressing or honorific ceremony

The relation of crises of vulnerability to the emergence or revitalization of religion is notable, but I also wonder whether there might be another source of innovation and renewal for religions today. It may well be that phenomenal success in the human enterprise itself eventually fosters another kind of religious interest, one that arises when having everything proves not to be sufficient for our living. Leo Tolstoy's own spiritual journey, as he recorded it in *My Confession*, suggests as much. While he had every advantage humanity could conjure and construct in his time, he found himself considering suicide. In the face of his own mortality, he could not find *meaning* in his own living. It was not his vulnerability, although death is the ultimate vulnerability, but his anxiety over finding significance in the midst of maximum human achievement that drove him to the brink. What Tolstoy's experience suggests is that, even with our most successful insulation against the tide of time and fate, we desire some way of construing life's quality, its worth to us.

Of course, not everyone is stirred by this question of meaning, at least not to the same degree, and many of us settle quite readily for the more pedestrian and mundane meanings we find simply in living. Nonetheless, where the question of meaning arises—and I believe it arises most acutely wherever and whenever our finitude encounters the infinite—the religious sensibility takes root. Thus, we might propose that the question of meaning and the encounter with vulnerability are the two most common sources for activation of the religious sensibility to take form as religion.

As I keep saying, I'm not speaking of the historical origins of religion, which belong to the receding and increasingly murky past. I'm speaking of the impetus for religion to take form by virtue of the conditions of human existence. It does seem that at either extreme of existence, the extreme of vulnerability and the extreme of human achievement, the likelihood that the religious sensibility will take form intensifies.

Perhaps not all religions begin with these promptings. Religions may well arise from the need for group cohesion, for granting some order to the dumbfounding mystery of things, or for personal or communal solace. The historical and cultural origins of religion are surely complex, but still, crises of *extremis* do most likely provide elemental motivation. This motivation most obvious in religions of oppression such as Rastafarianism. And this observation brings me once again to my perennial theme on this pilgrimage: the inevitable encounter of our finitude with the infinite.

I hear movement behind me and turn to see Frank coming up the hill smiling and waving. "Ivy and Delilah fell asleep," he explains. We walk in single file along the narrow path to the lake.

"Tell me about the Rastas' use of ganja," I say abruptly.

"Ah yes, the weed!" Frank exudes. "That's what everybody wants to know about. We have to watch for that because so many people, especially the younger ones, are attracted to that stuff instead of the movement itself. That's another reason they're. . . we. . .are so suspicious, especially of whites."

"Then how do you see the use of it?" I ask.

"Man, ganja is for the purposes of ritual and meditation. That's it." Frank speaks insistently and a little defensively. "I used to smoke for recreation. . .you know, for kicks, but I've stopped doin' that. It's too sacred. . ." His voice trails off.

I suspect that when religions emerge in the midst of oppression, the attraction of mind-altering substances may be especially compelling. They provide a means for rising above the conditions of the oppression and making contact with a higher (or deeper) dimension. I think of the Native American Church and its use of peyote, as well as the Rastafarian use of marijuana, or the use of *soma* among the Hindus. Other religious traditions also use mind-altering substances as part of their religious practice. Their use serves to separate them from the dominant culture against which they are reacting, but it offers more than that: it offers a more immediate access to a sense of engagement with the infinite. The same might be said of the so-called snake handling churches in Appalachia. The audacious immediacy of challenging normality is part of the religious quality. It moves the practitioner closer to *exstasis*.

****

The day is Sunday. The conference is over, and the people begin to scatter. The man drives away in a 1958 pink Chevrolet convertible, top down, with sun his only cover. New Mexico friends have let him use the exotic vehicle. He drives north, then east, toward Taos. He has a friend there, a maverick lawyer turned artist striving to survive on his vision and his hands.

In the foothills of a rising range, the man is so stunned by the splendor of the day that he pulls off the winding road and walks along a rutted jeep trail. He watches the earth being herself. He is moved to an unnamable joy, uncontrived and fathomable. He cannot remember such release—such liberation. He drives on, elated but not knowing why.

At the northern edge of Taos, the man notices people turning to stare at him. He wonders why until he realizes that it's the car. That pink 1958 Chevrolet convertible! Eventhough he had no plan to make a spectacle, he cannot escape his momentary celebrity. He parks on the plaza and asks where he might find his friend. Shortly, he is walking north to Bent Street and across the street, where he locates the friend's tiny store. He walks in unannounced and the friend looks up and beams at him. Tall, lanky, tanned, and wearing the customary dress of locals, the friend embraces the man with signature enthusiasm. Within minutes they are back on the plaza at a bar and drinking canned Tecate beer.

The man and the friend connect as though never separated, grinning and filling in gaps left by time and separation. The man will stay the night. The friend insists.

An acquaintance of the friend accosts him and they whisper. The man pays no attention but looks about at the earthy surroundings of a Taos tavern. When the friend turns back, he asks the man, "Have you ever seen acid?" The man says he has not. In fact, the man has been a purist about "chemicals" of any kind. He has seldom taken anything stronger than aspirin, never smoked, drinks sparingly. Childhood training in piety! The friend opens his hand, and in his palm rest two small squares of paper with a tiny dot in the middle of each, like a window in a wall.

"Have you ever thought of taking some?" the friend asks. The question is not coercive or even encouraging. Simply a question.

"No, but I think this might be a good time to do it," and with that the man reaches into the palm of his friend, retrieves a tab—a communion wafer at the cosmic mass—and begins chewing on it.

The friend, after gazing incredulously at his palm, laughs and says, "I might as well join you."

For more than half an hour the man and the friend continue talking. The man asks for a restroom and leaves. In the toilet there is a rude painting of a woman above the urinal. She is crying, and a balloon flows from her mouth with these words: "You'd cry too if you had to look at this all day." This churlish cartoon immediately incenses the man on behalf of the woman. He imagines ways to help her escape, including the use of a hammer to release her from the confines of the cinderblock wall.

The man returns to the friend, still thinking of the woman. He says nothing until he notices that the Tecate beer can has become a rose blossom. He points out the miracle to the friend, who looks at him with clownish delight and says, "We'd better drive home."

En route to the friend's house, the friend drives. He appears translucent to the man, as if from another planet. The man rummages in the glove compartment for no reason and pulls out a screwdriver. He studies it, impressed with the utter genius of the instrument. They pause at another home, an old school bus surrounded by bales of hay to stem the winter winds. They enter the bus, where children play and the woman stirs about. She seems irritable, busy. All of this disorients the man. He cannot fathom why he is in this place and why anyone would be disturbed by anything.

Abruptly, the man and the friend are outside, and the man looks west toward a splendid New Mexico sunset. As he stares, it becomes a perfect cubist painting, and he cannot stop gazing. When they arrive at the friend's house—an adobe with standard regional features— the man sits on a couch as the friend scurries about with coming-home routines.

The man has fallen into a deep sleep and is awakened in the dark of night by his friend. He sits up. The friend asks, "What do you need?" The man says, "I need to be rid of time." With that, he pulls a wrist watch from his arm and throws it against the adobe wall. It shatters and ceases to offer up time.

"What else?" the friend asks.

" I want to get out of these clothes." He wears a polyester jumpsuit. He stands and removes it, and the friend hands him large loose-fitting overalls. The man dresses.

"What do you want to do with your clothes?"

"Burn 'em," the man insists, and they go into the yard and burn his clothes in an outdoor oven. Both of the men watch the fire, intrigued.

With these rituals of purification, the man plunges into another world where all boundaries blur and limitations recede. He turns to the friend and says, "I've gotta get organized!" The friend says loudly, "Fuck organization!" And the man looks to the ceiling at a glaring neon sign: "Organization." The sign explodes, and the man slips further into a glorious alternative universe.

For eight hours the man swings between altered states—hallucinations—and intense perspiring interludes of recognition. At the center is the ceaseless lure of the anima-feminine. She is everywhere, imaged in the ordinary artifacts of the room. All women in his life rise before his face and float past him: daughter, former wife, mother, grandmother, aunts, lovers, and acquaintances. The force of this feminine energy springs from his psychic depths, tumbling before him and away into the abyss.

A woman enters the room. She is the friend's partner, but the man has not met her. She appears as a phantom, a bearer of the anima. The man is transfixed. He turns to the tiny corner fireplace, coals glowing in its grotto, and it becomes a vagina. He closes his eyes and sinks into the depths. He senses that woman and the feminine constitute the lifeline, the source and medium for life itself. He longs to participate, to be a means of life. He enters a trance that takes him to the place of births, and he finds himself giving birth—through his mouth it comes. An enormous cube stretches the mouth, then wrenches free, and he is astounded to see that on each of the six sides is one word: Yes!

Mouth as womb.
                        Birth of word
                                  words, words, words
                    The Word
           Word of Life
                        Life in Word
                Life.............YES

Far into the night, exhilarated and exhausted, the man drops away into psychedelic slumber. He sleeps on the floor. The friend awakens him early, knowing that he must drive to Albuquerque for a flight home. They embrace, and the man stares in the face of the friend and says, "You are straight! Now I know what straight really means." With a hardy breakfast as farewell, the man departs. A donkey looks at him from a nearby field, and he looks back. They know each other. The day is unbearably bright.

Driving through the canyons along the Rio Grande, the man is repeatedly overwhelmed by the heights, the expanses, and the rushing river. He stops to watch the water tumbling away as if fleeing the mountains. His attention is captured by a cluster of enormous boulders near the river, some in the river. He finds he cannot distinguish between the massive stones and himself. The union, though only momentary, is indelible. He has again encountered oneness, and he will not forget it.

At the airport the man calls the couple who had loaned him their car. He tells them where it is parked. He sits in the lounge, waiting for his passage home. He stares blankly, and the clear message dawns out of emptiness: the rest of this life will be unlike all that has gone before.

****

Frank agrees with my assessment and adds, "When your whole life is organized for you and you're constantly under the gun to follow rules you don't control and don't accept, you need a doorway out of the situation. The best escape hatch lies right here." He points to his head. "If you do it right and keep your focus, you can touch the truth." He appears serene in his confession. "This country's so screwed up that we need something to scramble our synapses and give us a new way of organizing things. I mean that literally. We do need to have our minds altered! Otherwise, we're gonna live and die in prisons we've just made up." His momentary eloquence matches his conviction.

"Then is your religion, your Rastafarianism, a form of escape?" I ask.

"Not at all!" Frank insists. "Well," he continues more thoughtfully, "it probably does begin with tryin' to get away from the mess, I reckon. But still, the religion itself, once you go deep enough into it, is an alternative...another way to live that's better than the one you're rebelling against." After a pause he adds, "The religion becomes its own thing for you...including the ganja. It helps you find your way through the maze, so to say."

I sense he is reaching for a language to convey what his experience has revealed to him. This is often the way people who have found their way speak. When pressed, they cannot *explain*. They must settle for acknowledgement. They wind up *confessing* more than anything else. As religion reaches for and claims to encounter the transcendent presence, language gives way to poetry, then to silence.

Ineffable! The form of the religion, made up of those elements I discussed earlier, finally proves too limiting. It appears to me that the aim of religion is to undercut itself, and I need to examine that idea more fully.

Frank turns to listen and hears the faint voice of Ivy calling for him. He walks toward the voice and I follow. When we reach her, she says Delilah is still asleep. She asks, "What're you doin'?"

"Just talkin' about stuff," Frank says.

"So, what's new?" Ivy responds with a slight note of playful sarcasm.

"Hungry?" I ask. They both nod, and we return to the camp and scrounge among the few remaining snacks. The baby stretches but continues sleeping while we eat.

"When'd you expect him, uh. . .Collins, back?" Ivy asks.

"Probably by four, if not sooner. He hikes like a jackal," I confide. They laugh, and without another word we separate. I reach in the tent and grab my notebook, head back downtrail to a sizable boulder and perch myself atop it. Somehow I always like these perches. They give me a vista.

For the next couple of hours I review my conversation of the day and insights gained. I specifically take note of the idea that came to me about the inadequacy of formal religion. I make some preliminary notations on various ways this idea can be examined. I begin with one general observation: *religion is as inadequate as it is inevitable*. And I decide that I want to understand what that means.

I can see the "holy family" moving about near the camp. They are not as unusual as I had assumed at first. Almost no one ever is. When all is said and done, we're pretty much members of the same expansive family strewn across the planet. In fact, despite their peculiar form of religion and their audacious attempt to live in these mountains all summer, they are actually simply folks trying to hew lives that fit for them. It's tempting and easy to see other people as so strange that we place them outside our circle of normality. And that's the source of most humanly induced plagues on humanity.

The going way to put this is to say we treat them as *other*. I don't really like this way of speaking because everyone who is not me is in one way or another the other. The real problem is more nearly how we relate to the others, whether we can include them as part of the *we* to which we belong, while acknowledging and encouraging their otherness.

Or, we might ask ourselves this question: how inclusive is my 'we?' We have always divided ourselves into groups of various sorts and then faced the consequence of how we relate across the boundaries we've created. This impulse to divide is as true of religion as it is of any other dimension of human life. In fact, with religion it may even become most acute because religions, at least some of them, tend to make superior, if not exclusive and final claims for themselves. I'll need to consider this characteristic of religions before we leave these mountains.

Shortly after the sun disappears behind Santa Fe Baldy, I hear Collins speaking to Frank and Ivy. When I reach camp, the pack is bulging, and an extra plastic bag hangs on the back of it. We have a fresh supply of food for the week, including whole potatoes and an assortment of vegetables. Dinner comes early, and we dine sumptuously.

As darkness settles around us, Collins says, "I called at the ski basin, and Peck'll meet us at Holy Ghost Canyon next Saturday." Then he turns to Frank and Ivy and adds, "You can hike out with us, and we can take you wherever you need to go."

"Not sure where that is," Ivy admits apprehensively. She looks at Frank, who shrugs with uncertainty.

"You don't need to worry about that," Collins says with that proverbial tone of mystery he often uses. With those words, another day begins its drift away. We scatter to find the oblivion of sleep.

Twenty-One

Penetrating so many secrets, we cease to believe in the unknowable. But there it sits, nevertheless, licking its chops.

                                                             H. L. Mencken

∼

Collins is up earlier than usual. I hear him stir and rattle pots. When I look out, he's perched on a sizable rock at the edge of our campsite, staring into the gray haze of dawn and sampling from a steaming cup. I watch him for several minutes, caught between feelings of admiration and mystification. I admire his solidity and silent resolution about everything he does. He continues to give me the feeling that he knows something I have yet to learn and need to know. And because I don't know it, I'm mystified. It's often that way with people who remain at a distance and seem to abide in themselves. We have the old saying, "still waters run deep," but I've learned that it's not always true. In this case, however. . .

He spots me and beckons. I wave back, clamor out of the tent and stretch upward, reaching for the pending day.

Collins points toward the hot water brewing atop his camp stove, and I grab my mug to join him. "I've been thinkin'," he begins. We don't wanna leave 'em." He nods toward the south, where our camp guests are most likely still asleep.

"Yeah, I know," I agree. "They're close to useless to themselves up here. Too much trust and not a clue."

"Yesterday I thought about it on the way down and back, and I'm ready to make 'em an offer."

"What kind of offer?" I want to know.

Collins doesn't answer for a while, satisfied to take a couple of draws on his coffee and stare into the timber below. "I've been by myself a long time, you know, since she died." Silence again, as if in memorial, and then, "Now it's about time I rejoined the race."

I think he's going to talk about a new relationship, but he says, "Frank and Ivy and their little girl need a place to be, and. . .Well, here's the deal. We have enough grub for another five days. Then, like I said yesterday, we can hike out to Holy Ghost and Peck'll be there to pick us up."

Since I already know this plan, I'm puzzled as to why he's reciting it again with such a serious tone. I finally respond tentatively, "That's what you said yesterday, and it sounds like a good plan. I'm anxious to check on Ethan anyway."

"Then," Collins continues abruptly, "I'm thinkin' about havin' them live with me for the rest of the summer. They don't have a place, and the cabin has enough room." Then he adds, "barely," and we both chuckle.

"You sure?" I ask, thinking of his penchant for solitude and silence.

"Pretty much," he says. "I'll keep thinkin' about it while we're hikin' these next few days. At least they can stay with me for the time bein', and if it works out, we can take the next step." He drifts away into his brooding domain.

I wonder at his proposal. Knowing him, he's simply concerned about these two waifs and their offspring. Collins has always found his home among the people at the edge. That's what drew him into the Navajo world, but it seems more than that. I find myself, to my own surprise, blurting out, "Are you lonely?"

He turns, momentarily taken aback. After some time he responds, "Never was, 'til she died. But all the time since then."

I'm stunned by Collins' confession. Another bit of the mystery, I suppose. I had assumed he was more self-contained, but then I should've known better.

"People are made for people," he begins, as if giving a soliloquy. "We come from people and we become ourselves with people. It's a plain fact, and we might as well face it. I like bein' alone, always have, but this ordeal's made me realize that, even when I'm all by myself and satisfied with it, it's mostly because I know they're there, waitin' in the shadows for me. Can't run away from that without losing your way." Again, he retreats into that mystery, but I've had a glimpse of it, and it's even more dense and complex than I'd imagined. "Those Navajos know that better'n most, but they don't talk about it. That's just how they are. . .I miss 'em."

Frank calls to us from atop the rise, and Collins waves. He turns to me and says, grinning, "They're hungry," and we both begin preparing breakfast. The baby, Delilah, is the leaven in the lump. She makes us more like a family.

After breakfast Collins suggests we stay here at the lake one more day and then hike around to one of our favorite spots, and our only destination, a hidden wedge-like meadow we found on that earlier trip and named it Arrowhead Meadow. Frank and Ivy nod in agreement, and we prepare to scatter for the day. Frank takes Delilah, saying something about giving Ivy a break, and follows me downtrail toward the boulder where I spent time yesterday. As we walk he says he wants to talk more about religion, especially about his being a Rastafarian.

"It still puzzles me, why I've become a Rasta," he begins. "Everybody needs a place to be. . .to be able to see the whole picture, I reckon, but it could've been somethin' else. Maybe anything! Why, I've asked, is it the Rastas? I asked Ivy that last night, but it makes her nervous. She thinks I'm about to take off into somethin' else."

I make no response. We reach the boulder and spread out two small blankets, one on top of the other for softness. Frank lays Delilah on her back, puts his hand on her stomach, and gently rocks her from side to side. She enjoys the sky.

"You said yesterday that it all started out of spite. You wanted to get at your father."

"Yeah, but that was only the beginnin'. I had no idea where it would lead, but this stuff's become serious to me. I don't just believe it; I really try to live like I believe it. . . That's how I know I do believe it."

"Isn't that how belief always works?" I propose. "What you really believe. . .and not just say you believe. . .is whatever you're willing to make the guide for what you do. I once heard it said that action completes belief." I pause, then add, "I'm not sure it's that simple. It could be that acting brings about belief, and then belief inspires more action, a kind of circle back and forth."

"Then what makes a person break into that circle?" Frank wonders.

"It's a kind of leap, I suppose. You find yourself acting in a certain way or entertaining a possible belief or way of understanding things, and bingo, you wake up inside the circle. Sometimes it's more deliberate, I guess, but it can come as a downright surprise. We wonder what happened. This one thinker calls it 'the shock of recognition.' I like that way of putting it."

"That's me," Frank admits. "I've come awake, and I'm inside this circle." After a pensive foray into his own mind, he continues, "But sometimes I begin to wonder what's outside the circle. . .about all the other circles. Maybe bigger ones."

"These circles, let's call them circles of trust. . .or of meaning. . .are very helpful, at least potentially, and the reason is that they orient us. We have the feeling that we know where we are in relation to that big picture you just mentioned, and this helps us face and make sense of all the buzzing and relentless chaos around us. But," I urge, "these circles are also potential traps. They can, and usually do, limit and confine us, while at the same time helping us locate ourselves."

We both ponder this paradox, and I find myself reflecting over my musings of the last few days and the way I've been laying out what I've called *formal religion*. Frank, I sense, is both enamored by the form he's living and disturbed, even if only slightly, by the boundaries it marks for him. Eventually this line of thinking leads me to ask myself, *What motivations prompt the formation of particular religions—specific circles of trust*?

At the risk of outrageous oversimplification I find myself pursuing two related types of answers. I explain them to Frank. On the one hand, I point out, we experience the infinite, not so much as infinite but as a turbulent chaos without edges or as the bottomless abyss—what I call the realm of *possibility*— and out of this primordial experience arises our urge to order. It may be more motivated by our own urge to protection than a solution to life's riddle.

On the other hand, we experience our finitude most precisely in the encounter with our fallibility, that is, the failure to realize our own idealized versions of finite existence. This elemental sense, that our existence is problematic—in some way amiss or off course—prompts us to reach for a schema of assurance.

These twin drivers conspire to direct the religious sensibility toward formation, and the most explicit form lies in formal religions.

I explain that this is not an historical explanation of origins at all, but as I keep insisting, if we can penetrate the existential human dilemma to the core, where we engage the polar pull between our own finitude and the infinite, these two motives unveil themselves.

To my slight surprise, Frank nods his comprehension and shows interest in what I'm saying. I decide to see how far he'll go with me. I continue to explain how I understand the sense of infinity and how it draws us toward formation, and especially toward religion.

Beginning with the image of *chaos without edges*, I'm led to think of this wilderness where we're camping. It contains us and lures us ever further into itself. Frank nods his head in agreement. Friends, I point out, often express consternation that I, or anyone, would voluntarily choose to spend nights sleeping on the ground and days carrying the resources for survival on our backs. The most common counterconfession goes something like, *My idea of camping is a luxury hotel with a sauna.*

If I've heard that once, I've heard it a hundred times. But the untamed character of this wilderness, its vastness and its self-sustained otherness, dwarfs me and confronts me with *the force* over which I have virtually no control and over which I need not seek control, let alone dominance.

I participate it! Those early American explorers, Lewis and Clark for example, experienced this. That could be why Lewis could never really adapt to civilization after the expedition.

I recall to Frank a recent occasion on this trip when in the late afternoon I strolled into a stand of timber near our camp. After finding myself enclosed among a phenomenal array of pines, mostly ponderosa, a sense of their pervading silence and power came over me.

One especially majestic tree confronted me simply by its ponderous size and its reach upward. I noticed its several bulging roots, larger than many of the other trees around it and lying along the earth's surface. The roots dipped into the soil and disappeared in the underworld that allows that massive tree to survive and soar.

I sat down on one of the roots, roughly barked and firmly set. As I took a draft of water from my flask, I recalled a passage from Jean Paul Sartre's novel, *Nausea*, in which he describes a root. For him, the root is alien and stark. It is not him but is nauseatingly *there* as a stark and absurd *thing*. But this root on which I sat inspired the opposite of alienation. I found myself utterly at home with the root, marveling at its hidden genius in transporting nourishment from the earth's depths into the canopy above me. This process continued even as I sat on the root and leaned back against the tree trunk.

My view of this root and Sartre's view of that root in Paris have nothing to do with the root. It has only to do with how we each relate to the root—and by implication, to the natural order it represents.

"What does the root have to do with infinity?" Frank asks with a puzzled look.

"Huh," I mutter. "Well, what I'm tryin' to show is that this encounter with infinity I'm talkin' about begins with experiences like the one I had with that root. One tree and its system of roots is enough to dwarf us in relation to all the things we do not originate and can't finally control. Oh, we could cut the tree down. We can plant trees and help them grow. But we're not the cause of trees and not necessary to them at all. Knowing that much, I'm already opening toward the boundless infinite.

"And we really can't stand facing the infinite for long. Actually, we can't even survive for long unless we organize enough of the infinite possibility to protect us and make us feel somehow important. But that's only the beginning. We want some kind of relation with the infinite. We want to make it more *available*. . .and more than that, we want to take away its terror. . .what one German thinker called the *tremendum*. That's what religion used to do. . .It addressed and responded to our terror. And in some ways, I suppose, it still does."

"Then what gives us a kind of organization now?" Frank wonders.

"The whole modern enterprise," I blurt out. "Technology mainly. Think about it. We're hell-bent to organize the whole earth. . .and beyond. . .to our specifications. Of course, it'll come back to haunt us, and maybe it already has, but we can still resist it for some time before the infinite laughs in derision over our puny push against it."

"But religion hasn't gone away," Frank observes. "It's still hangin' in there."

"Right, and in some ways it may be even more important to more people because, despite the many foibles and follies in all religions, they still serve to acknowledge the infinite in one form or another. But the point I want to make is that religions are just that, *forms*, and forms always both express as well as limit and bind."

"That sounds like a kind of double message, like we need and don't need form," Frank observes. "Don't we need form? Seems to me humans organize everything they put their hands on. Like when we set camp up here. We kept messing with things, tryin' to get everything just right."

I immediately agree, as Delilah whimpers and Frank snatches her up. He walks around on the boulder holding her lightly against his shoulder, then sits down to cradle her.

This idea comes to mind: giving form to things is inevitable for us humans. In fact, I think to myself, I've already formed this very idea in my mind. Wow!

We can't quit forming. It could be argued that the most fundamental gift of our species is this ability to form things, including ideas, and if this is true, then seeking to give form to our connection with the infinite and the general drive to form things are entangled with each other from the start. So, it's understandable that religion has taken form among human beings, and the process of forming, reforming—to say nothing of de-forming—is likely to persist.

What I'm more interested in grasping is the downside of our human penchant for formation, namely, the fact that it is both inevitable and at the same time inherently limiting and problematic. For example, culture—whatever else it is—is a process of forming social life for the well-being and continuity of those within the culture. And no one can do without a culture in this sense. It is utterly necessary to possessing a language and to the ability to continue relating to the people around us.

Culture is our larger necessary group home. At the same time, the bond culture provides is also a bind for those within it. Culture mediates social life but throttles the capacity to reach beyond its boundaries—or tries to.

Having said this, I recognize that culture confronts us with both boundaries and the possibility of moving beyond those boundaries. Cultures vary in their built-in capacity to allow for raids across its borders. It's like that circle I mentioned earlier. It's one thing to break into the circle of belief or trust, but it is also possible—perhaps even highly desirable—to break out of the circle.

If sufficient experience challenges our circle and we encounter what social theorists call *cognitive dissonance*, we at least must face the limitations of our circle and the possibilities that lie beyond it. Some cultures or circles of trust, especially those in relative isolation, may be much more reluctant to sanction challenges to their edges, but if cultures are *alive*, meaning open from within to modification in relation to changed conditions, then the edges are likely to be more porous.

With the increasing proximity of cultures to each other and their influence upon each other, this capacity becomes both more likely and more critical, but at the same time, cultural life is threatened by challenges to its boundaries. This threat is why we experience vivid crises of cultural—as well as personal—*identity* when boundaries are threatened.

The same is true within religions today. They are, one and all—regardless of how endlessly varied they may be overtly—inevitable attempts to give form to the encounter of human finitude with the infinite. As this formation takes place, however, the religions fall into the same bind as cultures—and usually in deep association with cultures: the power of religions to unify and mediate the energy of those participating in them is stifled by the confines placed upon the participants.

To put it starkly, religious forms are traps, and we constantly become lost in the details of them. They may be welcomed and comforting traps, but in the end they remain traps—unless. . .

"Unless what?" Frank urges.

"Unless the form includes an acknowledgment of its own limitations," I declare triumphantly. "A given religion can be aware of its own boundaries and even that it is at best an informed guess or point of view on the finite-infinite engagement. As a friend of mine puts it, 'Religions are at best only pointing gestures.' Some religions actually do this gesture and do it relatively well, but the more common outcome among religious practitioners of any persuasion is to assume that their own form is definitive, if not final.

There is a propensity in all religions—and cultures—to forget, ignore, or deny their own boundedness. Familiarity breeds confinement!

Ivy's call reaches us, and we turn to see her standing by Collins, waving. Frank says it's about time to feed Delilah, who's fallen asleep against his shoulder. He stands gingerly and picks his way down the boulder. At the bottom he turns and says, "We need to talk more about this. It's what keeps bothering me, but I'm still not sure why." He turns resolutely and moves up the trail. I pick up Delilah's blankets and follow.

Right, I say to myself, *religion is troubling, and one of the most basic reasons is that its strength, the capacity to "bind back," is also its weakness. The binding becomes bondage.*

These reflections take me back to something I once read by the philosopher Gabriel Marcel, having to do with marriage. He readily confesses that marriage is a "bond," but then he adds, "Marriage is a bond that sets us free."

This is as paradoxical as it gets. How can a bond be liberating? I suspect the secret lies in choice as deliberate commitment. As long as we are not committed, we are free in one sense. That is, we can do as we please within the bounds of our capability. But in the face of this ostensible freedom, we confront a most weighty question: *What do you want to do*? If we are not to be paralyzed, we will do something. Otherwise, we're not free, but when we exercise that freedom, we become bound by the decisive act that expresses our freedom.

This is why for some existentialist thinkers freedom is not a light-hearted matter at all but an enormous burden. If free, so the argument goes, we are thereby *bound* to exercise that freedom by taking one course rather than another. Moreover, we are then obliged to deal with the consequences of whatever course we take. If we freely decide on a deliberate commitment rather than endless arbitrary and momentary choices to do this or that on whatever whim occurs to us, we become free in quite another respect. We become free to respond and to act within a field of new possibilities unavailable to us on the other side of commitment.

To complicate the matter of freedom and choice even further, we cannot *unmake* a commitment. Even if we later rescind it, we are still caught in the framework of having committed. This is what Milan Kundera calls, in his powerful novel by that title, "the unbearable lightness of being."

Since religion always involves primary life-defining commitments, tacit or declared, then we should not be surprised that it both binds and liberates at the same time. But this is not the binding limitation I've been discussing. The problem runs much deeper.

If formal religion is the consequence of the drive to give finite form to the infinite—and I believe this is what all *formal* religions attempt to do—then religion is reaching for the impossible. Every boundary it draws becomes, if not arbitrary, truncated and, in the end, quite inadequate. As my friend says, at best, all religious forms are only pointing gestures to what lies utterly beyond the grasp of any form: the infinite.

These pointing gestures may be—and they do appear to be—crucial to the expression of the religious sensibility, but they are also inherently inadequate to the task. They cannot capture that to which they point and toward which they yearn.

It is rather like Zorba the Greek pointing at dolphins playing in the sea, and his friend, Boss, deciding to concentrate on Zorba's finger instead of the dolphins. Zorba is outraged that his friend misses the dolphins by staring at the pointing finger.

Religions may point to the infinite, but the pointing is not the infinite. No religion can capture, let alone tame, the infinite. To pretend to do so is the heart of religion's most profound failure: *idolatry*.

As I shall use it here, idolatry refers to taking anything less than the infinite and identifying it as the infinite. Thus, I come to a second contention: *given the finite boundaries of any and all formal religions, no religion can be final*!

The first contention, stated earlier, is this: *giving form to things (including religion) is inevitable for us humans*. Between these two propositions, formal religions inherently fall short of the task they set for themselves. No matter how liberating a person's commitment may be *within* their religion, they are still constrained by the religion from engaging fully the infinite for which they lust. Formal religion, even the best, abridges the boundless range of possibilities ingredient in the infinite.

Religions use one or a combination of two strategies to avoid the dilemma I have described. First, they may claim to rest on a received *revelation*; that is, they are founded on the initiative of the infinite, usually in the form of some divine agency, which enters the domain of finitude. The theistic religions, most notably Judaism, Christianity, and Islam, are especially drawn to this claim, but something similar may be found in non-theistic religions.

For instance, when Buddhism appeals to Enlightenment as the ideal end of Buddhist practice, it is not calling for divine revelation, but it is promising that illumination comes to a person, even if from within. Enlightenment cannot be conjured or coerced or caused by particular practices and certainly not by willing it. It can only be awakened or received. In this respect it is like revelation, though without divine agency being the source.

The problem with appeals to revelation or variations of it is that, for the revelation to be available to human beings, it must be *received*, and it can only be received under and within the conditions of finitude. Revelation itself is dependent on words and other symbols to be available to human receptivity. Thus, we are back where we began: *the finite cannot contain the infinite, and all finite attempts to do so are incomplete.* And since anyone can *claim* revelation but can never *prove* it to be revelation, it always remains possible that any revelatory claim is simply misguided or conjured.

A second and more helpful strategy is simply to acknowledge that one's religion is bounded and only, at best, a pointing gesture toward the infinite. To the extent that religions maintain this sense of their own boundedness, their followers may be able to transcend their formal religion as they continue to practice it. Otherwise, they become lost in the details of their own religiosity.

In order to sustain this second option, religions forfeit all claims to finality, absoluteness, and exclusiveness in relation to other religions. While this can be done, it is by no means easy or as common as we may pretend or wish. We may refrain from overtly urging our religion on others or claiming it to be definitive and final, but it may continue to be construed as fully adequate and perhaps even sacrosanct in actual practice. Insofar as this is the case, formal religions must cope with the potential evil in all formal religions, namely idolatry as I have defined it—confusing the finite with the infinite.

I reach camp and decide on a mid-afternoon snack. The camp is empty and no one is in sight. I look around briefly but then rifle through a hanging bag and come out with crackers and a small jar of peanut butter. That, and a handful of dried fruit, mostly apples, pears, and apricots, suffices. As I finish my flask of water, I turn to see Frank and Ivy coming out of the timber below. I wonder where Delilah is, but when I ask, they say she's with Collins.

"He's taking her on a little hike," Ivy says. Somehow I'm not surprised, but as always, he does the unexpected. *Bonding*, I think to myself.

"I've been tellin' Ivy about our talk, but I think I kinda' got it balled up, some of it anyway," Frank confesses.

"It just seems to me," Ivy contends, "that we need religion, even if it's limited. It just means that the one we've chosen is as good as any..."

I sense anxiety in her tone, and I hasten to reassure her. "I agree that we need a way to express our most basic longings, and religions have served that purpose for a very long time, probably from the beginning of humanity." We begin walking slowly toward the lake, luxuriating in the peerless blue sky above and the warming of the weather in these heights. It can still be bone cold in the night.

"I believe religions can and should continue to serve that purpose, but on one condition...and Frank, we didn't quite get to this. We must recognize and acknowledge that our religions are only *mediums* and not the thing they try to mediate. And they're frail mediums at that. Does this make sense?"

"Only a little...partly," Ivy admits.

"It comes down to this, at least for me. We cannot do more than imagine how things *ultimately* are in the vast universe and within our own deepest selves. At the same time, we are drawn to try, and the particular actual religions are among our most definitive attempts to do this. I call religions *formal* attempts, meaning that they have specific structures and processes we can all recognize. These religions strive to convey to us the very thing that is entirely beyond us. I call it *the infinite*. You may call it *God* or *the One* or something else.

"If I'm correct in this, then we're left with one great gift through formal religions." I pause, and Frank and Ivy both stop on the trail and look at me as though I'm about to deliver an oracle. "The gift is that we and everything available to us in the world is couched in *mystery*." I think to myself, *There's that bewildering word again*. Then I continue. "We stand within and on sheer mystery, and mystery is not to be resolved so that the mystery disappears. It becomes the stuff of our living, trusting, and hoping. Folk are usually more than a little disappointed when they first discover this. They want it all *revealed* for them, not realizing that if that could happen, they'd immediately take it for granted and proceed to ignore it."

Frank, obviously disappointed, says, "Mystery sounds like a cop-out to me. What can you ever do with it?"

Ivy, not convinced herself, is more pensive. "If you take it in the right way, it's kinda' comforting. It allows you to quit trying to put the last nail in everything. You know. . .figure it out once and for all."

"Yep. That's how it strikes me. Doesn't mean I don't ponder things and keep probing to make as much sense as I can. But it lets me off the hook of having to get things exactly right and then be able to prove it. In other words, I don't need to carry the burden of *certainty*. I like what you said, that a deep sense of the foundational mystery of it all is a comfort... And more than that, it invites me to really examine things in an open-ended way and to appreciate the little discoveries along the way. The mystery is not in *how* things are but the sheer givenness and force of them as they are. No matter how much I learn about things, I remain amazed that they are the way they are."

"What little discoveries?" The voice comes from behind and to the right of us. Collins is grinning as he approaches, Delilah slung in a carrier on his chest.

"Oh, we're just solving the problems of the entire universe," Frank boasts.

Collins waves a dismissive hand, then pointing at me, says, "He'll take you down that road to oblivion if you don't watch out." I can see he's relaxed and appears positively joyful, not a condition I've witnessed in some years.

We stroll to the lake, chitchatting our way along. We skip rocks across the otherwise placid surface of the water. It becomes a contest, and Ivy finally wins with seven skips. She's impressed with her newfound talent.

Back at camp, with dinner finished, the dishes put away, and Delilah changed, Collins speaks up. "I wondered if maybe you three," pointing at them, "might like to spend the rest of the summer at my place?"

They stare blankly at Collins, and finally Ivy asks, "Us?"

"Yeah. My place's not all that big, but it'll do the job. You don't need to decide right away, but. . ."

"Problem is," Frank says in a low voice, "we don't have any money or anything else that's worth. . ."

"I'm not askin' for anything at all."

"Well then," Frank promises, "we're gonna think on it and maybe give it a try." With that, we all settled into the warmth of the little fire and the consolation of twilight.

The evening ends with Collins mentioning that we'll move around Santa Fe Baldy tomorrow to the west side. Ivy and Frank nod enthusiastically and, lifting their sleeping daughter, hike off toward their camp.

Twenty-Two

As long as man is finite he will never by fully relaxed.

Woody Allen

~

I realized that no matter how irrational and distorted answers given by faith might be, they had the advantage of introducing to every answer a relationship between the finite and the infinite, without which there can be no solution.

Leo Tolstoy

~

Santa Fe Baldy rises 12,600 feet to the northeast of Santa Fe. It can be seen from some places in town. Pecos Baldy, a twin peak, lies just to the north. These mountains are not especially tall, and their rounded bald tops give them a modest appearance as peaks go. Yet, like any mountain, they offer their own peculiar majesty.

Today we'll skirt the foot of Santa Fe Baldy from the east to the southwest, a fairly short hike of about three, maybe four, miles. Collins likes it this way. He wants to check out how fast we can travel with the baby. He has us up and eating as the sun brightens the open space on the slope above us to the west. Frank and Ivy start to clean dishes, but Collins encourages them to go back to their camp and pack up.

Within the hour, we've packed, inspected our campsite for needless residue of our being there, and taken to the trail. When we reach the other site, chaos reigns. Collins gives me a knowing look. They're novices and void of any sense of organization. We decide to drop our packs and sit to wait for them. I start to offer assistance, but Collins takes my arm. "Let 'em figure it out. They're not gonna learn any other way."

I mutter under my breath, "You sure you're ready to take them on?"

"It'll be educational," Collins responds.

"Whose education?"

"We'll see."

Collins whittles shavings from a stick into a pile, and I make notes in my journal. An hour later, Ivy stands apologetically in front of us. Frank is behind her, oblivious. She has a lighter pack than he does, but she carries Delilah in the sling at her chest. Frank's pack bulges, and an assortment of bags and gear dangles on the outside of it. He looks like a wandering street peddler.

Collins picks up the wood shavings and stuffs them in a side pocket of his pack. As usual, he takes the lead, and I follow at the rear. He quickly moves ahead by some thirty yards but realizes he needs to slow his pace. Soon we settle into a rhythm that suits our tiny caravan.

My journal notes cover yesterday's discussion with Frank. I'm frustrated with what I've discovered about formal religion. Everything seems fragmentary and unfinished. If all religious forms are ultimately inadequate efforts to capture the infinite, I'm left to wonder why religion persists and why so many people actually define their worlds by the canons of this or that religion.

While jotting notes this morning, it dawned on me that the second motivation for religions taking form is as important as the first, and I need to think it through. The drive to overcome the incomprehensibility and threat of the infinite is only partly sufficient to explain how our lust for infinity takes the forms it does and why it persists. There is this other motive, not infinity, but the fact of our own finitude.

Possibly the most difficult burden for us to accept is our own finitude. While it's *there*, staring us in the face at every moment, we keep deflecting our attention from the fact. Ernest Becker speaks brilliantly of this dilemma in *The Denial of Death*, a book I've already mentioned.

He focuses on death itself, but we can immediately expand our consideration to the entire experience of our finitude. We actually deny it all, and denying death is simply the most focal point of the denial. Becker says that we endlessly create what he calls "immortality projects" to take attention away from human limitations, especially our mortality, and to pretend that we are an exception to them. Surely we can conquer, or at least side step, the boundaries that confine us. All human presumption, as well as arrogance and outright evil, can be traced to this foundational denial of our finite existence and its conditions. This is how we're trapped within ourselves.

Becker describes our condition with stunning accuracy: "humans are the creatures that write poetry and shit." We imagine ourselves reaching unfathomable heights of human grandeur while at the same time being obliged to endure the visceral drag of embodiment.

To put it another way, our finitude is not our problem. *Our problem is that in the face of the infinite, we find our finitude intolerable.*

Once again, we are the creature who imagines the infinite and thus finds finitude an insufferable burden. I once used a text that describes some of the more noted theories of human nature. I was struck that each theory includes the same sequence of presentation: the nature of human existence; the problem with human existence; a proposed solution to the problem of existence. Every theory of our humanity construes our human condition as inherently *problematic*. The theories do not agree on how to characterize the problem or how to solve it, but they all agree there is a decisive problem that belongs to our very humanity.

I contend that when all proposals offered to account for humanity's definitive problem are shaken to the core, they rest in the ceaseless effort to deny finitude—and to do so by capturing, in one way or another, the infinite. Because we engage the infinite (or does it engage us?) and imagine boundless possibility, we make every effort to transform our finitude into the infinite. Religion emerges in the vortex of this dilemma—as does science, art, and other attempts to grasp the whole—and offers a response to it.

Indeed, I discern in this truth the great paradox at the core of the human dilemma: our resistance to our finitude and our urge to escape from it is accentuated by the *fallibility* inherent in finitude.

Perhaps the best way to understand fallibility is to think of it as our propensity to err. We can and do get it wrong, probably more often than not, and if we expand the sense of the term sufficiently, it may include all the weaknesses to which we are heir. Our fallibility, in turn, motivates our construction of formal religions—or at least some form of "immortality project." If this is true, then we must understand fallibility more broadly and especially its manifestation in what we call sin or evil.

Ivy calls ahead to Collins that she needs to stop. She removes her pack and takes out a blanket. She places Delilah on the blanket and proceeds to change her diaper. Immediately I wonder how they take care of diapers. I ask Frank, and he says it's a drag but that they have about twenty, and every two days they boil them and hang them to dry. They're hardy people, even if foolhardy!

We guzzle water and then help Ivy with her pack. The baby whimpers, but as soon as we're ontrail, she drifts into tranquility. Frank hangs back and asks, "What're you thinkin' about today? I saw you writin' stuff this mornin'."

I review my reflections, and he nods and says, "Babylon. It's always there to threaten or pull us away. It's the way of the white guys...the Man."

"I'm not sure the problem's 'out there' in a particular kind of guy," I protest. "That's what we all keep doin'. We say, 'I'd be fine if it weren't for...Babylon or something...or someone...else." The trail has turned flat, and talking while walking is easier. "I'm sayin' that the problem starts with us, with our rejection of our own condition and our projection of the problem to something or someone out there. That's what I'm callin' *fallibility*."

"Fallibility?" Frank asks. "Not sure exactly what you're drivin' at. Don't you just mean you're not perfect and you can mess up? That's how it strikes me."

'Well, that's part of it, but it doesn't go deep enough," I insist. "We have too many ways of avoiding the weight of our fallibility. For instance, people can do the most outrageous things, and when they're caught, the maximum confession is something like, 'I made a *mistake*.' That word mistake, what an evasion! When I deliberately do something perverse or hateful or callous, it's not a mistake. Mistakes are doing things you didn't intend to do. More like an 'oops'!"

"I can see that," Frank agrees. "Or here's one I used until Ivy laid into me about it. When I used to goof up, I'd say, 'Well, nobody's perfect.' She hates that."

Ivy stops in the middle of the trail and turns to us. "As far as I'm concerned not bein' perfect is nothin' but a way of elaborating the obvious. Who can really say anything else, since it's always just how it is?" Then she turns to see Collins almost over a rise ahead of us and picks up her pace.

"That comes closer to my whole notion of fallibility," I note. "What such throw-away 'confessions' try to cover up is how fundamental our problem is and how we spend so much energy denying we are as we are, fallible. We not only are this way, we do not seem to be able to keep from being this way. We're not done in by our limitations so much as by our refusal to face them. We deflect, reject, project. . .or outright deny. . .who we are.

All of the talk these days about our potential and the dreams of human achievement and excellence. . .the full arsenal of defenses we carry against our own finitude. . .is about as American as can be, but it leaves out of consideration the brute fact of our finitude and how liable we are to one sort of failure or another. Dammit, we do fall short. . .or deviate from who we imagine ourselves to be. As a friend puts it, 'We judge ourselves by our ideals and other people by their behavior.' That's why we always come up smellin' like a rose."

I catch myself delivering this diatribe and wonder why I'm so exercised about it. But then I realize that I actually believe this line of thinking is taking me closer to one of the cornerstones of the process that turns the religious sensibility into religious schemes and structures. It really doesn't matter whether we label the dilemma of fallibility as *sin, attachment, immorality,* or the more graphic *evil,* all attempts to account for our fallibility within religion begin with the recognition that we cannot—or do not—avoid this condition. And we can't get over it or escape it by denying, ignoring, or summarily mastering it.

Religions propose pathways through and beyond the crippling effects of fallibility. However, the one thing they do not do is avoid the dilemma.

The nearest thing to avoiding fallibility through religion seems to be the notion in some religions that all matters of fallibility result from one fact: *finite existence itself is sheer illusion.* But even so, the aim of religions that take this route is still to provide a way to penetrate and overcome the illusion. In this sense, then, the illusion is *real*, and that's the problem itself at the core of our humanity. Whether we're snared by fallibility or the illusion of finitude as our fallibility makes no serious difference.

Of course, there are also popular versions of religion such as those that emphasize positive thinking or what William James calls "healthy minded" religions. In some instances they may try to evade all preoccupation of human fallibility, but more often they at least minimally acknowledge our propensity for culpability while promising ready strategies for overcoming it. These religious forms, I believe, are marked by superficiality in refusing to countenance the gravity of human finitude, and certainly of human fallibility. Still, even though their perspective may suffer from shallow analysis, they are nevertheless, as religious forms, committed to addressing the problematic character of finite existence.

My point is that religious forms, when probed to their foundations, appear to arise in response to the conditions of finitude and the human propensity to either dismiss or strive to overcome the fallibility attendant to finitude. In short, religions arise because existence is messy, and they strive to engage and resolve—or at least cope with—the mess!

Frank turns to me. "I have another one. When people get caught doing something they shouldn't, they say, 'I'm not the only one!'" He throws his head back in laughter, and I grin at him. "Or," he adds, "they say, 'Everybody's doin' it.' I've used that one myself, especially with my old man."

"Right," I agree. "I suppose we could say that fallibility loves company."

For the next half hour we trudge in silence, except for Delilah's slight stirring. We enter a wood, and I notice squirrels announcing us by fussing from their perches above. I think, *Even the creatures don't like their boundaries being invaded, but at least they don't have this burden of having to hide from their own limitations. They announce them with authority!*

Somehow I want to go deeper into this idea of fallibility. It's not the *idea* of it that needs to be grasped so much as the weight of it in accounting for how we human beings behave and snarl our existence so badly—and why religion is inevitable. This morning I jotted down four insights I've had about human fallibility. They may help cast more light on it and clarify its relation to formal religion.

First, there are at least three expressions of our human fallibility: frailty, folly, and fault. Frailty, of course, belongs to our finite condition as such. We are constrained by time, space, embodiment, and mortality, and all of these conspire to make suffering inevitable. Simple enough, but because of these tight confines, we are simply unable to do all we imagine or desire. Fallibility is not frailty as such but our constant denial or minimization of the frailty. Our fallibility makes its appearance as we strive to overcome these limits but fail to do so. Even when we momentarily feel we have broken the bounds, the transience of the breach becomes evident, and we slide back into the inevitable confines of finitude. Our fallibility lies either in denial or in summarily embracing the victimization that can come with failure. We are liable to failure for no other reason than the inherent frailty of our finitude, and I include all failure to be immortal, as strange as that may sound. This includes sickness, physical and psychic weakness, and the full range of suffering and anxiety to which we are prey.

I once became unexpectedly ill in New York's Kennedy Airport as I waited for a flight to Europe. My body went into rebellion, the result of shellfish poisoning. Try as I might to control my body and to endure what I could not comprehend, I utterly failed. I now recall my dominant psychological response throughout the ordeal: not fear or pain but embarrassment! Not only did my frailty take over my very body, but *I was publicly exposed as being frail*. My fallibility, in the form of frailty, was on display. (Eventually, of course, I became sufficiently ill to lose all interest in my being publicly exposed. I was forced to own my fallibility, manifest in my frailty.)

Religions often come most dramatically into play around issues of human frailty. Suffering and the desire for healing, death and the attendant rituals of closure (or transition), other life crises, evoke religious gestures. They are occasions when frailty cannot be hidden or ignored, and religious forms are marshaled to mediate the process of facing, enduring, and coming to terms with frailty's trauma.

Fallibility as frailty, however, is only one of three manifestations of our finite dilemma. A second is *fallibility as folly*. When I speak of folly, I do not mean ignorance or even stupidity. Folly entails our living obliviously toward our finitude. We simply pay no attention to the conditions of our existence. We stalk off blindly into our dreams of the possible, striving to preempt the infinite by pretending boundlessness. I once saw a card in a Tarot deck entitled *The Fool*. It portrayed a young swain, his knapsack over his shoulder, walking off a cliff. A perfect image of folly!

****

The boy-at-the-edge-of-manhood abandons home for college, the first in his family to do so. He matriculates at a small school associated with his religious tradition. A good choice. He is among familiar ways and at home there. On the surface it is an idyllic place to learn, but before he departs four years hence, he will discover the turbulent inner workings of this citadel of piety, which will reveal to him the stream of that turbulence within himself.

Within weeks of his entry into this new life the young man makes a dramatic decision. During a charged service of worship, pulsing with the fervor of youthful religious zeal, he "surrenders" to the ministry. He will become a "preacher," as everyone calls it there. Older folk have repeatedly told him that he had the gift of words and that he should follow this way. Moreover, he has discovered words and found force and solace in uttering them and writing them. He has been struck by Hermes, but he is only barely aware of it.

Over the next four years, while at study, the young man becomes an evangelist. Many of his peers follow the same course. There is keen competition among them as to who might preach the most. On weekends, the fledgling evangels fan out across the region to conduct revivals, youth rallies, and an array of churchly gatherings. By the end of his college years, the young man can boast of having preached more than six hundred times. Not a record but impressive.

But something happens during this preaching binge. The young man studies. He becomes ravenous for knowledge and for the ability to think clearly. His great love becomes philosophy, the art of critical and creative thinking in devotion to a reliable knowing. This subject is considered somewhat questionable at the institution. His teacher, also his primary mentor, confronts him more than once with the suggestion that the quantity of preaching does not matter so much as its quality. If one is a maker of words, does this not entail that the words be good ones? The young man begins to examine his words, and they are often found wanting. His preaching becomes, in the communities where he goes, somewhat eccentric. To some he is already suspect. To others he is "heady." To himself he is struggling for the synapse that connects words with understanding and worth.

The underbelly of psyche and spirit lies deep beneath the surface for everyone at the school. For him it lies deeper than for most others, because it is so ardently denied. Yet, it boils in the depths of the institution and those who live within it. Despite the young man's earnest intentions and ardent devotion to "the cause," these darker edges surface. They are not so much sinister as bewildering. He is taught a ready explanation: Satan. But this answer never satisfies him. He knows he is his own "satan," but no one dares admit this.

The young man, a member of the locally prestigious Gospel Team, is working with a young woman on day, a fellow student. He ardently strives to guide her into a state of grace. Other clusters are doing the same around the room. Suddenly, as he speaks with the young woman, he hears a distinct voice: "You are a phony." He whirls around to see who might have said this, but he sees nothing. He hears it only once, but the words are so disturbing that he summarily departs and returns to his room. He never hears this message again, but he does not need to hear it. It is indelibly sealed within. He broods on this for weeks. To be a fool is one thing, to have his folly exposed—to himself— is quite another.

****

Folly is often taken as a species of courage, but it lacks the sense of perspective and proportion that goes with courage. Aristotle defines courage as "knowing what to fear and what to dare." For him, courage is a middle way between two extremes: that of the coward and that of the foolhardy. The foolhardy presume upon the future and rush headlong into it, impervious to the strictures of finitude. The opposite, forethought, can be pressed to a neurotic distortion of prudence that becomes paralysis. This is cowardice. In this sense, cowardice is the negative of folly, its dark underbelly.

Perhaps we could think of it this way. On the one hand, religious faith or trust requires courage, that is, a kind of *risk* or daring, but if it is pressed too far into what is popularly called blind faith, it falls into folly. Faith is corrupted into presumption. On the other hand, if faith is taken simply as *security* in face of the "fell clutch of circumstance" known as human existence, it can easily degenerate into a hideout from that existence, into cowardice. In this way, both folly and its cowardly negation often manifest themselves in religion.

Folly cannot be eliminated by education because it is not ignorance. To address and overcome folly requires an *awakening*, a shift in consciousness away from the willful arrogance that denies finitude to a *willing* embrace of the burden of existence.

The third expression of fallibility is *fallibility as fault*. We cannot be charged with responsibility for being frail as such because it belongs to our finite condition. We are held accountable, however, for not attending our frailty either by hastily succumbing to it or by denying it. For instance, if we are morbidly obese, we may be charged with not adequately monitoring our diet.

When I speak of fallibility as fault, I have in mind conduct that *transgresses* finite boundaries, not by folly but through calculated and deliberate intent. We seek to breach our own finitude by invading and violating the finite domain of other human beings, of sentient creatures, or of nature itself. These are the actions for which human beings stand culpable before each other. All such transgressions, I believe, are expressions of a deeper urge, the lust for infinity itself. In ancient Christianity this lust was called cupiditas, the urge to take everything up into ourselves. The resulting transgressions are the basis of all that we call *evil*. It may be that not all transgressions are evil, but all evil entails transgression.

The endless discussions of evil, especially in philosophy and religious discourse, need not occupy us here. There are, to be sure, important and perennial questions: What is evil? Does it really exist? Who is responsible for it? How is it related to the ultimate order of things? These and similar questions are worthy of perennial reflection, but here I seek to establish only one general idea: evil lies in human fallibility understood as fault and is bound up in the longing to deny, reject, or overcome our own finitude by means of transgression. Evil begins with those petty behaviors that hardly register as more than human foibles and reaches to include the most heinous acts attributed to human beings. Moreover, this condition is the very condition to which the religions of the world strive to respond by variously addressing the encounter of human finitude with the infinite.

Second, there is an enormous gap between the roots of our fallibility and the surface behavior where we actually encounter it. For the most part we discern fallibility as fault only in our actions and especially in the actions of other people, what we and other people actually do. And we judge matters at that level. We may probe into motive to determine the extent to which the behavior is deliberate and premeditated, but we seldom go beyond that, except in cases of such horrendous behavior that we must separate its perpetrators from the rest of humanity—and especially from ourselves!

By dehumanizing such people, we separate them at a sufficient distance so they do not unveil our own capacity for doing as they have done. (When one young veteran of Vietnam was asked what he learned by fighting in that distant land, he responded, "I learned that you'll rape your mother and murder your father to survive!" That says it all.)

By the same token, I realize, we are quite as much dismayed by notable instances of ideal behavior. We are inclined to lionize those who perform such noble acts and to turn them into unreachable heroes. Rather than dehumanize them, we elevate them to superhumanity, to gods, where they cannot disturb our own strategies for denying the fallibility belonging to our finitude. Our elevation of these fellow humans may begin with envy we dare not admit, but this—and other unsavory efforts to sidestep confrontation with admirable conduct—ends with the elevation of exemplars into irrelevance.

Between envy and irrelevance lies a middle way. We may secretly identify ourselves with our perceived moral heroes, and this is actually quite easy. We do it by focusing on our idealizations and our excuses for not achieving them rather than on our actual conduct in contrast to theirs.

The roots of fallibility as fault lie far beneath the surface fissures of our conduct. They belong to our existential condition. That is, they rest at the point of encounter between our finitude and the infinite. The infinite exposes our finitude and sets in motion the endless jockeying for ways of capturing the infinite and avoiding or evading our finitude. All reprehensible human conduct, even the very worst, finds its origin here and nowhere else.

Furthermore, since religion takes form from exactly this same locus, it follows that religion rests upon and addresses the clash between finitude and fallibility. In short, religion arises in response to fault, to sin and evil. No one escapes this situation, nor can religion do otherwise than address it and propose avenues for overcoming or coping with it.

Third, however, we are amazingly hard pressed to acknowledge, let alone embrace, our own fallibility—particularly our faults. Or, if we do so, even that acknowledgment becomes a surreptitious tactic for making ourselves appear to rise above our fallibility by the grace of *confession*. The truism, "honest confession is good for the soul" stands, but the catch lies in the one word *honest*. When it comes to fallibility, the reach of our cunning to avoid it is endlessly convoluted and persistent. What's worse, we're blind to it.

Our most effective avoidance game is to make a sharp distinction between good and evil. We do this for one—or perhaps a combination of two—ends. On the one hand, we identify with the good against the evil. This option is by far the most attractive. It serves to objectify evil and to distance us from it. On the other hand, we admit our complicity in evil through "honest confession" in order to show how insightful we are in knowing the difference between good and bad. This backup plan works quite well, especially when we are caught "in the act," as it were.

Our most serviceable mode of *projection* is to identify evil with the worst, with only those actions so horrendous that virtually every "normal" human being is utterly repulsed. We then say, or leave the impression, that we could never countenance, let alone perpetrate, such vile acts. When we do this, we successfully separate ourselves not only from the acts under judgment but also from the roots we share with even those judged to be the most reprehensible of our species.

I readily admit that there is much conduct that properly should be clearly recognized as profoundly evil and that the evilness of it is not to be diluted by any accommodating explanation, let alone justification. Yet, I must insist that if the origin of these most reprehensible acts finds its roots, not in our finitude but in the perpetual denial or rejection of the fallibility of our finitude, then the worst is distinct only in degree rather than in kind from our more superficial attempts to minimize, reject, or wink at our own fallibility. My further point is to insist that religion takes form precisely in the attempt to honestly admit and confront our fallibility and to offer means to assuage it.

Fourth, and perhaps the most difficult factor to embrace regarding fallibility, is what may be called *the lure of transgression*. Behavior that may end in the most lurid evil, is actually *attractive*. By this I mean more than the proverbial forbidden fruit inclination. To put it simply, transgression implies boundary, and boundary implies finite limits. But we imagine the infinite, and we are caught in its aura and are under its spell. We lust for the infinite, and the madness of this urge lies in our propensity to transgress the conditions of finite existence to gain the infinite. That is, we are drawn to transgress upon the infinite itself—impossible thought that is!

All evil, as indicated earlier, finds its origin here. Because the artifacts of our lives, and more specifically the claims of other human beings upon us, confront us with our finitude and threaten to expose our fallibility, we easily succumb to the lure of crossing boundaries. Herein is the origin of the phrase, *playing God*. If we can but possess what lies on the other side of our boundaries, we can begin the conquest of the infinite.

Georges Bataille, another figure I have mentioned, captures this bent in the word *erotism*. The erotic is itself the urge to completeness, to overcome our fragmentary finitude by consuming what lies beyond our ken. Transgression is thus exhilarating! It provides the momentary thrill of being unbounded—of tasting the infinite. Herein, fault and folly join hands in leaping empty handed into the void. Of course, the effort fails, and it fails every time, but we have the utmost blindness and forgetfulness at just this juncture. One more reach, a slightly greater effort, and surely we will realize—what? We can hardly admit that the *what* is actually the infinite. Even the most strident overreaching arrogance can rarely go this far.

Still, every transgression—and the possibilities never end—uncovers the root problem: our finitude, especially in light of the infinite, is unbearable, and its gravity lies in the fallibility imbedded in our experience of finitude.

Religion takes form in the nexus of a shattering realization of this truth. We cannot escape either our finitude or its fallibility, but our principal longing, our lust, is to do so. Religion comes to the fore by offering a way out, or a way of solace, or a way of more profound engagement with the very reality that otherwise threatens and snares us in perpetual war against ourselves and against all.

When we stop for lunch, I'm lost in my ruminations and don't want to be distracted. I take a peanut butter sandwich and a pouch of dried fruit from my pack and walk up into the woods. I sit on a stump, staring into surrounding foliage. Presently a porcupine wanders into a small opening, sniffs the air, and ambles off downhill. I watch, intrigued by the creature's independence and nonchalance. This is far more its domain than mine. What an odd prickly creature, I think to myself, and I imagine it thinks the same of me.

Presently I have a flash of insight about all that I've pondered today. I ask myself: *But why is it that religion still seems to be as much a part of the problem of finitude as an attempt to resolve it? Yes, religion, the savior from the fallibility of our finitude, is itself also fallible*!

I write furiously in my journal about the obvious fact that much religion distorts its message and misleads people, that it can be pathological and can perpetuate the very evil it would challenge. Hosts of religious skeptics have publicized this obvious truth, and even devoutly religious people are quite as bewildered and disturbed by this sinister underbelly of religion.

Then the insight comes. *When religion presumes to answer conclusively for the infinite, it falls prey to the temptation to coerce other people in the name of its claims*! In other words, religion may suffer the delusion of possessing the greatest alibi of all for justifying evil. In such cases, it does not assuage or resolve the problem of fallibility as fault. It perpetuates the problem. Indeed, there is no more powerful sanction for evil than religious justification.

Religion, I find myself writing in bold letters, is not only inevitable and ultimately inadequate. *It is dangerous! And the danger rests in failing to accept its own limits and its ultimate inadequacy.*

Formal religion, I keep repeating ad infinitum, comes into play out of the existential encounter of our finitude with the infinite, but when formal religions lose their humility, they become liable to the evil they would overcome. Once I understand this, I become aware of the fragility of formal religion and the need for its adherents to be ever mindful of excess or of what I called earlier, using Rene Girard's language, "a deviated transcendence," which can legitimate the most heinous behavior.

Thus, the integrity of religion requires a delicate balance. Otherwise, *idolatry*, the singular religious curse and its consequent liability to religiously inspired fault!

Collins whistles from below, and I scramble back to meet the brood. Soon we're climbing a gradual grade through, first, a stand of aspen, and then pines dotted with occasional spruce. I assure Frank and Ivy that we'll arrive shortly. I can see our destination through the opening in the trees ahead. Rather unexpectedly, the brow of a ridge gives way to a sun-splashed meadow about a hundred yards across and perhaps half again that long. A hidden stream runs silently in a deep furrow through the meadow. "Arrowhead Meadow," I announce.

Collins heads for a cluster of especially tall trees across the open area and just beyond the stream. One of the largest of the trees has fallen since I was last here, and it partly blocks the stream. Its enormous trunk lies well above our heads as we pass.

When Collins drops his pack, the rest of us follow suit. After stretching and reconnoitering for several minutes, we choose various sites for tents at a little distance from the fire ring in the center of the seldom-used campsite. Frank takes Delilah, and Ivy whirls around, as if liberated from confinement. Within the hour we've set up tents and scavenged wood for a fire. Collins goes for water, and I clean out the firepit. To our considerable delight, it is only mid-afternoon, and we scatter in casual exploration of the meadow. Frank takes Delilah to the middle of a cluster of mountain lilies and waves back at us. Ivy follows behind Collins upstream where the rise toward Santa Fe Baldy begins.

I want to finish this process of thinking through the dilemma of fallibility because I believe it to be crucial to any adequate grasp of formal religion and especially of the reasons human beings pursue it with such persistence. With my journal in hand, I stroll to a large flat rock at the edge of the meadow, where I've spent long hours in the past. It rests in the sun. I sit facing west and for a time simply let the sun do its work.

After acclimating myself to the restful little space, I open to my notes of this morning and read them through, scratching out some passages and adding a couple. Then I turn back to the subject of how religions form in response to our existential crisis of finitude cum fallibility. I discern that religion employs three principal strategies to address our finitude, and every religion of which I am aware takes up one or, usually, a combination of them. These strategies are strictly formal and only serve to indicate the logical possibilities: religions that embrace finitude; religions that seek to overcome finitude; religions that mediate between finitude and the infinite.

In the first place, religions may form around the aim of consoling humanity within the confines of finitude. Every religion to some extent strives to provide such consolation, but this way, what might be called *the way of consolation*, concentrates on embracing human finitude while honoring the otherwise overwhelming burden of the infinite. I sense that many, if not most, indigenous religions serve this end. My guess is that their far greater sensitivity and attunement to the rhythms of nature and their devotion to those rhythms allow them to be less inclined to overreach their boundedness. For this reason their taboo systems are especially pronounced. They prohibit whatever they perceive to seriously challenge boundaries.

Sacrifice is the method used to atone or appease, to keep the infinite at bay or to keep it satisfied. Religions that involve sacrifice appear less inclined to transgression and conquest of the infinite. They remain more at home in their condition, while giving honor to the grander scheme that reigns over them.

In the second place, religions may offer a way out of the constraints of finitude with the promise of a more-or-less direct relation to the infinite. This approach might be designated as *the way of liberation*, that is, deliverance from the conditions of finitude and the curse of fallibility. Religions that offer this way out tend to emphasize the distance or gap between human finitude and the infinite.

To be sure, the emphasis on liberation is common within and among religions, and what counts as liberation widely varies. What I have in mind here are those that make explicit and confident promises about ultimate liberation, usually couched in redemptive ideas of *salvation* and *eternal life*. The monotheistic religions are especially inclined to emphasize this way of being religious.

In so far as religions promise a definitive resolution of the hiatus between the finite and the infinite, they tend toward doctrinal formulation, finality, and exclusive or absolutistic claims. In their most strident forms, these religions are ardently assertive, if not aggressive, in seeking adherents and in proffering their faith as the singular solution to the problem of human existence. Consequently, in extreme versions, such religions claim that their finite message is straightforwardly identified with the infinite. There are, of course, degrees and differences among religious claims of this kind, but insofar as they seek closure and finality on the assumption that they traffic in a unique intimacy with the infinite, they strive to overcome the inherent limitation of formal religion, albeit, without success. This extreme is what I'm calling the peculiarly religious expression of fallibility, *idolatry*.

Thirdly, religions may form around the aim of perpetual mediation between the finite and the infinite. This might be called *the way of participation*. Mindful of the abiding tension between human finitude and the infinite, these religious forms invite us to recognize that, in a sense, we already belong to the infinite. That is, while humanity remains a part of as well as *apart from*, they dwell partly within their finitude while *participating* the infinite.

This play on the root *part* suggests an inherent relation between our finitude and the infinite. Humanity is neither fully outside nor identical with the infinite. In this mode, human beings are at once called beyond themselves and at the same time ever more deeply to and within themselves. The aim is enlightenment! Further, the relation is dynamic and processive, as *participation* implies. My own sense of Asian religions in general, and specifically Hinduism, Buddhism, and Taoism, is that they are closer to this way of construing religion.

These three strategies are abstract and somewhat artificial, but they serve to indicate in broad strokes the range of possibilities among religions for coping with their own formal limitations and the condition of fallibility. Religions may, and do, mix these elements, but they tend to stress one or another of the three. We do well to keep in mind that religions have a mission: to address the problem of human finitude and the crises of fallibility in relation to the human encounter with the infinite. I find that. . .

"Hey," A voice comes from behind me. Frank approaches, still wagging Delilah on his hip like a peasant woman. He leans against the rock, and I reach down to take the baby. He releases her with relief. "Man, she's heavier every day," he says.

We visit casually for a while. He wants me to talk about my project, but I'm through with it for the day. Brain fatigue! I scoot to the ground, and we walk to the end of the meadow, pausing to notice small oddities. Delilah rests easily on my shoulder and is soon asleep.

Back at camp Collins is already setting the fire. He removes the wood shavings he produced this morning and uses them as the base to build a pyramid of twigs and sticks. Within minutes a tiny flame blazes. At this altitude the flames are subdued by the limited oxygen available, but we soon find modest warmth against the cooling twilight.

Ivy helps Collins prepare dinner while I hold the sleeping baby and Frank brings in more wood. He hauls up a relatively large limb, places it in the fork of a tree, and pulls it until it snaps and he screeches and tumbles to the ground. Delilah bolts awake, and we all guffaw at Frank lying splayed in the weeds with one foot in a recent deposit of cow dung. The baby whimpers until she spots her mother, and Ivy immediately takes her for feeding. I assume duties at the cookstove. We're becoming familiar with each other, a cozy clutch of shared humanity. I enjoy these mountain vagabonds, their odd innocence and good spirits.

After dinner Collins retrieves a harmonica from his tent and soulfully drags out tunes we know: "Home on the Range," "Somewhere Over the Rainbow," "My Only Sunshine" We sing along in fits and starts, with loud outbursts when familiar phrases come to mind.

Collins puts away his harmonica, looks at us clustered around the fire, and offers a kind of benediction, a Ute saying I think: "Today was a very good day to die." Then he adds, "But we didn't. So, we have something to look forward to in the mornin'." He turns and disappears into the night, and we scatter.

Fourth Movement: Transformation

Twenty-Three

> This need to shut out many aspects of reality in order to live as finite creatures that we are, not only limited but limited in our specifically human ways, also applies, I have been suggesting, to our consciousness of God. We have a system for filtering out the infinite divine reality and reducing it to forms with which we can cope. This system is religion, which is our resistance (in a sense analogous to that used in electronics) to God. The function of the different religions is to enable us to be conscious of God, and yet only partially and selectively, in step with our own spiritual development, both communal and individual.
>
> John Hick

~

"What if we climbed to the top today?" These are Frank's first words of the morning. No one responds as he stares into the trees hiding the ascent up Santa Fe Baldy.

Collins pours Frank a cup of coffee before speaking. "Well, it's today or never, I guess."

"Whatta you mean?" Frank asks.

I respond. "We'll need to start down tomorrow if we're gonna catch our ride."

Frank nods. Restive with enthusiasm, he urges, "Then let's go for it."

"I wanna' go too," Ivy's muffled voice announces from their tent. Her head appears through the frayed tent flap.

"Not sure about that," Collins interjects. "It's not a bad climb, but with the baby. . .I don't know."

Ivy is out of the tent and approaching the fire as she rebuts, "But I'll carry her myself. Nobody needs to bother. . ."

"And what about Frank. He's the dad," I add with a smirk.

Frank says, "Yeah, right," as if embarrassed at not having owned his status.

"Or, we'll take turns with Delilah," Collins concedes.

"I'm not comin' down 'til I make it to the top," Ivy declares. "I've wanted to climb up there since we came, and like you said, it's gotta be today."

I'm stretched between apprehension and admiration, but I stay out of the discussion and settle for handing around bowls of piping old-fashioned oatmeal, my one specialty. I sprinkle brown sugar, raisins, and a few nuts in each bowl as I release it.

While we eat, Collins explains that there's no trail up the mountain from this side but that we can fairly easily bushwhack our way to the top. He concludes, "We can make our own switchbacks up the steep places." Then he looks toward the sky to the west and adds a postscript: "We need to start right away. We want to be off the top before it storms. . .and throw in a jacket. It'll be cool up there."

Within minutes the campsite turns into a staging area: sandwiches made, dried fruit and trail mix gathered, water purified and distributed. Day packs are stuffed with extra shirts and jackets, then the food. Water bottles dangle on the outside of packs. Delilah, in a lively mood, is the last to be hoisted into the sling on Ivy's chest.

Ivy takes the lead until the trail disappears under our feet about halfway through the timber. Then Collins takes point. The climb is steady but not steep for a quarter of a mile. Just before we come out of the trees, the terrain becomes more demanding. We take the first of frequent breaks.

I lie on my back staring at wisps of cloud forming, dissolving, and reforming. Frank drops beside me and says, "I've been thinkin'. If religion's so important, like you say it is, then why doesn't everybody practice a religion?" When I don't respond right away, he begins his own answer. "Course, maybe everybody has a religion but some of 'em don't look like it." He sits up, shakes his head and says, "I don't know, but it sure seems to me that most of the people around me, except other Rastas, couldn't give a fig about religion. My generation wants to get drunk, stoned, or laid, and that's about it. . .or find a way to make lots of money while listenin' to music. And the regulars, like my ole' man, just want to be. . .well. . .regular. Anything to look good, including their religion." He shakes his head again, chuckles, and reaches for his water flask.

Before I can say anything, Collins calls for us to begin climbing again. The terrain is too steep for talking, but I begin to ruminate on Frank's question and his comments about it. Everything rests on how we take religion. If we make it general enough, then almost anything can count as a religion. It all depends on the degree of commitment, not what the commitment is. Whatever we make a matter of life and death and pour all of our energy into operates quite like a religion. Whatever we stake our very lives upon is our religion. If we look at religion Frank's way, virtually everyone has a religion by definition.

Although I do believe everyone has the elemental potential for religion, what I've called *the religious sensibility*, to make everyone religious by definition is not especially fruitful. In fact, it can be almost dismissive: *Oh well, everyone has a religion!*

As Ethan and I discussed back at the beginning of our pilgrimage, if religion's to be taken seriously, we need to distinguish between being religious, or having a religion, and not having one. As we've said, scholars have repeatedly made a distinction between two basic human orientations: *sacred* and *profane*.

The idea is that we humans live in two dimensions at once. The profane or ordinary orientation has to do with daily life, the process of staying alive and thriving. The sacred or holy transcends the ordinary or commonplace by designating and honoring our sense of connection to whatever gives comprehensive meaning and coherence to ordinary or profane existence as a whole. These two orientations are thoroughly mixed, especially in indigenous or tribal cultures, but modernity, especially in the West over the past three hundred years, has increasingly divided the sacred from the profane and proceeded to concentrate on the profane.

The most common term used for this process today is not *profane* but *secular*. I discussed it in a general way earlier, but it's important here for two reasons. On the one hand, the secular is now commonly used to distinguish religion from what is not religion, and on the other, the secular dominates our modern situation in which all religions find themselves.

The distinction between having a religion and not having one implies that one's religion is increasingly a matter of personal choice. We are no longer simply fated to follow the form of religion dictated by family or culture. One recent popular book, *Finding Your Religion*, goes so far as to advise us on choosing a religion for ourselves. True, we may commonly begin with a religion foisted on us long before we are able to decide for ourselves, but with the growing plurality of religions spread before us, we can, at least in principle, determine for ourselves whether to continue practicing a given religion or change religions or not practice any religion at all.

Religion as choice, however, is made possible by a larger frame of reference, one that belongs to modernity itself. Let's call it the *secular spirit*. We may best comprehend this orientation by considering the word *secular* itself. Like that other term, *profane*, the secular aspect of our existence refers to the concrete and mundane condition of our survival and the projects we pursue to that end. The secular refers to here and now and to human ingenuity and effort expressed for the sake of human interests. To put it simply, the secular is *earthly*. It focuses on what belongs to human capacity and control. What we call modernity is marked by increasing emphasis on this orientation until it dominates the way we organize our societies and cultures, the way we resolve problems, and the way we thrive.

In a fundamental sense we humans have always been secular. Insofar as we face the demands of existence with the conviction that we are capable of addressing and resolving the issues involved for ourselves, we are secular. Even among those who maintain an intimate bond between the sacred and the secular, the secular remains. Indeed, the most ardent spiritual ascetic must undertake some concrete domesticating duties in order to live. Or, at least *someone* has to undertake them on behalf of the most strident ascetic.

Western modernity, however, is marked by a concentration upon the secular orientation at the expense of the sacred. In other words, we have taken an aspect of life and rendered it fully adequate, sacrosanct. *Secularization* is this process of increasing the dominance of the secular orientation. Furthermore, secularization has spread from the West and is in the process of becoming planetary. Every civilization is affected, and while there is resistance to secularization and its excesses, it continues to set the rules for our globe.

But the impact of secularization upon the sacred, and hence upon religion, does not stop there. When secularization is employed to *reject* the sacred, and religion, it becomes *secularism*. It strives to undermine religion altogether or to marginalize the sacred strictly to the private sphere of personal decision. Secularism as extreme secularization seeks to bring the dimension of religion to an end, to render it obsolete, anachronistic, nothing more than vestigial superstition fated to wither away.

Wherever secularization devolves into secularism, a peculiar consequence follows. The secular itself becomes the final substitute for the sacred and for religion. Historically this substitution is most sharply evident in constructs such as Marxism and later, Freudianism. Other, more abstract candidates include scientism, materialism, aestheticism, and some versions of humanism. Attempts are made to have a self-contained scheme fully and finally adequate to explain everything without the need for the sacred. Put another way, the secular becomes itself sacred by substitution. I've called these attempts *surrogate religions*. They function like religions while denying transcendence as a dimension beyond our intramundane control.

Nevertheless, I insist that, even at this extreme, the religious sensibility remains. It still articulates itself as the drive to master the infinite and to bring it into form, harnessing it for human purposes. In short, secularism conquers the sacred by becoming the sacred. The Promethean dream fully realized! It swallows its dialectical other! From a more foundational religious perspective, however, this extreme is treacherous indeed. It is but another kind of idolatry—idolatry as ideology. The infinite is still confined under the thrall of a finite scheme declaring its own ultimate adequacy. Formal religion has not disappeared but has been driven underground by yet another form masquerading in its place.

All of this is to claim that secularism itself, despite the blindness of its advocates, is a form of religion striving to articulate the religious sensibility. As such, secularism is a competitor within the plurality of religions, standing against them all and claiming to have supplanted any need for them.

Not all who are committed to secularization are necessarily guilty of secularism. Some appear to be simply preoccupied with the grand secular challenges before them. They settle for the earthly immediacy that belongs to the lure of secularity itself. They live, as it were, in one long parenthetical distraction, mesmerized by the secular spirit. And as long as the lure of the secular maintains its promise, they may well leave the religious sensibility lying fallow and uncultivated. They are, apparently, *a*-religious. Nor will they necessarily realize this, but the extreme situations attendant to human existence can and sometimes do challenge the secular fixation and invite its devotees beyond the secular boundaries. Still, we must allow for the likelihood that some people—perhaps more of them in this secular age—settle for *sheer immediacy*. They do not recognize, or they have not attended, the capacity to engage, a dimension beyond their secular domain.

Still other secular minds, however, are aware of something more, but they remain unable or unwilling to embrace formal religion. They appear to be caught somewhere between the religious sensibility, which belongs to their existence, and the plethora of forms into which that sense has taken shape. A couple of examples come to mind.

The philosopher Ludwig Wittgenstein was thoroughly secular in his intellectual interests. Yet, he continued throughout his life to raise religious questions. He at times denied that he was religious, but at other times he recognized his whole philosophical enterprise was somehow religiously driven. I sense that he acknowledged the religious sensibility while refusing all efforts to give it form. He may well have realized that every attempt to give the impulse form is inherently inadequate and thus a potential trap. This interpretation of Wittgenstein is somewhat conjectural on my part, but based on how others have interpreted his religious sensibilities and his own writings, he stands as a secular man who remains genuinely open to the infinite possibility in its religious aspect.

Some years ago, while reading the autobiography of Loren Eiseley, *All the Strange Hours*, I sensed early that he was a thoroughly secular man. He was a scientist and enamored of the promise that comes through scientific investigation. Yet, his was a brooding mind that knew there was more to human existence than what the grand secular project of modernity could comprehend. Story after story reveals this subtle reservation in the face of his commitment of secularization. Near the end of his self-study, he entitles a section "Days of a Doubter," and in a startling passage he confesses that there is a place where his secular adventure comes abruptly to an end. While reflecting on the behavior of a Sphex wasp, he confesses:

> I am an evolutionist. I believe my great backyard Sphexes have evolved like other creatures. But watching them in the October light as one circles my head in curiosity, I can only repeat my dictum softly: in the world there is nothing to explain the world. Nothing to explain the necessity of life, nothing to explain the hunger of the elements to become life, nothing to explain why the stolid realm of rock and soil and mineral should diversify itself into beauty, terror, and uncertainty. To bring organic novelty into existence, to create pain, injustice, joy, demands more than we can discern in nature that we analyze so completely. Worship, then, like the Maya, the unknown zero, the procession of the time-bearing gods. The equation that can explain why a mere Sphex wasp contains in its minute head the ganglionic centers of its prey has still to be written. In the world there is nothing below a certain depth that is truly explanatory. It is as if matter dreamed and muttered in its sleep. But why, and for what reason it dreams, there is no evidence.

I found these words so astonishing that I keep them on a note card in my journal. Eiseley harks to a concept from Wittgenstein, that there is nothing in the world to explain the world. With this admission, both men acknowledge that the secular project, as impressive as it may be, comes to a jolting halt before the explanatory limits of a final why! All one can do, Eiseley admits, is to "worship...the procession of time-bearing gods." He knows the problem is religious in character, but he also knows that nothing whatever within the bounds of finitude—including the forms religion takes—can adequately explain that finitude. Thus, he finds himself standing in the wake of the religious sensibility but allowing it only the most tenuous possible form, "the unknown zero."

All of this is to say that, in the midst of this era of strident secularization and the excesses of secularism, there are those who discern the something more that finds expression as the sacred. They may be unwilling to confess more, but knowing it is there is quite enough to challenge the vast overreach of secularist thinking. Well over a century and a half ago, the Danish philosopher Soren Kierkegaard saw that religion is larger than its specific forms. He spoke of two religions, "Religiousness A and Religiousness B." The former he attributed to Socrates, and the latter he identified with Christianity. I suspect that "religiousness A" is close to what Wittgenstein and Eiseley embrace, namely the religious sensibility that cannot be satisfied by a secularist reduction of it to a human urge toward fulfillment.

By our third break we are all panting for breath. Ivy takes Delilah out of the sling and spreads a blanket. The infant is notably placid today. She seems to thrive on the climb, as if she knows its challenge and promise. I take out my journal briefly while snacking on a health bar and read the Eiseley passage again. I think of having Frank read it, but Collins has us up and walking before I can manage it. We are at another steep passage just below a false crest. Frank asks whether we're almost to the top, and Collins only grins and waves us upward. Novice climbers often want to reach the top before they're there. Pushing the envelope!

Mountains! I consider how they lure people and dare them to climb. Indeed, high places have long served as representations of the sacred. I recall a Hopi saying to me, as he looked west toward the San Francisco Mountains east of Flagstaff, that those mountains were where human life originated. Such stories are replicated in many religious traditions. Is it the mountain's height? Or its simple prominence and visibility? Or perhaps its sheer bulk?

I once climbed a modest mountain made famous by the paintings of Georgia O'Keeffe: the Padernal. Collins and I climbed together. The last hundred feet were vertical, and we had to find a slight opening in order to wedge ourselves up, pushing and heaving our backpacks and a three-day supply of water. Our reward was height, silence, and above all, *perspective*. We could see how the terrain unfolded for miles on every side. The vista expanded and pushed horizons into hazy distance. It could be that this capacity of high places ties it most closely to the sacred. High places bring people closer to an imagined God's-eye view of things.

Beyond the actual mountains religions use to disclose the sacred, other symbolic mountains rise in our inner psycho-spiritual domain. One such mountain is found in Dante's *Purgatorio*. It's a mountain of the inner life, and that's part of its genius. Much more recently Rene Daumal left behind an incomplete work at this death entitled *Mount Analogue*. The subtitle is more revealing: *A Novel of Symbolically Authentic Non-Euclidean Adventures in Mountain Climbing*. Here, once again, Daumal imagines a non-spatial height, inviting those who *find it* and who have the discipline to climb. Why? He answers with a singular metaphorical statement: "What is above knows what is below."

My excursus into mountains and their symbolic force is thrust upon me by our plodding expedition to the brow of Santa Fe Baldy. Ahead I can see my companions struggling for footing and picking their way among the rocks and scruffy vegetation. Ivy moves resolutely, on her own pilgrimage to the summit. For her, this mountain is more than its sheer bulk. It speaks to her, and this is how the mountain as sacred symbol arises in us.

These ruminations set me thinking about symbols as such and their relation to formal religion as I've been examining it. Ethan and I've discussed how basic and necessary symbols are for a sense of the sacred, and it strikes me now that symbols are the primary building blocks of all form. We form things through and out of our symbolic capacity. Thus, formal religion is made possible by the symbol, because the symbol is elemental form. It draws things together. That's what the word actually means in its Greek derivation. The mountain as sacred symbol most clearly takes form, I believe, in cathedrals, temples, mosques, and other rising edifices where religions make their homes.

The secularization project, and especially its secularist extreme, strives to minimize, if not eliminate, the symbolic order. Myth, as a concentration of symbols into story and vision, is especially subject to challenge and dismissal. Yet, science, the primary expression of the secularization project in the modern era, is saturated with symbol. The raw data on which science relies cannot begin to be comprehended without taking form through symbol. And when science itself moves beyond the evidence it uncovers and the attendant explanatory theories and begins to make vast generalizations, it, too, enters the province of myth.

But that's another story. Here it is sufficient to show that, even among the most secularist minds, the symbolic as elemental form remains. When secularism forgets this and seeks to render all knowledge one dimensional, understanding is reduced to *flatland*, and the perspective of high places is lost. Herein lies the folly of strident naturalism and its extreme, materialism.

Rather than dismiss the symbolically rich dimension of formal religion, as secularism is prone to do, would it not be more beneficial to recognize the universal role of our symbolic gifts in giving form to human existence? Once we take this step, we can then allow science and religion—along with other dimensions of the human enterprise, such as politics, economics, art, and social order—to participate in rendering life coherent and stable. Religion need not—and must not—dictate to science, but science ceases to be a threat to religion. They are each what Wittgenstein calls a "form of life," and insofar as both *take form*, they most nearly make contributions to the human project of giving order to life.

An additional benefit of this way of construing symbol and form is that it invites both daring and humility. We dare to give formal expression to our experience, and we are humble enough to recognize that every form is provisional and incomplete, if not downright fragmentary. I have been frank to pursue formal religion's difficulty with recognizing its own finitude. In such cases, as already noted, religion easily degenerates into the same fallibility it is formed to challenge and resolve. An even more graphic fallibility arises with secularism insofar as it presumes that human beings are fully and finally adequate to shape life as they see fit. Flatland strives to remove the mountains, but the symbolic heights unveil the sacred and allow what is above to know what is below, but not the other way around.

High above me I hear a muffled "Yo!" It's Collins' familiar call. He has the summit in view. Everyone picks up the pace, and within minutes we're clustered around a small bronze marker on which the United States Geological Survey assures us that this is the mountain's rounded peak. We look about to see the ground worn bare by previous visitors. I sense a subtle disappointment in Frank's voice, as though he had hoped we might be the first to reach the top.

Collins says to Ivy, "You're a real trooper," and we join in congratulating her. She grins.

Scattered boulders provide furniture and we sit briefly to catch our breaths. We are immediately entertained by scrambling marmots dashing about in hopes of food. The wind, already stiff, picks up its bluster, and everyone, including Collins, reaches for jackets. The sun bears down on us, but with clouds forming to the northwest, we know we cannot stay long at the top. Collins checks out a cluster of large standing boulders and beckons to us. We gather on the leeward side to escape the direct force of the wind.

Ivy moves aside to nurse Delilah, and we spread a poncho and our collection of food on it. As we sprawl around the edge of the poncho, Collins offers a Navajo blessing before we eat and chat about other mountains, deep valleys, and caves we've each explored. Collins treats us to a vivid description of spare lands he has visited on the reservation, but where few, if any, whites have ever ventured. Ivy joins us and places Delilah, wrapped in her blanket, in the midst of our "table." The infant smiles as she sits like a centerpiece before us.

Collins peers around the protective boulders at the sky and gestures that we'd probably best begin our descent. Immediately, Ivy stands and walks back to the summit. In ritual fashion she looks off into space and turns clockwise to view every direction. She points east and calls in a muted voice, "I think I can see where we stayed." Collins shakes his head in doubt but says nothing. Frank joins Ivy for a brief survey of the expanse. Collins takes the baby's sling and prepares to install Delilah in it, but we can see that she is pleased with her relative freedom. We wait.

"We made good time," Collins says as we begin our descent headed eastward. "There's a trail this way. It'll be a little longer but easier." We fall in line behind the gentle dictator as he hikes off, talking to the baby.

Frank drops back and offers the cliché, "Everything that goes up must come down."

I respond, "Yes, but, 'everything that rises must converge.'"

"What does that mean?"

I tell him about the Jesuit scientist and thinker Pierre Teilhard de Chardin and his ideas about evolution's being purposeful and moving toward greater convergence and unity. Frank likes this variation on the concept of evolution, and we discuss the idea of teleology and the possibility that everything participates in an overarching purpose. He concludes, "Well of course, nothin' like that can be proven, but it sure makes sense as a possibility. This guy. . .what's his name?"

"You can call him Teilhard."

"Yeah. He may have somethin'."

Frank asks me the same question he proposed this morning about why everybody's not religious. I tell him what I laid out while climbing up the mountain, and he listens intently.

"I've read some about the secular stuff you mentioned. Rastas put it all, 'specially where whites are concerned, under the one word, *Babylon*. They. . .we. . .talk over and over about how old King Nebuchadnezzar of Babylon led God's people away into slavery, and this same story still fits. Except now it's not just one guy. It's the whole thing, the 'power brokers,' as they're called. Babylon is now the way the world of the white man runs things, the secular way." Frank's voice rises as he speaks. "But what I don't get is how the secular business is a religion. It tries to stomp out religion."

"Sure, extreme versions of secularism do that, but not everyone is that extreme. All I want to show you is that wherever religion is taken away, something comes to take its place, and to do that, whatever it is becomes like a religion. That's what I meant by it's being a substitute or surrogate religion."

Frank nods his comprehension and then asks, "But what's gonna' be done about it? Rastas believe there'll be a great purging. I mean, we're talkin' end time. . ."

"Well, in a way there've been a considerable number of purgings in history," I acknowledge, "but any talk of apocalyptic end time seems to me too easy. It's a way of giving up and waiting for some great unknown cataclysm to sweep all our troubles. . .and our enemies. . .away. It's all about vengeance against our limitations and our sense of helplessness, what I call *frailty*.

"What actually happens over time is a movement to bring back a balance, in this case between the secular and the sacred. Once religion had too much of the power and abused it awfully. Now there's a danger that what I call the *secular project* will so dominate and flatten human existence out that we'll lose all sense of meaning. Everything vertical. . .the high places, as I described them. . .are being flattened. For instance, if you ask what occupies the minds of most people, especially in the West, and most especially in America, it can be stated simply: economic prosperity, consumption, and entertainment. Listen to the media chatter, and this becomes evident. We say that other things are important, such as family, security, and general happiness, but the emphasis dictated by the secular project itself and the powerful voices that keep it stoked is driven by prosperity, possessions, and pleasure."

"Yeah, Babylon!" Frank once again declares.

"And what's worse is that it. . .this secular Babylon. . .acts like a religion, and we easily turn it into one. Many of the more popular formal religions even contribute to the distortion and are co-opted to join in making the secular itself the sacred. If the secular project cannot replace the sacred, it strives to seduce the formal religions to become a sacred sanction for rampant secular dominion. And I believe this is taking place right now, as we hike down this mountain!"

"Then what're we supposed to do?" Frank asks the all-American question, while gesturing his frustration.

"That's why I came up here on this pilgrimage. I'd hoped to work through some serious questions about religion, the most basic ones, with an old buddy, but he decided to leave."

"When?" Frank wants to know.

"It's a long story, but the way I've handled it is to do some tough thinking for myself, what I call *fundamental thinking*. My aim is to arrive at the best understanding of religion I can muster. It won't be good enough. It never is. But at least I've begun to locate my own starting point and where it seems to take me. This way of doing things is not very popular these days. The trend is to abandon all such efforts and spend our energy only on the this and that of our experienced world. Most scholarship has itself fallen into this very trap. Thinking things through for their own sake is not applauded these days."

I pause as we negotiate our way through a field of scree. "This fundamental thinking I'm talkin' about begins with takin' nothing I've previously thought I knew for granted. It's more like starting at the beginning. It's something like this: we have this dimension of human existence we call *religion*. But it has so many ways of expressing itself that we have difficulty making sense of it. So, I begin with a simple question: *What makes human beings religious at all?*"

"That's a really good question!" Frank exclaims. "But it's damn hard. . ."

"Tell me about it," I pant in response.

Ivy has dropped back to listen. She asks, "Have you made any progress on your answer?"

"I'm not sure I'm seeking an answer, not in so many words. What I want to do is lay out the terrain and line up clues. . .or ways of seeing the larger picture.

"What've you found out so far?" Ivy presses. Frank chides her for her endless questioning. I insist that questions are especially good, often better than answers. "How's that?" Ivy wants to know, and Frank throws up his hands and walks off the trail as if leaving us.

"I've spent much time thinking about the way questions are primary and often more important than answers. If we experience life as a quest, and I do, then questioning is the way we give thought to our quest. Questioning goes with questing. It seems to me that if we can pose a really appropriate question, we must already have some hint toward an answer, because the question already proposes a direction to seeking its answer. So much of the time the reason we don't make progress in understanding. . .let alone living. . .is that we are asking the wrong questions or don't know what questions to ask.

"But still, don't you find some answers?" Ivy is anxious to know. "Because, if you don't, then what keeps you askin'?"

"Yes," I respond emphatically, "there are answers along the way, but they're always provisional and partial. The way I know this is that every answer only serves to open vistas for asking further and more helpful questions. Well, at least potentially more helpful. . ."

Frank intrudes with a question of his own. "Then there's no *final* answer?" He stresses the word *final*. "I mean an answer that ends the askin'."

"None that I can imagine," I answer.

"Just thinkin' about that makes me tired," Frank confesses. "Why start asking if there's no goal. . ."

I ponder before responding. We Americans are so goal oriented, as is often observed, that we are hard pressed to imagine embracing the process rather than fixating on the outcome. This is a true, although hackneyed way of putting our situation. Eventually I comment: "If there's a goal to questioning of the sort I'm doing, it is to deepen understanding in the interest of more expansive and focused living. It is rooted not in the mind but in the passion for life itself." I pause before concluding, "The quest serves life, and life thrives on the quest. And, I believe, the most life-defining quest of all is the religious quest."

Both Ivy and Frank pause in the path and stare at me. They share a look of baffled consolation at what I've laid before them. Delilah abruptly cries out, and we all look up to see Collins taking her from the gray-green sling on his chest. Ivy rushes ahead at a mother's pace and sweeps the infant onto her shoulder.

We sit for half an hour while she stirs a mix of cereal and pureed dried fruit she prepared this morning. She feeds the baby as we watch and applaud. Collins takes the opportunity to discuss plans for hiking out of the mountains. "I calculate that we have about two more days of food, and my buddy Peck'll pick us up down at the Holy Ghost campground."

"How far's that?" Frank asks.

"I'd guess ten miles, maybe twelve," Collins calculates.

"Can't we make that in one day?" Ivy asks, looking for a way of extending our stay in the mountains.

"Probably," Collins nods, "but if somethin' goes wrong. . ."

"Like what?" Ivy counters in her perpetually interrogative mode.

At just that moment, as if on cue, rain drops from the sky in an instant flood. We scramble for our ponchos. Ivy covers Delilah, and we huddle under a tree with low-hanging branches. I'm relieved there's no lightning. As we settle into our fragile protective covering from the torrent, Collins mutters to Ivy, "Somethin' like this might slow us down, for instance."

The rain ceases as abruptly as it began, and we throw off our rain gear and walk away from the dripping tree limbs onto our trail. We stuff our wet ponchos into the packs and hike. Our tracks in the wet earth betray our movement downward. We continue around the foot of Santa Fe Baldy to the southwest and back toward Arrowhead Meadow by the same trail we took yesterday.

Our campsite is as we left it. No sign of rain here. We spread ponchos on the grass at the edge of a marshy area and begin our late-afternoon preparations to end yet another Elysian day. Before preparing dinner, I walk over to the giant fallen ponderosa lying in repose across our tiny creek. I climb up the scaly skin of the dying tree, find a perch, and sit. Opening my journal, I write extensive notes on my musings of the day. I make one additional note to the effect that this age of secularization, while a potential threat to traditional formal religion, is also a challenge for religion to change its ways.

I see Collins stirring among our stores for the evening's food, and I'm about to join him when yet another thought imposes itself upon me. I turn back to the journal and write, *The only thing that challenges religion more than secularization is the boundless diversity of religions. If there are so many forms of religion, with new variations constantly emerging, the variety is implicitly a threat to the uniqueness—and even more so to the superiority—of any given religion over the others. But,* I add hastily, *that's for another day.*

After scrambling down the rough hide of the fallen tree, barking a shin on a protruding branch in the process, I report for duty at the fire ring. Ivy declares that the climb has energized her, and she wants to prepare our dinner. She insists. Frank takes Delilah on a sightseeing tour of the surrounding flora. Collins sits on a log and, in one of his rare loquacious moments, engages Ivy in a discussion of mountains and their allure. He begins with our earlier adventure up the Pedernal. She responds emphatically, "That'll be my next climb."

I go for more water.

Twenty-Four

Only the madman is absolutely sure.

> Robert Anton Wilson

~

It's early, not quite daylight, when I hear the rip of a tent zipper. The sound comes from Frank and Ivy's direction. I waken momentarily, but then doze off. In the dull background of light sleep I hear someone rummaging in our supplies. At first I wonder whether a bear, or more likely a raccoon, could be visiting, but in my somnolent stupor I resist checking.

"What're you doin'?" I hear Frank ask in a stage whisper.

Ivy answers softly, "I'm checkin' our food."

"Why? Whatta you want?"

"To find out if there's enough for us to stay another day," Ivy confesses as if caught in the act.

"Delilah's hungry," Frank mumbles.

"Then bring her here." Commotion follows, and I hear the baby muttering gurgles of good morning interspersed with whimpers of hunger.

Frank says, "I'm goin' to that rock for prayers. When you're done, come over." Sounds of his retreat fade to silence.

I hear these barely whispered exchanges as background noise in my sleep, but when I realize that we're supposed to start packing out today, I spring up and exit my tent. Collins has done the same, and we stare blankly at each other as if strangers. Collins spots Ivy some twenty feet away, sitting on a poncho nursing Delilah. Our food supply is scattered about the poncho in neat piles.

Collins walks toward Ivy, observing, "You must be pretty hungry."

"No. I was just checkin'," Ivy responds.

"For what?" Collins asks.

"I wanted to see if we have enough food to stay here another day," Ivy explains. "I'm not ready to leave yet." She proceeds to account for the various mounds of food packages and to assure us that, if we ration ourselves, we can do it.

Collins is impressed and says as much, nodding that she's probably right. Then he asks, "What about food for the baby?"

Ivy points to a small stash she has set aside for Delilah and says, "I know how to prepare that. I've become a bona fide baby food expert."

In the still moments of this early hour a consensus takes form through our silence. No one speaks of the decision, nor is there need. We all know and accept that we'll have one more day in this enchanted clime. Ivy walks over to tell Frank, but he already knows. His confirmation carries across the meadow on the morning stillness.

I ask Collins in a low voice about Peck and how he'll know when to meet us. He looks at me as if I'm dull witted and whispers, "He'll know. He's Navajo." I grin out of trust, not wisdom.

Immediately Collins announces with a rye grin, "We'll have our 'Last Breakfast' today. It's harder to cook a fit breakfast once we're packin' out. So, today's the day." With exuberance he launches into preparing pan biscuits, while I stoke the stove and heat the last of our freeze-dried beef strips. Ivy returns to start a small fire against the morning chill before stirring powdered eggs into something approximating the real thing. Frank shows Delilah what we're all doing.

Half an hour later we're in a circle around the beach towel, passing food to each other. We banter in free association about the climb yesterday and these idyllic environs.

I find myself musing over our little human cluster. We're such an unlikely collection of humanity. It's as if we were randomly picked by lottery and thrown together. Yet, it works. For all of our distinctions, peculiarities and idiosyncrasies, we're an instant family. Aside from the input of genetics, most families are that way, I suppose.

This dialectic of difference and likeness intrigues me, especially the fact that difference and likeness contribute to each other in forming a vital tension that makes up *life together*. We exist between the extremes of homicidal alienation and the pull of fusing into each other. Both extremes terrify us and can seduce us. The human drama is played out in the tension between them.

Again without speaking, we clean the campsite and scatter for the day. We know this will be a rare chance at the leisure assured by simply having no obligations whatever, and we take advantage of it. What does one do, when there's *nothing* to do? One option is to shift the focus altogether from *doing* to *being*. This sounds entirely un-American on the face of it, but it belongs to the core depth of human existence. When it is absent, we long for it, whether we are conscious of the fact or not, and when it is present, all longing abates.

I stroll across Arrowhead Meadow, up an incline, and down again into a stand of aspen. The terrain drops precipitately, until it flattens into a tiny secluded open area, where the sun slants through to spackle the grass. In the center of the space a decaying log stretches along the ground, pointing into oblivion. Placing my water bottle and journal on the ground, I occupy the log for some time in the waning shade, until the sun splashes my face. Then I turn away from its glare and cross my ankles. Presently I prepare for meditation, and soon the blankness of *being there* drains away the dross of mental busyness. A tingling numbness removes my embodiment from the center of consciousness. Only the vacuous mind abides. Mindfulness!

This state is ordinarily difficult for me to achieve, even briefly, but on a day such as this and after so much arduous effort at comprehension, it comes abruptly and as welcome release. How long I remain in this timeless inner space, I cannot calculate. That's how the *timeless* works; it counters all efforts at calculation. The sunshine has expanded, but I don't try to speculate how rapidly. No need.

When I open my journal, the last entry from yesterday greets me. After rereading it, I summarize the last few days by adding, *since we humans inevitably seek to give form to all of our experience, our experience of the religious sensibility itself inclines toward some formation. But form, as I keep saying to myself, is only a medium, and when this is not understood, form is misconstrued as a kind of terminus—an end in itself—and thus a prison. And surprisingly enough, prisons can be as much a comfort as a confinement. We profoundly need religion because, as*

I keep insisting, our finitude entails frailty, folly and fault, and therefore, fallibility. At the same time, the religious 'cure' so easily degenerates into a curse, the curse of finality, that is, idolatry.

Modernity only complicates the situation for religion by introducing a different form of life: secularization devolving toward secularism. Even more challenging for religion, secularism eliminates the sacred by becoming a substitute for it. For at least the past three hundred years, religion in the West—and increasingly around the world—has been reeling from this challenge. In face of this situation, what is the promise, if any, of the religious dimension of existence?

As I read, reflect, observe, and converse about religion, this much is becoming clear to me: if religion is to realize its promise, it must come to terms, on the one hand, with secularism and on the other with the fact that its formal character is inherently inadequate to its aim: religion, as finite form, cannot capture the infinite. Religion cannot in-form the infinite. At best all formal religions are <u>approximations</u>, and that may be stretching it.

I believe that the way beyond this dilemma is something like the following. Religion is more than the various forms it has taken and continues to express. Furthermore, one way to explore avenues for overcoming the limitations of formal religion is to concentrate on the remarkable plethora of forms through which religion has been and continues to be manifest. Before our era of modernity, the diversity of religious forms was known to some extent, but with the expansion—and at the same time the compression—of our planet this variety of forms is, as it were, 'in our faces.' Religions butt up against each other with growing intensity, and each affects the other, despite all efforts to maintain the uniqueness—or purity—of particular religious forms.

My hand is exhausted from furiously laying out the rough summary of where my pilgrimage has led me over the past several days. I close the journal and lay it aside. The exercise of summarizing has helped me concentrate my thinking. If formal religion is, in the end, always inadequate, then all forms, no matter how many and how distinct, are under the same—or approximately the same—limitation. As I've urged, no formal religion can be final, and given the grand diversity of forms, this truth becomes even more evident and weighty.

How could anyone adjudicate among the world's religions to determine the *one true form*? Or even the one *superior* form? Certainly practitioners of given religious forms will hasten to nominate theirs as the only, or principal, candidate, but this is simply special pleading and begs the question. No amount of intricate rationalization, let alone the more unsavory efforts of bombast—or worse, coercion—allows any religious form to stand above all others or to their exclusion. All attempts end in a self-referential circle. The cat vainly chases its tail.

Current discourse on this subject of diverse forms of religion distinguishes various attitudes toward religious diversity. One popular version proposes three common attitudes toward religious diversity: exclusivism, inclusivism, and pluralism. There are refinements of these three, but they will serve to express the options generally under consideration at present.

The first, *exclusivism*, signifies the view that a given religion, usually one's own, is the true form of religion and that all others are, at best, pretenders or imitators. While this perspective is common, often unconsciously, among practitioners of numerous religions, it is more acutely held in some religions than in others. I sense that the monotheisms are more nearly inclined in this direction. It has occurred to me that the "mono" in monotheism may be the clue. That is *singularity*, as in one and only one deity, may carry with it the implication of exclusion.

Further, exclusivism may either be held confessionally or become the basis for intense efforts at persuasion. Proselytizing! As noted above, this exclusivist attitude is purely declarative and simply cannot be substantiated, except in the minds of those who already embrace the form being touted.

Inclusivism refers to a middle position. It may range from bare tolerance of other religions to a "live and let live" attitude. Most inclusivists still tend to make their own religious form normative for authentic religion. Their own religion serves, if only informally, as the standard for judging the adequacy of all other religions. Yet, they are more open to acknowledging that other religions have at least minimal legitimacy and that their claims can to some extent be accommodated to fit one's own religion. People who are more nearly cultural or nominal adherents of a particular religious form are inclined to find this attitude appealing, but inclusivism may also express the way more serious devotees seek to "include" other faiths within the universal reach, something like this: despite their ostensible differences, any other authentic religion somehow belongs to their own faith. This is something of a model of cooptation.

Religious *pluralism* rests on the conviction that difference is to be embraced as the context for living together on the same planet and in the same community. Difference is not an enemy but a challenge with the possibility of becoming a resource for human community. If we can grasp that community does not rest on sameness but on seeing the "common" in and through—not despite—the differences, then we may move toward a "family of religions." Advocates of this attitude often stress the need for what is today referred to as "inter-religious dialogue." It is not always clear what this phrase means, but minimally it means that practitioners of any given religion should be able to speak openly with others about their own tradition, while listening to the way others understand theirs. The aim is not to dissolve differences into one mega religion but to allow differences to mediate engagement in the interest of community, something like a spiritual oneness beyond ostensible differences.

This pluralistic posture comes down to something like this: my religious convictions are authentic, but they do not exclude the possibility—or inevitability—that other religions and the convictions of their followers also participate in the same ultimate orientation to, as one thinker puts it, "the Real." This notion can be challenged on a number of fronts, but one that occurs to me is that it seems to take the intensity and passion away from *conviction*. If religions represent a smorgasbord from which we might choose any one for our own, then wherein lies the force of conviction?

My own response to this query is that, since we are speaking of *formal* religions, none of them contain the focus of conviction. Rather, each and all point beyond themselves to something more than any of them can claim for itself. In other words, the convictional focus lies elsewhere in the depths of mystery, and the religions themselves only point and mediate. Thus, to raise the question I posed above is to misplace the substance of religious conviction.

The same goes for all of the distinctions just considered: exclusive, inclusive, and plural. All religions, without exception, are *formal* manifestations of the religious sensibility, and as such, they all suffer from the same limitation in seeking to fulfill the urge of the religious sense itself. As I have claimed, these many forms may be historically, culturally, and yes, existentially inevitable, but at best they all remain confined within our finitude as "pointing gestures" toward the infinite mystery.

To be sure, religions make truth claims for themselves, explicitly and implicitly, and they tend to see those truths as categorical or "necessary" truths. But my point is this: every truth claim of whatever kind is made by human beings existing under the conditions of finitude and bounded by those conditions, and this includes the statement I have just made.

I, too, am guessing what the elephant actually looks like! At best, all of our truth claims—including but not limited to the claims of religion—are proposals to bring order to the hodgepodge and relentless immediacy of our experience, thus providing a viable coherence and comprehension in the face of the infinite and its boundless possibilities.

This need not by any means be the end of the story for religion, but if we are to go further, we best begin with the humility that comes by recognizing and living according to our limitations. This is true of all dimensions of our existence—political, social, economic, educational, etc.—but is especially acute in the case of religion. Why? The truth claims of religion reach for ultimacy and finality, for the consummate cosmic meaning in which we may personally and communally participate. The very audacity of the attempt can only be countenanced if it is grounded in humility. Religion takes form in striving to say more than can be said, and it can do so only if pursued with the perennial caveat: *we know only in part and always through a glass darkly*.

If indeed we are to go further, we must probe more deeply. Beginning with what is given, namely, the religious sensibility and the various forms of religion as we find them, we can examine the religions for whatever *common ground* they yield. In a sense, I already began this earlier by suggesting some of the common features among the religions. Granted, those common elements—beliefs, myths, rituals, etc.—are strictly formal, that is, they are more or less ubiquitous ways of expressing any religion. Some elements may be more central to a given religion than to others, but at least most of the elements are present in any religion and belong to our understanding of any religion as a *religion*.

A chronic controversy persists over the extent to which we can find a unifying substantive core to religion that runs through its many forms while not being reduced to any of them. I gave a nod to this debate earlier, and I took a clear position. Simply stated, there is more to religion than its various forms, and I add here that, even if we limit ourselves to the forms in their particularity, there is more imbedded in the forms than form can express. I am proposing that we no longer speak primarily of religious forms but of their intended *substance*. Another way of putting the problem is to ask this question: to what extent is religion *true*? To ask this is not to seek *the true religion* among the many forms but to probe for *the religious truth* possibly underlying, implicit in, or lying beyond all forms but foreshadowed, if not articulated, through the forms.

No word is trickier than true or truth, and most especially *The Truth*. Even to raise it is dangerous in that it can lead to an endless tangle of analysis to say nothing of controversy. I plan…

"What're you up to?" Ivy asks from somewhere above me. I look up the rise among the aspen but do not see anyone. Then she moves, and I spot her descending toward me. I'm slightly frustrated at the interruption of these concentrated reflections, but I set aside my project to greet her. She's alone. I gesture for her to sit on the log.

"I could ask you the same question," I retort.

"You first," she insists.

"Just my usual…thinkin' and writin'…" I hold up my journal as evidence.

"Yeah, *religion*," she says, emphasizing the last word with a tone at once quizzical and slightly anxious.

"I'll admit, it's a jungle, an endless tangle. I'm just tryin' to hack my way through it…or into it," I confess.

"Why do you need to do it? Why not just live your religion?"

"Huh!" I mutter. "I guess it all started by bein' born into a nest of seriously religious relatives, beginning with my parents. They ate and drank piety, and the whole business got into my blood."

"Fanatics?" Ivy asks.

"Not really. They were serious and intense about what they believed and how they lived, but they weren't blindly obsessive… They…"

"Are you still that way yourself?"

I shake my head emphatically. "No, no, no! I moved past that long ago…"

"Then why do you still spend so much time thinkin' about it all?"

Frank's frustration with Ivy's endless questions flashes through my mind, but I realize that I don't object to her inquisitiveness. Its part of her lively involvement in everything she does. Besides, I need her to push me. It helps me make better sense.

"Well, in the first place I believe religion's important, and if so, it's also important to make sense of it. Besides, I teach religion. It's my principal subject."

"I didn't know that," Ivy's voice carries a note of surprise. "So, you're not especially religious yourself, but you have to talk about it to your students."

"Actually, I am religious. I believe everyone's religious, but some of our ways of showing it are very odd… That's what I'm tryin' to figure out now."

"But you said that you'd left your religion." Ivy states it, but it's still a question.

I try to clarify. "What I meant is that I'm no longer following the particular religious tradition of my childhood."

"Me neither," she admits. "But now…you know…I'm not sure. About bein' a Rasta and all…" She drops her head, then looks up pensively. "I thought this'd be it. I don't like just floppin' around…"

"Flopping around?" I question.

"You know, jumpin' from this religion to that…or to not havin' one…" She is earnest. "Frank was nothin' when we met, except mad! Mercy, he had a temper, and we both 'flopped around.' But when he became a Rasta, everything changed. And it gave me confidence."

I see Ivy's dilemma, because I was once there at about her age. If we let go of something that has helped us but no longer works for us—if it has lost its "truth value" or pertinence, we may feel as though we're lost rather than liberated. But then, genuine liberation seems to include a feeling of loss, perhaps disorientation, for a while. That's why questing and exploring are necessary for those who are liberated to find their way. Otherwise, we're in danger of attaching ourselves to the next thing that comes along so we can feel safe. And then we're imprisoned all over again.

"Ivy, what you're goin' through is important. That's why it's not easy," I begin. "If you had stayed in the same place and with the same people from your childhood, you'd most likely still be practicin' the religion of your childhood."

"Yeah, probably," Ivy agrees.

"But when you left that security, you had to find your own way. That's what 'floppin' around' is all about. Some people, once they let go of what they received from childhood, spend most of their lives doin' just that…floppin'. But more often, people simply hook up with what is locally available and follow without much thought. Neither way seems to me to encourage us to adventure, if you know what I mean…to live with a capital 'L'!"

"Seems like a trap either way," Ivy observes dejectedly.

"But these are not the only options," I insist. "Oh, you can join this or that group to help you focus and begin. This may be especially important in the case of religion. People need each other. That's what community gives us. You can even stay with whatever group gives you a sense of home, but you don't need to be trapped in it."

"But like I said," Ivy responds, "it still seems like a trap to me… no matter which way you go."

"Well, you're married to Frank. Is that a trap for you?"

"Not really, but that's different." Ivy leans toward me for emphasis. "I want to be married to him."

"Right! That's the difference. Your heart's in the marriage. And you want that same quality in any basic commitment. Does Frank help you be more yourself, or does he keep you from being yourself?"

"Uh, most of the time he does help me, and he's better since Delilah… She helps too."

I do not respond right away. Ivy's dilemma takes me back to the same concerns I've considered this morning. She's seeking a way of moving beyond the confining aspect of religious commitment to its vitality and force as her very life, her *way of life*.

No religion can do that for her, but a given religion may become a vehicle, a medium for actually living the religious sensibility into its fullness. Here's a young woman, still strangely innocent, seeking the door into life itself, and the chosen religious form is not, nor can any form be, sufficient, let alone final. If she thinks it is, her religion becomes a snare. She's looking for a doorway through those boundaries without rejecting them.

"Okay," I finally propose, "you and Frank are Rastafarians. You're committed to this. But what's the heart and soul of your commitment? The Rastas are only one more of endless possible ways you might take..."

"God," Ivy says softly.

"What?"

"God. I'm committed to God." She pauses, then adds, "God's gotta be more than what the Rastas think, or what any religion thinks, for that matter. Or anyone, including me."

"Ah, see! That's the beginning of your way through this. As long as you don't focus on being a Rastafarian but on seeking your way to live in relation to God—including "God" by any other name—and as long as being a Rastafarian helps you do this, then you're not trapped." I don't try to explain that God is also a symbolic term and refers to the Infinite and its mystery, but this is good enough for now and perhaps good enough, period.

Frank's voice comes wafting through the trees. We answer and climb toward him. Back at the campsite he's prepared lunch. We scatter to find comfortable places to sit and eat. Frank wants to know what we've been discussing, and I review some of my thoughts of the morning and the conversation with Ivy. Delilah wakes up, and Ivy feeds her. Immediately afterward Collins takes the baby and without a word walks away with her, making his way down the meadow along the creek.

These mundane details of life in the wild unfold like the flow of the nearby stream. I decide to nap and interrupt this mental barrage raging inside my head. When I awaken half an hour later, no one's in sight. As I turn my head slightly, something catches the corner of my eye. Turning more slowly still, I see a coyote frozen in place and watching me intently. We stare at each other for several minutes, until it utters a low gruff bark and retreats into the marsh. No fear in the creature, only surprise dissolving into curiosity and then boredom.

I decide to hike up to an overlook above the meadow. After scrambling to locate the dim trail, I can walk easily. Presently I see off to my right what appears to be a large tent. On examination I find a makeshift hut covered in plastic. Inside are a few artifacts bearing witness that someone has lived here fairly recently, but the place is obviously abandoned. *Another adventurer*, I mutter as I poke through the meager stores left behind. The only item worth salvaging is a white quilt with the edges trimmed in green vine interspersed with roses. It is tucked in a relatively protected place and kept dry. I take it with me to the overlook, and when I arrive, it serves as a seat.

The spectacle of the meadow spread below me and Collins just entering it from far at one end occupies me, and my thoughts give way, once again, to feelings of gratitude for this temporary remote haven. Far removed from the fitful surge and chase of contrived living "in the world," all of this is entirely independent of me and does not rely on me. Yet, it includes and sustains me, like a mute *presence*. As I noted earlier, I have little doubt that the deep roots of reverence among our species lie in such experiences of this presence.

This morning's reflections, before Ivy appeared, only gradually come back to mind. I was about to take up perhaps the most difficult problem of this, or any, era of human history: truth. In our thinking, knowing, and understanding what is *reliable*? This is a peculiar way to ask about truth, but it makes sense, once we embrace the confines of finitude and the humility that comes with it. In the end we trust what endures and both promises and yields for us a thriving existence. Granted, at our most fully flourishing we live *in the moment*, what some have called "The Eternal Now," but we do not live *for* the spinning moments of chronos. Only as we discover what abides and is thus reliable—a living *truth*, in a word—does this Eternal Now arise.

But I fear that I've begun at the point I seek to reach. Truth enjoys a complexity and suffers complications that dare not be ignored. Here is one example. Some of my students, especially those whose strongest convictions are under challenge, sometimes assert simplistically, "But this is the truth!" That is, for them the truth is simply identified with what they seriously believe. Case closed. When

I ask them whether a belief, even the most deeply held, could be mistaken, they agree in principle that beliefs can and do turn out to be wrong or at best incomplete and in need of modification. Yet, the ones they currently hold are actually "true." If I point out, as I often do, that it is contradictory to say, "This is not true, but I believe it," almost everyone agrees. All I want them to discover is that our beliefs are what we hold true, but no belief is immune to the possibility that it may turn out to be false, and if false, then no longer believed—or in decisive instances, what was believed becomes *unbelievable*.

If we cannot accept this condition of all beliefs, we thereby fail to grasp the finitude of any and all truth claims. When I make this point, I'm sometimes accused of being a relativist, by which those using that word mean that I "believe" there is no truth and that beliefs are occasional, if not whimsical, conveniences. Those most exasperated by my point of view sometime accuse me of "believing" that "anything goes." If so, of course, I have at least one belief that I take to be true, namely, *anything goes*. This rather sophomoric snarl only serves to indicate the complex—and complicated—arena we enter, when we discuss the subject of truth.

I will by no means seek to resolve the many problems and confusions raised by any serious consideration of truth. What I wish to do is to take up the problem of *religious truth* in an effort to gain a deeper grasp of religion through and beyond its myriad forms. To serve this end, I have worked out an overly simplified scheme of three basic types of truth. The first is *factual truth*. These are truths that arise directly from our experience of the world and our social agreements on the interpretation of these common experiences. These might be said to be truths about time, space, and "stuff" and the relations among them.

The second kind is *interpretive truth*. The slightest move beyond specific facts by attempting to relate factual truths to each other and to organize them is an act of interpretation. We could argue that even factual truths are still interpretive acts, and it does seem to be the case that we are never interested in "mere" factual truth for itself. What counts as a fact is already decided by the interpretive framework that makes the factual truth interesting or relevant to us. Or, if we begin with "the facts," they must be "connected" through some scheme in order for the facts to contribute to our knowledge and understanding. The more complex efforts to establish interpretive truth are called theories, and the most comprehensive theories move far beyond the facts to construct large and inclusive explanations of our world, what we sometimes call *worldviews*.

The third kind of truth is *meaningful truth*. With the introduction of "meaning" into this discussion, its complexity increases exponentially. Before I can make clear this kind of truth, I need to offer one preliminary distinction between two types of meaning: *signification* and *significance*.

When we come across a word, any word, that is not understood, we undertake to define the word or find out how it is used. In defining we may simply point to some object or indicate some object or condition that the word *signifies*. Or, we more often use other words to indicate what the word we are defining signifies.

Put simply, meaning begins with the idea of signs and their use to refer to something other than the sign. The sign may be an abstract one, such as a word, or it may be a concrete object. This is why we speak of "road signs" or "stop signs." They serve to signify something. When we understand the relation between the sign and that to which it refers, we grasp the *meaning* of the sign, and this constitutes meaning as signification.

But signs may and often do provide much more than signification. To the extent that a sign takes on importance for us, it becomes *significant*. The sign makes a difference to us, because of its value and thus of our *participation*—that word again—in what is signified. We usually refer to significant signs as *symbols*. In this respect symbols are signs which bear significance, that is, importance, worth, value. We participate in symbols in a way in which we do not participate in sheer signs or significations. At the more profound depths of our existence we *identify* with the very symbols we employ, and these symbols, in turn, shape our existence.

Two examples may be helpful. As has often been observed, a nation's flag is both a sign to signify it as this nation and not another one. So far this is only an act of signification. But for people whose flag it is, this is not enough. People defend flags, die for flags, and protect flags from desecration. Why? The flag is more than the signifier of a given nation; it is a symbol for the significance or importance of that nation to those who participate in it. Taken literally, any flag is only pieces of colored cloth organized and sewn together to "represent" a nation or whatever body it signifies. Why should anyone become overly exercised about a given composition of colored rags? The reason is that people invest the sign with *significance* and find significance in and through it. The sign signifies something of significance! It is more than a sign; it is a symbol and thus a revealer of existential participation in the thing signified. Little wonder, then, that the enemies of a nation begin to show it by desecrating its flag.

Take the monosyllable "God." Although much more complex than "flag," it too is a sign, signifying...what? For starters it is a locution that simply signifies a highly abstract idea of a Divine Being, perhaps a "person" of a very special sort, or perhaps a non-personal Oneness. The possibilities are many, as the history of the word and its uses makes evident, but the point is that "God" is a sign that signifies. We may disagree on what it signifies, but its usefulness begins with its capacity to signify.

Granting all of this, any serious user of "God" is not satisfied with this explanation at all. The significance of the word dominates its signification. In other words, its symbolic meaning conveys an engagement with the *power* and *presence* of "God" for those who participate it! This is why the word is protected by taboos in some traditions and by special "sacred" contexts for its proper use in others. As a child, for instance, I was taught that the worst possible profanity is to say "God damn" or "by God" or any phrase which misuses the sacred symbolic significance of the word for a *profane* purpose.

If we return to our description of the three kinds of truth—factual, interpretive, meaningful, we are ready to insist that *meaningful truth* refers to the symbolically significant truths by which we live. Meaning as signification belongs to all three kinds of truth, and meaning as significance is to some extent present in both factual and interpretive truth. Insofar as value and importance attach to *any and every kind of truth*, then all truth participates in symbolic significance. Otherwise, we would not bother ourselves about "truth" in the first place.

But the dimension of *religious truth* remains distinctively concentrated on meaningful truth as significance. Religion does not seek to discover the way things are as such, but only as the way things are bears upon their significance for us. Religious truth addresses what is decisively significant about human existence. It is this understanding of "meaning" that we find in such phrases as "the meaning of life," or in the distinction between science as a discipline devoted to knowledge of how things are and religion as a devotion to the meaning—that is, significance—of the universe and human existence in relation to it.

Now that we have plowed our way through some dense undergrowth surrounding truth and its relation to meaning, we are faced with two additional complications. The first is the problem of *certainty*. It is one thing to claim truth and it is quite another to *arrive* at truth with surety. How can we be sure of any truth, regardless of kind? Rather, than work our way through this thorny patch, I propose some simple principles.

(1) The most certain truths are factual ones, which we can corroborate by direct experience or indirectly through social agreement sustained over time. However, these truths are the least significant, when taken in themselves as endless instances of "facticity."

(2) Interpretive truths seek both to explain and to make it possible to determine the significance of the facts to a greater degree by giving them a context for comprehension. At the same time, interpretive truths are inherently less certain than factual truths while investing factual truths with greater significance.

(3) Truth as significant meaning refers at once to the most important truths for our qualitative existential participation and at the same time to truths that have little or no demonstrable certainty. They are the truths by which and for which we risk our existence. We may have assurances based on subjective and communal participation, but we never have certainty. On the contrary, the drive for certainty undermines truth as significant meaning by seeking to circumvent its participatory character. As W. B. Yeats says, "We cannot know the truth; we can only indwell it."

Religious truth is primarily *truth as significant meaning*, and in the context of the religious sensibility and its articulation, both factual and interpretive meaning, while they may contribute to religious truth, remain secondary to it. The uncertainty inherent in religious truth is the result of the very character of the Primary Impulse as *encounter with the infinite*. When our finitude opens to the infinite, the great *unknowing* of participative immediacy prevails. We are beyond certainty and uncertainty, contained and sustained within the promise and peril of the "indubitable given," that is, the unbounded.

Of course, most of us can hardly grasp, let alone tolerate, this depth of participation. Thus, we hastily retreat into forms that tame and domesticate the infinite, rendering it more palatable by shrouding it in the rich fabric of symbol. Only those who are spiritually hardy enough to press beyond the forms of religion recover this participatory immediacy. We refer to them as *mystics*.

Exhausted, I struggle to my feet. My legs are momentarily unreliable, until I ambulate for several steps. I'm surprised to realize that the sun has set, even on this prominence, but before I can organize myself to scramble down to the trail, I hear voices calling my name in the distance. First, Frank, then Ivy, call to me, and I waft a response. As I'm about to leave, I see dimly the figure of Collins standing in the meadow and waving a white rag of some sort. I cry out again and descend.

"You gonna spend the night up there?" Collins wonders as I trudge the last yards into camp.

"Got carried away, I guess. Sorry about that." I look around the camp and spot early preparations for tomorrow's departure. Steam rises from a pot on the camp stove, and I can see that dinner's ready. We're all pensive with our separate reflections on the fact that we'll be departing the wilderness. But we've become sufficiently harmonious that little need be said. After dinner I clean up, and we sit around the fragile fire, snug under the garment of darkness. We cluster around the campfire a bit longer than usual, but conversation is light and inconsequential, a feature of growing familiarity. Chitchat gives way to mumbles, and after brushing teeth and the various rituals of the evening, we dissolve into the oblivion of sleep.

Twenty-Five

> The very insight at the core of this text requires an intimation of infinity. That is, I am to some extent standing outside the constraints of finitude in order to discern the fact that finitude can never master infinity.
>
> Rudy Rucker

∼

Before anyone else stirs, I'm awake, but I continue to keep my eyes closed and to let the mind have its way. Thoughts fire at random, as if seeking a point of concentration. They gradually merge into focus on the single word: *pilgrimage*. Today my descent into the cavernous regions of the religious sensibility and its spangled variations turns toward ascent back into "the world." But the journey back is itself part of the pilgrimage, the going home.

My pilgrimage, I recall once again, has been more interior than exterior, but that's the way with pilgrimages: the external journey is only the skeleton of the living inner journey. Whether the destination is a temple, a shrine, a mountain, or a sojourn in this cathedral of green spires, everything hinges on the disposition of the pilgrim. The inner pilgrimage cannot be coerced. It's not a forced march. It's more about paying attention than about seeking a destination.

Thoughts shift abruptly, as thoughts can do, to yesterday's marathon pursuit of truth and meaning in religion. I recall that I left something dangling, but I cannot retrieve it. *What was the last thing I pondered? It had something to do with …*

Frustrated, I reach for my journal and the rough notes I made before returning to camp yesterday. *Ah! Certainty!* I say the word aloud to myself. Then I remember my ruminations and how important it is to embrace uncertainty. Words such as "insecurity," "ambiguity," "uncertainty" belong to the lexicon of the religious dimension, and the reason is simple but stark: we are utterly bound by finitude, where only the language of incompleteness captures our condition in light of our longing, our lust. In religion all language remains, at best, provisional and tentative. It more nearly unveils than informs. We may experience profound spiritual *assurance* through participation in the sacred, but certainty is more nearly a curse to the fulfillment of the religious sensibility.

I spot in my journal entry the other problem I did not have time to consider yesterday, namely, that the meaningful truth of religion has levels or degrees of realization. Today I'll...

"Up, up, everybody," Collins calls from his tent, interrupting my reveries.

"I'm already up," Ivy shouts back, and we're shortly mobilized for the challenges of departure.

Breakfast is scant, granola cereal and dried fruit with the last of our hot chocolate. Collins has already dropped his tent, but the rest of us are busy folding and stuffing sleeping bags, mats, and assorted gear. Little mounds form outside the tents. Then the tents collapse in sequence and are folded and stuffed. We load packs.

Long before we're ready to depart, Collins disappears with Delilah. As usual, he has finished packing quickly after breakfast. When our packs are bulging and resting against trees, we look around the camp for the last time. I'm about to call out to Collins, when I hear Delilah behind me, chattering her gibberish.

"Come on," Collins says unceremoniously, and we start to don our packs. "Leave the packs here." We follow.

At the upper end of the meadow Collins halts, and we see a series of stones forming a circle some twenty feet across. He leads us around to an opening on the side, where the morning sun streaks through the timber. Collins enters and takes his place to the north. Ivy and Frank stare, until I gesture for them to enter and move clockwise. Ivey follows Collins's gesture and goes to the west, Frank carries Delilah to the south, and I take the east. We sit cross-legged and become still.

Collins moves from chanting to offering prayers, first in Navajo and then in English. He ends with an abrupt cry followed by sustained silence. We wait with him. Finally, he speaks: "This is the circle of the universe," he begins, "and also the circle of life. Everything is in the circle, and it is enough. Anybody who lives the circle and appreciates it is religious." He pauses before adding, "This is my religion and it's what religion boils down to." I immediately detect Collins' not-so-subtle response to my pilgrimage and our occasional halting discussions of religion.

After another quarter of an hour Collins stands, bows to the four directions and leaves to the east. We follow and continue behind him back to our gear.

Once we've packed out of the meadow and found the trail, Ivy asks Collins, "What was that ritual we did?"

"We said good morning to the universe and gave thanks for our time up here. We're supposed to be grateful for everything." This is all Collins says, and it's enough. We hike in silence for more than an hour, until Delilah calls a halt near a stream we'll soon cross. We drop packs, and I unlash the quilt I found yesterday and spread it for the baby. We munch on health bars, eating sparingly to stretch our dwindling food supply.

Frank sits beside me and abruptly asks, "Can you be religious without a religion?" Immediately I can tell that he and Ivy have been discussing my conversation with her yesterday.

As I start to reply, Collins throws up his hands, pulls out his razor-sharp pocketknife, and begins to create long even shavings from a stick. Once again, his point is obvious. Shavings! For him, everything's a message, mostly without words. I sense his exasperation. After the ritual this morning, he thinks any further discussion of religion is pointless, if not rude.

Undaunted, I answer Frank. "Religions are supposed to help us be religious, but as often as not, they replace the religious vitality with the stuff of religion, the details...the routine, repetition and habit of it."

"Okay, but do we need religion to help us be religious?" Frank wants to know.

"Most people seem to need one form or another, but I'm not sure it's necessary. What I do find is that no form of religion is sufficient. That's what I've been workin' on for the last few days. There are so many religions, and none of them, from what I can tell, can claim the high ground all for themselves. They're just avenues, and as long as they keep that in mind, they can contribute to the religious aspect of our existence." I stop before I begin to pontificate. This subject's so much in my blood that, when anybody shows interest, I'm inclined to over-respond.

Ivy adds, "And from what you said yesterday, you don't seem to care which particular religion a person takes up, so long as it helps and doesn't get in the way of really bein' religious. I mean, you know, *really* livin' it."

Delilah whimpers, and Ivy picks her up, makes a gagging sound, and says to Frank, "Whew! Can you change her? She's rank." Before Frank can respond, Collins comes over, takes the baby, and begins to change her.

I venture, "Well, it does seem to me that people can *choose* whatever form of religion they wish, at least in principle. But it's not really so simple. If we're born and raised in a particular religion, it'll be hard to shake, and if we do, we settle for nothing or for the opposite or for one that seems similar to what's been familiar to us." Then as an afterthought I add, "Maybe we don't become religiously mature, until we do actually choose our religion…or at least choose how we're gonna be religious and relate to religion."

"Well, I went for the opposite of what I grew up in," Frank says. "Rastafarians are about as different from Episcopalians as they come."

As Collins turns Delilah back on her stomach, Ivy interjects, "But Rastas still use the Bible. We're forever readin' *The Book*." She says the last phrase emphatically.

"That really had nothin' to do with it," Frank retorts. "Like I said the other day, at first I just wanted to piss off my ole' man. Takin' up a black African religion sure enough took care of that, especially when I went to his place in dreads."

I chide back, "But you're not a Rastafarian only because you want to rebel against your father…"

"Yeah, well, not now. This Rasta way is…" Frank searches for the right words. "My… uh…inspiration…and comfort, I guess."

I decide to press him. "Could you be religious without it?"

Frank stalls briefly then says, "I reckon I could do without it, but I'm not sure I want to give it up. Not yet, anyway."

The spell of our conversation breaks for the time being, when Collins stands and says that we'd better move along. He very deliberately takes the shavings he's generated and puts them in his pack.

Another message!

Our hiking picks up a casual cadence, mostly because we're walking on level terrain or slightly downhill. Our conversation, still stirring in my thoughts, draws me back to my theme. Religious truth, I begin, does not derive from the forms religion takes. On the contrary, religions are dependent on religious truth and at the same time incapable of containing it. The *meaning* intended and borne in every religious form eludes religion's attempt to possess and control it. When any religion claims otherwise, it easily degenerates and becomes presumptuous and self-satisfied. It falls asleep under the torpor of having arrived, and as it slumbers, spirit escapes!

Some religions appear to be more alert to this possibility than others. For example, I have long appreciated the Zen koan: "If you meet the Buddha on the road, kill him." The implication is that, to be a faithful Buddhist, one best does so by overcoming Buddhism, including adoration of the Buddha. The challenge is to become a Buddha. This does not mean a *rejection* of the religion or its founder but a *realization* of the meaningful truth imbedded in it but always remaining beyond it.

One way to characterize this *liberation* from religious form is to consider another level of religion, what I will call *transformational religion*. I use the word "transformation" deliberately. It contains the root "form," which I've considered for the past several days, but the prefix "trans" conveys the notion of "moving across," in this case moving across religious forms without denying the forms.

The metaphor "moving across" becomes pertinent the moment we realize that our own form of religion is one among others. Even though we may hold our form to be superior in one way or another, we find ourselves acknowledging that other forms also claim legitimacy as expressions of the religious sensibility. This realization is itself a first movement "across" religious forms, and it contains a threat, however mild, that our form is thereby somehow diminished. Neither our form of religion nor any other can be as definitive or final as we may have previously assumed. This threat, along with a pervasive secularism currently challenging religion's place, presents a potential disruption or diminution of the centrality of religion in personal as well as cultural life. Religion thus easily devolves into nominal and conventional tradition and habit, a sort of ritual decoration for an otherwise secular way of life.

But transformative religion presses further and moves beyond this relativistic account of all formal religion. Here the operational term is "beyond." We cannot move *across* without already being implicitly *beyond*! To stalk the depths beyond formal religion without denying its forms and the substantial contribution they make to our lives requires courage, courage to venture beyond the security of form. Why do I insist on going beyond formal religion while not leaving form behind?

Before answering this question of moving *beyond* formal religion, I first want to affirm the abiding role of formal religion by addressing its fundamental contribution: *community*. The founding religious sensibility, understood as our awareness of our finite encounter with the infinite—the Primary Impulse, is profoundly *existential* and thus intimately personal. As I've observed, however, personhood emerges only within the context of corporate shared life, beginning with family and reaching potentially to all of humanity. Without a community of persons there can be no *identity* as person. This may sound like an unfortunate "chicken and egg" dilemma, but the paradox remains necessary to an understanding of "person" or "personhood." Personal identity emerges within the context of persons, and the name for that context—in so far as it contributes to the emergence of persons—is "community." To put it another way, community is the cocoon of personhood!

One pitfall in this explanation of the relation between community and person is that personhood can easily become construed as a sort of *product*. Communities produce persons? Not at all! Persons are not products but emergent *responses* to and within the relentless presence and power of community, beginning with the "community" of even one other member of our species. The quality of any community, that is, whether it fulfills its character as community, may well be determined by whether it reduces persons to products or engages the potential responses that allow personhood to emerge and flourish.

The roots of personhood lie in this responsive capacity. All living things, of course, *react* to their environments and to their species. Response is more than reaction in that the human creature brings something to the context to which it responds. Response influences the context and indeed may come to shape the context to the point of generating novelty within the context. Community as the context of personhood actually thrives on this dialectic, this give and take between persons and community. Our ordinary term, "responsibility," refers to the "ability to respond." Without it, no one can be held accountable for actions. But communities constantly hold their members accountable, just as persons may hold communities accountable.

The responsive capacity that articulates itself as person is complex indeed. It includes the full range of conscious and unconscious resources: cognitive, affective, *conative*. I need not explain human responsiveness in detail. It is sufficient for my purpose to say that, among the responses humans make, one dimension of response lies quite beyond the communal context and derives from an encounter with the very stuff of existence, in other words, the finite encounter with the infinite—the Primary Impulse and what follows from it, *the religious sensibility*.

Because this encounter is integral to the condition of human existence, the community of persons reflects its force by giving form to the religious sensibility. Hence, formal religions! All formal religion, while including a deeply personal aspect—at least implicitly, is inherently communal. This is why it is sustained by the many ordering features of all communal forms, including institutions, hierarchies, limiting norms, sanctions, and so forth. Since personhood emerges in the communal context, religious form as an expression of the religious sensibility is simply inevitable and ingredient in the unfolding of religion.

We break for lunch as the trail opens into a broad meadow. Collins takes us to a campsite he's used before. Ivy and I dig into the peanut butter and preserves to make our last sandwiches. Our supplies are disappearing fast, and we are consigned to trail-mix with fruit bits as our dessert. Water suffices as our beverage.

"If we pushed a little, we could make it all the way to Holy Ghost, but..." Collins' announcement is interrupted by enormous raindrops pelting us. I snatch up the quilt, and we scatter to our packs to retrieve rain gear. It has been cloudy most of the day, but the rain surprises us. We each hunch in our respective postures to endure the squall.

Frank tries to talk, but the rain picks up, and he retreats into his shell. We sit for almost an hour, until rainfall decreases to occasional drops. We throw off our drenched ponchos and shake ourselves back into action. Within minutes Delilah is released from her wrappings and passed among us. Then we're back in formation headed down-trail.

My earlier reflections on persons and personhood return as observations about the distinct personalities in our little entourage. Even Delilah, an infant, is already becoming differentiated in her responses to us. She's beginning the long and arduous process of becoming a distinct person. She's not simply "another baby girl" but this particular diminutive person-in-the-making. *What, exactly, is personality?* I ask myself. *For starters, what is my personality?* Shortly I take a stab at answering my own question: *My personality is the I that presents itself to the other as me.* I chuckle at my clumsy attempt, and Frank, hearing, stares back at me. He stumbles on a root and turns to regain his balance.

But my self-definition of my personality still makes a certain sense. As I've insisted, there is no personality apart from the *other*, and when the other presents itself, the "I" that responds is a different "I," namely, a "me." Personality, then is a double sided manifestation of the I-me complex.

These reflections draw me back to my consideration of personhood, and I sense that personhood is the vital vortex for engaging its communal—in this case, religious—context and at the same time moving *beyond* it. Personhood emerges through a life process that begins with *differentiation*. The infant's discovery that its mother is not an extension of itself may well be the traumatic initiation into this process of differentiation, and it likely reaches a critical threshold in adolescence. In its mature expression, personhood may include a certain *detachment* from its communal context, while remaining always fundamentally dependent on that context. Detachment is the ability to trans-form the communal context, to see it at a distance and as "other."

This is what Carl Jung means by *individuation*, the capacity of the self to "stand apart" and on its own without denying its communal context. With detachment we begin to move beyond, while continuing to be nested within our context. This is true, even when our detachment takes the form of rebellion. Indeed, there is a minimal rebellion in the very act of "going beyond." This capacity lies at the heart of transformative religion in our ability of see our religion as one among others and the possibility of going beyond it without necessarily denying it or leaving it behind.

Detachment is my name for a person's maximum separation of self from community and, in highly evolved states, from the self. Perhaps another more helpful name for this latter capacity is *self-transcendence*, but before I take this up, I must add a warning. Detachment is always dangerous, because it can degenerate into isolation and a sense of being cut off from contextual community. Feelings of isolation are not the same as detachment but are more nearly neurotic or even pathological distortions of it. I shall call these distortions *dissociation*. When we dissociate, we lose our continuity with our world, our sense of context, and to do so, is also to lose ourselves.

But self-transcendence takes us beyond the nexus of personhood within community, and in this respect it takes us to another level of existence. Notice first that I am using another word with "trans" in it, and that prefix carries with it the weight of the metaphor, "going beyond." How is it possible to go beyond one's self? Since this is a tricky idea, and an even trickier existential process, I want to make some distinctions.

I have encountered four distinct uses of "self-transcendence." First, it may be used existentially to mean that the self is always more than it appears to be at any given actual moment. The self transcends itself by its own possibilities not yet realized. Thus, selves continually create themselves through their decisive acts. This is the viewpoint of the philosopher Jean Paul Sartre.

Second, self-transcendence may refer to a psychological participation in unconscious 'archetypes" we share with humanity through the "collective unconscious." Carl Jung presents this view of the human psyche. It is another way of saying that the self is inherently rooted in "deep communality" as noted earlier.

Third, self-transcendence can be interpreted relationally through the claims other persons make on the self. In the words of Martin Buber, the other person is a "thou" encountered as transcendent to self. In short, other persons are irreducible and cannot legitimately be reduced to functions of myself or my own interests. As I noted earlier, to encounter another, a thou, is to touch the edge of infinity itself.

All of these ways of construing self-transcendence, whether existential, psychological, or relational, point to the responsive capacity as the basis of personhood. (I use "person" and "self" as virtually synonymous. A person is a self-standing forth as self in its communal framing.)

But there is a fourth use of self-transcendence that makes the term crucial for religion. It could be called *ontological* self-transcendence, but I prefer to speak of it as *ultimate* self-transcendence. Understood in this sense, self-transcendence has its roots in the original Primary Impulse, namely, the finite encounter with infinity. This is the definitive instance of self-transcendence as the "ultimate" context beyond all finite contexts. Self is grounded, contained, and sustained by the infinite whole in which self nevertheless participates.

When formal religion comes into play as the articulation and delimitation of the infinite (ultimate) transcendent, the radical character of self-transcendence becomes muted and focused upon and through the mediating form. Transformative religion enters the picture at the point where formal religion proves inadequate to its task, namely, to its inability to articulate the full significance of self-transcendence.

Let me describe this dense process another way. The elemental finite encounter with infinity and what I call the consequent religious sensibility may be described as *primary immediacy*. That is, it is the initial direct and stunning sense of boundedness, of encapsulation in time, space, and body over against infinity. We can hardly tolerate the graphic exposure accompanying this primary immediacy, and we strive to escape into the forms that contain us and assure us. Hence, among other strategies, formal religion! But as the finite limitations of formal religion itself become exposed, we may press further by moving across and beyond the forms. This is transformative religion, which recovers and penetrates the original self-transcendence in a *second immediacy*, that is, the shock of more fully recognizing and engaging our original position as finite creatures in the *presence* of infinity. The unmediated immediacy of the Sacred stands forth and draws us through and beyond forms.

Of course, we may never make the move from formal to transformative religion. We may never so much as attend the original religious sensibility. We may ignore or deny it through an array of finite distractions. Or, more likely, we may respond by settling for mundane forms, of whatever variety, that provide us with security against the weight of our finitude in light of the infinite. None of what I've said is automatic or necessary. When religion manifests itself, however, its existential origin and cultural-historical process appears to unfold as I suggest here. Moreover, since our finite encounter with infinity is ingredient in human existence, the religious motif constantly hovers in the wings, awaiting the triggering occasion that may bring it to consciousness.

All of this intricate analysis has been pursued with one end in mind: *transformative religion goes beyond formal religion without necessarily denying it.* In other words, transformative religion involves religion coming of age and maturing through the self reaching beyond itself and the forms by which it secures itself. Perhaps a better way of stating it is to speak of *Religion beyond religion*.

In the last quarter of the twentieth century some psychologists, especially those known as *humanistic* or *existential* psychologists, developed a special word for this capacity of the self to reach beyond its limits. They came to call it *transpersonal psychology*. Here again we have another "trans" word. In this case, "trans-personal" refers to that which is mediated through personhood but which is not confined to person or to the ego-self. When I speak of "transformative religion," I have the same capacity in mind in relation to Transcendence, that is, in relation to the infinite encountered as Presence.

At this juncture our capacity to rationally explain grows thin. We begin to appeal to immediate experience and to others who speak of such experiences. We move more nearly toward an "unknowing" than simply another level of knowing. In fact, we are beyond both knowing and understanding, toward being grasped by visionary unveiling. Or, as I prefer, our awareness becomes decisively *participatory*. The distance between knower and known recedes, and we *discern* but not to the extent that we can convey the *insight* to another by means of explanation. After unusual experiences in our mundane world, when we later seek to explain them, we sometimes end in frustration, saying, "You'd have to have been there." Participative understanding can only invite others to "go there." It can only point.

Nevertheless, I continue to point and to find confidence and guidance in those who have, in the words of Abraham Maslow, explored "the farthest reaches of human nature" and beyond. Thus, I do believe it possible to probe our way into this more refined and rarified atmosphere of transformative religion. Much of what I can say is yet beyond me, and I can only discern its contours by anticipation and as a potency emerging toward potentiality. Its throb is already present in our elemental lust for infinity and the vital possibility implicit in it.

"Clear the trail! Horses!" I hear Collins calling out and look ahead to see a retinue of half a dozen horses making their way up the now slushy trail. We step aside and stand, as if reviewing the plodding animals. Their bodies steam and their earthy horse-smells remind me of their primal energy. Indolent riders slouch in their saddles and nod to us in passing. Only the trail guide pauses to speak to Collins. He assures us that there are unoccupied campsites not more than a mile below. We wave our thanks. I still do not like so many horse caravans mucking the trails, but then again, as I'm reminded, it's a free country, especially out here "west of the Pecos"—literally—where horses rule.

Less than an hour later, Collin leaves the trail and heads off to the left. The wet grass slaps at our legs, leaving our socks soggy above our boots. It is not all that late, but we're looking for a place to set camp.

"It's too far to the next place to camp," Collins says, "and besides, the baby's got to be tired. She'll do better tomorrow if we stop now."

"How long will it take tomorrow?" Ivy asks as she takes Delilah from her pouch and holds her facing the rest of us. Delilah grins in gratitude for her release.

"It depends," Collins responds with one of his stock answers to most questions. "Weather…how fast we walk… Most likely it's about three hours. Downhill helps."

We continue through a stand of aspen and into an open space with a fire ring in the middle and a couple of logs arranged on two sides of it. Collins drops his pack, and we follow suit. After we stretch and move about in relief from the weight on our backs, we start the routine of making camp. Clouds continue to hang heavy, and we hurry to prepare our tents in case of more rain. After I pitch my tent and toss my bedroll inside, I help Frank do the same. Ivy is busy with Delilah.

No sooner do we complete our tasks than drops begin to splat against the tents and the tops of our hats. We duck into our respective dwellings to wait it out. The pelting increases and drowns out other sounds. My senses grow dull from the constant drone, and I later awaken with no sense of how long I've slept. All I know is that the rain has stopped. When I look out, Ivy's standing beside their tent. She waves and, as if on signal, our little tribe moves to converge at the fire ring. Hunger draws us.

This will be our last evening meal, and we scrounge to cobble together enough food. Collins pan-fries the remaining batch of cornbread, and it, along with honey to smother it, becomes the main entre. Freeze-dried green beans laced with carrots completes the offering. Just enough, no more. Fresh water helps. Fatigue outweighs hunger.

With dinner behind us, we sit around a sluggish campfire. Most of the wood is too wet at first, and we have to dry it out before a stronger blaze warms us. I appreciate Collins' stash of dry shavings. They set the fire going. By dusk we're toasty, but an atmosphere of low-grade depression pervades. We'll re-enter "the world" tomorrow. No one is exactly somber, but we're slightly withdrawn and pensive as we stare into the flames. Delilah makes occasional baby sounds, but otherwise, the earth enters once again the stillness of transition between day and night. As I've often observed, only in the wilderness do we sense this hallowed change. Back in the world the jangle of human busyness drown it out.

"Coyote, the trickster, is always messing with our minds," Collins begins out of the blue. No one moves or looks at him, but we're listening. He knows it, and he says no more for several minutes.

"Yes, old coyote gives us fits," Collins continues, "but he's always tryin' to help us see things clearer. This one old trickster was so good at it that he kept doing his work even after he died." More silence, then, "You see, before he died, he made an agreement with some members of his kind. It happened this way.

"When he died, the elders called for a ceremony to honor his passing to the spirit world. But when everyone came to the pole, his body was missing. Folk began to speculate. They said he must've still been alive and had probably walked away. Another one of his tricks! Some of the children started to go and hunt for him, but everyone was mostly confused and a little scared. How could a dead man, even a coyote, play such a trick?

"While everyone was milling around the pole and wondering what to do next, because they couldn't have their ceremony without the guest of honor being there, suddenly there was a loud thud on the ground behind the crowd. When people turned around, there the old dead coyote was laying in front of them. His fellow coyotes had fulfilled his last trick and the whole community broke into laughter."

Collins pauses, as if this is the end of the story. Then he continues, "But the trick wasn't over. When the people finally quit laughing, they took Coyote's body back to the stand near the pole, and the ceremony started. An elder began with a prayer, crying to the winds. Then he turned and said some words to everyone. After that, a drum began to speak, but at that moment Coyote's two assistants, the ones who threw him from the roof and onto the ground, walked up to the body. They stood solemnly to show respect for Coyote, and after standing a long time, when everyone grew quiet, they urinated on the body and walked away. It was a long time before the ceremony could continue. Everyone laughed most of the night…and celebrated."

The rest of us giggle at Collins' story but say nothing, until Frank asks, "What was the trickster…Coyote tryin' to say?"

Collins stares at him in disbelief, then says, "Well, I'm not sure. I know what I've learned, but I really don't know how to tell you. Who knows? You might need to learn somethin' else. I wouldn't want to confuse you." Collins stands and stretches. "Maybe if you sleep on it, the message'll come to you." With that he walks off to hang our pitiful food supply in a tree, and as the fire dissolves into a complex of gray and glowing ashes, I sprinkle water on it and watch steam waft upward. The dense black of mountain darkness takes over.

Twenty-Six

True resignation consists in this: that man, feeling his subordination to the course of world events, makes his way toward inward freedom from the fate that shapes his external existence. Inward freedom gives him the strength to triumph over the difficulties of everyday life and to become a deeper and more inward person, calm and peaceful.

Albert Schweitzer

∼

For much of the night I sleep fitfully, waking repeatedly. My mind gears toward home. I keep thinking of Ethan, of the likelihood that he has gone back to Oklahoma, of how I will travel home, of my wife's return, family and the summer ahead. I marvel at how intoxicating this wilderness has been and yet how pervasive and relentless the images of that other world have become in the night. When I try to dismiss them in favor of sleep, they become all the more insistent. My own mind, I realize, is not truly "mine." That is, I actually—whoever this "I" is—do not have mastery of "my" own mind. It mocks me, but when it does, am I actually mocking myself? Nothing is so bizarre as this psychic abyss that I am.

As the tent lightens dimly with the promise of dawn, I decide to give up on sleep and simply let my mind run freely. Later, when I awaken abruptly, daylight is inside the tent. I realize that I have just dreamed my next move. Yesterday, when I introduced the idea of *Transformative Religion*, a notion I've pondered for some time, I realized that I really did not know how to describe it. I couldn't locate the core of the idea. No. It's more than an idea. It's an awareness, something I barely grasp—or does it grasp me?—but cannot ignore. But the illumination came to me in my sleep. Transformative religion moves beyond form by the agency of *inwardness*. I scribble hurriedly in my journal, until Frank whispers from outside the tent, "You awake yet?"

"Yeah," I assure him and climb out to a sparkling crisp high-country morning. Ivy nurses Delilah and Collins stokes a morning fire to life. We're in no hurry. It is only three hours to the Holy Ghost Campground, where Peck will meet us.

We conjure our final meal out of very little. Unknown to us, Ivy soaked our remaining dried fruit overnight, and she now prepares a compote, using honey instead of syrup. Tasty! Collins divides the remaining granola bars among us. Two each with two left over. I eat one and keep the second for later, topping off breakfast with an herbal tea.

Collins surveys our few remaining bits and pieces of food. "I guess that'll motivate us to hike out today," he concludes. With that, he begins the familiar routine of folding, stuffing, and stashing gear for our final haul.

As usual, we all work in silence. Frank takes Delilah, and Ivy plunges into their preparations. I notice how tattered their gear has become and wonder what is soon to become of them. Collins has solved their problem for now, but how long can that last? Abruptly, Frank announces to no one in particular, "The point is that life and death happen constantly, and no particular death is so important that we cannot laugh about it."

I have no clue what he's talking about or why, until Collins responds. "That's one way to look at it. In fact, that's pretty good, but is that all there is to it?" Only with this comment do I remember last night's story of the coyote trickster.

"What else could it mean?" Frank asks insistently.

"Many things," Collins teases. "For instance, maybe coyotes don't die but live on through our laughter. As long as people laugh, the coyote is alive, and as long as his story's told, he's alive. I kept him alive last night. What about that?"

"Well, but that's not what really happened in the story..." Frank declares. "When people die, they don't continue living. They're gone..."

Collins stops loading his pack and sits on a log near the fire. "Okay. Let me ask you somethin'. You Rastafarians believe that Haile Selassie, your messiah, still lives and that he'll return to save his people. How does that make sense? Is he somewhere just waitin' for the right time? Where? Is he in suspended animation, waiting to be called forth? How can that begin to make sense?"

"Actually, I'm not real sure I believe that, not exactly. I mean about Selassie and all…" Frank admits.

"Then what do you believe?" Collins asks. "The last time I spoke with a Rasta that belief was pretty firm."

"But it's symbolic. He'll return in spirit…" Frank urges.

"Good!" Collins exudes. "That's also true of that old coyote trickster. His body's long since decayed, but his symbolic power is still with the people. It's present in the story and in their pleasure over it. You met him again last night. And that's the only way Selassie's gonna' appear, or Jesus or anybody else we keep lookin' for. Native people know this. Anything else is too spooky for words. Hallucinations!"

I sense that Collins has exhausted his indirect approaches to solving the religious puzzles we've been pondering. Now he's taking the head-on approach. I'm fascinated. When the packing's finished, we gravitate to Collins, but he says nothing more, waiting for Frank.

"Huh…I guess. You're probably right," Frank ventures haltingly. "But just because it's a symbol doesn't mean it's not real…"

Collins sits there, like a skinny Buddha, letting Frank soak in his words. "You remember that circle of rocks yesterday," he begins. "What was it?" He waits for Frank to answer.

"What do you mean, 'what was it?' You said it was the universe, or somethin' like that."

"But really," Collins asks, "Wasn't it only a circle of rocks. There was plenty of universe left outside that circle. And until I said what it was, you only saw a circle of rocks. But then, when I made it into the circle of the universe and all of life, you bought into it right away."

"Yeah, because I knew what you meant," Frank agrees.

"And what did I mean? How can a circle of rocks ever, ever be 'the universe'?"

"Well," Frank answers, "It represents the universe. It's a symbol for the universe."

"Then is the circle of rocks as the universe 'real'?" Frank nods in response, and Collins continues, "I believe symbols are the most real things there are. And they're the only interesting things we have goin' for us. What's real has to be shaped out of the raw stuff available to us, and we give it shape by the way we participate in it."

That word "participate" leaps at me, and I lose track of the conversation. I'm immediately preoccupied with the idea that the old notion of "objectivity" and of subjects—ourselves—seeking to overcome ourselves through connection (knowledge) of what's "out there." That project just does not work. Our participation in "the world" shapes the world, and symbolism is the medium for doing so. Symbolism participates the world, as well as Transcendence, and that is our only source of connection. There may be an objectivity apart from us, but we'll never connect to it as such but only through our capacity to participate it symbolically.

By the time I finish my mental excursus, the conversation between Collins and Frank has ended, and they're scrambling to don packs and depart. I want to pursue the discussion and ask about whether there might be some way of penetrating the symbolic, but the focus has shifted to the task at hand. In any case, this is where my concept of Transformative Religion comes into play, and as I dreamed in the night, the clue appears to rest in this inwardness.

On the trail we assume our usual order in single file, but this time Ivy hangs back just in front of me. She says, "I want to talk about what they were sayin' just now, but I'm not sure I get it…"

I assure her that we can discuss the subject later, and she turns to pick up her pace. I'm left with this often used—and frequently misused—notion of inwardness. What am I to make of it?

Perhaps I can begin by sorting through some related concepts. First, it appears that, when anyone encounters me, they see the surface: my physical presence and my behavior. That's about it. But if they then claim to "know" me on that basis, I profoundly object. They do not actually "know" me at all. The reason is that I associate myself with far more, with capacities they do not and cannot access. In other words, the "I" of which I am aware is only superficially manifest through my embodiment and behavior in the world. Granted, these are necessary and significant *surfaces* of my presence in the world, but there is so much more. These surfaces are rather like the proverbial iceberg: most of the "I" remains *below* the surface. In other words, I have an "inner world" largely hidden from external engagement, and much of it can be hidden even from me. This is where inwardness comes into play. There are ways to make this interior world more available, but it remains largely below the surface, even when my behavior betrays it—which it often does. Some people can interpret these betrayals better than others, and some are even trained in doing so. Psychiatrists and psychotherapists come to mind. Or the far more mysterious shaman!

Second, this interior existence below the surface "feels" most nearly like the *real I*. Yet, it takes on two aspects that complicate matters. (1) This interior existence has a life of its own. "I" may presume to be the master of this interior domain, but it actually operates in very peculiar ways that I do not control, at least not easily. Take daydreams or fantasies, for instance. I frequently catch myself allowing my mind to free float in directions that, when I catch myself, are surprising and sometimes disturbing. I don't seem to be in charge of these mental meanderings at all. I can only, as noted, catch myself and strive to concentrate more deliberately, that is, in a more controlled focus of my attention. But although I may to some extent master my daydreams and fantasies, I also dream during sleep, and with the rare exception of "lucid dreaming," I cannot take charge of my dreams. My dreams take charge of me.

Moreover, I can fixate on particular thoughts, which, no matter how much I pledge to think otherwise, continue to occupy my mind and prompt my feelings. It's like being put to the old test: stand in the corner and *do not* think about a white bear. Until some resolution is achieved, these fixated notions prevail against every effort to eradicate them. In extreme cases I experience such fixed ideas as a kind of possession. They will not let me go.

These inner states, and others like them, suggest that the interior life is to some extent chaotic, beyond "our" control, and more ominous than comforting. Most theories of the unconscious, beginning with Freud, have been attempts to address this condition and find ways to bring its threatening pathological extremes under management through a more unified and "conscious" awareness. To do so can be an arduous process, as both therapists and spiritual teachers know. Therefore, when in the present context I speak of "inwardness," I'm not speaking of daydreams, fantasies, sleeping dreams, or fixations. These conditions are more nearly barriers to inwardness or distractions from it than expressions of it.

(2) I have an urge to express my inner states, to allow them to "escape" their confinement within my inner life. Of course, I monitor and strive to control this process, and in extreme cases of shame, guilt, or simply fear of exposure as such, I deliberately seek to prohibit the expression of these inner states. Yet, despite this counter tendency, I have an urge to manifest, to become known, to unveil the inner self that lies so hidden beneath the surfaces of body and behavior. The way I manage this urge is determined by disposition, nurturance, and life conditions, and because I do not consider myself unique in this, I suspect the same is more or less true for all of us.

This sort of urge to self-revelation remains a tense time-release process. On the one hand, I believe that our kind suffers the urge to be known, at least among those we trust. On the other hand, this is also where we often find ourselves most anxious and reluctant. I recall reading a small volume entitled, *Why I Am Afraid to Tell You Who I Am*. The answer to this "why" question was simple: *I am afraid to tell you who I am because that is all I have, and I do not know what you will do with it.*

This suggests that our urge to express our inner lives is also resisted by a low-grade anxiety—and sometime terror—of the exposure. Again, this psychological tension between self-revelation and self-protection has little to do with the inwardness necessary to Transformative Religion.

Third, if we are to grasp inwardness as I wish to introduce it here, we must allow it to unveil itself in relation to other conditions we may easily confuse with it. We may, for example, consider inwardness as simply another name for *subjectivity*. Since the Enlightenment, if not before, we in the West have been preoccupied with establishing objectivity, that is, a reliably confirmed domain outside and over against our subjective limitations. In this historical context subjectivity—and especially "subjectivism"—has been our nemesis. This is dramatized in one of the charges often made against us when we assert something to be true: "Oh, that's purely subjective" or more commonly, "That's only your opinion."

This dilemma of how subjects can know objects and thus liberate themselves from "subjectivism" is as pervasive in modern thought as it is unfortunate. The project of *overcoming* our subjectivity is both impossible and undesirable. It is like asking us to leap out of our own skin. If 'objectivity" is taken to mean overcoming our subjectivity, then there is no objectivity. At best, what we designate as objectivity is actually, at most, *intersubjective agreement*. When there is sufficient agreement among us, based on our interpretations of shared experience that something is the case, then we take it to be true. Objectively! But of course, as much as this may be a source of personal and corporate assurance, *we can all be mistaken*. Furthermore, we often are, especially regarding complex matters of consequence.

In contemporary religions this is exactly the grave error in what is popularly called *fundamentalism*. Every version of this point of view suffers from an exoteric fixation on "objective truth," whether located in a text, a person, dogmas, or a combination of them. In this respect, I sense that the fundamentalist mind, if we can speak of such, is horrified at the prospect of inwardness. It is too uncontrollable, too fraught with the uncertainty that comes with the very idea of any direct unveiling. What fundamentalists lack and what they resist is inwardness. In this regard they are rather like sociopaths, who, because they are dissociated from their own interior orientation, externalize their behavior without regard to other people as having claim on them.

Rather than deny or reject our subjectivity, I propose that we take it seriously and press it to discover its potential. This is not to collapse into subjectivism but to plumb the fecundity of the singular resource available to us: *ourselves*. Inwardness comes to our attention only as we embrace and move into our subjectivity rather than pretend to escape it.

The moment we say this, however, a further confusion arises. We are most likely to be accused of advocating for ego-centricity, that is, self-centeredness or, in its worst manifestation, "selfishness." Narcissism, the self's preoccupation with itself, is most assuredly one dominant and ubiquitous way of engaging and distorting our subjectivity, and there is surely some degree of narcissism ever present in us. Thus, I am not speaking here of the self-regard necessary to our very existence but of our propensity to self-preoccupation at the expense of, or disregard for, other selves. Let's acknowledge that this kind of self-absorption is a profound and persistent temptation for our kind. But, when I speak of inwardness, I'm referring to an orientation that actually challenges our self-preoccupied narcissism. Only through inwardness can this threat of self-absorption be penetrated and overcome.

To press this theme to its extreme, consider *solipsism*. This notion, that the self is the only thing known to exist, is the ultimate trap of the self-within-itself. This way of thinking takes subjectivism and narcissism to the brink of madness. It is more nearly related to a theory of knowledge than an attitude. In the end, solipsism maintains, all we can *know* is the self, period. We are trapped in isolated atomistic existence. The Greek term from which we derive "idiot" carries exactly this weight: "to be totally alone." It remains important to press our discussion to this extreme, because it reveals the potential danger in all subjectivity, namely, the degeneration into narcissistic self-isolation beyond even the kin of subjectivism. Solipsism!

Once again, inwardness stands in sharpest contrast to self-isolating solipsism. On the contrary, inwardness is the locus of encounter with the *other as presence*, whether the "other" is other selves, the flora and fauna of nature itself, or Transcendence as Presence. Rather than inwardness further isolating us from the other, it is the point of meeting. When Martin Buber declares that, "All real living is meeting," he has in mind the depth of meeting which both constitutes and expresses us to ourselves in and through what he designates as "Thou." In the crucible of inwardness we move through ourselves to the other as constitutive of ourselves. That is, the other claims us and thus becomes presence.

To put the case one other way, our encounter with all that is not simply reducible to ourselves takes place in two domains: *extrinsic* or *intrinsic*. When we ordinarily engage the other in common experience, the other remains "there" as that which modifies us in some way, minimal or profound, but which we may enlist to serve our interests or oppose when they challenge our interests. This extrinsic domain of relations leaves the other as other and is more akin to what Buber calls the "I-It" relation. Only when we begin to understand the mission of our subjectivity as inwardness can we engage "internal relations" and participate in the other as presence grounded in intrinsic hiddenness.

This move to inwardness is frequently prompted by 'going abroad" in the world and encountering the strange and uncanny, that which does not fit with our assumptions and expectations. The alien may serve to drive us inward, especially if we strive to overcome the alienation. While some of us have a predilection to inwardness, most of us must be driven or drawn there by the demands and threats of extrinsic relations. These two domains of relation need not conflict or contradict each other, so long as the intrinsic, born of inwardness, under girds the extrinsic surface. To sum up, inwardness is not an escape from the other into an isolated condition. Rather, inwardness is the ground out of which the other discloses itself as presence. The other makes claim upon us as we participate it.

Finally, I discover inwardness as a serious source of fulfillment and wellbeing only by awakening and devoting myself to it in a disciplined way. This strategy might be designated in general as *introspection*. Some of us are surely more predisposed to disciplined interior attention than others, but all of us are, in principle, capable of attending ourselves from within. But introspection is not itself inwardness, only the tool for engaging inwardness, seeking to "see" or discern inwardly. The word itself, meaning, "to look within," indicates as much.

Abruptly and without forewarning, we break into an open meadow, and I realize we are entering Holy Ghost Campground. We have not stopped for a break, mostly because Delilah has resigned herself to a life of endless hiking and because the trail has descended steadily. Collins stops ahead and removes his pack. As I draw nearer, I see a picnic table on which he stacks his gear. We do the same, and Collins strikes off to reconnoiter the campground and look for Peck. He's gone for so long that I wonder whether he's decided to walk the ten or so miles back to his cabin.

Before we see him we hear the drone of a vehicle coming toward us. Within moments a disheveled ancient grayish pickup appears with Collins squatting in the back and Peck driving. Without a word, only a nod, Peck leaves the truck running, goes to the other door and begins pulling out of the front seat what looks like debris. He piles it all in the truck bed and puts the spare tire over it to hold it in place. He then ushers Ivy and Delilah into the cab, as we retrieve the gear and lift it to Collins standing in the back of the truck. We climb aboard and without the least fanfare trundle through the campground and toward the main road. I have not been in a vehicle for almost three weeks, and the sudden jolts and bumps take on a surrealist character. They affect my bones. I keep wondering how Peck knew when to show up, but it all remains shrouded in a mist of Native intuitive magic.

Still in the campground, we round a curve, and Peck stops abruptly. I peer over the cab to see a grown mountain lion standing in the road. It's not spooked in the least but only stares at us. There it is again, *nature red in tooth and claw*. We watch until the beast strolls casually off the road and disappears in the underbrush. I find myself muttering, as I did in the mountains, *Tyger, tyger, burning bright/ In the forest of the night*... Ah, the mysterious depths in those eyes!

I feel my beard. Rough and scraggly. And I realize how good it'll feel to bathe after so many spit-baths and occasional dunks in the frigid mountain streams. I say as much and Frank retorts, "Yeah, but for us it's been a lot longer. Ivy's been talkin' about it the last week."

We turn right onto the road that meanders with the Pecos River toward civilization. I ask, "How long did you think you could stay up there, I mean, before we came along?"

"All summer..." Frank admits with a hang-dog countenance. "That was really stupid, since Rick never came back... We'd decided to hike out in a day or two, but then you showed up." Then after a pause, "Saved our necks, I guess."

For the next half-hour we lumber southward, down through the narrow passes, around sharp turns, the river guiding us. Only the drone of the truck penetrates the silence, until I hear Delilah whimpering in the cab. Frank looks in the rear window and, satisfied, sits back.

We bounce along the gravel drive to the cabin. As we pull up, Collins' dog bounds off the porch, our welcome committee. Off to the right and under a tree near the river I'm surprised to see Ethan's truck parked. Immediately I imagine that he must have stayed here at the cabin, and I look around to spot him. He doesn't appear. Peck exits the truck and goes around to help Ivy and Delilah. We all reach for packs, Peck taking Ivy's, and haul them to the porch.

Inside, Collins shows Ivy and Frank where they'll be staying. They're astonished at the tiny loft and the door-sized skylight above their bed. They respond as though they've been invited to a five-star hotel. Within minutes Ivy takes Delilah into the bathroom that will be theirs. Collins shows Frank the other one, and they are all luxuriating in warm water before I can go back outside.

Collins tells me about an outdoor shower near a shed he calls the bunkhouse. Peck grunts that he's about to leave, and I thank him for meeting us. He nods, holds out a limp hand for me to shake, and departs with a wave at Collins. I take my pack out to the bunkhouse, where I'll stay tonight. As I prepare to go out to the shower, I realize that, although I'm out of the wilderness, it's not yet out of me. This is all more nearly a dream. The shower outside in the early afternoon breeze of dawning summer caresses me and leaves me at the edge of drowsy. I dress in shorts and stroll down to the river, trying to make my way back to "the world." When I look up at the cabin, I see Frank sitting in a porch swing and holding Delilah. Ivy stands out in the sun, drying her hair with a towel. Collins strokes the golden retriever, feeds her from a bin, and disappears inside. I find the abrupt return to this routine at once welcoming and alien.

As my sensibilities gradually revive and catch up with me, I stroll along the Pecos, occasionally reaching down and chunking a stone or twig into the lilting water. At once my mind returns to so much unfinished pondering. Has anything been settled by my explorations into the dense web of religion? Not really. The subject's too vast for that, but I'm still convinced that I've pushed the matter along, especially with this breakthrough idea of Transformative Religion and more especially with the insight about inwardness as the portal into it.

The actual practice of most formal religion itself invites introspection and thus inwardness, but it cannot cause introspection or inwardness. Worship itself, its rituals and endlessly varied liturgical processes are designed to evoke—and to invoke—introspection. The extrinsic gestures point to and call forth the intrinsic plunge inward. But formal practices cannot *cause* introspection and engagement with inwardness. They can only, at most, be the occasion for the process. I think of two particular instances of this. (1) Rituals, as religious expressions, are externalizations of what lies hidden in the invisible reaches of inwardness. Granted, rituals often leave those practicing them with only the external husk. There is no *ex opera operato* in ritual—nothing automatic, only a prompting of a possibility. Hence, rituals may, and often do, become "empty" gestures, but their intent is to invite congregants into introspection in the interest of inwardness.

Another way of understanding ritual is to see them as dramatizations of the myths on which they are based. This means that ritual is an acting out of the mythic meanings we embrace. Indeed, without the mythic under girding I imagine rituals would be quite empty.

(2) Wherever formal religious practice encourages *contemplation* or *meditation*, the invitation is more direct. These practices are interior as such, and the discipline of doing them promises to quicken the introspective orientation toward inwardness. Likewise, *solitude*, *stillness*, and *silence* have the same potential, and they often go hand in hand with contemplation or meditation.

Although formal religion points to and may prompt inwardness, this is also its boundary. Not only is formal religious practice unable to *cause* the move to inwardness, it also has no *control* over inwardness. Herein is found perhaps the great irony of all formal religious systems: they invite deeply personal response and experience, which no system can dominate. While formal religion can offer *interpretations* of these experiences—these encounters with inwardness, there is no assurance that any such interpretation is definitive or final. In other words, the very thing formal religions encourage can become unwieldy within the system. Inward spontaneity inevitably threatens to become more than systems and structures can contain or manage.

Hence, Transformative Religion is both related to formal religion and intimidating for it. As long as the inner voices of Joan of Arc spoke messages consistent with the "orthodox" interests of the Catholic hierarchy, they championed her, but when her voices proved contrary to the church, she became anathema and was consigned to the flames. Inwardness cannot be controlled by external form, but neither is inwardness necessarily the nemesis of formal religion.

Let's state the situation one other way. Transformative Religion entails an orientation to inwardness, but inwardness creates, at best, a tension with formal religion, even though formal religion may seek to invoke and evoke the inwardness. Because forms are extrinsic and provide context and security against unbounded infinity, we are easily drawn to settle for formal interpretations and meaning over against the wild immediacy of inwardness. Why? Inwardness haunts the borderland between our finitude and the infinite. This is why I keep warning that formal religion, in so far as it would confine the infinite, too readily degenerates into a trap—an idol—rather than a medium. But if inwardness possesses this potency, this capacity to break free of form without denying it, we are obliged to examine it more fully.

Thus far, the concept of inwardness remains empty. I have said little or nothing about what it actually entails. I have only suggested that it is the primordial locus of *meeting*, where the other as presence reveals itself. This claim alone deserves more attention, but is this all that we mean by inwardness? If so, is it enough? For what? If not, what more remains to be examined? I find these questions frustrating, because they are the most weighty I've considered, and here I am nearing the end of this pilgrimage. Alas, I suppose Robert Frost has it right: the only interesting business is the unfinished business.

As I turn to walk back upstream, Collins comes toward me with Delilah on his arm. I hold out my arms and he delivers the infant into my care. We stand for some time, watching the river, the constancy of its ever-changing flow. I break the silence. "I wonder where Ethan is. He wouldn't leave the truck…"

"There's a note inside the cab, but I didn't read it," Collins reports. Another of his traits: always meticulous to mind only his own business. "He's a big boy, ya know. He can look after himself."

I nod in partial agreement, but then I remember how he left in a fit of turmoil. I want to be sure he's all right. Collins picks up my agitation, and turns back toward the cabin. I follow with Delilah cradled on my arm. She locates my beard and pulls at it.

At the truck I reach inside, take the note, and shut the door. Written in Ethan's peculiar back-slanted scrawl on yellow lined paper, it reads, *Come to the monastery. You can drive the truck. The key's in the regular place.* He signed his name. I hand the note to Collins. He reads it and grunts, "Better wait 'til tomorrow. They close up shop to outsiders pretty early."

Back at the cabin Ivy and Frank lie back, sprawled in canvas chairs, the late afternoon sun warming them. Frank looks up. "This is the first real chair I've sat in for about two months. I forgot how they're made to fit your body..." No one takes up the conversation. The halcyon gift of early summer steals our attention, and we all lounge quietly until the sun nears the rim of the mountain. Delilah is content to sit on the porch and pick at the odds and ends available to her. I watch her.

"Wanna' eat somethin'?" Collins asks, and I realize for the first time how famished I am. The thin fare of the last two days has caught up with me, and from the enthusiastic responses of Frank and Ivy, they're in the same condition. "Well, I put on some beans when we got here. We'll have beans and rice. All I need to do is th' cornbread." He disappears inside with Ivy following and insisting that she take care of the cornbread.

As twilight creeps onto the porch, Collins appears, swinging two pots by their handles. Ivy follows with a pan of cornbread in one hand and metal camp dishes in the other. They walk past us and toward the grove near the sweat lodge. Frank picks up Delilah, and we follow the aroma of fresh-cooked beans, stomachs turning cartwheels. Soon everything's laid out on a rough picnic table in the grove. After we've helped ourselves to generous quantities of food, a rude assortment of outdoor chairs invites us to gather in a circle. The first meal after a pack trip is always especially succulent, and this one's no exception. Everyone takes seconds, and after such indulgence we become lethargically satiated. Delilah nurses with gusto!

Frank points behind Collins and asks, "What's that?"

"Sweat Lodge," Collins responds.

"What's it for?"

"Purification." Collins sets aside his taciturn mood but only barely.

"From what?" Frank continues.

Ivy intervenes with her own question, "Now who's askin' all the questions?" She says it lightheartedly, but I can tell she's been waiting for the right occasion. Frank grins but keeps staring at the sweat lodge as though it might reveal an answer.

"Whatever's pollutin' you," Collins continues with his cryptic responses.

"Well now, that could be downright useful," Frank observes.

Ivy counters that she really doesn't much like words like "polluted," because it means that we set up everything as a conflict between what's pure and what's polluted. She argues that we're actually expected to deal with all of it…everything, the pure and the polluted, and even if we purify something, it only becomes polluted again.

"All right, but why not see it as a cycle," Frank suggests. "That's what life's really about, living and therefore getting polluted…I mean, you can't actually do anything without things becomin' contaminated. Then you need to purify so you can go back at it again. Maybe everybody needs a purification place, a…what is it? Sweat house, like that one." Then, after a moment's reflection, he turns to me. "That's why I need religion, to help me be religious. A sweat lodge is a house of purification."

With that comment, Collins stands unceremoniously and begins cleaning off the table. Shortly he's carrying the pots with dishes stashed inside them and walking to the cabin. It's another sign of how fed up he is with our discussions of religion.

Eventually I respond, "Could be. Most of us probably need a place and a people to help us set things right. They at least constantly remind us of what needs to be done. But I've been workin' the last few days on the possibility that we can move beyond that sort of religion to somethin' more…more…adequate or fulfilling, I guess."

Ivy stands. "I'm gonna' put her down. She's already asleep, but don't talk any more 'til I come back."

Frank tries to comply by asking me, "Do you think it'll be all right if we stay here for a while? We don't wanna' to be any trouble…and Ivy's worried a little about that."

"Here's what I know about Collins," I begin. "If he didn't want you to stay, he'd be the first to say so…and when he wants you to go, you'll know. He doesn't say much, but he always means what he says, even when he's bein' a trickster." After a pause, I add, "You can learn from him. He knows things, different kinds of things than we think about, but they're important. And he'll leave you alone. He won't try to get you to do or be anything. Of course, he sure does have his own ways and his own thoughts. That's for sure."

"Yeah," Frank agrees, "I like that about him. But why does he get so perturbed about religion?"

"Huh," I say. "It's mostly 'white man's religion' that bugs him, and he thinks that's all I'm talkin' about. He thinks that Native people have a better grip on it and without nearly as much fuss…"

"Do you disagree?" Frank asks, as I proceed to kindle a small fire in the fire ring to put the evening chill in retreat. He gathers some twigs and small limbs to help. Ivy returns and listens enthusiastically.

"To some extent," I admit, "but in his world, the Native world, everything's still somewhat integrated. Religion weaves itself in and through the fabric of how they live. That's why there's not much fuss. We've discussed it many times, and that's how he feels. He thinks that, if I'd quit trying to understand religion and join the medicine circle, everything would be fine. Only when the outside religions…and he always means European and American Christianity…come along and interfere, do the Native people become confused, or more nearly, distracted and corrupted."

"Do you agree?" Ivy wants to know.

"Somewhat," I confess. "But still, this is how things actually are. Nobody can really hide from all of those other ways of living. We're all bein' affected by each other, whether we like it or not, and with so many religions existing in the shrinking space of this planet, we cannot avoid dealing with each other, and by the same token, we'll automatically need to deal with our own take on things, including religion. And I believe, especially religion!"

"But you said that you're workin' on how we can get past all this…well, mess that religion seems to me to be." As always, when Ivy's considering something vital to her, she speaks with a barely muted passion. "That's what I want to know about."

"Well, it's difficult to move beyond the trappings of religion, and I suspect that only a few are capable of it, at least at the present time. It's like climbing Mount Everest: the closer climbers are to the top, the fewer the climbers. The air's thin, and it takes hardy souls to dare those heights. Still," I say with conviction, "I believe this is the wave of the future. Religion's ready for…I'm not sure how to express it, but…ready for the next evolutionary leap, if I can be that presumptuous. If it comes, it'll come slowly and painfully and with great resistance. The resistance is already so loud it threatens to drown out the subtle shifts takin' place."

"Sometimes I have this feelin' about the whole thing," Ivy declares. "It's like there's something more, something hidden right below the surface. When I meditate at some of our gatherings, I come close to it, and it's exciting. But…" Ivy stands unexpectedly and whirls toward the cabin. "I hear Delilah!" And she charges off. I hadn't heard a thing, but I note how tuned a mother is to the sounds of her child. Amazing! And comforting!

Ivy's sudden departure breaks our mood. I can tell that Frank wants to join her, and I encourage him to go. "All of this," I reassure him, "is the unending conversation. We'll mark it to be continued… And that's the way it'll always be."

Twenty-Seven

Presence has force and authority. It is the all-but union of James Joyce, the *advaya* of Hinduism, the *coincidentia oppositorum* of Nicholas of Cusa. It is not monism or dualism; it is the unitary experience and an experience of totality in the midst of shattering differences.

Ralph Harper

∼

...imagination and the final participation it leads to, involve, unlike hypothetical thinking, the whole man—thought, feeling, will, and character...

Owen Barfield

∼

I start toward the bunkhouse, picking my way in the dark, when I hear Collins' voice calling. His "Hey" is at first disembodied, but when I stare toward the cabin, I see him silhouetted against the lone light cast through the kitchen window. He gestures for me to come, and we ease into the canvas chairs.

After the obligatory silence from which he gains succor, Collins asks, "Ya wanna' hang around a few days?"

"Probably not," I predict. "Tomorrow I'll check on Ethan and see what he wants to do, but I'd like to be home when my woman returns from Europe."

"Europe?"

"Yeah, like I told you, she's teaching in this travel program..." I pause, then add, "If she'd been available, she would be with me. She likes packin' as much as I do."

Collins suddenly looks lonely to me, hunkered in that low-slung chair. He nods but doesn't speak. Just as I'm about to stand and go for my first night in a bed in weeks, he says, "I'm glad Ivy and Frank are gonna be here for awhile. We might all be able to help each other out."

"You gonna ask 'em to work for you?" I wonder aloud.

"Yep. I'm askin' them to be company. That's their job."

"And yours?"

"The same," Collins says with a grin. "That's really the only job anybody has...bein' company and havin' company."

"How long do you think they'll stay?" I ask

"How long's a piece of string?" Collins responds, with that trickster look in his eye. Again, he changes the subject. "Did you find what you're lookin' for in th' mountains this time?"

"Well, more clues anyway...and a breakthrough or two..." I answer cautiously, not wanting to claim too much.

"As I keep remindin' you, it'll all come clear as a mountain stream, when you come back to the Native way." Collins' comment can no longer surprise me. It's his mantra. He's been saying this in words and deeds for the last couple of weeks, and besides, I already knew his take.

"Ya know, you're partly right. I believe the most basic...original humans, the ones nearest our roots, probably know much that we've forgotten or rejected. But, Collins, there's something really goin' on in the world that's new, and its loaded with promise, problems and downright peril. But one thing's for certain, we're not goin' back to somethin' earlier. We have to move into possibilities we've only imagined at best. The world's gotten much more complex—and complicated, and religion's interlaced through all of it. If we're gonna' simplify, we've got to do it by wading through the complexity and the complications of a planet that's both expanding and shrinking at the same time. We cannot run away from the mess. We *are* the mess...and so is religion...yours, mine, and everybody else's. Maybe, if we've got the guts to muddle through the complexity, we'll find another kind of simplicity on the other side."

After a silence punctuated only by tiny night sounds, Collins says, "Probably. But I'll tell you what I'm plannin' to do. I'm waitin' right here 'til you all come back home."

We stare at each other, and I sense that Collins, as solidly reliable as they come, will continue to stand his ground. Knowing this reassures me, and I can stroll off to sleep with the comfort and confidence that his kind is still around. Waiting.

When the country sounds of morning invite consciousness, my first thought is of Ethan. I still wonder why he told me to come to the monastery. He must be visiting until I can pick him up. These thoughts drive me from bed, and I walk over to the cabin. No one else is awake yet, and I quietly begin breakfast. Not many supplies in the house, I soon discover, but I find the makings for pancakes, and some ham in the freezer. By the time I've finished and set the coffee brewing, I hear Delilah stirring her parents. Collins enters, looks at the coffee pot, and goes for it. We sit, tasting and smelling without words.

Frank brings Delilah into the room, and I start the pancakes, serving plates one at a time. Shortly, we're circled around the table on the first day of a new venture for this peculiar "family." When we've finished eating, I announce that I plan to go to the monastery to see about my friend. Ivy asks, unabashedly, "Can I come?" When I nod, Frank adds his own request, and the morning's set. I wait while Ivy bathes Delilah in the kitchen sink and they repack gear for her needs.

I slip out to the porch and sit with my legs dangling over its edge. Chama, the golden retriever, joins me lying close and occasionally yawning. As I stroke her, my thoughts wend their way back to yesterday and to this phenomenal condition that rests in the depths of existence: *inwardness*. This singular quality comes to consciousness with our sense that we have no hiding place from the self-transcending other, indeed, from Transcendence itself. And the consequence follows: we have no hiding place from ourselves. At our very core we stand *exposed*, despite the constant effort to pretend otherwise. In fact, I've come to sense that we spend most of our life's energy and interest in hiding away as though the hiding granted us security. Another delusion of the "immortality project!" Much that passes for religious fulfillment, especially in formal religion, only turns out to offer another place to hide from our own unveiling.

But paradoxically, inwardness is itself a quite different sort of hiddenness! Inwardness invites us to escape, or at least retreat from, the realm of extrinsic concentration—and often, distraction—with its endless appeals to surfaces, especially those which dominate modernity: consumption, entertainment, the surprises of technology, the thrill of the immediate crisis, the seething planetary ferment. "Getting and Spending," Wordsworth calls it, and he adds, "...we lay waste our powers." There is so much to see and do and, above all, to own.

How can one *hide* from these alluring charms? How dare we? The entire machinery of modernity is orchestrated against such hiding, against inwardness. And this includes the machinations of formal religion as well. While it is true that formal religion invites us toward inwardness, or claims to do so, at the same time it succumbs to the madness of exoteria and employs the same noisy din that belongs to the world at large. Thus, we find ourselves obliged to hide from even the busyness of religion in order to encounter the inwardness that religion claims to represent and to promise us.

Consequently, to enter upon the inwardness that marks Transformative Religion is daunting. Perhaps this has always been so, but given today's obstacles to it, inwardness is more than daunting. It is experienced as illusive, ephemeral, unavailable—at best beckoning but just beyond reach. Perhaps this is why, to use the words of one of our great sacred texts, "Many are called but few are chosen." In short, engaging inwardness is rare, especially deliberate and sustained engagement, but this is no basis for dismissing or diminishing its centrality to human fulfillment and wellbeing.

Nor is inwardness inherently rare. Recently I ran across a phrase in a quotation. I don't recall where, but this phrase leapt at me: "a new collective interiority." I'm not sure what to make of this notion, but some references come immediately to mind, such as *esprit de corps* or tribal consciousness. What caught my attention most was the word "new." Could it be that there is a way of being in community that is unrealized as yet, and could it be that the clue to it lies in inwardness? I believe this is a promising way to pursue the recovery of inwardness in our time, because, as I've already stated, it is as simple as it is confronting: *inwardness is not isolation and separation but the locus of authentic meeting*.

Given this description, I take inwardness to include three elements: *presence, participation,* and *mystery*. While these terms have already been put in play, they have not been quite clear to me. Nor have they been adequately described, particularly in relation to each other. Each has a long history and each is controversial, but my aim is not to enter the debate about them. Rather, I have simply found myself drawn to their use as necessary to understand the idea of Transformative Religion beyond (formal) religion and of inwardness as the key to moving beyond the later without discounting it.

Presence, "to stand before" or "to stand forth," entails the connotation of being called out, but of being not so much "there" as "here." In elementary school, when the teacher used to call the roll, we often answered with either "present" or "here." As I use "presence" it bears the sense of a unity between *identity* and *intimacy*—or better, identity *through* intimacy. Postmodern literature never ceases to engage such terms as "difference" and "other." The stress is always on the "over against" and irreducible givenness of identity and the constant threat of its loss in the "postmodern" world. But inwardness is precisely the domain where presence overcomes the hiatus between difference or otherness and the possibility of *connection*. With presence the oppositional character of the engagement of identities is not dissolved, but the competitive dominance or *othering*—so touted in the exoteric domain—is overcome.

Ivy comes out on the porch to announce they're ready to go. Frank follows, holding a demonstratively pleased Delilah. At Ethan's truck I pull the seat forward and reach into a toolbox to retrieve the keys from his hiding place. Ivy slides into the middle with Frank following and holding the baby. "How far is it to the monastery?" Ivy asks, childlike, as we pull up out of the drive and onto the road. "Eight miles, or about that," I answer, and the rest of the drive is laced with random comments and observations. They are ecstatic at the opportunity to stay in the cabin with Collins, and animated conversation betrays their pleasure.

We pull through the gate into the monastery compound, as Ivy reads the sign over the entrance: *Benedictine Monastery, Pecos*. She says, "I've heard good things about the Benedictines. Their thing is hospitality. That's what I read." The large parking area in front is only sparsely populated with three vehicles, and the edifice of the center invites us with its casual, almost sonorous, appearance.

We file through the front entry and look around. A large circle of chairs suggests that there has been a group activity, but otherwise, there's no sign of life. I walk to the dining hall, then look in a tiny chapel. No one. Finally a young man, thin to the point of emaciation, appears, and I ask for Brother Xavier, the one we met before. "He's in the garden," the young man says, indicating the direction with a gesture, "but I'll call him."

He scurries away and within five minutes the bustling and perspiring brother appears. Before I can speak, he recognizes me and greets me with a robust embrace. He does the same with Ivy and Frank and then talks with lively gestures to Delilah.

"Our pleasure to have you here. What are your needs?" Brother Xavier inquires.

I speak up. "My friend Ethan left me a note to come here..."

"Ah, yes indeed! So you're Ethan's friend. I remember that now. He told me you'd come. He'll be pleased."

I wait for Brother Xavier to say more, but he looks at me as if expecting me to respond. "May I see him? We're supposed to be heading back to Oklahoma in a day or two...and I..."

"Ah, then he didn't explain things," Brother Xavier says as if enlightened by my request. "To tell you the truth, Ethan's not seeing anyone. He's staying at one of our hermitages these days."

Incredulous, I ask, "For how long?"

"The way he put it is that he's going to stay until, and I quote, 'that damned war is off my back.' Viet Nam. That's his monkey... But he's taken to the discipline, and I believe he'll find what he's lookin' for here. We've had other veterans...a good place for them to heal..."

"But what about his truck and his business back home?" I ask with some urgency. "And his dad will be...well...out of his mind. He didn't want him to come out here in the first..."

"Oh, he called home and all of that," Brother Xavier says with a wave of his arms. "And he did leave a note for you. Not sure where I put it but...give me a moment." With that, the wiry monk exits the room and leaves me in consternation. Frank wonders if Ethan's all right, and Ivy tries to reassure me.

"Here it is," Brother Xavier says, waving another piece of lined yellow paper. He gives it to me and stands close beside me panting. I read:

I guess you found the truck at Collins' place. I came straight here. This is where I need to be for a while. I almost lost it in those damn mountains. Too much like Nam and too many demons of the wild. I've got to find some relief, and they told me that the secret is to quiet my mind and "go inside." That's what they kept saying.

One day I told this young monk that the one place I cannot go, because it is so full of ghosts and monsters, is inside. I thought that would be insane. But they kept working with me, got me into their schedule of prayers and gave me some chores to keep me focused. Believe it or not, it's working. Or, I think it will if I give it enough time.

Anyway, I've decided I can't see anybody for now. And I don't know how long this will take, but I'm here for as long as I need to be. I called Dad, and he knows about it. Take the truck back to him and be sure to explain that everything's all right with me. I might write, but don't count on it. I'll see you when I get back.

The note is signed with Ethan's left-slanting script. I'm stunned but fascinated. "Can I see him before we leave?"

Brother Xavier shakes his head. "No, he said he's not visiting with anyone until he overcomes his 'curse,' as he calls it. You can see his place...where he's living. Come." He hurries off beckoning to us over his shoulder.

We walk through the dining room and out a back door onto a patio-like porch. Brother Xavier points across a field of radiant green growth to the far side, where a small adobe building stands. "That's his place. He stays there most of the time. For now we're taking him his food, until he's ready to join us."

I stare in a confused muddle of disbelief and admiration, but presently I realize that this is exactly what I've been thinking and writing about these last days. And Ethan has needed something like this for...how many years? Things were never going to improve for him, not as long as he kept running with the same friends, working all those hours, and living in bars. "Good for him," I declare after several minutes. "I do regret not getting to see him, but if that's what he wants..."

"I know. It's difficult for outsiders to understand," Brother Xavier begins, "but if you're wounded in your soul, there's no easy cure. Taking an aspirin and hoping for a better day tomorrow just doesn't work."

"I agree," Frank chimes in. "It takes a radical move to head-off a radical problem."

We continue to chat with our host as we head back to the front door. I'm reluctant to leave, but I realize there's nothing more to do. We load ourselves into the truck, drive into Pecos, and buy a week's supply of groceries; using a list Collins gave Ivy. He also gave her money. On the way back to the cabin I confide in my companions that Ethan is actually doing what I've been thinking about for a couple of days. We discuss what I mean by inwardness and how difficult it is to understand, let alone to actually encounter. Ivy startles me at the end by noting that to understand it we must first have the encounter. "We have to actually go there," she says, pointing to her heart. "Otherwise, we're talking through our bonnets."

When we return, I look for Collins to explain Ethan's decision. When I find him, he's working on the tractor he borrowed from Peck, preparing to mow the field between the cabin and the road. Collins nods his approval of Ethan's decision. "He knows what he needs. We all do. We just don't listen." With that, he steps up onto the tractor and slides into the seat.

After grabbing my journal and a rucksack, I walk over to the cabin and take a piece of fruit and a canteen of water. I tell Ivy I need some time to think things over. She smiles her confirmation. Ethan's been my friend for a long time, and I had looked forward to seeing him and telling him what I'm learning. Still, he's doing the one thing that might help him break free of that damnable disaster in Nam. I appreciate his courage in facing up to it after running from it for so long.

I head up the mountainside east of the cabin, a place I've been before. It offers a captivating vista. When I reach a small outcropping, I stop and look around. Below, the canyon spreads, split in a jagged line by the Pecos. Along the river houses, cabins, barns, and small fields appear to be hacked out of the otherwise pristine dominance of wilderness. To the west a ripple of ridges mark the boundary of the vista with a horizon.

Beyond the horizon, less than twenty-five miles away, Santa Fe sprawls at the edge of the mountain range and onto the high desert. The old town, with its roots in an odd spiritual antiquity that haunts and invites, is being swallowed by America's upscale crowd. Like locusts, they move from one idyllic place in the country to another, drawn by the vibrations they find there, only to undermine the very quality that draws them there in the first place. They seek inwardness, but it eludes them, because the sacred geography of this whole place, while it calls for inwardness, does not assure it. Exoteric distractions are powerful. One must see through the surfaces, read the signs.

Today I haven't meditated, and I begin by stretching and relaxing. The body, I've learned, is partner to meditation. Then, stillness. Eventually, the dissolution of sensation follows. Time and space recede, and *being there* takes over.

As I re-emerge and sit with myself, that one word again rises to consciousness: *presence*. What power it bears! When presence prevails, it is immediate, consuming, and inexplicable. We are drawn beyond ourselves in such a way that we come to ourselves. In presence we do not *lose* identity but find it constituted in the *availability* of the other as presence. We are grasped and shaped by the other, claimed! And thus, we ourselves can be *present*.

To say more is possible only if I introduce a second term, one used repeatedly in my reflections: *participation*. This word speaks of the other side of the coin and is best comprehended in relation to presence. From what I've said earlier about participation, it should be clear that it is about knowing, or better, about understanding—or better still, *awareness*. No, that's not quite sufficient. It is better to speak of something like *engaged* awareness, for it bespeaks an awareness caught up in definitive connectivity.

A distinction is sometimes made between two kinds of knowing: "knowing about" and "acquaintance with." The first is formal and distancing, that is, *objectifying*. It suggests a separation, a cleavage, between the knower and the known. In modern usage most, if not all, knowing is of this kind. The second, 'acquaintance with," bears the connotation of engagement, of intimacy. As such, it suggests an inwardness unveiling itself through engagement. In English translations of the Hebrew Scripture, passages referring to a man having sex with a woman, describe the encounter in this way: "And he knew her." I find this description of one of the most potentially intimate moments of human interaction especially telling. The man "participates" the woman. (I had rather say, of course, that they participate each other!)

Participative awareness, then, is a knowing in which the knower and the known are mutually grasped and shaped by each other. They do not "find" each other so much as they find themselves in each other. Sexual "knowing" only offers one of the more definitive instances of the possibility of participative awareness. It applies to all knowing grounded in inwardness, and *that which* we participate through inwardness is presence.

Participative awareness is both *receptive* and *responsive* with the former always coming first. Receptivity precedes responsivity! This is rather like Buber's contention that in genuine dialogue listening precedes speaking. (Hence, the rarity of dialogue!) Participative awareness is not assertive—and never aggressive, because it rests in the gift of presence and its reception. Only then can one fulfill the participative engagement through response. In participative awareness, we wait upon the unveiling of presence as the cue to respond. In this respect, all knowing deriving through inwardness is revelatory, but revelation is impossible without both our reception and our response.

This foray into the deep waters of inwardness is rendered more complex and dense by the introduction of a third element: *mystery*. Again, I have already considered this persistently troubling term, one that is often used in religion to avoid the demands of clarity. But, as I've noted, mystery is not about the unsolved—or irresolvable—puzzles and perplexities of life. If all such muddles were settled to our satisfaction, mystery would remain. Mystery originates in the Primary Impulse itself, in the original finite encounter with the infinite. Mystery does not dismiss the riddle of infinity but embraces it and luxuriates in it. Mystery is not about solutions but about the wonder of the way things actually are. Inwardness is the locus of mystery, because the vortex of astonishment lies in the givenness of presence and our participation in it.

Before moving beyond these reflections on inwardness as the *mystery of participatory presence*, I should note something about the multidimensional complexity of presence. When we ordinarily consider presence, we have in mind the engagement of human selves with each other. This is presence *par excellance*, in its most immediate and concentrated expression! That is, our most focal and direct experiences of presence are of the human other, but a comprehensive understanding and appreciation of presence requires that we recognize every encounter with other, including the sense of self as other, are potential occasions of presence.

For this reason, when I speak of presence, I have at least four dimensions in mind. First, in so far as we transcend ourselves—whether psychologically, existentially, relationally, or ultimately—we are open to experience ourselves as presences. We employ many odd phrases to express this, such as "he came to himself" or "she's not herself." What can this mean but that we can be more or less available to ourselves, that is, *intra-personally present*?

Second, as I have already mentioned, we may be present to other persons. I only add here that we may be, and often are, present to one degree or another. Much depends on our capacity for inwardness and its orienting ground of presence. What ostensibly appears to be presence, as when we tend another person, may not be articulated out of inwardness. In other words, we can—and often do—feign presence, but this is a matter for psychology and sociology to examine. When we feign it, I believe this is due to our sense of its importance, even if we cannot or do not participate it.

Third, we may acknowledge *the world* as presence through our experience of it. This is probably the most difficult realm of presence to engage or appreciate. In the West, as we have assumed dominance over the world as it presents itself to us, we hardly treat it as a presence. We objectify the world in order to control it. Again, to quote Wordsworth, "Little there is in nature that is ours." This is one reason I am drawn to the uncontrived order generally referred to as "nature." When I venture into the wilderness, this presence is most immediate. It confronts me with its uncontrollable otherness, its mute insistence that we re-cognize it and re-spect it. We may either become driven to overcome the otherness through conquest, or we may allow inwardness to prevail and open us to participate the presence of the world itself. It is here that the pre-modern voice still has most to say to us. It is here that the deeper intonations of modern ecology find inspiration.

Finally, and most important to our consideration of religion, we may engage Transcendence itself as Presence. We do this through our efforts to cope with the infinite. The unbounded abyss I am calling "the infinite" is greater than can be conceived! It beggars comprehension. Yet, it is "there" or "here" in its unfathomable givenness, thrust upon us through the Primary Impulse. Inwardness opens the possibility of embracing the infinite as Transcendent Presence.

Of course, this quickly and easily degenerates into objectifications such as gods and varied *dogmas* in order to bring the Presence under finite control. Casual attention to the endless formulations and controversies over Transcendence among formal religions is enough to make the case.

Yet, the Presence need not degenerate into finite objectification, if we keep our engagement at its wellspring: inwardness. And when we do succumb to objectifications to help sustain us in face of our finitude, we may properly do so only with the constant reservation that we never seriously know what we're talking about. We dwell, as noted earlier, in that great *cloud of unknowing*. If we confess to this, we embrace the mystery of inwardness itself.

Perhaps this is the best place to offer two caveats to my description of inwardness. First, as with all primary categories, the elements of inwardness can be—and often are—distorted. Nothing within the purview of human potential is incorruptible. Yet, inwardness remains the land of promise for connective relational possibilities and for the higher reaches of religion itself.

Second, inwardness is not in any respect alien to the external or exoteric dimension of our existence. They are, indeed, correlative; that is, they belong to each other. But if inwardness is not the ground of this co-relation, the external overwhelms the *inner voice* and, finally, devolves into superficiality and triviality—or even to what Hannah Arendt brilliantly calls "the banality of evil." What is called for in this regard is a harmony between the inner life, inwardness, and the outer life of manifest existence. The ground of such harmony remains inwardness.

My consideration of inwardness and the elements that constitute it are in the service of what I've been calling Transformative Religion. Religion, taken in its original sense of "binding back," calls us *back* to inwardness. Our original "moment" of inwardness is the Primary Impulse, but our consummate encounter with inwardness lies beyond all artifices of religion, that is, all of its formations, in our conscious and deliberate return to inwardness. Formal religions may point to inwardness and urge us to it, but formal religions cannot take us there. Only by "cutting across" and "going beyond"—that is, transforming—the forms can Religion fulfill the longing of all forms of religion.

When I speak of Transformative Religion, I do not have in mind some new unifying formal religion, taking the best of the myriad forms into a higher harmony. Nor do I propose that we examine the religions to discover Transformative Religion in the underlying patterns that bind them together. These may be interesting and informative possibilities, but they remain bound to the notion that the secret lies in, among, or out of the formal religions.

Transformative Religion is related to formal religion in so far as formal religions acknowledge and point toward inwardness, but formal religions do not and cannot control inwardness. They are, at best, exoteric surfaces pointing to what lies beyond them. To use a rude analogy, they are rather like "water witches" who claim by their art to locate water below the surface of the earth. They may be able to spot the proper locus for the digging, but they do not dig the well.

I write furiously in my journal, munching on an apple as I compose my notes. The sun touches the rim of the mountains. Sundown comes early in the valley, and I watch its shadow engulf the cabin. Frank and Ivy are in the yard throwing something back and forth. I hear their muffled shouts and laughter. Collins has mowed the field, and the weeds and grass lie slain in vague patterns dictated by the blade. I sit here wondering when to leave this place, wanting to see my wife but reluctant to depart—especially without Ethan. I realize that I can stay one more day and still be home one day before she arrives. Yes, that's what I'll do.

As I make my way down the mountainside, creating my own switchbacks, I see Collins coming from the bunkhouse. He speaks to Ivy and then walks toward me. When I'm close enough, I call out, and he waves. Just as he reaches me, I stumble and fall into him. We both take a tumble, and for an instant, we're giggling children again.

We sit up, and Collins says, "Ivy wants us to do a sweat tonight. You up for it?"

"Sure," I answer enthusiastically. "These bones need some loosening."

"Did you talk to Ethan?" Collins asks.

"No. Brother Xavier says Ethan's going to live alone for awhile, until he comes to grips with things." Collins nods agreeably, and I add, "I hate to leave without seein' him, but he's one stubborn bastard, when he's made up his mind."

Collins, standing and pulling me up, says, "Good for him. Look, every few days I'll go down there and check on him. You can call me to get reports…"

"How about his dad?" I ask.

"Yep. Give him my number," and with that we stride of together, down and across the bridge to the cabin.

It's Frank's turn to cook, and we sit down to a stew. Our conversation revolves around the sweat. Ivy's endless questions pick up their pace. Collins, tongue in cheek, says, "We do the sweats without clothes. You all right with that, Ivy?"

"No problem," she answers almost boastfully. But Collins says that since she's the only female here, we should probably wear shorts. Ivy responds, "What about Delilah? She's a *female*." She says the last word with a scoff, as if throwing down a gauntlet. I have a hunch that she'll hold her own in this household.

As we finish eating, Collins goes to the phone and I hear a muffled conversation. He returns to the table and says, "Peck's comin' over with his wife and another woman, and he's bringin' a younger guy and his girlfriend. That way, we'll have enough folk for a good sweat." With that, he walks out into the twilight to build a fire.

By the time we've finished the dishes and Delilah is prepared for the night, we can see through the window that the fire is roaring. Ivy watches, asking more questions about the purpose of the sweat and whether it's religious or not. I suggest that, for Native folk, everything's religious in one way or another. Ivy likes that.

We stroll casually down toward the lodge nestled as it is among a grove of cottonwoods. Ivy carries Delilah and Frank follows with a playpen that Collins has managed to dredge up from the bunkhouse. That will be the baby's bed out here in the night's calm. We sit in folding lawn chairs and wait. We watch as the fire diminishes toward embers. I recall an old movie, *Quest for Fire*, and muse over the centrality of fire to our very humanity. The licking flames, dance bluish, yellow and orange across their "victims" recalling my earlier ruminations on mystery. Fire, no matter how thoroughly explained, remains an elusive presence. It is there and not there at once, utterly dependent yet all consuming.

Peck's truck lumbers to the cabin, and five people pile out giggling at some comment. I wonder how they managed in that cramped space. They join us, and Collins makes introductions. Little is said, but despite the reserve so characteristic of Natives, everyone appears comfortable. Peck inspects the dying fire and nods to Collins.

It is now quite dark with the low glow of the fire our only source of light. As if on cue, two of the women and the younger man begin to undress. They fade into the shadows and drop clothing into small piles. First Ivy, then Frank follow suit, and Collins and I are last. Within moments we find ourselves lined up, a naked parade about to enter another dimension. Collins takes the lead, and Peck stands behind at the end of our line of Stoic pilgrims. Ivy steps aside to make sure that Delilah is asleep and returns to her place.

As I listen to Peck behind me, uttering something prayer-like in a low moan, I marvel at this gentle spectacle. Being naked in a cluster of friends and strangers, I note, has nothing to do with shame, and it is a shame that we do not realize this. Rather, being naked has to do with the potential for presence exemplified in the manifestation of our embodiment. Yes, it does include our being *exposed* and thus vulnerable, but under conditions such as this we may best discover something of the very character of presence. We cannot do this, if we focus only on surfaces, on the nakedness itself, but if we are privy to inwardness at all, we may meet the edge of presence in this condition.

Collins lifts the flap of the lodge and enters, stooping low, then crawling through the darkness. We follow, until all are seated in a circle around the edges of the lodge. We sit on old pieces of carpet provided for comfort. Peck goes to the fire, and with a shovel brings into the lodge our first stone, glowing red. He places it in the deep pit in the middle of the space. Three others are added before he enters and pulls down the flap. We have once again entered the deep womb of this spiritual gestation. A symbolic inwardness, no less!

First, silence. Then, the initial sprinkling of water over the stones and the upward and downward surge of steam, cascading over our heads and shoulders. Peck leads in prayers, spoken in Navajo. Collins offers additional gratitude in English. More steam, and the heat increases. By the end of the first round, when the flap is opened, the heat already challenges us.

More stones are gently dropped into the pit, and the flap drops again. We begin, during this round, to express gratitude. Each person speaks, as they are inclined. Mostly, they are grateful for someone or some recent benefit. Peck, however, offers appreciation for being tested today, when his truck broke down on the road. Frank gives thanks for Collins and our meeting in the mountains, and Ivy speaks of her daughter and the gift she represents. Collins weeps quietly and offers thanks for unnamed memories. I end with gratitude for my friends, Collins and Ethan and for my wife. At the end of each statement, the speaker says, "And all my relations."

By the third round the sweltering steam is draining us, as we offer personal petitions. The young woman asks for guidance in seeking employment, and the young man seeks wisdom in coping with his alcoholic father. Peck's wife struggles with smoking and her friend with weight. Ivy wants illumination about how to express her gifts. Frank breaks down as he asks for a way to reconcile with his father. Collins longs to live "in the moment" more fully, and I ask guidance in supporting my friend Ethan. A long silence follows before Peck asks to be kept fearless and loyal. In the quiet space hands find hands and we make a circle of contact.

At the end of the fourth round, after we've celebrated our being together in this cocoon, the flap opens for the last time. We are so weakened by the drenching heat that we crawl outside into the rush of crisp night air. Peck and Collins help each of us to our feet. Then they place life vests on each of us—were these come from I have no clue—and lead us to the river. From a prominence of rock hanging over a quiet pool in the stream, they direct us to plunge into the chilly but utterly refreshing water. We float on our backs with random utterances of delight.

I am barely aware of climbing from the river and locating my clothes. We all amble off, muttering our farewells and moving toward dreamless sleep.

Twenty-Eight

In the future Christians will be mystics, or they will be nothing.

Karl Rahner

∼

Mysticism is not part of intellectual life today. By its nature, kit is kind of elemental thought that attempts to establish a spiritual relationship between man and the universe. Mysticism does not believe that logical reasoning can achieve this unity, and it therefore retreats into intuition, where imagination has free reign.

Albert Schweitzer

∼

Collins finds me sitting up in bed, writing in my journal. I'm confessing to myself how much I long to see my wife and at the same time my reluctance to leave the haven of these mountains and to depart without Ethan. Life can be such a jumble of desire, delight and dread, and I'm enthralled with all of them. Now, at this moment!

The door to the bunkhouse abruptly opens and stands ajar, ushering in the morning chill. Collins stares, wordless, but I know he's come with words. "You stayin' today?" He asks.

"Yeah, I think so. I'll probably head out tomorrow."

"I'm goin' into Santa Fe to pick up some things. Wanna come along?" Collins asks, in his typically open-ended way. Immediately I find myself enthused at the prospect. My longstanding affection for the town continues, despite the way it's been compromised by the intrusion of wealth and privilege. Even the overlay of glitz cannot cancel that more profound and elemental throb belonging to the place. One must only pay attention for it to show itself.

I bound from bed and rush outside to the shower. Pulling the thin veil of plastic around the curved rod, I wait for the water to warm. By the time I'm ready for the day, breakfast is on the table and everyone is waiting for me. When breakfast's finished, we find ourselves filing to Collins' truck. The three of them slide into the cab with Ivy holding Delilah, and I vault into the bed of the truck and lean against the cab. An old seat cushion provides a makeshift shock absorber as we, once again, bounce away and up onto the road.

We pass the monastery, and I stare out across the green field toward the adobe house, hoping to catch a glimpse of Ethan, but we pass too quickly for more than a momentary recognition of the structure. In Pecos we make a right turn toward the interstate. We move past Glorietta, an enormous center for the gathering of Baptists from this part of the country. The buildings are in colonial style, strikingly out of place in this terrain. Odd.

In town we drive to the square. Everyone has an agenda except me. As I climb down to the street, Collins asks whether I need anything, and I shake my head and gesture that I'll probably just scout around, "unless, of course, you need me."

He responds, "Say, there's a Zen center not far from here. If you'd like to see it, take the truck, and we can meet back here at noon." I nod, and he gives directions. I take the keys, and we all scatter.

I follow Collins' directions, as circuitous as a labyrinth. They take me winding back on dirt roads, until I find myself at a drive and a modest sign, Upaya Zen Center. It is an utterly quiet place, composed of a scattering of low reddish brown adobe structures. Crisp and orderly but without pretension. No one is to be seen. Stillness prevails. I enter tentatively what appears to be a main entrance, and a young woman with shaved head, a black robe and Birkenstock sandals greets me in a soft voice. When I explain that I'm only here to visit, she smiles and welcomes me. She asks, "Would you like to see our meditation room?" When I indicate that I would, she leads me around to another building and at the entrance she gestures for me to remove my shoes. I enter to see a pristine space, displaying an ordered simplicity and bearing the markings of the Zen world. Santa Fe always gives me the sense of an alternative dimension, and this room focuses and intensifies that sense.

The young woman backs out of the room and leaves me standing. I move to one of the cushions on the floor and sit. Following a lengthy meditation, I observe again the appointments of the room and take solace in their constancy. I begin to contemplate my pilgrimage, what I had anticipated in contrast to how it has unfolded. *Everything,* I say to myself, *depends on having expectations shattered by surprise.* Almost none of the anticipated external processes have been according to plan, and the internal process has taken on its own character. I would never have predicted that my reflections on religion would lead me to the conclusion that the fulfillment of the Primary Impulse lies in Religion that goes beyond religion, what I'm calling Transformative Religion.

My key discovery has been the centrality of inwardness. I should have known. Now it appears to me as self-evident, but I had long been suspicious of the interior life as an escape from life in the world. Not until I realized that exactly the opposite is the case, that only through inwardness do we seriously meet and engage the world, did insight come.

Religion, in its Transformative expression, is composed of two poles. One pole is the immediacy of direct experience of Transcendent Presence. Inwardness is its locus, and traditionally it has been most expressly realized in *mysticism*. The other pole mediates life in the world by providing quality in the encounters between and among people, along with their relations to their habitat, the world itself. Inwardness is its source but life in the world is its articulation. It has been called *morality*. Only in the dynamic between the mystical and the moral does Transformative Religion find its fullest expression.

Several years ago, when my wife and I took students to Italy on a travel-study program, we focused our study on "St. Francis, St. Catherine, and the Spirit of Medieval Monasticism." I mentioned this adventure earlier, but our study prompted me to read a number of biographies and interpretations of St. Frances. One abiding tension is reported in more than one account. He continually wrestled with two callings he found to be contrary. On the one hand, he longed for the life of *contemplation,* where he could spend his days in prayer, sacred reading, and other forms of inner concentration. On the other hand, he sensed a need to participate in the world through perpetual *compassion*. He was never able to satisfy the relation between these two attractions, and he constantly moved between periods of intense contemplative withdrawal followed by encounters with the world through compassion. Put another way,

St. Francis found himself caught between the mystical and moral poles of Transformative Religion.

My own pilgrimage into this labyrinth of the religious dimension has brought me to the realization that there is no necessary conflict between the two poles. Although the mystical grounds the moral, the moral is crucial to the concrete manifestation of the mystical in the world. In this respect, they are correlative. The mystical without the moral devolves into pious narcissism. The moral without the mystical is without grounding to keep it focused, inspired, and perpetually transformed.

Having ventured out on this proverbial limb, I am compelled to examine these two poles of Transformative Religion. First, mysticism!

I have been puzzled and perplexed by the frequency and intensity with which mysticism is discounted or dismissed in religious discussion. Likewise, people who wish to dismiss religion in general often reduce it to "mystical gibberish." I can understand why formal religions tend to be suspicious of the mystical. It is too "subjective," that is, the mystical cannot be adequately controlled by the demands of form. It is immediate direct experience. How can such experience be brought to heel?

One way is to insist that the mystical experience be *interpreted* through the forms associated with a formal religion. Since formal religions at least claim to be interested in inwardness and in our actual engagement with Transcendence, they may allow the mystical so long as it is interpreted to fit the formal character of religion. Likewise, from the point of view of the mystics, their experiences often—but not always and not necessarily—take place within the context of some formal religious orientation, and they may turn to their formal tradition to help them make sense of the experience. The frequently noted *ineffability* of mystical experience often prompts the mystic to seek a framework for making interpretive sense of the experience, and thus to *formalize* it to some extent. This is why so many mystics write incessantly about it, even as they deny that language can convey what they mean.

Still, the more highly structured and objectively constituted a formal religion is, the more suspicion it is likely to express toward mystical experience. For instance, in all three monotheistic religions there are mystical traditions and movements, but they are largely ancillary to the central thrust of these religions. Other traditions, Zen for example, are much less objectively formed and indeed center upon inwardness and direct engagement toward Enlightenment. It follows that the centrality of mysticism in formal religions varies, but the point is this: *because the mystical element in religion is dynamic—that is, lived immediate experience of Transcendent Presence, it can never be fully contained in or limited to the forms employed to interpret it.* In just this sense, the mystical is inherently *transformative*, cutting across and moving beyond the forms. Yet, as noted repeatedly, the mystical need not deny the religious forms but may rather employ them for some measure of orientation and understanding.

In William James' monumental analysis of religion, *The Varieties of Religious Experience*, his focus on experience at the expense of formal religion leads him to his decisive lecture: "Mysticism." In the end, he concludes that, because religion is primarily found in a variety of experiences, its mystical expression is its most definitive articulation of religion. I find this helpful with one proviso: as noted earlier, he denigrates and neglects the place and force of formal religion, especially its communal importance.

By contrast I do not want to diminish the significance of formal religion, and the reason is that, if we are bound within finitude while engaging the infinite, part of our condition is the *urge to form*. Mysticism saves us from being trapped in forms, but it does not thereby simply reject form altogether. The moment we strive to *say something* about mystical experience, we enter form, and when we seek to *do something* based on the experience, we manifest form. The only way to sustain this tension between the dynamic of experience and the formality of its interpretation is to keep their relation open and dialectical. That is, experience transforms forms and forms articulate and make manifest our experience.

Perhaps an analogy helps. Ernest Becker observes that there are but two fundamental types of psychopathology: over organization and under organization. The over organized person succumbs to a rigid insistence on form, on one form, and on judging everything by the artifice of that form. The under-organized person lives in constant rebellion against all forms and every attempt to establish a consistent orientation. The relation between the mystical and formal elements in religion is similar. The danger of the mystical lies in under organizing, while the danger of the formal lies in over organizing. Each is a pathology only overcome by maintaining a conscious dialectical tension between them.

My understanding of mysticism is already implicit in these reflections, but I should state it more forthrightly. First, mysticism has to do with a particular kind of human *experience*. Not every religious experience, however, is mystical. For instance, we may experience a profound sense of release by simply being affirmed by a religious community or another person, and this may have the character of a religious experience in drawing us closer to what we take to be sacred or divine.

Second, the mystical experience is *direct* and *immediate* and not necessarily dependent on a community, a set of beliefs, or some causal chain of events. Mystical experience breaks upon us. We may prepare for it, but we do not cause it or conjure it. We receive it, and the reception is possible through inwardness. One oft repeated confession of the mystic is the utter surprise of mystical encounter. To use a phrase introduced earlier, it comes as a "shock of recognition."

Third, the subject of mystical experience is not the *self* and not the *experience*. It is *Transcendence as Presence*. This is why mystics frequently report either a diminution of self or its actually dissolution into what may be described as Oneness or Wholeness or Godhead. The emphasis is on an ecstatic harmony in which all distinctions recede. This state is ineffable and beyond explanation. Only those who have had the experience can, to some extent, comprehend it. I realize, of course, that there are also moments of *mystical-like* experience, such as a sudden flood of wellbeing or the ecstasy of falling in love, that may provide helpful analogies for understanding, or at least appreciating, the mystical experience.

Rising from the cushion, I stretch and bend low. I have no idea what time it is, but I want to be back to the square by noon. Not wearing a watch—my modest rebellion against returning to the mechanistic excesses of modernity—has its drawback. As I step out the door and bend to lace my boots, a monk passes. At first he says nothing, but then, as if remembering some etiquette he has been taught, he turns and asks if I have any needs.

"I was only meditating for a while," I confide. Then, without forethought, I add, "…And reflecting on the mystical experience…"

The man's eyes, calm and trance-like, fix on mine. He is American, but he might as well be from the farthest monastery in Japan. "I see," he intones. "Mysticism is a western idea I think. It depends on another idea, belief in God. In Zen we do not hold such beliefs, only the self-emptying that brings Enlightenment." He delivers these words as though it were a lesson he has been carefully taught.

He turns to walk slowly away, but I come to his side and fall into step with him. "Then you believe in Enlightenment?" I ask.

"Enlightenment is not a belief but awareness," he declares, and I sense that he has been well schooled in this explanation and has used it before. "By following *zazen*, we awaken to Enlightenment."

"Have you experienced Enlightenment?" I find myself asking before censoring the question. I wonder whether I'm being rude.

"I wait," he says quite simply and resolutely. Then, after a period of silence, he adds, "Enlightenment is not an experience. It is beyond experience…"

We walk into the sunlight and follow a path through a small garden. A crisp dome of blue, the New Mexico sky's trademark, seems close enough to touch. It contains us like a protective covering. We do not speak, but I wonder how, given our finite condition, we can move beyond experience itself. We may move beyond our sense of *ordinary* experience, but isn't this itself another level or dimension of experience? I do not ask this question but am content to stroll with this resolute but seemingly modest stranger as we move toward my truck. I want to ask him the time but sense that he neither knows nor cares about chronos.

I park near the square and walk to the corner where I left Collins. As I scan the ever-moving parade of tourists and traders, I see no one at first. Then all of them materialize as if I'd willed them to be there. Collins announces that he wants to treat us to some "real food," and we follow him, maneuvering across the square and along a grid of sidewalks, until we reach a small outdoor café. I see immediately that we're having Native American cuisine. Ivy and Frank sit enthusiastically, eyes glistening.

After eating, I volunteer to bring the truck around. Collins nods agreeably, and I hike back the way we'd come. As I pull to the curb, Ivy finishes nursing Delilah, and we all find our places in the truck. Collins asks, before we move, "Would you like to see a place I found last year?"

"What is it?" Ivy asks.

"A surprise," Collins teases, and we drive away heading north toward Espanola.

On the way we turn off to the left toward the Jemez Mountains. We're driving along, in open rolling terrain, when Collins abruptly pulls onto the shoulder. He scans along to the left, as if searching for a clue. When he sees what he's seeking, he crosses the road and we pull up and park near the roadside fence. We step out, and Collins tells Frank to take the baby sling for our hike. Collins reaches for his rucksack, with a rolled blanket lashed to it. Still we don't know what awaits us.

After crossing the fence, we follow a dim trail back through the pinion trees, climb through a narrow passage between boulders, and up onto an enormous flat surface of red stone. Ivy rhapsodizes in her astonishment, pointing to an array of natural wonders strewn across a shallow valley. Behind us a modest bluff rises, and we're soon making our way toward it. I'm wondering how we plan to scale the stone face, when a ladder appears ahead. Made of logs and reaching thirty or more feet upward, it will take us to yet another prominence. Collins takes Delilah, and we climb. He points out a series of ancient etchings in the stone wall beside us, a symbol of the sun, some animals, and a stick figure of a human. They are all dimmed by time and erosion but clear enough.

The vista is even more spectacular from this higher vantage. After staring in silent awe at the expanse before us, ending with the heights of the Jemez to the west, we turn to explore the mesa. Collins indicates sites of possible dwellings and some dished out stones likely used for grinding corn. "Probably an Anasazi village," Collins notes. "But this is not the most interesting stuff."

Climbing down another ladder further south, we walk along a narrow trail at the base of the bluff, until Frank shouts, "Look, there's a cave." Collins laughs at him as Frank rushes to the dark hole in the side of the bluff. Within minutes we discover that the entire area is pock-marked with tiny caves hued out of the soft stone. After exploring for half an hour, we settle on one of the larger caves and enter. It is no more than five feet high and black soot covers its ceiling. Around the upper wall a snake-like design can be seen, but when Ivy points to it, Collins suggests that this is more likely a modern addition.

Collins spreads the blanket on the dusty floor, and we sit, watching each other and peering out the small doorway and the valley below. No one speaks for a while, then Ivy wonders, "Who were these people and how did they live here? How did they see things? I wish I could talk to them?"

Frank rolls his eyes, but Collins responds, "They were in most ways pretty much like us, I think. …except they saw the world more directly without so many grids between them and it." After a pause he continues, "We have too many words and models that explain everything. They had the world itself, and it spoke to them."

As Collins and Ivy continue their conjectures, she in a kind of reverence and he committed to claiming his kinship with that other ancient world, my mind retreats to the morning reveries at the Zen center. That monk may have been saying that he seeks something—a direct awareness unencumbered by mental activity—much like Collins believes these earlier folk possessed. I wonder whether we have taken a long distracting journey into what we call "the modern world," only to be now trying to recapture something we lost along the way. Not that we have made no advances or that we need to retreat into some idyllic past. I'm only thinking that we have perhaps forgotten something fundamental in our dash toward progress, whatever that means.

This leads me to the possibility that the mystical dimension of experience might belong more nearly to our natural state that persisted until we turned to manipulation and explanation as our way of controlling our world. I can't be sure of any of this, but it does leave me wondering.

Frank exits the cave to look around at others, and I follow him. We discuss my thoughts of the morning in relation to the earlier inhabitants of this site. He asks what I mean by "mystical experience," and when I finish a brief description, he says, "Yeah, that's important. It's how I really became hooked into the Rastas."

"What do you mean," I ask.

"Well, in the early days, when I was so busy thinking about how being a Rastafarian would drive my Dad up the wall, I kept going to these mass meditations in Taos. We'd prepare by smoking Ganja, but that didn't really distract us from our purpose, to meditate on Scripture and find our relationship to God. After many tries at this and when I got over dealing with my Dad all the time, I began havin' what I've called 'visitations.' I don't have another word for it, but I could tell that something or someone was with me. I mean right there. And when that happened I could be peaceful. I didn't need anything else, and my ole' man was no longer in my way. Ask Ivy. It happened to her, and she can testify to it."

"Oh, you don't need to convince me," I say, throwing up my hands. "I've had too many of my own encounters to question yours."

"That's why I decided the other night in the sweat that I'm goin' to see my father. We've gotta' mend things…or at least I need to do it…for myself and Ivy."

"When?" I ask.

"Probably next week," Frank says. "But I'm gonna' call first and then hitchhike. Ivy's all for it. She says it's about time…"

"Where to?" I want to know.

"Indiana…Gary. He's a muckity-muck in this big company." Frank thinks before continuing, then confesses, "I'm goin' to tell him straight out that I've been a butt and I'll ask him to forgive me… And if he won't, then I'm plannin' to forgive him anyway. I already have, but he don't know it. No point in him carryin' me on his back for the rest of his life, and I sure as hell need to put him down so we can both walk on our own."

"What's changed your mind about him?" I wonder aloud

"Visitations. I had another one in that sweat…" And that's all he says, because he hears Delilah whimper and makes his way back to the cave. He takes her, and we are all soon following the trail back to the big rock, down the narrow passage, and to the truck.

Bouncing along in the back of the truck on the way To Collins' place, I brood over Frank's one word, "visitation." A curious choice of terms, I think. Is Frank making the visit or is he being visited? Or both? In any case, Frank's experience speaks to my ponderings on mysticism.

****

The man is lost in mid-life. Older convergences, wrought in youthful enthusiasm, dissipate into divergences. All that has been learned, ordered carefully, and employed as guidance now lies strewn, like debris from a storm, across the inner landscape of mind and heart. His cluster of orthodoxies, carefully and critically crafted, are under assault.

In the spring the man departs alone for Europe. He has duties there and will find consolation in the quaint artifacts of cultural difference. He is there two weeks, lecturing and embracing the ethos of a distant land. He enters into the novelty, forgetful of all else. The gift of immediacy is quickened by ceaseless novelty. He exists as though suspended slightly beyond the earth-bound contingencies he left behind. There he enjoys relief from the relentless press of forces conspiring to make his existence fit some predetermined mold generated by...himself? Fate retreats, if only a step or two.

Back home, the man plunges into the complications so briefly dismissed by the stratagem of distance. He travels to New Mexico, lecturing again. In a remote and seemingly restful retreat, along with a host of conferees, he finds himself inwardly turbulent without being able to calm the forces that impinge upon him. When not officially at work, he walks the remote land of buttes, gorges, and vistas.

He strolls on the high desert, wandering and wondering. Barely contained emotion rises to the lip of expression at every instant. A self-generated weight presses his head, shoulders, chest. The barren landscape is broken by an animal trail. He makes his way along it, only occasionally raising his head to note the expanse spreading out to far horizons.

Presently, the man looks down to see a lone white blossom nestled among scraggly green shoots, the only sign of vitality within view. The man drops to the dusty desert, sitting cross-legged before the tiny flower. He is enthralled by its audacity in being there and being alive.

"How did you make it here," the man asks. He senses a communion with this pale bit of life clinging to the earth while reaching upward.

"You are like me...or maybe I'm more like you. What gives you the courage to rise and bloom in this place?" The man wants to cradle the blossom, to dig it up and take it to safety. It becomes his alter-ego staring back at him, drawing him.

The man weeps. He cannot cease weeping. He convulses with a vast voiceless scream from a depth he has seldom visited. How long his catharsis continues he does not know, but when he at last looks up, the sun rides lower in the sky. He looks around, as if to determine whether anyone has seen him. He has been opened up from the inside out, lured by a waif of a blossom.

For three days the man walks and climbs to sit high on massive boulders, and every day it is the same. Emotions, untempered by civility, break forth without provocation or warning. He's coming loose at the center, and he knows the great constraints of ordered life are dissolving from within.

He cannot, he dare not, leave this or go back to...anything.

****

The whole field of mysticism is strewn with interpretations and analyses from disparate traditions. To make sense of its surface variety and its complexity is not my aim. What I am more interested in claiming is that the mystical dimension is ubiquitous across traditions and thus one possible avenue for finding and exploring common ground among them. In other words, when religion—any religion—becomes transformed through inwardness, it enters a spectrum of universality that most nearly realizes what the Primary Impulse originally awakened in us.

If this claim about mysticism is sound, then what will be most helpful is an understanding and appreciation of this, the depth dimension of religion as Religion, as Paul Tillich refers to it. To this end, I want to explore the idea of levels or degrees of mysticism. Or, to put the matter as a question, what is the spectrum of mysticism, that is, its range of possibility?

After reading and reflecting on mysticism for some time, I've come to the conclusion that it enjoys a process from more elemental expressions to the most ethereal. Furthermore, in that process those who are prepared to make the arduous trek of inwardness become fewer and fewer. Yet, these hardiest souls call back to the rest of us with inspiration and promise.

Of all attempts to grapple with this sense of mysticism, I am most aided and encouraged by the work of a maverick self-taught thinker by the name of Ken Wilber. I need not examine his scheme of thought as a whole. Although it is complex, evolving, and provocative, I am not advocating his system. Nor am I interested in criticizing his work. Rather, I want to borrow one notable insight from his larger scheme having to do with the place of mysticism in it.

Two insights from Wilber contribute to my pilgrimage into the heart of religion. First, in the evolution of human consciousness—his obsession—he finds a fundamental transformation occurring, when we move from personal to what he calls "transpersonal" consciousness. The transpersonal refers to our realization that personhood is contained and transcended by its necessary connection to the whole of which it is a part. Once we awaken to this truth, the boundaries of self and personhood become porous and flexible. We literally move beyond ourselves without denying or losing ourselves. He speaks of this in psychological terms primarily, but he also acknowledges that it is spiritual in character. When I speak of "Transformative Religion," this is the grand shift I have in mind, though I am describing it differently and for a different purpose. Once again, the locus of this transition is *inwardness*.

Second, according to Wilber, once the "transpersonal" orientation comes into play, the mystical dimension of spiritual life emerges and moves through four levels or "spheres" as he calls them. I find these levels or spheres, while perhaps somewhat artificial, helpful in understanding the expansiveness of the mystical dimension.

The sphere of *nature mysticism* refers to the direct experience of the realm of nature, or the "gross" manifestation around us. As I've found during the past three weeks in these mountains, nature itself provides a direct engagement with a species of wholeness. This is not to hark back to Romanticism, although that movement did grasp something of this sense of our union with the earth and the cosmos.

Today, when Collins spoke of his view of ancient tribal people such as the Anasazi, he had this sort of understanding in mind. It involves the capacity to directly engage the world as it presents itself without filtering it through the artifice of interpretation and explanation. Indeed, as I rattle along in the back of this truck, wind swirling about me, I look up at the brilliantly illumined forthrightness of nature still palpating here, despite our growing effort to domesticate it, and I know something of the mystical presence in its vital throb. Yet, I do confess that, as a modern, it remains veiled by the "mind-forged" grids I place on it.

A second sphere, *deity mysticism*, as Wilber speaks of it, breaks with the immediacy of nature and moves toward that which grounds and accounts for nature. Herein begins the experience of Divine otherness as Presence in the great paradox of distinction with closure, transcendence with immanence, as the literature often puts it. As is obvious, theistic religions are inclined to this order of mystical experience. Most Deity mystics, with the possible exception of Meister Eckhardt, while emphasizing connection and closure in the Deity, also strive to maintain the distinction and difference between humanity and the Divine. Closure but without identification!

Third, the sphere of *formless mysticism* refers to a union of the self with "emptiness" or with "the abyss"—common in mystical language—in such a way that a dissolution or merger of self into the "All" is experienced. Eastern religious traditions are more comfortable with this sphere of mystical experience, but mystics such as Eckhardt and Rumi also confess to a virtual identification with God, as in the phrase, "I am God." It is worth noting that the opposite of a word I've used in describing structured religion comes into play: "formlessness."

Religion as form, the dominant exoteric face of religion in the world, is here most decisively transcended as formlessness overrides form. In this case, I propose, finitude becomes indeed thin and the infinite itself is more fully realized as Presence. This profoundly challenging mode of mystical experience leaves us more tenuously related to the finite order of existence. Thus, it is correspondingly rare because of its tendency to shatter our finitude, beginning with our selves and reaching to all ordering through distinctions. Like orgasm, it is simply too ecstatic to last long, given the persistent pull of our finitude.

Finally, the sphere of *non-dual mysticism* represents a union of the formless with all form. It is that sphere of mystical experience in which the whole and the no-thing unite as one. This is the basis for the ethereal declaration: *All is One and One is All*. A few holy voices, mostly found in the East, speak of this elusive capacity for liberation from finitude while existing under the conditions of finitude. Frankly, while I can imagine the first three modes of mystical experience, I find this last one a fearsome and perplexing delight, a vague and indistinct possibility. Thus, when I read those who bear witness to it, I am left at once infatuated and dumbfounded.

Even thinking about these levels or spheres of mystical experience leaves me bewildered. They at once call me to myself, through myself, and beyond myself in a "mystifying" challenge to the limits set by finitude, specifically my own. Yet, what keeps me coming back to their power and possibility is their implicit promise of liberation from—but within—the finite boundaries within and against which I otherwise vainly strive. Mystical experience allows me to be at home in the world and invites me into it, shorn of the *incarceration* it commonly represents. But strangely, mystical experience does this through the immediacy of Transcendence. Astonishing!

Through the veil of dusk, I make out the monastery as we rush past it on our way to the cabin. Ethan again leaps to mind, and I'm reminded of what he would say to all of my musings about mysticism. He'd warn me: *Anything and everything easily becomes an addiction. Obsession with experience, any kind of experience, is about as dangerous as ignoring it altogether.* Then he'd speak of the "holy rollers" and their endless quest for the next experience. "Goosed by the Holy Ghost," he'd say with rye amusement. And I would agree, because anything authentic can be easily distorted or corrupted through excess, denial, or neglect. Even so, distortion, corruption, and counterfeiting only underscore the genuine article by contrast.

Furthermore, the fact that the higher mystical orientations are correspondingly rare is no grounds for dismissing or diminishing their centrality in understanding the true aim of all religion. The more sanguine practices of formal religion still have as their inspiration and promise the possibility, nay longing, for the immediacy of Presence—or the haven of Divine Abyss. Even amid the many forms, one may find, through the prism of inwardness, muted momentary glimpses into and beyond the veil of form and finitude.

The truck lurches to a halt in front of the cabin, and the film of dust following behind catches up and settles around us. Delilah is restive, and Frank takes her into the cabin for solid food. We lift groceries and other items from the bed of the truck and trundle them inside. Ivy, having already memorized the kitchen, stashes things, while Collins and I cobble together a meal of leftovers and fresh vegetables. Collins opens the windows, and night sounds, echoes from the wilderness, sneak in to serenade us as we dine. The food, the sounds, the gentle rude setting bear all of the markers of home, save one. My wife and mate flies back across the ocean in two days.

Twenty-Nine

Love is Being's gracious consent to Being.

Jonathan Edwards

~

Collins, up and stirring before the rest of us, calls me from the front porch for breakfast. The hour's earlier than I expect, and I stumble bleary-eyed into the kitchen. Frank serves us authentic old-fashioned oatmeal, unlike the pasty globs we endured in the wilderness. When Collins joins us, he makes a proposal, that Frank ride with me as far as Amarillo, where he can catch a plane to Dallas and on to Indiana.

I turn to Frank as he looks at me, trying to organize my day sufficiently to understand Collins' suggestion. It takes me so long to respond that Collins asks, "You're goin' home today, right?"

"Yeah, sure," I say, while pondering the fact that I had looked forward to trying one last time to see Ethan before enjoying the long solitary drive home. Then I observe Frank's silent enthusiasm for the idea, and I corral my ego enough to offer him a formal invitation.

As soon as he finishes eating, he kisses Ivy in passing and heads for the loft. She says, "I'm real pleased that he's goin'. I want him to deal with his father, and this is the first time he's even admitted that he needs to." Then with a pensive stare beyond Collins and me, she adds, "Maybe he'll come back a lot lighter."

"And he'll have a companion part of the way," Collins notes, clapping me on the shoulder in an uncommon show of barely muted exhilaration. I can tell that he's becoming more and more invested in the welfare of his new instant family.

"Think I'll go pack. I wanna' stop by the monastery on the way out." Then, addressing Collins, I ask whether he knows about flights out of Amarillo. He says there are three or four into Dallas, and that Frank shouldn't have to wait too long. When I ask, "What if they're full…" Collins looks at me condescendingly and says that after all it's the middle of the week and Amarillo. Enough said.

By the time I locate and stuff my gear into the backpack and drive Ethan's green pickup in front of the cabin, Frank, Ivy, and Delilah are waiting at the gate. Frank and Ivy take up the rituals of separation, as Collins steps from the porch. He and I embrace, grin and nod our pleasure at having been together these past weeks. I hug Ivy and kiss Delilah on the forehead. As I slip behind the wheel of the truck and Frank clamors in from the other side, Collins says, with only a trace of irony, "I sure hope you worked out your thinkin' about the whole thing…God or whatever you're tryin' to get right. No matter what you figure out, you'll always wind up pretty much where you started. It's a circle, you know." He grins as the engine stirs to life, and we lumber up the long rutted drive to pavement.

"I want to stop by the monastery and see…leave a note for my buddy," I say as we follow the twists and turns of the road along the Pecos River.

"Right. Ivy said you probably would. Wish you could've seen him the other day." A mile or so later he adds, "Maybe I'll get to meet him when I come back."

"Probably," I agree. "One thing's for certain: he's cut from his own pattern" We remain silent until we pull into the monastery parking lot.

Inside, Brother Xavier talks to a small circle of people in a corner of the spacious room. He spots us and excuses himself to greet us with Benedictine hospitality. When I whisper that I'm leaving and want to check on Ethan, he gestures for us to move through the room and to the porch. He assures me that Ethan's making progress but that he's still in extended retreat. I nod my agreement—or at least acceptance—of the fact and ask if I can write him a note. The monk responds by rushing away for that yellow-lined pad of his and a pen.

At the end of the porch I spot a small table where I sit, while Frank wanders back inside. I write:

Ethan—Today I'm leaving for home. Tomorrow morning I plan to take the truck over to your dad's place. Brother Xavier says you're all right, and

that's what I'll tell your dad. I wish I could see you, but I have high hopes for your decision.
   Stay with it...

I add the last sentence with the reluctance of uncertainty, but when I remember his long bouts of drinking and raving over what he calls the "unmitigated outrage of war," I can accept his courage to face up. I end the note with one sentence designed to stimulate his venture into solitude: *I learned in the mountains that the secret is inwardness.* I underline that last word and leave it to his imagination.

Through the village of Pecos and eastward toward Interstate 25, Frank and I begin our drive. I'm retracing the pathway that led Ethan and me into these mountains and on our pilgrimage. It's as though I'm easing my way back into the world after a sustained absence, rewinding the spool. Decompressing! Frank says little, only asking occasionally about this and that, especially about the Pecos Monument as we pass its entrance.

Once on the interstate Frank says, out of nowhere, "It all comes down to bein' responsible, I guess." I wait for him to say more but he only stares out the side window at the mountains already diminishing toward prairie.

"Whatta you mean by that?" I ask.

"My old man...my Dad...used to drive me nuts with that word. You know, 'responsibility.' And I thought he was crazy, that it was an old man's dusty word. It always had jagged edges for me.... designed to cut me down. But it turns out he's right. Ivy says I've gotta quit blamin' my life on him and take it up for myself. That's what I see in that word now. Bad as I hate to admit it, he's right... even if he's not a very good example of it himself."

I can see that Frank's in his own travail over this journey into the past. He sees it as his way into a future he could not see before. He talks about it and I ask questions for the next half-hour. At one point he revisits his recent breakthrough. "The other night in that sweat I had another visitation, like I told you about. It felt like an end and a beginning, but I couldn't tell what the end or the beginning was. Then I see this whole thing we've found...Collins and you and all of it, as a present put in our lap. That's a beginning, but I had a hell of a time findin' out what the end was. All I could see—can you believe it—was my own dad, standin' by this friggin' big window in his office, smokin' one of his fancy, disgusting cigars. But this is what came to me...the visitation. 'He's standin' there, waitin', but for what? Then it hit me. He's waitin' for me, watchin' to see if I'm gonna come to him."

"Ah," I find myself exclaiming, "as in 'the prodigal returns'!"

Frank stares at me and then with a sudden remembrance of the ancient story, he slaps his knee. "That's it! In the visitation he's doin' exactly what a father's supposed to do...what I'd do if Delilah..." He breaks off, his insight outflanking words. "Yep, that's what it is...and it may not be what he's really doin', but it's what I'm goin' up there to do. Man alive, that's..." Then, as if his own thoughts rebel against him, he speculates, "Hell, he's probably not waitin' at all. On the golf course with buddies or somethin' like that." Then his words dissolve again into his own inner examination. He says nothing more until long after we've turned off toward Santa Rosa.

When Frank speaks again, sobered by whatever discovery he's made, we take up the idea of responsibility, and I begin sharing where I've come in my own pilgrimage into the labyrinth of religion. We talk about inwardness, about mysticism, and then I tell him about this other dimension of Transformative Religion, the one I'd left dangling. The other side of inwardness, I tell him, is life in the world, and that's where the mystical force of religion comes to expression and testing. I guess it could be called something like 'responsibility.'

I once read Robert Pirsig's statement in *Zen and the Art of Motorcycle Maintenance* on the meaning of life: "The meaning of life is to live it." That says everything and almost nothing at once. On the one hand, he's right. Meaning, whatever else it is, is not an abstraction or set of ideas we can impose on our existence. Meaning more nearly wells up from the "grass roots" of living. True, but "to live it" is far more burdensome and complicated than that sentence suggests.

We find our orientation to the living from somewhere, and I find that the true end of the religious sensibility is to help locate that *center of gravity* or *still point* from which to break into the world...to live it. Experience! Inwardness! The mystical! Therein lies the depth of our existence, but we dare not hide there. Out of the deep well of inwardness comes the echo calling us to return to the muck and mud of life in the world.

Qualitatively this is what I mean by *morality*. I'm not using that word to refer to a narrow notion of how to behave and "do the right thing" or "be good." These may be included, but I'm actually sensing that far more is at stake. Morality has to do with the *quality* we bring to life in the world. Unless it's rooted in inwardness, I can't really imagine how morality, understood in this way, can flourish.

True, we may "behave" because we've been taught to behave or because we fear the repercussions of not behaving or because of simple strategic reasonableness. But that seems to me, in the end, too shallow to serve as an adequate foundation for moral quality.

Frank's virtually writhing in his seat as we talk. "That's what I'm tryin' to do now," he blurts out. "That's what I mean by becoming responsible." I agree that he's taking up a helpful word, that its root is 'response' and it suggests, first, that a person is awake to the world and engaged and second, that attention is being paid to what is going on so as to respond to it. Hence, re-sponsible! Frank probes his newfound perspective as though he's found the goose that lays the golden egg.

And I realize during our conversation how much my own thinking about morality and ethics has shifted in recent years. I taught ethics for years, only to become increasingly frustrated with it. The whole subject was far too conceptually ethereal, too laden with traditions of explanation, too disconnected from the actual demands that we act with integrity in relation to other people, as well as to all sentient creatures and the good earth. My dissatisfaction became more disconcerting as I was invited to address medical, environmental, business, educational, and other forms of what everyone calls "applied ethics." All discussions of ethics start on the surface, where our actions occur, and the task is to provide adequate guidance to help people behave and to assess their actions in order to determine whether behaviors are "right" or "good."

In all of this there is some talk of *motives* and *intentions*, but it remains only slightly below the surface. More recently much attention has been given to what is called *virtue ethics* or *character ethics*, and these efforts do try to probe more deeply on the premise that good actions in the world flow from people of virtue or character, not the other way around. To put it simply, we must be moral in order to *act* morally, even if we must first *act* morally in order to learn how to *be* moral. Although this line of inquiry is attractive, I find that it does not go to the heart of the matter.

Once again, *inwardness* becomes a clue to the way out of this morass. When I considered it earlier, I urged that inwardness not be seen as an escape from relations but exactly the opposite: the locus of human meeting and presence. Our attempts to relate and to act well toward other human beings and toward the world are fraught with complication, and at best, only fragmentary success. The reason for this, I do believe, is that we attend only the surfaces of action and reaction, only the rules for doing it in such a way that we minimally avoid exterminating each other. And when we stumble, we "try" to do better...or be better.

I hasten to add that we must never ignore these surface issues of how best to conduct ourselves when our actions affect each other. On the contrary, these obvious dilemmas attendant to the active life in the world are precisely the conditions that prompt a more fundamental engagement with the basis for them, and I offer this possibility: our moral dilemmas and ethical confusions are ultimately grounded in our lack of inwardness.

Before I'm charged with that presumed curse of *subjectivism*, I hasten to emphasize, as I have insisted, that my view of inwardness is exactly contrary to the common way it's construed. All genuine meeting of the other must be from the inside out and thus rooted in inwardness. I once read that the word "intimate" comes from the Latin *intimum*, meaning "open from the inside out." Now there's a challenge for us!

I will go further. *I am a subject*, and never merely an object. In a certain sense I am literally incapable of becoming an object to myself, except perhaps in the province of deep psychopathology. My subjectivity belongs to the very condition of finitude from which I cannot escape. Rather, I relate to the world and to all others in the world in and through this gift of subjectivity. Further, every relationship to other subjects—read, "human beings"—is *inter-subjective*! I may treat another as an object, but when I do, I am not acknowledging "who" they are, namely, human beings, subjects just as I am. Inwardness is the locus of our realization of the other as subject.

Granted, in order to achieve inter-subjective engagement I am obliged to learn a certain *distancing* of my self from myself. This may seem like doubletalk, until we recognize that through self-reflection and our awareness of ourselves being aware, we do enjoy a convoluted thickness of self. This is why genuine inwardness has nothing to do with ego-centric self-fixation, let alone self-absorption. Rather, it is the proper source of authentic subject-to-subject engagement.

If what I contend here is sound, then the problem of morality is fundamentally a religious problem. No doubt this will be immediately misunderstood, unless all that I have discovered and discussed to this point is kept in mind. When I say the problem is religious, I'm not speaking of formal religion, "the religions." These are all derivative of the Primary Impulse and the religious sensibility as given form and lived out in an array of cultural settings with corresponding grand diversity. Once again, what I'm addressing here is Transformative Religion, grounded in inwardness, manifest in the mystical immediacy of Transcendent Presence, and lived out in the moral domain where subject honors subject.

We stop for lunch in Tucumcari. In a local eatery we sit in a booth by a large window offering us a view of the parking lot. The town, giving the impression of being in perpetual siesta, spreads beyond. Just as our lunch arrives, we hear muffled voices outside. Three men in work clothes are talking loudly and gesturing broadly. One of them, the smallest, suddenly swings at the largest one, who immediately drops to the parking pavement. The third man kicks the fallen man in the stomach, and they both walk off to a pickup and drive away. Before we can respond, a woman from a nearby car rushes to the man sitting on the ground wiping his face with his sleeve. She tries to help him, but he pushes her away, stands, and walks ahead of her back to the car. Our young waiter, watching the drama with us, shrugs and dismisses the incident with one word, "Drugs."

"Lot of drugs here?" Frank asks the waiter.

"Whatever's your poison, you can get it here," the young man says as he withdraws.

I again gaze out at the town, a seemingly peaceful way-station for people on their way east and west. But surfaces are always deceiving.

"I wonder if those guys would be interested in what we've been talkin' about," Frank says, a note of irony punctuating his words.

"Huh, not likely," I rejoin. "We're back in what they keep callin' 'the real world,' but it's only the one we seem to have conjured. Nothing says it has to be this way, even if we hide behind, 'Well, it's always been like this.' What I've been talkin' to you about is only a possibility for the most part, an ideal and as rarely realized, even partially. That's the way it is with ideals."

"Then what good are they?"

I say nothing for some time, while we eat. "Ideals are like measuring sticks. We can check ourselves against them." After a pause, "You're probably idealistic right now about how your father's gonna' act, when you talk with him…"

"How's that?"

"You're hoping it'll lead him to act in a different way and you can begin a different kind of relationship with him. And it might, but you can't count on that. In fact, I'd wager against it. But of course, I don't know him. All I can say is that you gotta' do what you're gonna' do and leave it at that. Who knows? He could come around right away, but what if he doesn't? What if he never does? The question is, have you come around?" After a moment I add, "You'll be face to face with the infinite that's inside your father, and it's totally beyond your control…and beyond his."

We leave the café, still discussing ideals and how we're easily disappointed when we expect them to be easily realized. We agree that it's not just other people. We disappoint ourselves, and I remind Frank that, if he's not paying close attention, he can stumble over his own ideal of doing the responsible thing. The two biggest stones over which we tumble are perfection and certainty! Under our finite condition they only paralyze us.

As we drive back to the interstate, a passage comes to mind from Jesus' sayings in The Sermon on the Mount: "Straight is the gate and narrow is the way that leads to life, and few there be who find it." Or something like that. What leads me to think of it is that last clause about so few finding it. Transformative Religion is not commonplace, because inwardness is so murky, lying beneath our egos and all the trappings that protect us from taking such a plunge. Even when formal religion is at its best, encouraging the plunge, "few there be who find it."

Experiences of Transcendence, especially the more definitively mystical ones, and the morality that rests on them, are even rarer.

Many of us may have glimpses or moments of lucidity, but we're mostly sucked back to the surface demands so quickly that forgetfulness takes over. At best most of us are left with intimations, hints of the possibility. It takes hardy souls to find and follow the arduous way into the depths.

Yet, the ideal remains. It haunts our subterranean awareness as a longing...a lusting. And it is located, as I've insisted all along, in the Primary Impulse born in our finite encounter with the infinite. At the highest mystical registers we come back to this place, but we are now at home in our suspension between our own finitude and the infinite. The threat of it becomes promise, inviting us back into the world, no longer as aliens but as genuine inhabitants, that is, as morally present there...in the world, subject addressing and being addressed by subject. Moral schemes and ethical theories reach for this, but none of them can set it forth, because its basis lies elsewhere. They remain at best provisional gestures, awaiting the unveiling of an existence grounded in inwardness. If religion, so pervasive and persistent among our kind, has any justification for continuing, it lies here. Out of the depths, where Transcendent Presence encounters us, we rise to meet the transcending other, our neighbor.

I suspect that my effort to ground the moral life beyond itself could leave the impression that I believe all morality is somehow necessarily religious and that religion makes us moral. But this cannot be the case. Religion provides about the same degree of fragmentary success as any other dimension of human existence, and besides, there is more to the point I seek to make. Although I do hold that the Primary Impulse is ubiquitous, that is, elemental, lying at the core of human awareness itself, it can be, and usually is, a fearsome engagement indeed. Thus, we tend to flee from it—from its *mysterium tremendum*—and rush headlong into the trappings of external existence, into life in the world and into our own version of its cultural trappings. But we are singularly unprepared for the world, that is, we are ungrounded. Disorientation *par excellance*!

Yet, we are obliged to face the other and to act toward and in response to the other. In this respect ethics is just another attempt to formalize a response to infinite participated by the others. Hence, our continuing and ceaseless effort to make moral sense by endless ethical theorizing and application! This is inevitable and, given our finite condition in the world, potentially useful. It at least keeps our attention directed to our dilemma: the moral quality of our actions and responses.

Religion comes properly into play only beyond the forms and constraints of the religion that is also very much a part of "the world." At its best, then, formal religion can offer a moral orientation and inspire the moral sensibility. But not all moral orientations come from formal religion, at least not directly or primarily. Formal religion may even point to and encourage us—again, at its best—to move beyond its own boundaries into the Transformative. But it cannot and does not take us there. It can only be a context, an occasion for the realization.

Nor is it necessary that we go through the crucible of formal religion in order to discover Transformative Religion. Formal religion—again and again, *at its best*—is only mediational, never the thing itself. Indeed, formal religion is only *at its best*, when it limits itself to this role. But by whatever means, those who dare to plunge into inwardness itself discover the threshold of Transformative Religion and the liberating illumination it affords. Herein lies the "chamber," where we find ourselves by losing ourselves in Transcendent Presence and are made ready to live in the world unencumbered by our overreaching egos that generate all moral bedlam. Not that the ego is lost, only that it is brought to heel and reoriented to…what? The other!

To this point I've avoided one obvious term associated with everything I have pondered: *love*. The omission is intentional, not because it is expendable but because it is of such profound significance that I dare not approach it until this juncture. If there were ever a case of *word inflation*, the word "love" is it. Its expansive and overstretched use, however, speaks to its primacy in human self-understanding, as well as our longing for it. I do not wish to add to the burden of the word by entering upon yet another discourse as to its grandeur and standing in the perennial effort of our kind to make sense of ourselves and our relation to the order of things. Yes, it does, in the end, speak to a *connectedness* that persists against all efforts, commonplace or diabolical, to split and splinter "reality" into bits and pieces, this over against that, the self over against all others. To make distinctions, the passion of modernity, is indeed a useful enterprise, but only in so far as it *remembers*—no, re-members, as in putting the members back together—connection. Love is about this truth.

A personal anecdote will suffice. As a college student, I became imbued with the idea of love. To be sure, libido was the immediate driver. After all, this only demonstrates that love is organismic and foundational, but love need not be *reduced* to this, its most primordial expression. Libido is more nearly like a beginning, a launching forth into the mystery of connection. Had Freud not been so… so…Victorian, he might have discerned this. Of course, as a young man, I covered over this primal interest by considering love in the context of religious discourse. I thus romanticized it grandly! The Greek *agape* and its relation to other Greek terms for love especially drew my attention. But the more I pondered and sought to sort through my own multi-layered sense of love, the more convoluted and entangled the word and my feelings became. It had too many levels, too many bewildering intersections. For instance, the close connection between divine love and sexual love puzzled me repeatedly, especially in a religious tradition where the two had been wrenched apart so graphically.

****

The father dies when the boy is barely a man. He is too young to contain the loss. Only distraction with serious matters of growing up and on saves him from paralysis. Love for the father runs so deep, down to natal sources, that he knows it but cannot find it until years pass.

It begins with a story told by the mother. She tells the man of his birth:

> You were actually born dead. The doctor could not revive you. He put you, first, in cold water, then in warm. He worked against time. I looked up through a cloud of left over pain from your birth, and I saw your father praying on his knees near you. You will never imagine the comfort that gave me. I knew you'd be all right. Then the doctor breathed into your mouth—you know, like God did for Adam—and I saw you quicken and begin to cry out.
> Your body changed from a pale gray to a rosy color. You were alive and so was I…and your dad.

That's how tight the love was between the boy-cum-man and the father. Only the man could not reach that far down inside to locate the love that was covered over by death. It was too deep for thinking, let alone for words.

Only with the assistance of mescaline does the man once again 'find' the father. Under the spell of sacred medicine, the man finds himself in the father's grave, digging for him. All he can find is a jawbone, which he holds aloft for all to see. The man says to companions in the room, "He's not there. All that's left is one bone." This makes sense only to the man.

In his next vision the man is carrying the limp body of the father, and he is wading into the water of a deep and boundless lake. He calls for a canoe. It is made of crystal, transparent with infinite elegance. The man places the father in the canoe, moves out to where the water is shoulder deep, and pushes the canoe into the lake. The water bears the father away. At long last, years after the anguish of loss, the man bids farewell to the father, and the splendor of love breaks forth.

Only by penetrating to the death does the love heave into view.

****

Much later, as I sat in a graduate seminar on Jonathan Edwards, the breakthrough came. We were reading his work, *On the Nature of True Virtue*, when the insight visited me. The teacher, offering comment on a passage, said simply, "For Edwards the center of true virtue is love, and he had a specific understanding of it: 'Love is Being's gracious consent to Being.'" Even when, after so many years, I tell this story today, that simple definition sounds odd. For most of my friends it was entirely too ethereal, too abstract. How could anyone cozy up to a statement like that? "Love is Being's gracious consent to Being!" This pushes far beyond any sort of romanticism.

But after several years of my bewildered reflection, Edwards' words came as a revelation. *Love is Being's gracious consent to Being.* The Being that I am acknowledges its own other in the Being of the other! Mercy! When we cut through the morass of images of love, from *libido* to *agape*, the utter immediacy and pristine clarity of Edward's simple statement takes us to the still-point in love's vortex, to connectedness itself. Inwardness, then, when allowed to do its luminous work, unveils this mystery of mysteries—*connection*—and we are prepared for the world.

Frank searches the truck's glove compartment for a piece of paper. He wants to write down the definition of love. He scrounges a scrap and the stub of a pencil, but he cannot write with the truck's road shudders. At about that time I spot a local spectacle on our right, a series of ten Cadillac buried in a field near the highway, nose down in the earth. Periodically they are repainted with a fresh color. Frank wants to stop, and we pull off the highway. He hastily writes down the definition, asking me to say it again, one word at a time: *Love-is-Being's-Gracious-Consent-to-Being*. We exit the truck and walk along a well-worn path to the curiosity. A couple stands nearby, and we all gawk.

"Why's that art?" Frank asks

"Look what we're doin'," I point out. "These cars stuck in the earth like this invite our attention and interest…"

"But they're not…pretty…or even attractive," Frank insists.

"Watch out! You were attracted. That's why you walked out here. Art's not always 'pretty,' as you put it. Maybe the best never is. It's simply another way of arranging things to surprise us…and to bring delight or to confront."

"Yeah, I guess, but it's sure a screwball thing…"

"There you have it. Art!"

We both chuckle as we turn back toward the truck. Soon Frank is surveying signs directing us to the airport. We're through the town, rising conspicuously against the endless flatness of surrounding prairie, before he spots the arrow pointing our way. Within minutes we're pulling into the parking lot in front of the terminal.

As Frank retrieves his small bag from the back of the truck and we make our way to the terminal, I'm already feeling lonesome. I've been with him for weeks, longer it seems, and for some uncanny reason I'm reluctant to leave him. Down deeper I know that the more basic loneliness is my realization that it's been a month since I last saw my wife, and I'm longing to be home to greet her. But Frank's become part of the fabric as well.

He stands at the counter, discussing his passage and planning. I hang back, until he calls me to join him. He can leave in about an hour and a half but have a four-hour layover in Dallas, or he can leave on a later flight and have a closer connection. I tell him that it depends on where he wants to be trapped, here or in Dallas. I remind him that, when it comes to airports, the options are not especially exciting. He looks around and decides on Dallas. When he takes out his carefully stashed money, I note the meager trove and decide to pay half of his ticket. He objects before relenting. "Collins gave me most of this," he confesses, "and when I resisted him, he said it's rude to refuse a gift. He said if I was Red Man, I'd know better."

When I start to walk with him to the waiting area, Frank insists, "Hey, you go ahead. You've still got quite a drive. I'll be all right." He claps me on the shoulder with an air of authority, as though gently guiding me to do the right thing. We stand in the midst of the open space of the airport, dancing farewells. Then we embrace and within moments I'm back in the truck. It feels hollow.

I retreat as we'd come, to Interstate 40 and turn east. *When does the pilgrimage end, or has it ended already*, I wonder to myself. Maybe never. Maybe it's constant, only at another level of travel. What should I call it? "Soul travel?" Sounds too New Agey, too much like that out-of-body lingo, I guess, but it's something like that. Anyway, I'm about to decompress into the world, the world I've kept talking about today. That's the test.

Made in the USA
San Bernardino, CA
29 October 2015